Outstanding prai

"No one tells a story like Lisa Jackson. She's
headed straight for the top!"
—Debbie Macomber

"Lisa Jackson takes my breath away."
—Linda Lael Miller

Outstanding praise for Cathy Lamb

"A story of strength and reconciliation and change."
—*The Oregonian* on *Henry's Sisters*

"Lamb delivers grace, humor and forgiveness . . .
positively irresistible."
—*Publishers Weekly* on *Henry's Sisters*

"*Julia's Chocolates* is wise, tender, and very funny. In Julia Bennett,
Cathy Lamb has created a deeply wonderful character, brave and
true. I loved this beguiling novel about love, friendship and the
enchantment of really good chocolate."
—Luanne Rice, *New York Times* bestselling author

Outstanding praise for Holly Chamberlin

"Nostalgia over real-life friendships lost and
regained pulls readers into the story."
—*USA Today* on *Summer Friends*

"An honest, forceful novel about love, family, and sacrifice."
—*Booklist* on *One Week in December*

Outstanding praise for Rosalind Noonan

"Written with great insight into military families and the
constant struggle between supporting the troops but not
the war, Noonan delivers a fast-paced, character-driven
tale with a touch of mystery."
—*Publishers Weekly* on *One September Morning*

BEACH SEASON

BEACH SEASON

LISA JACKSON
CATHY LAMB
HOLLY CHAMBERLIN
ROSALIND NOONAN

KENSINGTON BOOKS
www.kensingtonbooks.com

KENSINGTON BOOKS are published by

Kensington Publishing Corp.
119 West 40th Street
New York, NY 10018

All Kensington titles, imprints, and distributed lines are available at special quantity discounts for bulk purchases for sales promotion, premi-
ums, fund-raising, educational, or institutional use.

Special book excerpts or customized printings can also be created to fit
specific needs. For details, write or phone the office of the Kensington
Special Sales Manager: Kensington Publishing Corp., 119 West 40th
Street, New York, NY 10018. Attn. Special Sales Department. Phone:
1-800-221-2647.

Kensington and the K logo Reg. U.S. Pat. & TM Off.

ISBN-13: 978-0-7582-6563-0
ISBN-10: 0-7582-6563-8

First Kensington Trade Paperback Printing: June 2012
10 9 8 7 6 5 4 3 2 1

Printed in the United States of America

CONTENTS

JUNE'S LACE

BY CATHY LAMB

To Jimmy, Wendi, and Noah Straight
With Love

May the best you have ever seen
Be the worst you will ever see.
May the mouse never leave your grain store
With a teardrop in its eye.
May you always stay hale and hearty
Until you are old enough to die.
May you still be as happy
As I always wish you to be.

CHAPTER 1

Ten Things I'm Worried About

1. Too many wedding dresses
2. Not enough wedding dresses
3. Grayson
4. Going broke
5. Losing my home
6. Never finding an unbroken, black butterfly shell
7. The upcoming interview with the fashion writer
8. Not having peppermint sticks in my life
9. Turning back into the person I used to be
10. Always being worried

CHAPTER 2

"No. Absolutely not." I gripped the phone with white knuckles as I paced around my yellow studio. "I will never agree to that."

"Ha. I knew you wouldn't accept those unacceptable terms, June," Cherie Poitras, my divorce attorney, cackled. "Your soon-to-be-ex-husband has a monstrous addiction to being a jerk but don't worry, we're not quitting. Quitting causes my hot flashes to flare."

"I don't want your hot flashes to flare, Cherie. And I'm not quitting, either. I can't." I yanked opened the French doors to my second-story deck as lightning zigged and zagged across the night sky through the bubbling, black clouds, the waves of the Pacific Ocean crashing down the hill from my blue cottage. "If I could catch a lightning strike, I'd pitch it at him."

"It would be thrilling to see that," Cherie declared. "So vengefully Mother Nature-ish."

"What a rat." I shut the doors with a bang, then thought of my other life, the life before this one, and shuddered. I could *not* go back to it, and I was working as hard as I could to ensure that that wouldn't happen. There wasn't enough silk and satin in that other life. There wasn't any kindness, either. Or softness. "I so want this to end."

"He's sadistically stubborn. I have been buried in motions, requests for mediation, time for him to recover from his fake illness, his counseling appointments, attempts to reconcile... he's tried everything. The paperwork alone could reach from Oregon to Arkansas and flip over two bulls and a tractor."

"That's what we're dealing with, Cherie, bull." I ran a hand through my long, blond, messy hair. It became stuck in a tangle.

"Sure are, sweets."

"He's doing this so I'll come back to him."

"That's true. He's a tenacious, rabid possum."

"I don't ever want anything to do with the rabid possum again." I was so mad, even my bones seemed to ache. Cherie wished me a "happy wedding dress sewing evening," and I wished her the best of luck being a ferocious attorney who scares the pants off all the male attorneys in Portland and went back to stomping around my studio.

My studio is filled with odd and found things. I need the color and creativity for inspiration for the nontraditional wedding dresses I sew. Weathered, light blue shutters from a demolished house are nailed to a wall. Two-foot-tall pink letters spell out my first name. On a huge canvas, I painted six-foot-tall purple tulips with eyes, smiles, and pink tutus. I propped that painting against a wall next to a collection of mailboxes in the shapes of a pig, elephant, dragon, dog, and monkey. The monkey mailbox scares me.

I dipped a strawberry into melted chocolate and kept stomping about. I eat when I get upset or stressed, and this had not proved to be good for the size of my bottom. Fifteen extra pounds in two years. After only four more strawberries, okay *seven,* and more pacing, I took a deep breath and tried to wrestle myself away from my past and back into who I am now, who I am trying most desperately to become.

"Remember, June," I said aloud as my anger and worry surged like the waves of the Oregon coast below me. "You are in your sky-lighted studio. Not a cold, beige home in the city. You are living amidst stacks of colorful and slinky fabrics, buttons, flowers, faux pearls and gems, and lace. You are not living amidst legal briefs and crammed courtrooms working as an attorney with other stressed-out, maniac attorneys hyped up on their massive egos."

My tired eyes rested, as they so often did, on my Scottish tartan, our ancestors' tartan, which I'd hung vertically on my wall. When I'd hung it in our modern home in Portland, he'd ripped it down and hid it from me for a month. "Tacky, June, it's tacky. We're not kilt-wearing heathens."

I am a wedding dress designer in the middle of a soul-crushing divorce. I am a wedding dress designer who will never again marry. I am a wedding dress designer who has about as much faith in marriage as I do that the Oregon coast will never see another drop of rain.

A blast of wind, then a hail of rain pummeled my French doors.

I ate yet another chocolate-covered strawberry. I have been told my eyes are the color of dark chocolate. Not a bad analogy. I washed the strawberry down with lemonade, then ate a carrot.

No, I have no faith in marriage.

None.

It was a bad day. A very bad day. And I knew there were more bad days to come with my ex.

I did not see the wave erupting from the ocean like a sneaky, amphibious water assault. The Oregon coast, stunning and breathtaking, can, infrequently, whip out dangerous waves that arch and stretch and cover anyone in their path with freezing cold water, a bit of foam, and a mouthful of long seaweed. If you are lucky, it will not pull you out to swim with the whales.

But I had committed the cardinal Oregon beach sin: I put my back to the ocean. Never do that.

An hour before, I'd pulled on a raincoat and rain pants and headed out for my usual five-mile "Sanity Walk," which I do each day to settle my worries. I need to get away from work and my sticky workaholic tendencies, and an overload of *him*, whom I try not to think about because he contaminates my brain synapses and makes them explode.

Between the raindrops, off in the distance, I could see rays of sun slanting through the clouds, a promise of a reprieve from an early summer rain. To my right, near the rocks and tide pools, I saw a black butterfly shell and turned to pick it up, to see if it was whole, unbroken. I am always searching for whole butterfly shells. I have never found one. The left wing of this shell was halfway broken off . . .

And boom.

I was soaked and choking as a wave poured down on my head. Another wave knocked me off my feet, then covered me in salt water. I struggled to find my footing, to figure out which way was up, as I fought vainly against the pull of the waves and the freezing cold. My face at one point was planted straight into the sand.

I tried to pinwheel my arms, but that didn't work. I tried to hit the ocean floor with my feet, but they were tossed up and over my head. I was under a wall of water, heading out into the ocean, a rock scraping my back. The water sucked and spun me out and around, as if I was a black butterfly shell and it was trying to crack me in half.

I tried to breathe and choked, inhaling water, the cold claws of panic paralyzing my mind as I fought against drowning, seawater pouring over me, my head bopping through to air, then churning waves covering it again. I struggled and fought against the undertow, still not sure which way was up.

I felt a hand grab mine.

A hand.

Grabbing mine.

Within a millisecond, I was hauled up as if I weighed no more than a seagull. An arm curled around my waist, and I was thrust up against a wall of steel, the freezing water pouring off my body. A hand pounded my back as I doubled over and indelicately wretched out sea water and, I think, part of a shell, maybe a seahorse or a shark, and sand. I made another gagging sound, more water poured out, that strong arm still linked around my waist as body-freezing water swirled around us. I wretched again.

And again.

I spit out sand, my whole body going into semishock as I shook and shook. Sucking in air with a gurgly, gasping sound, my lungs totally depleted, my legs shaking, my hair glued to my head, I held on tight to the wall of steel as another wave rolled in. The wave receded, as fast as it came, the chilly water circling our thighs.

"It's okay," the wall of steel soothed, both arms tight around me. "I got ya. You're okay." He hit me on the back again, and once more I released part of the Pacific Ocean. I inhaled again with a jagged breath, vaguely thinking I sounded like a hyperventilating octopus, however that would be.

Seconds, that was what it took. Seconds before my life was suddenly in danger. Seconds after that and I'm being pounded on the back.

"Sorry about that," the man drawled. "I've never hit a woman, but this seems to be an occasion where it might be beneficial."

I leaned against his chest, arms around his waist, my whole body trembling, and between long strands of sandy, soaked hair, I eyed my rescuer.

He was a giant. I was being rescued by a green giant with blondish wavy hair.

"How ya doing?" he asked, his emerald eyes concerned, brow furrowed. "Can you get enough air?"

I studied those eyes for a minute. Honestly, they were hard to look away from, bright and intense, steady on. "Yes," I gurgled out, "I have air." I then leaned over, coughed in a particularly disgusting fashion, and this time spit up seaweed. I dragged one end of it out of my mouth until I had about six inches hanging from my fingers.

"Better now." My voice was still hoarse, sand crunching between my teeth. "I had not planned on seaweed for lunch."

"Good." He still held on to me so I wouldn't collapse. "I personally prefer clam chowder. Garlic bread. Less green, more flavor."

Ah. A man with dry humor. If I wasn't busy spewing out more sand, I would enjoy the verbal sparring. Leaning over again, his arms supporting me, I choked out yet another piece of seaweed and a mouthful of water. "Tastes terrible."

"Some people eat it with a dash of salt. Me, personally, it has never held appeal at all. At least you didn't swallow a fish."

"For that, I am grateful." I wiped my mouth. I was stunned. Overwhelmed. Two seagulls squawked above. "Thank you very much."

"You are quite welcome. Any time."

"Thank you," I said once again, my teeth now chattering, as he guided me out of the water and onto the sand, an arm still slinked around my waist. He took off his green rain jacket. "Here, take off your jacket, we'll put this one around you instead."

"That's chivalrous, but I'm soaked. You take it. It'll get wet." My body jerked as if it was being electrocuted.

"Please. Wear it. Let me help you. You're shaking too much to do it yourself."

That was true.

He unzipped my jacket and took one of my arms, then the other, both rattling around from cold and shock, and pulled my rain jacket off. He threw his jacket around me, stuck my arms back in, and zipped it up. I was instantly dwarfed by the giant's jacket. He pulled the hood over my head.

"But you'll get wet now," I gasped.

"I am not going to get anywhere near as wet as you already are. Please. Wear it."

He was wearing a blue sweater and I noticed that his chest was flat and the type you could sleep on, not that I would sleep on a man's chest ever again. *No way.*

"Thank you. I'm so, so glad you were here." A sense of utter relief, utter gratefulness flooded over me. Had he not been here, not taken action . . . *I could have died.* That had not been on my agenda for today. I bit my frozen lip and tried not to cry.

"Happy to be here. I did have to run faster than I've ever run in my life, but I've got my exercise in. I'm renting a place up the hill, just arrived today, came out for a walk, and saw that huge wave hit you. It came out of nowhere, didn't it?"

"As if it dropped out of the sky." I pushed my dripping hair out of my eyes and stared at him, the wind lifting that blondish hair around a supertough and strong-looking jaw and prominent cheekbones. "Good of you to make a run to rescue me."

He bowed. "My pleasure."

Those green eyes stared right into mine, as if the drowned rat in front of him was interesting and appealing. I could not look away. The rain sprinkled down, and there we stood, staring at each other. My, how his eyes were a light and wondrous color, bold and sure, as if he wasn't afraid to look away from life . . . the trustworthy, strong, *I have a deeper side to me and I want to know the deeper side of you* sort of gaze.

He shook his head, blinked a couple of times, and smiled again, his eyes crinkling in the corners.

Wow. Rough and tough and manly. Wow.

"Take off your shirt."

What? I felt myself prickle under his jacket, a blast of fear shooting through me.

"No, no, no." He put his hands up. "I'm sorry. I didn't mean it like that. But you're all zipped up under my jacket. Can you take off the wet clothing on your upper half so you don't get colder on our walk back?"

"Oh, okay." That made sense, since I was shivering so spasmodically.

"I'll turn around to give you some privacy and keep an eye on the ocean while you wriggle out of whatever you can."

I thought of taking my clothes off in front of this macho he-man. One graphic picture jumped into my mind after another, and my breath quickened. *Honestly, June. You almost drowned and you're thinking about getting naked? You haven't thought about a naked man in over two years.*

"Are your hands too cold to do it?" His face creased into worry lines.

"No. Yes. No and yes to you." I coughed. *Please, June, don't embarrass yourself.* "I'll be fine."

The water off the Oregon coast is so absolutely freezing it hurts your brain, even in summer, but as we stared at each other from inches away, my head tilted back; I felt a blush climbing up my neck.

He blinked again, as if he was somewhat rattled, too, then turned around. I started to strip while sneaking peeks at his backside. Huuuuge shoulders. A solid man, not skinny. Tall, rangy.

I wriggled underneath the jacket, still warm from his manly man heat, and managed to pull my sweater and T-shirt off. I hesitated on my bra, then thought, *what the heck.* I was going to freeze to death if I didn't. The rain coming down wasn't helping. I dropped everything in the sand, stuck my arms through the jacket's sleeves, then rolled my soaking, sandy clothes into a ball.

"Okay, I'm undressed," I said, then stopped. *Come on, June! Think! Don't say it that way!* "I'm undressed but dressed. I'm dressed in your coat. Not naked undressed."

He turned around and I could tell he was chuckling on the inside.

"I mean, I'm ready. Ready to walk."

"All righty, off we go." He pulled the hood over my head again. "We've probably got a couple of miles to the steps. I'm worried about you getting cold. Walking will keep you warm."

He was worried about me? Worried about me? *That was so darn sweet.* I smiled at him, even though I felt my frozen lips wiggle.

"I'll hold that." He held out his hands for my clothes. "Wrap your arms around yourself to keep warm."

As a river of ice ran through me from head to foot, I handed him my clothes, and of course, my bra had to drop to the sand.

I bent to snatch it up but because I was a frozen popsicle, I didn't move real quick. He moved quicker, and my brassiere was soon in his huge hands.

"Oh no," I groaned. It was my black-and-white–spotted *cow* bra. There was a pink cow across each cup, surrounded by polka dots. It was a funny gift from my sister September, because she said I was an "udderly" wonderful sister. "Put your girls in these two cows!" she'd giggled.

"I'll take that back." I put my trembling hand out for the bra.

"Polka dots?" He raised an eyebrow. "And two cows." He held the bra up with both hands.

"I am so embarrassed. Please blame my sister. She sent it to me."

"It's original!" he declared, smiling at me. "It's a cow bra."

"Yes, oh me, oh my."

"Me, oh my, too," he said softly, and oh me, oh my, I could tell that man was struggling hard not to laugh.

Who was this man? And why, after almost *drowning*, was I all aflutter?

He held the pink cows up again. "I don't think I'm going to forget today."

"Me, neither. And not only because of the cow bra."

Soaked, freezing, a summer rain drenching us, we laughed.

And that was the beginning. The laughter was the beginning.

The beginning of Reece and me.

CHAPTER 3

Later that night, wrapped up on my bed in my blue crocheted feather-filled comforter, eating only a small piece of apple pie with whipped cream, okay, *two* pieces, the waves pounding on the surf, I reentertained myself with the rest of my conversation with Reece . . .

He tucked the wet cows into the wad of clothes. I took a deep breath. "It's a long walk; you don't have to come back with me. I can return your jacket."

"No way. I'm not letting you walk back alone. I'll see you home to get something dry on, then we're going to the hospital."

"The hospital? Not a chance. I don't enter hospitals. They make me nervous."

"Me, too, but you're going. You swallowed a lot of water, and I want them to check your lungs and make sure you didn't take a knock to the head."

"I can take myself to the hospital."

"I'll take you." He smiled with nice white teeth and stuck out his hand. "Reece O'Brien."

"Nice to meet you, Reece." I shook his hand. My hand trembled. "I'm June MacKenzie."

"June? Were you born in June?"

The light rain suddenly turned into a deluge as we headed to the stairway. I was a double-drowned rat. "No."

"Oh."

He seemed pleasantly baffled.

"It's a family name, then?"

I didn't want to explain. It was a wee bit embarrassing to talk about sex in front of him. "June is the month when my parents conceived me."

"Ah. I see."

I stared straight ahead at the pounding surf.

"Do you have brothers and sisters?" he asked.

"Yes, three of them."

"What are your sisters' and brothers' names?"

I could see the hazel flecks in those green eyes, a crooked scar by his right eye, another on top of his left cheekbone. *I want to kiss the scars....* Whoa, June! Had I just thought that? *I want to kiss the scars.* Where the heck had that come from? I was off men, completely! Done with men!

"Did you forget your brothers' and sisters' names?" He smiled at me.

I smiled back. He had such nice... lips! "What? No. No. I know their names."

Yes, I did. I knew my brother's and sisters' names, but my, how would it feel to hug a man that size? Oh, shoot! *What was I thinking?* "I know their names," I said again, with a bit of defiance, but I heard my voice come out as a whisper. "I do."

"Good." His eyes dropped to my lips. It was a flicker, but I saw the drop. My mouth suddenly felt like it was on fire. *What?* I couldn't be on fire for him, or any man. That was . . . that was . . . *bad!*

"Their names are . . ." Who was I talking about again? Whose names?

"Your brothers and sisters," he prompted, still smiling.

I accidentally made a funny sound in my throat. "Yes! I have a brother and sisters and they have names." I looked at the ocean for answers.

"That's fortunate. If they didn't, what would they be called?" His voice was low and husky.

"I don't know what they would be called without names." *What was going on?* I was freezing, I was in shock. Ha! That was it! I had almost been pulled out to sea. He'd saved me. Now I was transferring my emotions to him.

"So. My brother's name is . . ." *Quick, June. Your name is June . . .* "His name is March. March. And I have a sister named . . ." Reece was a cross between Poseidon and Zeus . . . he needed only a chariot to complete the image. "August. She's an August." I shook my head to clear it. "Her name is August. She's getting married soon. Her fiancé's family is proper. Scary proper. Blue-blood proper. I have another sister . . ." Chariot. Horses. A sword. Did Greek gods have swords? What would Reece's sword be like? *June, come on!* "The other sister has a name. She is a September." I bit my wet lip. "I mean, her name *is* September. She is not *a* September. It's just September. One word."

"Just September. One word."

As an ex-trial attorney I have been in court hundreds of times. I was never thrown, never intimidated, never embarrassed, even when the judge was threatening to charge me with contempt of court, even with obstinate juries or screaming opposing counsel. No, never, but this *man.*

"Do you have brothers and sisters named for the months of the year?" *What an inane question. No! No, he didn't. You and your odd MacKenzie clan are the only ones who are all named after months!*

He chuckled, deep and masculine. "I have two brothers and two sisters. Their names are Shane, Jessica, Rick, and Sandy. Dull compared to yours. Your parents must have enjoyed the months of June, August, September, and March."

I stumbled a bit on a rock, and he caught my arm. This time, I avoided locking eyes with him so as not to be possessed by his handsome magic. "I'm sure they did enjoy those months. Every month is a happy month for my parents."

"That's a rare thing to hear. Tell me about them."

Okay! I could do that! A normal conversation! "They met when they were sixteen and ran off and got married after they graduated from high school. My oldest sister arrived a year later, then my next sister, me, and my brother. We're all eighteen months apart, give or take a few months."

"Young parents."

"Oh yes, and they're way cooler than any of their kids. They're ex-hippies."

"Outstanding."

"Yes, we had an outstanding childhood. Different. Wild. Nomadic."

"Tell me about it."

"You want to know about my childhood?" I pushed a strand of wet hair off my face.

"Yes, I do." Those eyes were sincere. I was being pulled into a green pool, only the pool was warm and sexy and had big shoulders. *Look away, June. Look away! Remember, you do not believe in lust at first sight.*

I shook my head to clear my burgeoning passion. "My sister August was born on a commune in California. My next sister, September, was born in the back of our VW van. I was born in a hippie colony here in Oregon. There's some difference, not much, from a commune. My brother was born about fifteen feet over the U.S. border."

"Fifteen feet?"

"About that. We had been in Mexico, living on a farm with

other Americans, but my nine-months-along mom decided at the last minute that she wanted March born on American soil, like the rest of us, so they drove through the night. My brother was born on the other side of the customs building."

"That must have been quite a ride."

"It was. I remember it. We packed up the van on the fly. We were all wearing tie-dye shirts and sandals. We also had three mutts, two cats, and a bird who flew loose in the van. We had a box of apples and a box of bananas. I slept on the floor of the van between my sisters with our dog, Give Me Liberty or Give Me Death, asleep over my legs. Our other dog, Flower Child, snored away on a seat, and the third dog, Fleas, because he had fleas when we found him, my sister was using as a pillow."

"You are making my childhood sound as boring as heck. I can barely stand it."

"We were traveling gypsies in a VW bus." I drew my arms tight around my freezing, shaking body, the rain relentless.

"So, your brother made it to the U.S. border?"

"Yes, he did. My poor mom. No drugs at all during childbirth. She wanted it natural. All of us were natural. My father grabbed two tartans out of the back of the van for her to lie on."

"Tartans?"

"From Scotland. Our ancestors are from Scotland, and our family takes our love of Scotland seriously. Afterward, my father's face was whiter than my mom's. I remember my sisters and I had to stay in the van and there were a bunch of men in uniform helping my mom, and all of a sudden one of those men was holding our brother, March, who was screaming his head off, but, I'm sure, delighted to have been born in America."

He laughed again.

My, what a seductive and deep and gravelly laugh. *My!*

"And after he was born?"

"A doctor had been passing through customs and one of the guards ran him over to our mom, so he was able to do some sewing up, so to speak. A couple of hours later, after the border guards fed us, we were back in the van, March squawking in my mom's arms where she lay on the floor. Within two hours we were in a fancy hotel. It was strange. Our childhoods were so nomadic, we worked on farms and communes, and the basics, electricity and plumbing, often weren't there, but once or twice a year we'd go stay in a hotel with pools, hot tubs, and free breakfasts where we stuffed ourselves silly with pancakes and waffles. After March was born we had seven nights of complete luxury."

"Then back on the road? You didn't go to school?"

"Not traditional school. We weren't homeschooled, we were bus-schooled."

"What does 'bus-schooled' mean?"

He smiled. I melted further. For a moment I faltered again, couldn't speak, lost my train of thought. I coughed. "We learned all about geography, geology, and the history of the earth from our travels. We're all fluent in Spanish. Our father loved math, so in fourth grade we were doing basic algebra. He thought it was fun, so there we'd be, up at two in the morning, doing algebraic equations after learning about the constellations. My mom had us write in journals every night and we read the classics."

"A family of readers, then?"

"We ate books. It was required. We would visit other MacKenzie relatives often, and read their books, too. Books are your friends, my mom told us."

"How did your parents make a living?"

"My father is a talented painter so he would set up a stand at open markets, or in small towns we were passing through, and people would hire him to paint pictures of themselves, their homes, their pets. Once word got out, there were long lines. Sometimes he would paint murals at schools, churches, even civic buildings. He'd go in with a design, they'd love it, and all of a sudden they had a mural in their hallway and we had a check."

I laughed despite the cold that seemed to be living in my body from the inside out. Could blood turn to icicles? "My mom is an incredibly talented seamstress. She made all of our clothes and called it Hippie Chick. One time she took yards of beige material bought at a garage sale for fifty cents and sewed my sisters and me dresses with six inches of lace at the hem. People loved them, they stopped us on the street. My mom sold a lot of clothes when we were in that bus. Her flowered shirts, flowy and bright, sold well. She'd buy used jeans for twenty-five cents, cut out patches from colorful material, and sew them on. She added beads and feathers to plain blue shirts. She could turn anything into a fashion statement, and she did."

"She was a clothing artist, then."

"Yes, and she taught us. We would all spend hours together sewing into the night. There wasn't a formal bedtime. We'd use a lantern and she showed us how to make a boring dress unique, how to make a normal skirt something special. Ruffles, sequins, embroidery, shortening, lengthening. And lace. Oh, the lace was always in abundance. Our favorite. We used it all over everything. Satin was our second favorite. Sewing was a fun game for us."

"And you learned a lifelong skill."

"That I did." I sewed until I decided, insanely, that I should let that part of my life fly off into the wind and disappear over the mountains. Part of me flew off then, too, and I was soon a miserable cog in a legal machine. I went back to sewing to refind my lost self. How strange to say sewing recently saved me, but it had.

I was so curious about his family, but we started climbing the staircase and all I could think of was that I didn't want to go first because I didn't want my rear in his face, but I didn't have a choice. A gentleman, he had me go first.

I wanted to grab my bottom and hide it. It is not *overly* large, but let's simply say that I enjoy eating, have never desired to be model slim, and believe my curves, instead of the skinny, intense thing I used to be, signal a healthier eating life. Besides, I could die tomorrow. Why deny myself the finer pleasures of life like chocolate, fresh lobster with garlic butter, and clam chowder?

I tripped up a step, started to tumble forward, my freezing feet and legs not responding, and that strong arm whipped around my middle and pulled me back up. Again.

But this time my back was tight against his chest. The chariot chest. Hard and tight, a thigh partly between mine.

Oh, mercy.

His face was so near to mine. Inches. Oh, inches.

He smelled delicious . . . a combination of the beach and sunshine and musk.

Mercy, mercy, *mercy* me.

*   *   *

"Boil me dry, and hang me out on a laundry line like a dead possum," Estelle said, shaking her white curls. "It is a miracle. You have brought a man to this house. Who is he and what does he want and do you even know how to talk to a man without telling him off?"

"He is a tall drink of water," Leoni whispered, as if Reece could hear her talking through the window as she spied on him from my second-story studio. "And he's getting back in his truck and driving away! Oh, no! Run after him, June! Get him, get him!" She whirled around and started pushing at my back. "Go, go!"

I wanted to sneak into my light blue bedroom and take a hot shower, but if I did that, my two employees, Estelle, who is seventy-eight and blunt because, "Why waste time at my age?" and Leoni, blond, twenty-seven, and a single mom, would simply trail after me, probably right into the shower. Yes, they are *that* nosy.

"I am not going to run after him, Leoni." I dripped on my wood floor. I knew where Reece was going, he was going home to get changed. He said he'd be back up at my house in ten minutes. Ten minutes! Hardly any time to put my face and hair and myself back together!

"Why not?" Estelle asked. She used to be the mayor of a large city. "Politicians' middle names are Crooked and Creepy," she'd told me once. "I would only go back if I was allowed to throw things at annoying people's heads." She is also a most excellent seamstress, taught by her grandmother, who was taught by her grandmother. She shook her pointer finger at me. "You need a man in your life to get rid of that excess energy you're always sizzling off. Keeps a body young."

"You're wet, June!" Leoni declared, as if I didn't know it. She stomped a red, knee-high boot. She dresses in retro style and buys only used, vintage clothing. "Wet and soaked. Did you go swimming in your clothes? That's dangerous, June. You should know better."

"A wave ran after me and tackled me to the sand."

"One of those sneaker waves?" Estelle said. "The curse of the Oregon coast. They sneak up on you and rip-rap, rip-rap." She snapped her fingers.

"That would be it."

"Are you all right?" Leoni asked.

"Didn't hit your head, did you?" Estelle asked, peering over her glasses at me. "You don't want to lose your marbles. Some of yours are broken already. You weren't hurt, were you?"

Leoni squealed, as understanding dawned. "Did that tall drink of water rescue you?"

I bit my lip.

"He did! I can tell by the guilty expression!" Estelle pointed her scissors at me. "And it all started with a semidrowning. You look terrible. Makeup streaking, hair a wreck. Could you not have kept yourself dry for this one man?"

I almost giggled, couldn't help myself, then turned on my heel toward the bathroom.

"Where are you going?"

"I'm going to get the seaweed, whale poop, and salt water off of me."

I heard Leoni whisper, "Maybe for the first time in a million years she'll get a date out of this," to which Estelle said, voice on full volume, "That mouth of hers is a whip. She scares men. She sews wedding dresses that women kill for, but she swears she'll dress as a gnome before she be-bops down the aisle in one herself."

I rolled my eyes and skeedaddled for the shower, turning on the radio as I hurried in. My favorite song was on. It was about a small town on the river, sunshine, hope, and a cheating boyfriend who was locked up in jail for running naked through the streets, his girlfriend threatening to shoot him from behind and, "blast his butt to Jupiter." It was hilarious.

I sang along as I showered, washed the ocean out of my hair and dried off, quick as a lick, then jumped into jeans and white sandals. I pulled on a white lace shirt and a flowing white lace blouse, both of which I'd sewn, a rope belt I'd wound together with gold ribbon, and gold hoop earrings. I pulled a comb through my blond curls and dried it. I added lotion, liner, mascara, and lipstick. I reached for a lotion that smelled seductive, called Amber Moonlight, and rubbed it on my neck and wrists.

Fifteen minutes tops, I was new, improved, and done.

"He's been back for five minutes," Leoni whispered, again worried that Reece had bionic ears. "He knocked and I left him downstairs in the family room. He must live nearby. He's not wet anymore, either. He is a piece of heaven. A piece of handsome work. A stud."

"What are you two going to do?" Estelle said, again not bothering to curb the volume of her ricocheting voice. "If I were you, I would dispense with the preliminaries and invite that tiger to my bed."

I waved my arms at her, as in, *be quiet!*

"In fact," Estelle mused, "I think I'll invite him myself. He probably has a hidden thing for women of a certain age and experience."

I tried not to smile like a fool at the thought of my taking the chariot driver to bed. "He's taking me to the emergency room."

"How romantic!" Estelle dramatically clutched her chest. "Maybe you can take X-rays of each other's bottoms. Or you can give each other colonoscopies. Tar and feather me, you can get your pap smear and he can wield the tools . . . or," she used her fingers to form two guns, "you can practice giving each other stitches and shots in the butt!"

I rolled my eyes.

"Go, go!" Leoni insisted. "Before he escapes! Before he runs off or is intimidated by your harsh and ghastly view of men in general. Please do not go into one of your harangues about how men are comparable to vermin, spiders, or orangutan spit. Please don't tell him your history. Please don't lecture him on the faults of his 'species,' and for Godzilla's sake, don't list the problems that men have caused in this century, or in the last century. Try to be nice . . ."

"I'm going to be nice. I'm always nice."

"Not with men, you man-decimating wreck," Estelle said. "You're a charging grizzly bear with night sweats."

"I'm not going to change who I am because of a man."

"No one's asking you to change," Estelle argued. "Heck, I have never changed one iota of my charming personality for a man. We're telling you not to assume he's inherently a monster because of his plumbing and I'll bet he has big plumbing. *Big* plumbing!" She semishouted the last two words.

I blushed again. *Darn it!*

"Don't bring any of your sewing needles with you, is all," Leoni said, wringing her hands. "Figuratively or literally."

"We're going to the emergency room. That's it. I'm not going to poke him with needles or give him a shot."

Estelle threw her hands in the air. "You have a date! You had to almost drown to get one, but you have a date!"

"When are you coming back?" Leoni asked. "Don't rush. You need to savor the sweetness and sparkle of the date."

"It might not happen again for years," Estelle said, crossing her arms. "Years. Maybe even this millennium."

"I won't be gone long. As you both know, we're swamped in work and I don't even have time to go to the emergency room."

"Go anyhow!" Leoni said as she cupped her hands into a heart shape. "No matter what they do to you, even if they give you an enema, it'll be worth it!"

"Don't screw this up, June," Estelle said. "When you're my age, you take romance where you can get it and be grateful for it. Take life by the horns and swing it around and dance with it, that's what I always say."

I turned to head down the hallway. I stopped at the photo of my family's VW van, with all of the MacKenzies in front of it. There were purple peace signs painted on the sides. We were in Montana then. I'd taken an old photograph and blown it up to a three-foot-by-four-foot canvas.

I held two fingers up. Peace.

On my way down the hallway, I ran into an astronaut.

"Hi, Morgan," I said. Morgan is Leoni's seven-year-old daughter.

"Hi, June," she said through her white NASA astronaut's helmet. It wasn't an authentic NASA helmet, obviously. It was an oversized, battered white motorcycle helmet that she'd stuck a NASA sticker to. She wore a white astronaut jumpsuit, an ex-Halloween outfit, in red and blue, and carried a clipboard and pen. "Where are you going?"

"I'm going to the emergency room."

Through the eye shade I could see her confusion. "Are you dying?"

"No. A wave got me."

"Oh." She wrapped her arms around me. "Are you okay?"

"Yes, I'm fine." I hugged her back. Downstairs Hercules was waiting.

"Good. Do you know about astronauts' toilets on their space shuttles?"

"No, I don't."

"There's a vacuum for solids and there's a hose for liquids. There are two bars that hold your thighs down because there's no gravity up in space and you don't want to float away from the toilet doing your private business."

"No, that would be a mess. Sweets, I have to go." The chariot was here!

"I met that man downstairs."

"Oh, ah. Good."

"He's tall. I think he's smart enough to be an astronaut."

"You do?"

"Yes, I asked him if he understood why NASA astronauts need spacesuits and he told me why. We discussed why I need a camera on my suit, a headlamp for seeing outside of the shuttle, an oxygen tank, and a battery and water supply for a life-support system."

"Wow. I'm impressed." Aha! He was kind to kids!

"Yeah, me, too. Is that your boyfriend? My mom doesn't have a boyfriend. I'm going to go upstairs and study my astronaut books." She tilted her spacesuit helmet up at me. "He's going to be proud of me, you know."

My stomach clenched. "Morgan, I'm proud of you already. So is Estelle and your mom and your teachers, who all say you're bang-up smart. You know more about space shuttles and astronauts, the galaxy and astronomy, than almost anyone on the planet and you're only seven."

"Well, when he knows I'm an astronaut, he'll want to see me again."

My stomach clenched again. Morgan's father, the loser, the bottom-dwelling algae/larvae, had left Morgan's mother when she was five. He told Leoni he was going to the store for a cherry pie and never returned. Leoni noted that he remembered to take his golf clubs, hunting gear, camping tent, expensive bike, and he cleaned out their bank account. Ever since, Morgan has dressed, almost each day, as an astronaut because her father was interested, however mildly, in space. She wants to be impressive so he'll be impressed with her and come back and live with them again.

It breaks my heart. I hugged her again. "I want to see you every day, right here, because if I don't see you, I don't have a good day."

"Yeah, I know. The kids made fun of my astronaut suit again."

"What do they know? They're too young to understand brilliance when they see it."

"They think I'm weird."

"Who cares what they think? All that matters is that you recognize that you're wonderful and cool." I tried not to cry for Morgan. "Your mom made peanut butter cookies because she was supermad at the bodices of the yellow, twenties-era flapper dresses. Have a couple, read your space shuttle book, and organize the pink lace drawer for me, will you?" I give Morgan jobs all the time to do. It makes her feel wanted and needed. I pay her, too.

"Okay." She smiled at me through the dark visor. "I'll tell you about a new design for a space shuttle I sent NASA last week. The one I worked on for about three months with all the details and about twenty pages of explanations. I think they'll write me back."

"They might, Morgan. As least *they* know brilliance when they see it."

I tried not to let my heart squeeze too tight when I thought about the pain of abandonment that kid's selfish father had caused her, then turned to tromp down the stairs toward Hercules.

Chapter 4

"Thanks for taking me to the emergency room. I can't say it was fun, Reece, but I'm glad I went." I took another bite of clam chowder. Marlene's Chowder, a restaurant located on a blue-gray river that roars into the ocean nearby, is the best in Oregon. Creamy, not too clammy, dollop of butter on the top. Add hot garlic cheese bread for dipping, and you are in clam chowder heaven.

"You inhaled a lot of sea water and I don't think I could have slept tonight unless I knew your lungs were clear. And now we know for sure that you didn't swallow any fish." He grinned.

"Based on the amount of water I unwillingly swallowed, anything could have slipped down my throat, including an octopus and a treasure chest."

He laughed. "You are a funny person, June."

"No. I'm not." I didn't think I was. I was sarcastic. But funny? No. Some of the funniest people, it is said, are or were outsiders, so they see things differently. That's me. I have never felt as if I was part of this natural club that some Americans fall into so seamlessly, as if they were born to fit in. I was born to be that odd link. But maybe that made my sarcasm funny . . .

"Yep, you are." He winked at me.

How totally endearing. "Thank you, again, for saving my sorry butt today."

Reece picked up his coffee mug. "Happy to oblige you, ma'am. And your butt is not sorry, so to speak."

I tried not to blush, but the heat I felt between this man and me was sizzlin'.

"Cheers, June. To a meeting we'll never forget."

"Cheers." We clinked our coffee mugs together and I distracted myself by staring out the windows, hung with white twinkling lights and fishnets for curtains. The sea lions were on the sand bar, lounging about, sometimes rolling into the river, then out to sea to gobble fish.

"So you heard about my wacky family. Tell me about your family, Reece."

"Two brothers, two sisters, I'm in the middle. Not all living in our small farming and ranching community in eastern Oregon, where I own a ranch. My grandparents and their parents were all born there. My parents have four and five siblings each, so there's a ton of aunts and uncles, grandparents, cousins. I'm related by family, marriage, or long-term friendships to almost everybody there. Everyone knows everyone else, and their business, and their parents' and grandparents' business, too, and they can recite all the family scandals, dating back at least a hundred years."

"You have scandals in your family?"

"Heck yeah. Where do I start? There have been gunslingers and stagecoach robbers, eye-popping affairs, secrets, children fathered by men who weren't their biological fathers, but were related *to* the father. Feuds that lasted decades, stolen bulls that started family wars. Millionaires that were generous, millionaires who visited boudoirs. Practical jokes that are legend. There's been a whole lot of love and friendship, too."

"Tell me about the practical jokes."

"Let's see. My brother's truck ended up on top of the elementary school. Horses were led out of a barn late one night and replaced by cows. My cousin snuck chickens into his uncle's living room." He told me more jokes, and I laughed so hard, I had to cross my legs.

"And your siblings?" I wiped the laughter tears from eyes.

"My oldest sister designs saddles and western wear and sells it in her store in town. The next kid, my brother, has a tea company in Portland and it's going gangbusters. My younger sister is a full-time mom, lives in town, has five kids, and her husband sells plumbing equipment, and my other brother is a cameraman for major motion pictures. They live in Los Angeles."

"All doing something different. Same house, same parents, completely different occupations."

"And all married, except me, the rebel son, and they all have children. My parents have fifteen grandkids."

"I bet they're happy with that."

He winked at me. "Always room for more O'Briens."

"Ah, well, good luck to you and your siblings and your fertility. I'll do a dance to the fertility goddess for you."

"It would be exciting to see that. But if you're on the beach doing your fertility dance, make sure you watch the waves. Scratch that. I'll be with you, and I'll watch the waves. You dance."

I thought of dancing in front of him and blushed. *Honestly.* Blushing? Wasn't I a little too old for that? A little too mean for that?

"By the way, I'll pay your emergency room bill," Reece said. "I know you didn't think you needed to go, but I feel better that you did and since I insisted, it's on me."

I dropped my spoon into my clam chowder and it splattered out of the bowl. "You'll do no such thing. I have money. I can pay it and I will pay it."

"Please. Allow me."

I could feel myself getting frazzled and angry. It had started that way with *him*, too. Being chivalrous. Manly. Take charge. He'd fling it back in my face later, asking for compliments and thank yous. It was all a ploy to pretend he was someone he wasn't.

"No. I'll pay whatever my insurance doesn't pay myself."

"I'd like to pay it." His expression was determined, but gentle.

"Why? That's ridiculous."

"Because you went through a hard time. It's traumatic. You're going to have nightmares for weeks, maybe longer, and I want to do something for you that brings one good thing to this situation, and if that good thing means I pay your bill, then—"

No. "No. I'm not going to owe you anything." My voice was tense and a bit screechy. "I'm not going to let you have that over me. I can pay for myself. I don't need a man taking care of me. Do I give the impression that I need a man to pay my bills? Do I come off as weak? Poor? Helpless?"

"Whoa." He held up a hand, his voice surprised. "Whoa. That's not what I meant. I want to do something nice for you, that's it. There's no other ulterior motive here at all."

I gritted my teeth, then took a breath, knowing I was bringing in way too much of my past baggage. "Maybe I needed help when a sneaker wave tried to eat me, but I don't need help otherwise and I certainly wouldn't put my trust in a man to help me."

"You wouldn't put your trust in a man to help you?" He leaned forward. He was genuinely saddened, I could see it in the lines of his face. "Why not?"

"Why not? Because I don't trust men." I could hear Leoni's and Estelle's voices echoing in my head, *Be nice!*

"All men? There's no man you trust?"

"I trust my father and my brother."

"What happened to you to make you not trust men?"

"I don't want to talk about it because it might make me throw something at the captain's wheel or the buoys hanging from the ceiling." I could feel my anger bubbling away.

"I'm sorry you don't trust men. I'm sorry for whatever happened that made you not trust men."

I tried not to get drawn into the sincerity I saw on his face, the strength in that squared-off jaw.

"It's not something you need to chew on for long. One drowned rat of a woman named June doesn't trust men." I pushed my blond curls back. "It's not a big deal."

"There's only one June, I can reassure you of that."

"What do you mean?"

"There's only one of you, and I wish you trusted men."

"Why? What's it to you?"

"I like you."

I hardly knew what to say. He liked me? "How can you like me? We don't know each other." But I liked him. I knew I did. How can you not like a man who risks his life to drag you out of a frothing ocean, then insists on getting you warmed up, listens to you chatter on about your hippie family as if it's the most fascinating tale he's ever heard, then whisks you off to the emergency room and waits, listening carefully to what the doctor says, before taking you for hot clam chowder, garlic bread, and onion rings? How can you not get a tingle?

"This is what I know about you so far, June."

I put my coffee down because I was getting *hot.*

"You like walking on the beach during rainstorms. Me, too. You get distracted by butterfly shells, I'm surmising, because you find beauty in small things. You pull seaweed out of your mouth after almost drowning, but you don't seem a bit squeamish about having it in there in the first place. Your dry humor shows even after a terrifying event, you never once skipped anywhere near hysteria, which most people would have, you didn't complain about being soaked and freezing, you were pretty darn calm actually, and in fifteen minutes flat you go from being soaking wet to . . . utterly lovely. Not that you weren't lovely soaked, you were. You were a soaked, lovely sea lady."

He thought I was utterly lovely! Oh, calm down, my heart!

"I saw you hug Morgan on the stairs, you were nice to the two boys in the emergency room with giant bumps on their heads, patted one of their backs after they vomited in a wastebasket, then hugged the worried mother. You spoke kindly to the nurses and doctors. You're strong, you're brave. How can I not like you?"

I was semistunned. "Do you always figure people out this quickly?"'

"No." He smiled again. "And I haven't figured you out, either. I'm learning about you, and I can tell you're a complex person. And interesting."

"I'm temperamental, moody, abrupt, and blunt, and I'm not in a good mood at this time of my life."

"Why not?"

"Because that's how it is. Eat some garlic bread."

"I love this stuff."

"Me, too. Eat it."

"You can tell me why you're not in a good mood at this time of your life on our next date," he said.

"Date? This is a date?"

"Let's call it a date."

"No." Oh no, I couldn't do that. It wasn't right. "This is not a date. Nope and nada."

"What is it, then?" He had such a manly voice, low and controlled . . . sexy.

"It's an . . . it's, well . . . it's a survivor's luncheon. You saved me, so we're eating together."

"Great. Let's have a survivor's luncheon again. How about it?"

I ignored a heavy weight, a trunk of lead, on my heart. "No."

He studied me for a few seconds. "Okay."

"That's it, then." I squashed down a terrible rush of disappointment. He was going to give up that quick? Not surprising for a man. Slightest bit of resistance and they back off. No, you're not worth the work or the worry, they'll find some other two-legged female to pursue. Darn, I do not think much of most men.

"No," he chuckled. "I'll ask you again. Probably tomorrow. Maybe you'll be in a better mood and more open to a survivor's luncheon?"

"I doubt it." My voice was snappish, but I smiled, then covered my smile with my napkin. He wasn't giving up! He was rebooting, so to speak.

"Maybe I'll sing to you."

I laughed at the image. "Maybe I'll sing back."

"Maybe I'll play my guitar under your window."

"I'd still say no." But I wanted to say yes.

"Don't press me, I'll do it. That's a beautiful shirt, by the way."

"Thank you."

He peered closer at it. "It's . . . can I use the word 'elegant' without you thinking I'm one of those men who's into fashion?"

"You sure can." I eyed his "guy clothes." This was a man who dressed in an outdoorsy, bring-on-the-fishing-and-hunting kind of style.

"It's all lace, isn't it? The whole thing, same with the shirt underneath it. Very feminine."

I wanted to yell, "I made it!" But I was too shy for that. Instead, I felt myself growing hot again. I would probably melt by the end of this lunch.

"Stylish. Maybe you'll wear it again when you give in and go out with me. There's this great restaurant down the road, ocean view, candles, excellent steak . . ."

"No." *Yes.*

"And stuffed baked potatoes that are incredible."

"No." *Yes.*

"And a seven-layer chocolate cake that is the best I've ever had."

I hesitated. *Yummy!* "No."

"No and no and no," he sighed. "Break my heart, June, break my heart. The cake is mouthwatering, and I have to say I'm a bit of an expert on cake because I eat it all the time."

My mouth was already watering, and it wasn't for the cake.

I drove home from Marlene's, after insisting and arguing with Reece to let me treat him to lunch, which he refused. Reece followed me down the road, his truck following my truck. That's how we'd gone to the hospital, too. I figured that someone who had saved my life, got a kick out of my nomadic childhood, and had eyes that made my heart kick-start into heaven was probably safe. If he and that sexy smile had asked me to climb into a parked space-ship bound for Pluto, I probably would have said yes.

But there was no invitation to Pluto; instead, Reece said, "I know we just met and I know you don't want to be in a truck with a man you don't know . . ."

With you I do! Bring on the spaceship!

"So I'll follow you to the hospital. It makes me nervous having you drive alone, but I'll be right behind you and it's only a ten-minute drive. If you feel the slightest bit sick, pull over, okay?"

I'd nodded on automatic. I would have liked being in a tight spaceship with him.

And that's what we'd done. When we left Marlene's, I said, "You don't have to follow me home, Reece. I'm sure you're busy."

"Not busy at all."

"But I'm fine."

"I know." He smiled. "You're more than fine."

I smiled like a drunken, love-struck fool, though I'd had nothing to drink.

So, we drove down the highway, through the town and shops filled with kooky souvenirs, ceramic lighthouses, fake shells, and taffy, the ocean sparkling on our left. We entered the residential area where I live and drove past my neighbors' houses, down around a curve, and up the hill to the end of the street. I turned into my driveway and watched his truck in my rearview mirror.

Reece turned into the driveway next door to mine. I assumed he was pulling around. I climbed out of my old, rumbly truck and waved at him as he got out of his new, black truck. "Thanks again for pulling me out of the ocean. I would not have wanted a shark to eat me for a snack. It would have been painful. For me," I clarified ridiculously. "Not for the shark."

He laughed; oh, the man was a laughing sort. Was I that amusing?

"I didn't think it would be painful for the shark. I think he'd find you quite tasty."

I turned to enter my little blue cottage, the cottage I so didn't want to lose, and instead of backing up, he headed for the front door of the home next door.

The home was two stories and the quintessential beach house, with shutters and shingles, the view of the ocean from the floor-to-ceiling windows incredible. Inside, it was modern with wood floors, an open floor plan, and two fireplaces.

"What . . ." I called. "What are you doing?"

"I'm going into my house." He smiled. My heart flittered. "I've rented it for eight weeks."

"You rented that house." I pointed at it dumbly. "That one. Right there. You rented *that* house?"

"Yes, I did. For eight weeks."

"For eight weeks?"

"Fifty-six days, give or take."

Oh, no. This was going to be a problem. "So I'm going to see you, then?"

"Yes. If you want to. I suppose you could always close your eyes when you saw me. Drive blindly down the street, run from my presence screaming, wear a bag over your head to hide, but neighbors do usually cast eyes on each other occasionally."

"Well, I'll be damned."

"Damned you won't be. I'm positive of that. Thanks for going to lunch, June."

He turned to open his front door. I didn't move.

The Greek god was living next door to me.

Oh, man. This was not gonna be good.

Or, maybe . . . it was going to be good.

Very good.

No, it wouldn't be good. It couldn't be good. When he knew the truth about my life, we'd be done.

And I had to tell him.

That I knew.

I'd met Grayson when I was working as an attorney.

I became an attorney because I wanted to fit in with The Establishment.

I wanted to be "normal."

I didn't want to be poor, I didn't want to travel around in an old VW bus, I didn't want handmade clothes, I didn't want to live in communes or hippie colonies or on farms with no electricity or plumbing.

So, at eighteen, as a rebellious teenager who decided she wanted to live a "normal American life," I attended a top-tier college on a full-ride scholarship. The college was apparently impressed with how much we had traveled, my fluency in Spanish, and my SAT scores, which were near perfect, comparable to my brother's and sisters' scores, a reflection of our parents' skills as educators.

I missed my family. I loved them. I cried every night for weeks.

But I was going to be Someone. I wasn't going to be on the fringe of society anymore, I was going to *be* society. I wasn't going to have long, messy hair and wear rainbow colors, or the tartans of our Scottish clan, and dance at midnight. I was going to be fashionable and mainstream.

In my quest to be Someone, I gave up sewing, a hobby that had brought me a sense of delight and accomplishment, and a camaraderie with my family. I powered through college, powered through law school, graduating second in my class. The valedictorian was Mindy Shadowhorse, who lived on a reservation in between her stints at school. She is now a state supreme court judge, the youngest ever in her state. She is my best friend outside my family.

I was hired to work as an attorney under crushing student loans and soul-sucking stress. I worked seventy-plus hours a week for five years. I made a lot of money and paid off my student loans at the end of those years.

Grayson was a partner in a hard-charging law firm on the floor below me. We met in the elevator. I thought he was sleekly, cooly handsome and successful. He had plans, he had ambitions. We would not be traveling around in a VW bus. We dated for six fast months and got married.

I then had what I thought I wanted: Normalcy. I had all the outward stuff that said, "You fit in. You belong. You've arrived. You're successful. You're respectable. No VW bus for you."

I wanted to be normal.

Normal made me bury all my unhappiness until I couldn't bury one more inch of it.

Normal stripped me of me.

Normal made me die internally, inch by inch.
It was not pretty.

"We have another order," Leoni said from a chair near the computer. She pushed back her white-blond hair. Today she was wearing a proper, lace-collared pink dress, fifties style, and black knee-high boots.

"Good." I took pins out of my mouth and readjusted the sequined wedding dress on my lap. This bride was an oceanographer and had ordered a jade green mermaid-style wedding gown with sequins swirling down the front and a flowing train that resembled sea waves. I loved how it was turning out.

"Bite me hard," Estelle muttered. "As if we're not all going to suffocate in piles of flounce at this studio already."

I love being in my studio. I love hearing the ocean waves outside my French doors. I love the three skylights that let the sun in and the pitter-patter sound of rain on the glass. I love the two old rocking chairs and the matching crystal chandeliers I'd added blue and pink glass beads to. I love sitting in my plushy red chair with a crazy quilt or working at the humongous table down the center of the room or at the numerous sewing machines. There are four half-naked, naked, or fully dressed mannequins, and we have shelves and piles of lace, satin, velvet, and other sleek, silky materials used to make wedding, bridesmaids, and flower girls dresses, veils, and beribboned hats.

"It's an odd order, though," Leoni said, her brow furrowed.

"Even better." I love odd orders. I am delighted to be in business with my odd orders. A bad day with odd orders is still far superior to a "good day" fighting with other strung-out attorneys in open court.

"It's rather witchly."

Witchly?

"Is she a Bridezilla sort?"

"I don't think so."

"But you said the word 'witchly.' "

"Witchly," Leoni said. "But not witchy."

"Did you tell her about the anti-Bridezilla contract?"

"I did. She signed it and will fax it back."

I have each bride sign a contract before we start to reduce the chances of my having to deal with shrieking, hysterical women. It reads, in part:

1. I will not be a Bridezilla.

2. I will remember that this is one day of my life, one day. It should be a joyous and happy day about my husband and me and when I am tempted to throw a big hissy fit, I will remember that there are people starving in the world and scrambling for water or for protection from war and wrath and hideous extremists, and I will keep myself and my highly exaggerated importance of this one day in line.

3. If I am obnoxious, June has the right to ban me from her studio forever. I understand there will be no refunds under any circumstances.

I also do not start drawing a design, or sewing one single stitch, until I have all the money, up front and paid for.

I do not mess with brides. I insist they not mess with me. Frankly, they're so happy with the dresses, and most of our clients are so edgy and free-spirited to begin with, that *most* of the time they're a pretty friendly bunch of women.

"The order is for eight bridesmaids' dresses," Leoni said. "The bride said she saw the dresses you made for her friend, Dahlia. She didn't even want to talk to you first, said her mind is made up. You're the wedding dress designer for her, her words. Her credit card has been charged and it went through."

Ah, Dahlia.

"Who can forget the bride Dahlia Parker and the dahlia bridesmaids' dresses?" Estelle said. "The walking, talking flowers." She fluffed out a gold skirt she was sewing. "Looking at Dahlia's dresses was akin to looking at Alice in Wonderland versus the War of the Flowers. An epic battle for the meadow."

"They adored them," Leoni said. "Dahlia cried. Remember how she said to the other girls, 'Now we're all dahlias' and how they cheered and danced around our studio in their Dahlia dresses?"

I put aside the mermaid wedding dress and flipped a page in a scrapbook on my desk. I have all my clients send me photos of themselves and their bridesmaids on their wedding days. Each bridesmaid in the Dahlia wedding had a different vibrantly colored dress in fuchsia, lavender, burgundy, lime, you get the point. There were eight of them. The dresses were form-fitting to the waist, then flared out under netting, the hem cut into the shapes of delicate, multicolored dahlia petals. We spent hours cutting out and sewing on delicate dahlias over one shoulder strap and down past the waistline.

Dahlia herself wore a white dahlia dress. I went to that wedding and I actually heard the guests gasp when they saw her walking down the aisle.

"They were gorgeous, earthly, garden-y," Leoni said, her eyes soft, lost in flowerland. "Blooming flowers of eternal love. Admit it, Estelle. We outdid ourselves."

"I dreamed of dahlias chasing me and smothering me with their petals," Estelle humphed. "It went on all night. They were evil dahlias, cursed and cursing."

I chuckled, then drew a finger down the dresses in the photo. As strange as the design sounds, the dahlia flower dresses were a hit. In fact, the state newspaper featured them on the front page of their Style and Fashion section.

"What does this bride want?" I asked Leoni.

Leoni pushed a stray lock back into her bun. "She wants her bridesmaids to be dressed in her favorite color."

"What is her favorite color?"

"Bright orange, like an orange."

I almost choked on a pin. "Orange?"

"That's right. She wants a smidgeon of black squiggling through the dress, too."

"I feel a headache coming on in my cranium," Estelle droned. "We have a boopsy bride. A pumpkin bride. A melon."

"Orange and black? Is it a Halloween wedding?" I asked.

"No. It's in July."

"And cramps. I think I have cramps," Estelle droned again. "Me. Way past menopause. But cramps."

"Is she an Oregon State Beaver football fan?"

"I asked that, too," Leoni said. "No, she's not. She has an affinity to orange because it reminds her of Popsicles and she embraces black because she has an aunt who's a witch."

"A witch?"

"Strike me down dead with a spell," Estelle groaned. "Down dead. Why do we get all the bridal wackos?"

Estelle knew why. We specialized in nontraditional bridal wear.

"Yes. A witch," Leoni said. "She wants to honor the witch aunt. I don't know if she calls her Aunt Witch. I didn't inquire further."

"Orange and black," I said. At first I balked, then I stood and opened the French doors and admired the ocean, the breeze cool, the sun golden candy in the sky. It would be a spectacular summer sunset.

The sunset would have orange in it. Flowing, bright, soft, creamy, dramatic, and romantic . . . orange. My imagination took off. I thought of sherbet, roses, and Costa Rica. I grabbed a pad of paper and five different shades of orange-colored pencils. I worked for fifteen minutes, not realizing that Estelle and Leoni were peering over my shoulder.

"Every single time," Leoni sighed. "Every time, my imagination bows to yours when I watch you work, June. Your mind is a mass of color. I could tell you we had an order for bridesmaids' dresses in dark brown and blah green, and those girls would wear dresses you'd see in *Vogue* magazine."

"You've got a hole in your brain where talent was poured in," Estelle said. "We get a witchly order from a half-cocked, ditzy bride, and you turn it into elegance. No sign of a witch or a spell or a black cat anywhere."

Estelle and Leoni worked for me, had for twenty-two months, but they were friends, too, and I became a bit snuffly with their sweet compliments.

Leoni patted my back. "Be gentle on yourself. Kind to your soul."

Estelle said, "Buck up, June," but not in a mean way. "Shoulders back, chin high, quit sniveling."

"She received another phone call today from Cherie," Leoni pseudo-whispered, as if I couldn't hear it, though her mouth was six inches from my ear.

Estelle said, no volume control at all, from my other side, "That'll upset her hormones. She gets in an emotional tornado and baby bawls each time."

"And she got a call from you-know-who about the you-know-what," Leoni said, then hissed. "Grayson!"

"Not good. He gets her panties in a twist, too. Two twists of the panties today."

"And, you know we have that writer coming from the magazine who's going to feature all our wedding dresses," Leoni said. "She's all jacked up about that, too."

"She should be," Estelle said loudly. "We can't screw that one up. That'd burn our butts."

"And she's stressed about her sister's wedding dress. She wants it to be perfect, more than perfect. She wants it to be a wearable dream."

"She still hasn't finished the bridesmaids' dresses, either, she's got to get it right for the clan. Go, Scotland."

"I'm right here, ladies," I said, still drawing, the oranges blurring and smearing, until I grabbed a black pencil and added a streak of black to the orange Popsicle/sunset/Costa Rica colors. I wouldn't think about the scary reporter, I already had enough to worry about.

"She has a lot going on." Leoni's breath ruffled my hair.

"Too much," Estelle agreed. "But she'll manage. She's a woman with iron panties."

"Iron panties? Gee, thank you," I said. I held up the drawing of the non-Halloween orange-and-black bridesmaids dresses. Not bad.

"Gorgeous," Estelle said. "If women must get themselves swindled into marriage, if they lose their minds to lust and society's rules of what a woman should do, they must come to you, June. Panty power, that's what it is."

"Panty power," Leoni breathed. "That is stunning."

That night I circled the work tables in my studio, again and again, while Reece jetted in and out of my head.

I have part of a blue rowboat in the corner where I've stacked all my favorite books. I have a blue cheetah lamp stand and art supplies stacked on open shelves painted yellow. I have two six-foot-tall white dressers filled with wedding dress paraphernalia.

I need all of it to keep me creative and focused.

But it sure wasn't helping me keep my mind off Reece.

Reece, Reece, Reece. June and Reece. Reece and June.

Oh, for heaven's and Pete's sakes, June!

When I was done I crawled into bed and wrote in my Worry Journal.

Seven Things I'm Worried About

1. Another sneaker wave.

2. Sharks in a tidal wave that might land on my deck. What would I do?

3. Business failing because no one wants to get married anymore because they realize it is a silly thing to do, akin only to prison.

4. Not being able to resist the Greek god.

5. Never being able to divorce Grayson, the process dragging on and on until I give up because I am too broke and too much of an emotional wreck to deal with it anymore. Then Grayson gets what he wants, and I will be tied to him for life until I am an old and feeble woman collecting plastic bags and chatting with spiders.

6. The article. What if the reporter thought I had a sponge for a brain and said so?

7. Estelle. Is she lonely living alone? I think I'll make her a lace shirt.

I played online Scrabble. I play online Scrabble with anonymous other people across the world. I almost always win. I did not win a single game that night, though I did spell these words:

"nymph," "lust," and "green." I could not get the gentle eyes of a man on a chariot out of my head to save my life.

I ate a Pop Tart and a teeny, tiny handful of buttered popcorn.

Okay, two Pop Tarts.

CHAPTER 5

"This divorce could have been settled months and months ago," I said, my anger simmering.

"But I don't want a divorce," Grayson, my soon-to-be-ex-husband replied, clipped and definitive. His hair was brushed back, nice and tight. Some women thought he was attractive, in a well-groomed, fashionable, rich attorney sort of way.

I did not.

I grunted with deep frustration and tapped the conference table in Cherie's office. It was new. Another divorcing couple had had a fight on it over a lizard or something, and the table had split in two. "That's out of your hands. We're not living in the caveman era where a man can refuse to divorce his wife, then go out and slay a dinosaur for dinner with a spear."

"I don't think he'd be able to slay a *big* dinosaur," Cherie said, beside me. She was wearing a tight, red dress with a plunging neckline and a silky, animal-print scarf. In the legal community, she is a legend. Cherie held up her fingers, one inch apart. "His spear isn't big. He'd only be able to slay a dinosaur this big."

I did not miss the hidden reference, and neither did Grayson, who protested by saying, "Hey! Keep it civilized."

"A teeny, tiny dinosaur. A weak dinosaur. A floppy dinosaur. A dinosaur who has to fake how big he is, because he is so small . . ."

"We get it, Cherie," Grayson's attorney, Walid, said. Walid had the same slicked-back hair as Grayson. He is five foot, four inches tall. Cherie and I always wear our heels when we meet with him.

Walid and Grayson had been friends for years. I thought he was my friend, too. That was incorrect. "Knock it off."

"I was explaining to your client, the teeny dinosaur, how things are." Cherie leaned her elbows on the table. "Grayson, June wants out. She will never want back in. I have handled divorcing couples for many years and trust me when I tell you that she is not changing her mind. This is a fair deal we've offered. Sign it."

"No," Grayson bit out. "June, we can talk this out. I'm still waiting for you to sit down and listen to me. You refuse to do it. You've been rash and emotional. You took a vow, in sickness and in health, good times and bad, blah, blah. So, we had a few bad days, now you walk out? You were tired from work, overwhelmed, it was too much for you, and you take it out on us."

I actually laughed. It was ludicrous. He was ludicrous. He didn't even surprise me anymore with his ludicrousness. "I'm done arguing, Grayson. Sign the papers."

"I hardly recognize you anymore," he said.

"I hardly recognize who I used to be."

"What's that supposed to mean?"

"It means that woman is gone. She landed somewhere off Neptune. We sell the house, we each take half. We each put half of the money down, so that's fair. I left you half our savings and half of what was in the checking account. You got your Porsche, I got my Porsche."

"Which you sold."

"Yes, gladly." I bought an old and grumbly truck with a lot of personality and a deep growl. I had needed the proceeds from the Porsche to start my business.

"Grayson, El Monster," Cherie delights in calling him and Walid "the Monsters," "you are ticking me off. All chat, no action. All style, no substance. All slick, no brain. All schmooze, no thinking person in there. Let's wrap this up or I'll have to get nasty."

"Hey, Cherie," Walid said. "No threatening."

"I'm not threatening him, El Monster, I'm telling him. This is a simple divorce. The simplest one ever. Sign the papers."

"We need to talk about the paper signing," Walid said. He wriggled in his seat, shot Grayson a glance, and Grayson wriggled, too. Two wrigglers. "We think the house should go to Grayson."

"What?" I semishrieked. Not that I was surprised. They are ruthless and sneaky.

"No way," Cherie said. "Fifty-fifty. On what insane grounds would you think we would give you the house?"

"Because of June's business."

That sentence, that *one* sentence, and Grayson leaning back in his chair, fingers steepled together as if he was smart and savvy, smirking, had my blood flowing, the ole MacKenzie temper flaring. "What about my business?"

"You have a business that you started when you were married to my client," Walid said, his dark eyes condescending.

"I started sewing clothes, at night, and if I had time, on the weekends, because I was stressed-out," I protested. "I wore the clothes."

"It was a business," Walid said, tapping his pen. "You sold clothes. You designed dresses, wedding dresses, other clothes. You started the business while married, which makes your business, June's Lace and Flounces, I believe it is," he fiddled with the paperwork to give me the impression that my company's name was of zero consequence to him, "communal property."

"Ha! Incorrect, El Monsters!" Cherie said. "June was sewing dresses for herself to wear, purses for her to carry her things, her guns and knives and a book on how to take revenge on small husbands." She seared my ex with a meaningful, mad gaze. "It wasn't a business."

"I disagree," Walid said.

"So do I," Grayson said. "You get your business, I get the house. You started the business in my home. We aren't divorced. We're still married. You developed this business during our marriage. I was supportive of you and encouraging. I helped with the design, the inspiration, the early development of your company. Without me, you would not have launched it to the point you're at now."

I actually saw red, I was so steamin' mad. "You didn't encourage me. You barely asked what I was doing. I worked on my dresses at night until two in the morning. I worked weekends. You told me once that it was embarrassing to be seen with me when I was wearing one of my lace skirts. You called it too 'redneck country.' You said the wedding gowns were too 'repulsively unconventional. A bridal circus.' You said nothing I ever made would sell, and that I should wear my ruffled shirts only at home in the bathroom where no one could see them."

"Nah," Grayson said, shrugging his shoulders. "I don't remember that. I remember long nights being up with you while we worked. I remember analyzing your designs and making corrections. I presented a plan for marketing and making contacts in the wide world of fashion..." He smirked again. He knew he was lying. He knew I knew it. He was simply using lawyer talk to pressure me into capitulating.

I grabbed a law book off a nearby shelf and heaved it at Grayson's face. Cherie sat back, relaxed. "Nice one, June."

Grayson ducked.

"Control your client!" Walid shrieked, rather high-pitched for a man who tried to present himself as a manly man.

I threw another book at Walid. He squealed and bent under the table.

"I will sprout wings before I give you the house, Grayson. Half of it is mine."

"Then start sprouting wings," Grayson said, running a hand through that perfect gob of slicked-back hair.

I pelted another law book.

"And I will take my business with me." My voice pitched high.

"The house for the business, June," Grayson said, ducking again. "That's the deal."

So that was it. That was the exchange. I would lose all my money in the house in exchange for a business that I was barely making money on. I thought of how much equity I had in that house. "No. Never."

I grabbed another book as Walid's pokey head poked above the table.

"That's for you, you freak. I thought you were my friend, Walid." He hid again and squealed.

"Never," Cherie said. "Ever. Ridiculous. Tiny dinosaur man, you are ridiculous. Small and flippy-floppy ridiculous."

Grayson flushed again. He was mad, but I saw what I always

saw in his beady eyes: relentless stubbornness and a sick desire for control over me. "Then no divorce. That's what I wanted anyhow. We're still married, June."

This time I didn't bother to grab only one book, I grabbed two and threw them at the same time until he and Walid scuttled out, like infected warthogs. Both books smacked Grayson in the butt.

"Monsters!" Cherie called out. "Limp monsters!"

"I'm afraid, June," Cherie said later, as we both nursed Bloody Marys at a bar around the corner, "that you're in a bad place."

"How can I be?" My hands were still shaking I was so infuriated. And I was mad at myself for letting Grayson make me infuriated. "I was sewing at night when I was married to him, I didn't have a business, I wasn't even planning on a business for a long time . . ."

"But you made patterns for about a year before you left him. Patterns for wedding dresses, bridesmaids' dresses, the white lace shirt and skirt you have now. You started selling your clothes when women came up to you and asked how they could get what you were wearing. That's an issue." She ate peanuts. I knew she was thinking hard. She's a bulldog with sharp teeth. "I will harass him for you repeatedly, and I don't think he has a solid case, but he clearly doesn't want a divorce and he will drag it out and drag it out and eventually you're going to have to settle."

Financially, I knew that. Cherie and I were longtime friends and she'd discounted the divorce costs, but hey, I'd had to write her a check with several zeros. If Grayson and I went on much longer it would be more economical to eat a hundred-dollar bill for breakfast each morning for two years.

"How badly do you want this to end? How much longer do you want Grayson in your life, manipulating your emotions, bringing all this negative stuff in?"

"I wanted him out of my life years ago. I can't stand that the guy is renting space in my head. I have to work to never think of him and it takes so much energy. Plus, this divorce is so wearing. Sometimes he'll send something, like flowers, or call out of the blue. He does it deliberately to antagonize me. It's sick."

"You have a magazine editor from *Couture Fashion* coming to your home to photograph your studio and dresses soon, is that right?"

"Yes."

"That's big-time. It's imperative that we get the papers signed before then. Your sales are going to skyrocket. The more successful you are, the harder Grayson will hold on. He's seeing money, June. He's smelling it. He doesn't get how flippingly successful you're going to be, but he will soon. He'll demand half of June's Lace and Flounces and then he'll be in your life for years to come."

Gall. "I will hand over proceeds and control of my company to Grayson only after I have constructed a home-built spaceship and launched myself off my own roof."

"Then, my friend, we need to talk about that house."

I ordered another Bloody Mary.

Early the next afternoon, a florist truck rumbled up to the front of my blue cottage.

Leoni rushed to the window to join me, as did Estelle, our faces plastered to the glass. They both bounded down the stairs and brought up a huge bouquet of roses and lilies.

"It's for you, June," Estelle said. "Hopefully it's not from that leach of an ex-husband of yours; you lost your mind when you married that one. What were you thinking? Had someone taken a hatchet to your head? Were you bleeding?"

"Probably, Estelle," I said. "Probably."

"Don't be so tough on her, Estelle," Leoni defended me. "She didn't know he was a vulture. Vultures can hide their vulture-ness. I should know. I married a vulture myself."

"I hope our ex-vultures eat each other one day, Leoni," I said.

I ran a finger over the fragrant roses and lilies. Flowers! As old as time. You send your justifiably raging wife flowers and she swoons and forgets that you were a wicked beast. Did Grayson honestly think I was going to swoon over his bouquets? Did he honestly think we could erase the last hideous two years as he incessantly fought our divorce, not to mention the two years before that, with *flowers*?

"I'll drive them down to the assisted living center again," Leoni said. "We don't want the vulture among us."

"A bleeding head," Estelle said, tapping her forehead, "is no excuse for marrying him. Don't you forget that, June. Use your noggin next time."

I ripped the card from the flowers and tore it open, my anger zip-zapping along my body, head to foot. He'd done this before, and each time it made me more mad that he could intrude on my life, my time, whenever he wanted.

But . . . but . . . it was from. . . . I gaped at the card and made a choking, gulping sound in my throat. It was not from *him.*

It was from *him.*

The chariot rider.

Him.

That him.

Estelle and Leoni leaned over my shoulder.

"By gum and golly, this is a miraculous moment. It's from the sneaker wave rescuer," Estelle said. "You should get knocked over by sneaker waves more often. What's a life-threatening event when you can meet a muscled, seductive rancher?"

"You obviously didn't tell him that the male species will soon die out because of flaws in their genetic makeup," Leoni gushed.

I stared at the roses and lilies, delicate, sweet, elegant.

"The note says," Leoni said. " 'Looking forward to our survivor's luncheon.' "

"What's a survivor's luncheon?" Estelle asked. "I think, at my age, I should go to one of those daily. But I don't want to hang out with men my own age. They're boring. They complain all the time about their aches and pains. They have bladder problems. They have intestinal problems. They're fascinated by their bowels. I want to hang out with the younger men. I want to be a cougar." She curled her hands into paws and made a cougarish sound.

I was not a cougar. Reece was not younger than me.

He sure was cute, though.

Estelle made another cougarish sound.

Leoni and I laughed.

Leoni pawed her hands in the air, too.

I growled back at both of them. "Grrrr..."

"To cougars!" Leoni shouted, holding up an imaginary champagne glass.

"To cougars!" We clinked glasses.

"Thank you for the flowers."

"You're welcome." Reece smiled at me, dwarfing his doorway, his blue buttondown shirt somehow making those piercing green eyes even brighter.

It had taken me hours of encouraging self-talk while I sewed my bridesmaid's dress for August's wedding—and an online Scrabble game where I spelled the words "fear," "loathe," and "prick," and therapy-eating where I downed five warm chocolate chip cookies—before I could gather up enough nerve to slink next door to thank Reece.

And to tell him what he needed to know immediately.

On my way over, Estelle leaned out the studio's window like an avenging gargoyle and yelled, "Don't mess this up. It's not like you're going to get a lot of other chances to prove you can be nice to a man. You had to almost drown to meet this one."

Leoni said, wringing her hands, "Be gentle, kind... feminine. Do you know how to do that?"

Estelle said, "Don't be a cougar, be a cougarette!"

"Grrrr," Leoni called out. "Grrrr..."

I was almost shaking with fear.

"They're beautiful," I said into Reece's handsome, chiseled face. "Sexy."

He blinked.

"I didn't mean that." *Not again, June. Focus, focus!* "I didn't mean the flowers were sexy. I meant that they're beautiful. The flowers. Not you." He was a tall and broad specimen of a man. "Not that you aren't, too. I mean! Aw." I felt myself boil up like a furnace. "I have to go."

"Please don't go," he rumbled out, still smiling. "Come on in. I thought you might need some color after you took a tumble in the ocean."

"I do. I did. I do need them. Yes, and color. That was nice.

Well." I ignored the fact that my knees were shaking. If only he was a temperamental green centaur, this would have been easier. "Thank you again."

"You're leaving already?"

"Yes and no. No and yes. No, no." Sheesh.

"How about no? Come on in. I have lobster."

Lobster was my favorite. I love lobster. Heaven is filled with lobster in tiny oceans where you can reach down and grab one at any time and they *want* you to eat them with a side order of coleslaw, thick, hot, white, buttered bread, and lemonade. They do.

"You do?"

"Bought it an hour ago. Come on in, June."

I hesitated. That man pinned me down and shook me up. He turned me inside out. I berated myself, out loud. "Who's the boss here?"

"I'm sorry?"

"Nothing. Nothing at all." I waved a hand in front of my face.

He stepped back, welcoming, and opened the door.

I tripped a bit in the doorway as I bumbled on in. "Nice, June," I muttered.

"What's nice?"

I turned to him. I thought of him naked. I blushed. I thought of him in bed naked down the hall. I blushed further. I thought of us naked in the bed down the hall. I turned away and said, again, so ridiculously, "I love lobsters in bed naked."

He laughed. I blushed further. "Stop blushing, June!" I muttered out loud.

Humiliated.

"So, you're renting this home?" I took another bite of lobster, dipped in butter and garlic sauce. It was absolutely delicious.

We'd set up a table outside on his deck, the ocean panoramically displayed for 180 degrees in both directions, the summer air warm, the smell of salt wafting in and out.

"A friend of mine's mother owns it. Her name is Frankie Schaeffer. Frankie fell in love with a man she met on a wild girls' trip to

France and stayed in Paris. Sixty-two years old and she said she's found true love for the first time in her life and isn't leaving."

I laughed. "Good for her. So that's what happened. I've never met the owner and no one is ever here."

"She's here in spirit." Reece laughed.

"I doubt it. The woman fell in love with a Frenchman in Paris. She's having the time of her life eating croissants and coffee in tiny white cups."

"Okay, you win. Her spirit is in France. By the way, I like your hair."

"You do?" I self-consciously pulled on it.

"Yes. I can only compare it to gold moving."

Gold moving.

"With sunshine and sparkles thrown in."

Sunshine and sparkles. "Are you a poet?"

He laughed. "Not quite. I say what I think."

"So, you're a flirt." I ignored a stab in my heart. Darn it. Flirts were dangerous. Teasingly, attractively dangerous. Light and fluffy and you are one of a harem . . .

"Not at all. You're the first one in many years."

He said it sincerely, so straight on. Could it possibly be true? I took a deep breath so I could spit out the truth. This was not gonna be fun. "Reece, I need to be completely honest with you."

"Please do."

I gathered my strength by studying the cliffs in the distance and the tide pools below it, then turned back to him. "I'm in the middle of a divorce."

Reece's eyes widened slightly and his expression froze, that hard jaw not moving.

"Or, I should say, I'm at what I hope will be the end of my divorce. It's a mess. I'm a mess. I left him two years ago. He doesn't want a divorce and he is fighting it with all he has, every loophole, every delay tactic."

I hoped the sun, bright and bold in a deep blue sky, would warm up my scared-stiff and frozen body. "I should have told you at lunch, but I didn't want to."

"Why didn't you want to tell me then?"

"Why?" I heard no judgment in his tone, only a question. "Because I wanted . . ."

"You wanted what?"

"I wanted to go to lunch with you, to talk and laugh, and I didn't want to discuss the black, frothing muck in my life, this constant sadness, this fight, this disaster." For once I was not awash in lust while looking at him. My sadness was squashing the lust. "I didn't even know if we would see each other again, and I wanted to take a break out of my life and just be with you."

He thought for a while, watching the ocean. *Maybe I should leave now?*

"Within ten minutes of talking to you," he said, "I knew we'd see each other again."

"Because you knew we were living next door to each other?"

"No. Because I wanted to be with you again."

I wanted to cry. I had so wanted to be with him, too.

"As far as your soon-to-be-ex-husband. Do you still love him? Do you hate him? Is the marriage over in your mind, or are there a whole bunch of things that are still upsetting you?"

"I have been through a mind-numbing range of emotions with this divorce, with the ending of my marriage, and I feel nothing for my ex-husband except this anger and frustration that he's holding things up. There are no other emotions left from the marriage itself. I don't love him, I don't hate him, I don't like him. I want him out of my life. He's controlling this situation, as he did our marriage, because he can. I can't stand that anyone is controlling me at all, especially him."

"He's on a power trip, then."

"Always has been. But am I over him? Yes. Long ago I was over him."

"Why did the marriage break up?"

"Definitely at least half my fault. I never should have married him. I was acting as someone I wasn't, reaching for things I didn't value, and I worked incessantly to build my career. I was part of an image that I thought, for years, I wanted. Grayson fit into the image. He was the perfect fiancé, and the perfect husband for about three months. We wanted the same things. We had the same interest in work. My mistake."

"What did you used to do?"

"I was a lawyer in a law firm on a partnership track. He was a partner in another high-powered firm."

"How'd that go?"

"I was unutterably miserable."

"And your marriage was miserable."

"Yes. I won't get into the sordid details, but I will say that it was the criticism that killed it, an incessant onslaught of negative, until I shut down. Down and out." I studied the break of the waves, the way the blue-gray water shot out in both directions. "That's when you know you're done with a marriage, I think, when there's no fight in you anymore, no arguments. You acquiesce, you give up, you dive into self-protection mode, arms over your head, knees to chest.

"He went on a business trip once, for four weeks, to New York. That was when I understood, finally, that I had a problem. Sometimes the problem has to leave before you realize you're in an emotional war zone, fighting to keep yourself together and constantly battling emotional manipulations. What is abnormal and not mentally healthy has become your normal, but you're too mentally unhealthy to see it. Your normal isn't normal. It's not a place where you can grow and live and create. It's a bad, bad spot.

"When he was gone and I wasn't constantly ducking for cover around him, and could breathe, and think, and finally be brutally honest with myself, I started to recognize how much my marriage had smothered me."

"What was the final moment, when you knew you were done with the marriage? Was there a last straw?"

"There was. I told you I loved sewing as a kid with my family. Even my father could sew. During college and law school and my years of building a career, I stopped sewing, I didn't have time. In the midst of my misery, a year into my marriage, I started sewing again, at night, as soon as I could sneak away from Grayson. It was my only respite, I lost myself in whatever I was making. Soon my uptight lawyer suits had a rim of lace. The skirts had ruffles. The sleeves were embroidered down the sides. I made flowers out of dyed leather and attached them to the toes of my heels. And I sewed dresses, long and flowing or short and snazzy, mostly out of lace, which I love, as I had done with my mom and my sisters.

"Through waves of pain and loneliness living in that barren marriage, in that barren job, I sewed and sewed. In every stitch, every scissor cut, every piece of thread that passed through my fingers, every touch of lace or satin or velvet or leather, I felt myself coming back to me. As if I'd lost her and she'd been packed into a sewing box in my head and the box had been nailed down and hidden.

"To court one day I wore a pink skirt with a ruffle and a bit of taffeta underneath it with a pink lace shirt I'd lined with satin trim, and I knew I was done. Even the judge noted, 'Hmm . . . I think we're feeling a bit pinkish today, Ms. MacKenzie.' "

I laughed out loud; so did Reece.

"I loved that judge. It was a woman and later she called me and asked where I'd bought my suit. That day I tore apart the lying witnesses, attacked the defense's case with ferocity, nailed my opening and closing arguments, and won the case. It was a high-profile case.

"I headed back to my office and was stopped three times by women who wanted to know where I'd bought my clothes and the handbag I'd made out of leather and lace. I had an epiphany and I quit my job fifteen minutes later. I left with a check and decided that part of my life was over."

"That was it?"

"That was it. It took a day in court with pink lace and satin trim."

"That's brave. I admire you. You were taking a new direction, didn't know where it would lead, but it had to be better than what you were living with."

"Exactly." Man, he was so smart. "Sometimes ya gotta walk . . ."

"And the walk may have no clear path . . ."

"But you have to get on it anyhow." We understood each other.

"Then what happened?"

Oh, those green eyes. I could feel the lust coming at me again, darn it.

I cleared my throat. "On my way out of the law firm, Grayson came tearing after me. He yelled, 'What the hell did you do? What happened? Have you lost your friggin' mind, June? Do you expect me to support you? Do you expect to sit around and eat chocolate all day while you sew your white-trash Halloween outfits? I'm not giving you a dime of my money, now get back in there and tell them you made a mistake, because you have, June, you have!' "

" 'No,' I said to him. 'I have not made a mistake.' "

" 'You quit your job!' He's screaming at me now. 'Why? What are you thinking? *Are you thinking?* And why are you dressed in *pink*? You didn't wear that to court, did you? You're an attorney, not a pink cake!'

"And I said, 'I'm quitting a lot of things. The job was first, you're second, and now I'm quitting this city.' And I did."

Reece abruptly stood up, his face flushed, and started pacing the deck.

"What's wrong?" I asked, alarmed.

He couldn't even speak for a minute. "I believe," he bit out, still stalking around, "that even though you don't hate your soon-to-be-ex-husband, I do. I can't believe he said that to you."

I about cried right there, his anger was so touching. Reece ranted for a few minutes, protective, furious, and when he settled down, we talked for another forty-five minutes. I was as honest as I could be. I told him how afterward I went to visit my parents for a week.

"I walked through their fields and down to the river. I took off my shoes. I went barefoot. I rode their horses and petted their cats and dogs with strange names like Christmas Wreath and Mr. Scoot and Admiral Crow.

"I stared out their windows and watched sunrises and sunsets on their porch, something I hadn't paid attention to in years. I wouldn't have even sworn that we still had sunrises and sunsets anymore. I watched leaves flutter through the fields. I watched flowers unfold. I studied a blue heron and blue jays. I listened to the river bubble and sat in absolute silence. At first the silence was so noisy I couldn't concentrate, but then I breathed the silence in, so I could figure my way out of the disaster of my own making.

"My parents asked me to come and work for the family company, but I declined, with a hug, because I wanted to sew wedding dresses and build my own company. They understood, and we spent hours working together, planning my business, discussing designs, drawing, coloring, penciling...my hands shaking, shock slowly leaving my body to be replaced by this light of hope I hadn't felt in years."

The kite flyers were out and I envied them their playtime. "I came to the beach and rented my house because I am passionate about the Oregon coast. I can think here, *be* here. Most days I'll put my rocking chair right next to my French doors, cover myself with my crazy quilt, and sew. I'm as happy as I've ever been when I do that."

"What else makes you happy, June?"

"My family, as odd as we all are, as imperfect as we all are, they make me happy. What makes you happy, Reece?"

"Right now."

"Yes, right now. Anything. What makes you happy?"

"I just told you. *Right now* I'm happy. I'm happy talking and watching the waves with you. Thanks for being honest, June."

"You're welcome. I probably should have told you the second I was dragging seaweed out of my mouth, so please forgive me."

"Forgiven."

So quick, without a second thought. The man did not want to play games. "Thank you. So, Reece. If you want, we can be friends. Ah...good friends. I'm still technically married, so I don't feel it's right to date. I don't think I could handle being involved with anyone, it's too stressful, I'm not a whole person yet, and I especially could not date you." I shifted in my seat. "Not that you would want to date me. I'm not trying to be presumptuous, I know you probably wouldn't want to date me, but—"

"June, I want to date you. But why would you not want to date me if you were free?"

I bent my head, wrestling with my thoughts, then looked up again. "You're sexy and too much of a man to get wrapped up with. I think I'd lose my head around you. There. I said it. More honesty for you."

"I don't want you to lose your head. You have a pretty head."

His mouth tilted at the corners; nice lips. Such nice lips. I tried to put myself back together and not think about his lips. "I'm a fast-moving train wreck, but if you want to be friends with a wreck, sign me up."

"I'll sign you up. I've always wanted to be friends with a wreck."

I smiled at him. He was such a cowboy/rancher sort of *true* man.

"I can do it," he said, almost to himself. "I can control myself. I can resist. I can stop myself from pulling you into my arms and kissing you on our midnight walks along the beach, counting stars together lying in the sand, hot tubbing . . . yep, I can control all those thoughts. But maybe, June, when this is all over, and you're ready, you and I can start as an *us*. We can be an *us*. Going slowly."

My stomach flipped and flopped in a happy, skippy way. "I think we might could do that. I haven't scared you off?"

"No. Not at all. To the contrary."

We sat in silence, my brown eyes on his green, neither looking away, both smiling like silly goons, my heart galloping about.

"It's an incredible day, isn't it?" he said, his voice carrying over the gentle ruffle of wind.

"Yeah, Reece, it is an incredible day." *And, June, you will not fall in love with him! You won't!* "Okay, I'll try not to," I said out loud.

"What?"

"Nothing. Oh, nothing."

He reached for my hand, yes he did. His hand was strong and muscled. Even though I believe in treats and chocolates, my body would seem small underneath the stroking of that hand. At the thought of that strong hand slipping over my entire body, I felt myself heat up again, as if a match had been lit right under my feet and the rest of me was now engulfed in flames.

I placed my hand in his.

"Now I'm even happier, June."

He winked at me.

Oh, for heaven's sakes.

CHAPTER 6

"It'll be a disaster!" she screamed. "A disaster of epic and long-lasting proportions!"

"What? Who is this?" I pushed blond, messy curls out of my eyes. It was six o'clock in the flippin' morning. A horrid hour to be awakened by the phone. "August? Is that you? Why are you screaming?" I'd had four hours of sleep. I had worked on August's wedding dress until I fell asleep and my head slammed on my work table.

"The vision! Them, and us, altogether! We could be a nightly television reality show! A reality show about two families who go to war with each other . . . the loons on the fringe of society against the uptight, snooty rich people."

"August, calm down, honey, please."

"How can I?" she moaned. "How can I?"

August is an accountant for our parents' company. She went to college, then graduate school, was hired at a major corporation, but the corporation snuffed out "my Scottish Highlands soul." She finally gave in to our parents' pleading and now runs their books. After work, August is August: unconventional, wild, sweet, and plays in a band called Ladies Loo Loo and wears leather.

She met a man named Ben online. One thing they have in common is that both families hail from Scotland and are into their genealogy, tartans, kilts, and all things Scottish. In fact, his grandfather was born there. The families are from different clans, however.

"Do you know what time it is?" I groaned.

"Yes, it's time to be up. Rise and shine, June, and help me! Help me! I'm getting married and we're about to witness the total breakdown of Scottish-American civilization on my wedding day."

"What's the problem, hysterical bride?" I propped myself up on a pile of pillows. Anyone getting up earlier than 7:00 is almost committing a crime, as far as I'm concerned. It's uncivilized to be up before then. "Do tell."

And there she went, whooshing into orbit. My liberal, free-thinking sister was petrified to death of her fiancé's family and they were all flying in for the wedding. Even Grandma with her pearls and her blue bloodline, and the stern and gruff grandfather who owned companies and the sisters who always had perfect hair all piled into a chignon and high heels and top-of-the-line fashion. "Their faces never move. They've been Botoxed to death. They're always composed. Intimidating. Cold. *Brrrr . . .*"

"At least they're Scottish," I mocked.

"They make me want to swim in a whisky bottle."

"You don't drink, August." I held my hand to my head. Hardly any sleep. Again. I would probably melt from exhaustion. I thought of Reece. Ah, I would take any opportunity to melt on him. . . .

"They don't spit watermelon seeds." She released an anguished cry.

"Uncle Taylor won last time," I mused. We have a family watermelon-seed spitting contest every time we're together. Not just the six of us, the whole MacKenzie gang. "Remember it made Aunt Mary so mad she accused the judges of cheating. The judges were her own children."

"And what about the scavenger hunt with the crystal fairy wands!"

"They might like the wands. They're shiny."

"And all our wild cousins and their parents are coming, June! Who knows if the twins will dress up as monster twins again with those vampire teeth. And I bet Cousin Carrie will insist on doing a Ouija board with them, and I hear that Uncle Sal is into witchcraft now. Witchcraft!" August shrieked. "I told Auntie Debbie she had to make him not do it at the wedding, but she said, 'Honey, it's better than his voodoo doll stage. He was mad at your father once and your father had terrible gas all year. Don't knock the witchcraft.' She actually said that to me, June!"

"Don't forget that a whole bunch of our family will be in kilts and tartans."

"I know, freak me out, and Ben's family will be in three-piece suits. Prissy and buttoned up . . ."

"August, this is one day. It's at Mom and Dad's. It'll be a gorgeous day, the tents will be up, and the families will only be together for a few hours. The attention is on you, August, and mildly, on Ben. Be yourself, loving and kind, and funny. This is the day you don't worry about anyone else—"

"But what about Grandpa Bill! You know he says that all MacKenzie weddings should have a three-gun salute and he and Bill Jr. and Mack are going to bring their .45s and shoot them into the air in celebration—"

I groaned and scrunched back into my blue crocheted comforter as August continued her harangue for ten more emotional minutes.

"But I love my wedding dress, June. It's Scottish and American and so me. Thank you so much. And I love the bridesmaids' dresses, too."

"I am so glad you love them, August. Hearing that makes me feel like yodeling." I yodeled to lighten the moment.

She sniffled. "You and September rock as sisters and knowing you'll both be on the stage Buddy's building for us will take some of my deathly fear of Ben's family away."

"I'm so happy for you, August." And I was. My marriage had been miserable but hers had all the makings of a sixty-year marriage. The groom was a winner, kind, funny, natural, and totally enraptured by August. He loved her semihysteria, her fascination with antique furniture, her food pickiness, her leather, her rockin' band, her worries. "It's a gift. You have a gift in Ben."

"I know. And you, June, are a gift to me. Okay, let's compare Worry Journals now."

I rolled over to my side table and grabbed my Worry Journal.

We go through our journals together at least once a week. It's neurotic, we know it, and we get more neurotic together, but we've done it since we were little kids in the VW bus, and we do it now.

It's a MacKenzie sister tradition.

"I have twenty-four things I'm most worried about, all equally worrisome, so this is not in exact order, that's important for you to know, June," August said. "Here they are . . ."

Later that afternoon I rocked in my rocking chair as I worked on a pattern for another wedding gown, this one for a bride who loved her motorcycle and would be riding off from the wedding in the gown. She wanted white lace, a black leather belt, and two midthigh slits. My French doors were open to the cool breeze wafting off the ocean, my crazy quilt covering my lap, Leoni and Estelle off to buy us hot crab sandwiches and raspberry lemonade.

"I'm an old woman," I muttered, pushing my reading glasses up on my head for a sec. "All I need is a cat beside me and a knitting basket."

I was trying not to think of my divorce. I was trying not to think about losing this blue beach cottage with its view of cliffs, surfers, and crashing waves. I was trying not to think of the reporter coming soon and whether or not she would hate or, worse, laugh at my alternative wedding dresses.

Most of all I was trying to stop thinking about Reece because I didn't want my mind all twisted up by a man. I would especially not think about kissing him.

I thought about kissing him, ocean water swirling around our ankles.

I shook my head and tried to concentrate.

I thought about hugging him down by the tide pools.

I stomped my foot and told myself to "reconnect" with the pattern.

I thought about him naked, on the beach, at night . . .

"Argh!" I said, out loud. "Stop it!"

I pictured myself taking a red wedding dress off in front of Reece down by the cliffs. I swallowed hard.

Now this motorcycle bride needed to straddle her bike so we would need . . .

What if I straddled Reece?

"Oh, for goodness sake!" I semishrieked out loud at myself. "Think about . . . think about cats! Small cats, black cats, gold cats . . ."

I put the pattern down.

"Dammit," I whispered, holding my head, as a 3D image of kissing Reece, three black and gold cats purring beside us on a boat in the ocean, branded itself onto my poor brain.

But this time, following the lust, I felt a wave of acute sorrow, then a deep, penetrating sadness, the same sadness I had fought through many times.

It was the Grayson sadness. *I must get him out of my life.*

* * *

"You never mentioned being married, Reece, so I assumed that you hadn't been, is that right?" Reece and I sat on his deck, the sunset only beginning its magnificent display across the white crests of waves, an art form in itself.

"No. Not married, no kids. Engaged once." He put a plate of omelets and French toast in front of us. Breakfast for dinner. My favorite.

"What happened?"

"It was years ago. I was twenty-two. She's a great woman. Our families have been friends forever, generations back. She was cute."

I tried to stamp down a rising red tide of jealousy.

"She was smart."

The red tide rose.

"She was fun and loyal."

The red tide was now frothing.

"She would have made a great mother."

Now the red tide was arching over my head in wave form, ready to make an ugly crash. I had no right to be jealous, but I was.

"And I would have been bored to death."

The red tide receded, pulling back down into a puddle. I almost gasped for breath. "Why?"

"I left when I was eighteen for college and I've worked and traveled between places for years. Quite frankly, I'd like to settle down in one place, have a home." He smiled at me. "Maybe the beach. Or Portland. Anyhow, as you know, there's a whole world out here and she wasn't interested in it and didn't want to see it. Her conversation was limited to what she loved best. She could talk about her family, her horses, and how she was a rodeo queen. That was about it. I knew what we wanted out of life was completely different and we broke up. She's married to an ex-rodeo cowboy, has lots of horses, and six kids. She's a kind woman."

"But not for you."

"That's right."

He sung part of a song about a perfect woman, but he couldn't marry her, he had to open the door and run, the world was there to live in, not hide from. The chorus was about mountaintops, rushing rivers, and adventures. "I know that song! It's called 'Running for the Rivers' by Jordy Daniels. He won an award for that."

"Yep, you're right."

"Sure fits your situation, doesn't it?"

"Yes, it did."

"Do you like country music?"

"I love it, listen to it all the time. Do you know this song?" He hummed a few bars, then sang the words.

"Yes! That's 'Tough Caroline Baker,' about a woman who slugs it out in bars to cover a hurting heart. I love that one, too."

"And this song . . ." His voice rose, strong and deep.

I laughed and sang along with him about the cheating boyfriend who was locked up in jail for running naked through the streets, his girlfriend threatening to shoot him from behind and "blast his butt to Jupiter."

"That is one of my all-time favorite songs."

"Mine, too. So, lovely June, you know I am a rancher."

"I know, cowboy. And by the way, you make the most excellent French toast."

"Thank you. My granddad taught me. But I have another job, too."

"Let me guess." I tapped my forehead. "You're a cowboy clothes model."

"Not even close, but thank you."

"You're a secret high heel shoe designer."

"I wear cowboy boots and beach sandals. That's about all I know about shoes."

"Hmmm . . ." I studied him. "You're a kindergarten teacher."

He simply laughed at that one, then hummed a few bars of another country song.

"That's 'Cowboy Lady.'" I sang the next two verses, about a lady that was tougher than men and no man could catch her, she rode hard and long, her heart broken way back when.

"So, June, when I'm not out on my ranch, or hanging out at the beach with a girl who wears lace, I write country songs."

I stopped. "You do?"

"Yep."

"For fun, right? You make up your own songs?"

"I do make up my own songs."

"Ah. Sing me one."

"I did. I sang you a few."

I put my fork down, hard as it was to stop eating that scrumptious French toast with powdered sugar. "I am not understanding this."

"The songs I sang you, I wrote."

More confusion. "But those songs are sung by huge country stars."

"I guess they want to sing my words."

I couldn't get a grip on this one. "Are you kidding?"

"Nope. I'm not."

Seeing my shock, he stood up and brought over his laptop. He typed in his name and millions of hits came up, along with photos of him.

Reece O'Brien was a famous country music songwriter.

"You didn't Google me, did you?" he asked.

Oh. My. Golly. There he was. "No, I didn't."

"I Googled you. I love your website, June, the photos of all the wedding dresses, bridesmaids' dresses, you, Estelle, Leoni, your studio. Can I see it soon? I feel like I've been able to take a step into your mind through your studio, but I want to know more, how it works, how you think—"

"Thank you, but—" I ran my hands through my hair. "You're a country songwriter."

"Yes."

"Is that why you're here? You came to write? I would think you would live in Nashville or L.A."

"I'm in and out of both cities, and I do go to my ranch. I came here for new scenery, but for the first time in my life I find myself distracted." He leaned toward me and I caught my breath.

"Want to hear my next song, June?"

"Yes, of course." I couldn't quite believe this one, my mind all baffled up. He wrote country songs?

Reece went into the house, came back with his guitar, and strummed.

The song had an upbeat melody, a *come and clap your hands to this one* tune. It was about a woman with blond locks who wore lace and loved tide pools, sunsets, and watching the weather roll over the waves. She believed that getting up early in the morning should be illegal. She had a temper.

His baritone voice rolled over and around me, snug and huggable, then burrowed deep, deep inside.

"What do you think?" he asked, and I could tell he cared. He cared what I thought of his song.

I was so touched, I could hardly get my throat to work. "I think that the woman with blond locks who wears lace and loves sunsets will love it."

He was silent for a second and we had one of those moments, close, raw, and romantic, where we were the only two people at the beach, the only two people anywhere.

"Good. I want her to love it."

"She does." I tried to catch my breath.

"June." He threaded his fingers between mine. "He loves it, too."

My soul did a heel-kicking dance, a rush of joy tripped around my body, and tears flooded my eyes.

And there we sat, the sunset a grand artist's display, our French toast covered in syrup and powdered sugar.

"Are you almost ready, June?" Mr. Schone said, his voice crackling with age over the phone.

I love Mr. Schone, Mrs. Schone, too, although I dreaded his calls. They own the blue cottage that I've been renting. They live up the street. I hike up once a week to check on them. I recently brought Mrs. Schone swatches of intricate lace for her tables because she loves them.

"I am so sorry to press you on this one, my dear, but my begonia is not feeling well, and I do need to get her off the coast by winter . . ."

His "begonia" was his wife of sixty years. Mrs. Schone needed to move. Her health wasn't good. She was one of the kindest people I have ever met, but she was weak and frail and they wanted to be near their two daughters who lived down south.

"Mr. Schone, I am so sorry, but I don't have enough money to buy this house." Even saying the words aloud, which I'd said to him several times, hurt. I wanted my blue cottage. I loved the creaking staircase, huge windows, the deck outside, and the flat roof over the garage that I sat on underneath a red-and-white–striped umbrella. It was the home of my heart, but I didn't have near enough money to buy it without the equity from my Portland house. "Please put it up for sale with a realtor. I'll get it cleaned and organized so you can move."

"Keep trying, my dear, keep trying. We can wait a few months. You're who we want to sell the house to. My begonia wants to know that you'll be in our home, it makes her happy. . . ."

I wanted to make the begonia happy, too.

I so did. For her, and for me. We hung up after a few minutes.

I hoped they called the realtor. I would lose the house to someone else, but they needed to move. I thought of Mrs. Schone. I would make her a lace wrap for her shoulders. She would feel pretty in that.

"Hi, June," Morgan said, her NASA helmet on her head. "I'm going to read you some information on spaceships while you sew."

"Superb. I can always learn more."

She put down her pen and clipboard. "You know, June, I don't fit in with the other kids at school."

"I don't think I've ever fit in, kiddo." I gave her a hug. "Don't try to fit in. Be yourself. List ten things you like about yourself. If you force yourself to be someone you're not, you will be one unhappy caterpillar."

"Yeah. I know." She fiddled with her white space gloves. "A lot of the other kids have dads."

"They do. But you have the coolest mother on the planet."

"She is pretty cool. Do you think my dad would like me if he saw me again?"

"Definitely. What's more important is, do you think you would like *him*?"

She didn't say anything for a minute. "I don't know. He left us. I'm going to have to think about that."

"Okay." I hurt to see Morgan hurt. What hurt the most was seeing her emotional dependence on a father who had skipped out of town, oblivious to the demolition he had brought to her life. He did not deserve her adolation. "Remember that supersmart kids like you can open the door to a world filled with adventure. Like the adventures you'll have at NASA. Now, tell me about the wings of a space shuttle."

"It's incredible," he said, his voice low. "Incredible."

Reece the chariot rider sat on a stool in the middle of my yellow studio. My French doors were open, the stars up and twinkling over the crashing waves, the lights of two fishing boats flashing in the distance.

"I am absolutely in awe, June."

Amidst the lace, flounce, silkiness, and sewing machines he looked steamrollingly masculine. Hard-core man. Sexy and huge. He was a manly man in a woman's territory, yet in some incongruous way . . . he fit in.

"I . . . well, I have to be around color." I thought of the colors in the home I shared with Grayson: Beige. Black. Soul-deadening. "Color helps me to think, and bright and interesting things— whether they're bird nests or a collection of odd teapots—help me create."

"I understand. I do." He nodded, and I knew he *did* understand. We're both creative; he *got* it.

"You are amazingly talented, June. This whole studio, these dresses . . ." He shook his head, indicating the mannequins that were draped with August's wedding dress and our bridesmaids' dresses. "Wow. That's all I can say, wow. How do you make a wedding dress?"

"You're kidding."

"No, I want to know."

"But you're a . . . you're a man."

"Yes. Last time I looked." He ran a hand through that thick blondish hair. "Could have changed on the long walk over from my place to yours, but I think not. Shall I check?"

Whew! Another graphic image! I shut that one out.

"No, no checking." I took a wobbly breath. "Okay, I'll make it short, don't want to bore you right out of your skull."

"I won't be bored. Start with what you do when someone calls and wants a wedding dress."

I told him. I watched him closely for signs of nauseating boredom and acute distress. I watched to make sure his eyes didn't glaze over and he didn't fall asleep, his head banging on my work table. None of that occurred. He wanted to know how my ideas sparked to life, how I worked, thought, imagined. The conversation was a huge turn-on.

Grayson hadn't even wanted to know about my sewing, calling it "June's 1950s backwards housewife hobby."

"To launch my company, I sewed straight through for weeks until my eyes were burning, my body a limp noodle from exhaustion. I designed a traditional, exquisite white wedding gown, then three nontraditional, eye-popping sorts of wedding gowns, and August, September, my mom, and I modeled them for a professional fashion photographer. I threw a humongous amount of money at advertising, online and in print, and I was, miraculously, soon in business."

"But why wedding dresses? You were divorcing at the time."

"I love the love, the passion for each other, the eternal hope that this couple could get married and stay together, possibly for seventy years. They could have a love like my parents' love. A love for forever. I want to make a dress for the bride that reflects her, her personality, her new life, and that shining hope."

"They're perfect. Like nothing I've ever seen before." He closed one of my bridal scrapbooks. He'd studied every dress.

"On my wedding day I was wearing a regular suit." I tried to sound offhand, but it hurt. *Still.* I bit my lip. *Why did I say anything at all?*

"You were wearing a regular suit?" Reece was aghast, his mouth open, eyes confused.

"Yep. A suit." I thought of that suit. It wasn't even my favorite suit. It was my fifth favorite suit. It was beige. I had left it behind when I left Grayson behind.

"*Why?*"

"Because we were married at the courthouse."

He hardly knew what to do with that one, his face frozen in shock. "Why did you get married at the courthouse?"

"Because it was convenient."

"*Convenient?* What the hell does 'convenient' have to do with a wedding?"

"We were busy. We worked a lot. We were married on our lunch hour."

"On your lunch hour? You've got to be kidding." Reece's disbelieving, appalled expression was enough to tell me what he thought about that.

"No." Grayson had been late. He'd hurried up the steps. He was in trial, buried in work, didn't "have time" for a nice wedding. "And they're so expensive, June. A fortune. I don't want to spend all that money. The result is the same, right? We're married. But this'll cost almost nothing and we're done."

Done.

Yep. We were *done.*

I remembered standing in front of the judge. I knew the judge. Grayson had forgotten my flowers.

"You forgot the flowers?" Judge Allery admonished Grayson.

Grayson blushed.

I said it was okay.

Judge Allery was absolutely flabbergasted. "It's not okay. *No flowers?*"

And yet, that was the least of what we were missing.

"Do you have the ring?" Judge Allery cocked an eyebrow at Grayson, as if he thought there was a distinct possibility that the brick in front of him had forgotten that, too.

"Of course!" Grayson puffed up and displayed our rings. Two thin gold bands. Inexpensive. "I'll buy you a diamond later, June. I don't have time now. We'll shop together," he'd said. I never had a diamond ring. It wasn't the diamond I wanted, it was the care and thought behind it and the fact that he had not kept his word that was the problem.

We were married. *It was done.*

The judge spoke very slowly during our vows and stared hard at me. He later told me that he knew Grayson, knew me, and hadn't a clue why I was marrying him. "A pigeon had clearly plucked your brain out of your head without you noticing," he'd admonished over a shared beer at a bar.

"My parents were appalled," I told Reece. "So was the rest of our Scottish clan."

"I bet they were. Weddings are for families. The whole thing is sad, June, and I'm getting all ticked off at your ex again." He stood up and stalked around the studio, his cheekbones flushed. "A courthouse! At your lunch break? Damn. He didn't care, did he? He wasn't thinking of you at all." He ran a hand in frustration over his hair. "That had to hurt you so much, and yet you make wedding dresses."

"Late at night, when I was still married to Grayson, I started sketching wedding dresses, dress after dress, with colored pencils. I know it was wedding dress therapy. As the marriage became, for me, more and more sad, I worked out my grief, my loneliness, my anger at him and at myself, through drawing. I lost myself in that marriage, but I'd really been lost for years.

"I drew pages and pages of dresses. The more I drew, the more original the gowns became. They started reflecting the core of the woman, her identity. It was fun. The next day I'd go back to whipping people in court, blasting the other side, inwardly knowing my life was rotting and something had to give."

"I'm sorry, June." Reece wrapped his arms around me, folding me into his warmth as if I'd been there a million times before.

"I'm over it." My voice wobbled. "I am. It was a long time ago." I sniffled.

Then he sniffled.

I snuggled into his warmth and sniffled and he sniffled again. I felt a tremor in his chest.

I pulled back and studied those green eyes, through the tears of mine. "Are you . . . you're not crying, are you?"

He coughed, then wiped a hand across his face and turned away. "A few tears only."

"What?" I scooted around in front of him. "Why are you crying?"

"Why? Isn't that obvious?"

"What? What is obvious?"

"You were married in a courthouse, on a lunch break, in a work suit, without your family. That's sad, June. That's sad." He gave me another comforting hug. "He never should have allowed that, June. You deserved more."

I couldn't even see through the hot water in my eyes, not because of the lunch-hour wedding but because Reece, my Reece, my friend who I was trying ridiculously hard not to fall in love with, was upset *for* me.

"You should have had your dress, your family, the whole huge, fluffy thing." His voice dipped and split, pained.

My shoulders shook. I tried to hold it in, tried to control myself, tried to wrap up the pain and put it back in the sewing box, slamming the lid tight, as I'd done hundreds of times . . . but it didn't work.

I burst into tears.

Yes, it had been sad.

It was still sad. I was still a mess because I'd caused the mess.

And yet, what was making me really cry was how compassionate Reece was. He understood, he grasped the pain and the loss, and he was upset *for* me.

He wrapped me up tight again in his arms, his chest heaving a bit, and soon all thoughts of my cold and lifeless past with Grayson left, whizzing out the French doors and into the frothing ocean, where I imagined they drowned in the waves, and I smiled.

Yep. I smiled through my tears.

Leoni, Estelle, and I worked for endless hours on August's wedding dress, the bridesmaids' dresses for September and me, and other orders.

We had fittings, calls, e-mails, some frantic, some panicked, some utterly grateful for their beaudacious dresses . . .

And in between the crush and the rush, I smiled.

I felt it. *Happiness.*

Seven Things I'm Worried About

1. Since I am still, technically, married, I can only be friends with Reece, but there is no way I can be "just friends" for much longer because he is delectable and that is a problem.

2. But! I don't want to be involved with any man. I don't trust myself. I don't want to get hurt. I am not all together, I'm still emotionally wobbly.

3. Besides! He is only here for eight weeks total. I will not get involved with a man for eight weeks and then be discarded. I am not a beach toy.

4. How poor will I be by the time I get divorced?

5. What if the reporter giggles in a mean way at my dresses?

6. Earthquakes. Strange diseases. Weird sounds at night.

7. Morgan. Leoni. She works so hard. I want her to be happy. I'll make her and Morgan matching lace skirts.

I played Scrabble. I spelled these words: "ache," "alone," "lace." I lost.
I ate a cream puff. Okay, two cream puffs.

CHAPTER 7

Reece and I headed down to the beach one sunny, golden afternoon to visit the sea anemones in the tide pools for yet another date.

He picked up a black, broken butterfly shell and tossed it back into the ocean.

"I have never found a butterfly shell in one piece," I mused.

"And you want one?"

"Yes. I'm down here all the time and mostly I see half of the shell, not the whole one, and if it is whole, it's chipped."

"I'll find a whole beach butterfly for you."

He grinned at me. He was so overpoweringly masculine he, well, overpowered me. Sometimes I think our society has beat the man out of men, but this one, no. He still had all the man roaring around in him.

He hummed a few notes, soaring and light. "I've found my butterfly girl, between the sand and the sea . . . but she keeps running away from me . . . baby we can be together, if you'll trust in me . . ."

The man was too much. Too much for my poor heart, which was pitter-pattering on high speed.

He took my hand and I ceased to be able to think. When you're holding hands with a singing cowboy, it's hard to think.

"Remember I've told you that since we're friends, we can hold hands," he told me.

"Yes. You told me that." I was breathless.

"Let's dance down to the tide pools, June."

"Dance?"

"Yep." He wrapped an arm around my waist, my hand in his, and pulled me close. His heat burned me, head to heart to toe, those bright eyes flirty, sexy . . . disastrous.

I should say no! *Say yes, June!* "Okay, cowboy. I'll dare it."

I put my hand on his huge shoulder, not an inch between our bodies . . .

I dared to dance in the arms of a singing cowboy, on the beach, in Oregon, on a summer day, my blond curls flying in the breeze, my white lace, ruffled skirt swirling around my knees.

Later I reminded myself, *again*, that I was not falling in love with Reece.

No, I was not.

I was not going to fall in love because I am not divorced and Grayson has turned my life into a relentless nightmare that he controls. I told myself it was lust, I was rebounding. I was passionate and needed attention.

I could not fall in love.

No, I couldn't.

Heck no.

Reece twirled me through the sunshine, sand between our toes, singing a song about a butterfly girl. *Baby, we can be together, if you'll trust in me.*

"This article is going to be huge for my career."

"Good. Hopefully for mine, too," I said. The reporter from *Couture Fashion* and I clinked our glasses, filled high with pink lemonade. Her name was Virginia Bescotti, named after her grandmother. "All the girls in our family are named after grandmas, great-grandmas, or great-aunts. Tradition. Our other tradition is marrying bad men the first time around. We call them starter marriages. The second marriages always work out."

She was about twenty-eight and wore red-rimmed glasses, her dark hair piled on top of her head, where it refused to stay. She had a toothy smile, a dimple, and had been divorced for a year.

We sure had a lot to talk about. By the end of the interview and photo shoot, after the photographer left, we were well into our sisterhood, my nerves calm, my laughter back. And I'd been so worried!

"My article on all your wedding dresses is going to get about six pages of coverage in *Couture Fashion*. It's gonna set your business on fire. Flames flyin'. We've got a style-busting national audience, with a zillion international readers, plus we're online, and this is gonna be big-ola. Big-ola. You need to get the snake to sign the divorce papers before it comes out."

"Don't I know it." I thought of all the bills I'd paid during my marriage with the snake. The mortgage, food, utilities. How Grayson had always said, "I'll write you a check, sugar, you don't think your own husband is going to cheat you on that, do you?"

I learned quickly that, yes, he would. He did.

When this article came out, he would realize I'd made it, instead of sensing there was success there, or would be there, and he'd hold on to our marriage with sharp claws, as Cherie predicted. Would he win in court? Probably not. Did I want to risk it? No.

"Get him to sign if you have to sit on him and prod him with a smokin' hot cattle brand," Virginia said. "I hijacked my husband's boat until he signed."

"I need a cattle brand," I muttered.

She flipped through my wedding scrapbooks. "You are an out-of-this-orbit talented designer and that is a freakin' awesome dress. A white wedding dress with feathered wings. Who would have thunk that up?"

"The bride worked at the Audubon Society. She loved birds. Her husband worked there, too. I made matching wings for his tux."

"And this prancy-dancy one!" She pointed again. "The tutu effect. How long did it take you to sew the gauze?"

"The gauze was endless. See how it sparkles?" Think of Sleeping Beauty's flying fairy godmothers in blue, purple, and pink and you have the dress.

"This is my favorite, this gold sheath, Cleopatra-y style, with the white veil and long train. Makes me want to climb a pyramid."

"That was an Egyptologist. Studies Egypt. Has a doctorate. Her husband is a neurosurgeon. Better to make a dress from her studies than his."

Virginia laughed. "You could have sewed a brain and cranium dress, but yuck. If I had known what was going to happen to me during my marriage, I would have walked down the aisle with my wedding dress on fire." She tapped her forehead for a second. One of her quirks. The other quirk was cracking her gum. She'd chewed an entire pack while we were sitting together. She tapped her pen on my table. "Maybe an enflamed wedding dress would have gotten my attention."

"Well," I quipped, "then you might have danced a jig for Teresa Terrio's dress. Within the folds we placed tiny white lights. It was a night wedding, all the lights were off, and she made quite a statement walking down the aisle."

Virginia blinked at me. "You are so funky in the head. Make sure you forward me that photo, too."

"I'll do it. I think of her as the Firefly Bride."

"You just wrote my caption." She cracked her gum. "You're gonna be busting out with work soon, June. Get ready and remember to get those papers signed pronto; hip hop to it."

The next morning I dealt with a Bridezilla.

She came for her fitting with her bridesmaids from Portland.

I could tell that her frazzled bridesmaids had come to hate her.

She was bossy, abrupt, and gratingly difficult. I told her bridesmaids to go downstairs and handed them a bottle of wine, even though it was only 10:00 a.m. They practically skipped down my stairs. I kept the screechy bride upstairs and told her that unless she wanted a bridesmaids' revolt, she needed to start pretending she was a human. She started to protest and I held up my open scissors quite close to the bodice of her dress.

"Calm down, Elise. Be nice. This is one day out of your life. One—"

"It's my day, my wedding! My day! My wedding! Me and my wedding! I've planned it for years, since I was a little girl. It's about me!" She actually stomped her feet and clenched her fists, tears bursting forth.

"And you're a little girl throwing a temper tantrum. You need to make your wedding day the day people remember you as being the kindest, most peaceful bride ever, not the day that your bridesmaids drank themselves under the table because you unleashed a drooling monster with sharp teeth."

She cried, told me all her problems.

I wiped her face, gave her lemon sugar cookies and a glass of white wine. (No red wine allowed in my studio.)

"Now shape up, Elise. You need to enjoy this time of your life, not tear your hair out, or worse, your bridesmaids' hair out, by the roots."

"Oh, I know! I love you, June! And I love my dress! Have I violated the Bridezilla contract?"

"If you stand still so I don't deliberately poke you in the boobs with this pin, I'll pretend you were docile today. Last warning, though."

I dealt with other brides and bridesmaids, I sewed on supersonic speed, I e-mailed and took phone calls.

And not for a second did I forget about my dear and smokin' hot *friend* Reece.

He'd done it all, that's why I teared up.

A bonfire on the beach would keep us warm as the sun dipped into the sunset, sparks flying, shadows dancing. Reece had laid out a red-and-white tablecloth on the sand for us and our pasta Alfredo, garlic bread, clam chowder, salad, and chocolates. He opened a bottle of wine, placed daisies in a glass mason jar, and lit two candles.

I couldn't even speak.

"Hey," Reece said, slinging an arm around my back. "What's wrong, June?"

"Nothing." I turned my head and studied the white caps of the waves, dusk drawing handfuls of liquid blues and crimsons across the horizon.

"There is something wrong. Tell me, June, please."

I wiped a tear from my eye, and another one, bending my head so my curls would cover my face.

"June . . ."

So embarrassing.

"Did I say something wrong?"

"No, oh no, Reece. You didn't say anything wrong." I sniffled and snuffled and he made sympathetic sounds and that made me cry more. I used my sweatshirt sleeve to wipe my tears. "I try not to cry and blubber about too much."

"Why do you do that? Let it rip, that's what I think."

How do you tell someone that you tried to stop crying a long time ago because you were so hurt, so despairing, that tears didn't work anymore? How do you say that without sounding pathetic? How do you say you try not to cry because you'd taught yourself not to when the loneliness was about to kill you, without sounding completely closed off emotionally? How do you say that for a long time anger has burned all of your tears away without reminding him of an anger freak?

He turned my face toward him and wiped my tears with his thumbs. "Tell me why you're crying. It can't be the food, because I didn't cook it. If I had cooked, that would be a reason to cry."

I laughed, then let the tears flow again, and his fingers caught them.

"I'm crying because you put so much effort into this dinner for us."

His face grew quizzical. "I don't understand."

"It's so thoughtful." I made a weird gulping sound in my throat. "It's so considerate and kind."

"I wanted to do this for you. You work too hard. You make me tired watching you work. And I wanted to hang out with someone funny who knows a lot about lace and sewing needles, so you're it."

"Oh, Reece." He had walked straight into my heart that first day. "I love pasta Alfredo, you know that, so you brought it."

"You have good taste."

"And I love chocolates."

"A woman needs chocolate in her life."

"She does, she does."

He handed me the golden box of chocolates. "Enjoy."

"And I told you that I love daisies, too, because they're so simple, and there they are."

He clipped off the stem of a daisy and tucked it behind my ear, then stuck a daisy behind his ear, too. "June MacKenzie, you are the most open, sincere woman I have ever met."

"And Reece O'Brien, you are . . . you are . . ." *You are a man I could wear daisies with each day for the rest of my life.* "You are a man who needs a daisy chain crown and I'm going to make you one."

"Good. I'll wear it. But first, let's eat. There's hardly anything on this planet that can't be made better by pasta Alfredo."

Later, when the stars were twinkling, scattered with magical abandon across the heavens, and after we ate the pasta Alfredo, which did make everything better, and talked as if we'd known each other forever, as usual, Reece said, "Here, hon, snuggle in." He lifted up a blanket, crawled under it, then pulled me toward his chest. "Let's rest."

I scrambled under the blanket. He pulled two more over us as the fire sparked, the waves crashed, and the moon glowed bright and white.

Let's rest. That's what I needed to do. I needed to rest. Not worry. Not fret. Not analyze him or us or the future that I was still so scared to step into.

"June, I think you're the only person I could talk to forever."

"Same here, Reece, same here." I readjusted his daisy crown.

I ignored that blast of pain in my chest that said forever wasn't going to happen with Reece. I lived at the beach. He lived in eastern Oregon. I was an emotional crackpot with a pile of anger and a long divorce.

"I think the moon needs some of our attention," he said.

I tilted my head up to him. He smiled, soft and gentle, sweet and sexy. He couldn't help igniting my rampaging passion.

Don't fall in love, June, you'll only get hurt again.

I gave the bright white moon my attention before I lost control and divested myself, and him, of all our clothes and invited him to roll through the sand buck naked.

I absolutely could not do that.

Yet.

My friend Reece and I continued to see each other. Each time, he sizzled my body and sent my spinning mind into a spiral of . . . love.

A love that I tried hard to smother.

My smothered love made me laugh when no one was looking.

"Good to see that you've lost your head," Estelle said, taking a pin out of her mouth one sunny afternoon, the kite flyers out in force on the beach, two surfers braving the waves. "Didn't think you could do it. You were a wedding dress designer who didn't believe a woman should ever wear a wedding dress. Now you're a wedding dress designer who is dreamy and woozily distracted and only half thinking, all the time. Yoo-hoo. Are you there?"

"She's in love!" Leoni said.

"I'm trying not to be in love," I said. "Trying hard."

"You have an aura of love," Leoni said. "And quit trying not to be in love, embrace it with open arms, bring the sparkle to your life."

"And you're in raving lust," Estelle said, pointing a needle at me. "What woman wouldn't feel lust with that bull of a man with steel-you-know-whatsits strutting around in heat?"

"He's not a bull, he's not in heat." I was a bullette in heat, though. I fanned myself with a paperback book on Victorian lace.

Leoni nodded. "Have to agree on the bull comment. He's got the equipment! And he's romantic. Always bringing you lunch, and the flowers, ooh la la! And the cushion for your back on your rocking chair so your back wouldn't get sore . . ."

"And the new light that hangs perfectly over the rocking chair," Estelle said.

"So your eyes don't get tired." Leoni patted her chest and sighed.

I sighed, too. In a happy way.

My friend Reece made me happy.

And nervous.

Morgan walked in with her NASA outfit on. "What is 'lust'? What do you mean about a man being a bull in heat? And what is the equipment of a bull?"

We froze. Oh, sheesh.

"Hey!" She tapped her NASA helmet. "I wrote another letter to NASA. This time I included information on why I think we can get to Mars, based on my studies. Nine pages plus drawings. I think they'll write back. I'll show the letter to my dad when he comes and visits me. I'm going to be a famous astronaut and he'll say, 'That's my daughter,' and be proud."

I stifled a groan, then patted Leoni's back as her eyes filled up with tears.

CHAPTER 8

"I've changed my mind," Grayson said, thumping a fist on the conference table in Cherie's office.

"What do you mean, you've changed your mind, El Monster?" Cherie asked. She tapped both sides of her temple. "You been thinkin'? Did it hurt?"

"I mean, that I've been on your website, June, and I think you've got a sweet little business going. I could see it making a lot of money. So, I've decided that I want half the business. You developed it during our marriage, after all."

I honestly thought my whole body had been invaded by an iceberg. The last time we met, he was using my business as a bargaining tool: the house for June's Lace and Flounces. I choked on my own words and had to cough through my shock. "I will not give you any part of my business ever."

"So keep working," he went on, as if I hadn't spoken. "The better June's Lace and Flounces does, the better I do. I might even buy a beach house! Is there one for sale by you? We could live right next door!"

I swore under my breath. This divorce, after all this time, was actually getting worse, not better. My legs, under the table, started to shake and I felt nauseous, the room starting to tilt.

"I do believe, Grayson, that June would rather stick her head in the open mouth of a Tasmanian devil than share June's Lace with you." Cherie crossed her legs. Zebra-print skirt today and a black leather jacket. Underneath the black jacket, zebra-print shirt. She is so cool.

I was wearing a white lace dress with a white liner and a jean jacket I'd added lace to on the cuffs, with silver bangles up one arm. I had made the dress. Grayson had gawked at me when I walked in, eyes moving from head to toe, then had swallowed hard. He hadn't stopped staring at me.

"That ain't gonna happen, Grayson." Cherie chortled.

Grayson flushed, high on those cheekbones that I'd come to hate. I remember kissing those cheekbones. Sometimes he'd tell me how many times to kiss the cheekbones, then how many times to kiss him in other places, where to run my hands, how to move. He had a playbook for sex. Yes, a playbook. He'd say, "We're going to have Sex C tonight," and then he'd show me the moves.

Gall. And I followed those instructions. I was a female robot. A robot in a suit who had lost all emotion and lust for life the second she quit sewing.

"The thing is, June, I know you. I think you're going to make this business successful, and I want to be a part of it. We'll share the profits. We'll spend time together."

That comment chilled my bones so hard I thought they'd crack. The thought of him leaning over my shoulder, making comments and suggestions, paying him a monthly check off the profits, made me ill. I wouldn't do it. I couldn't do it. "Never. No."

Cherie leaned forward and glared at him. "Take the few brain cells in your head that are still working, and let's figure out a deal that does not involve torturing you."

I needed the money from the house I owned with Grayson. I needed it for the down payment for the beach house. My chest felt tight, I couldn't breathe. I did not want to give in. I didn't want him to win, simply because he could bully me down. I didn't like living in a stress tornado.

But as I sat and listened to Cherie dive into full-throttle battle, I thought of the view of the waves, the seagulls, and the tide pools. I thought of all the orders I had stacked up, how I would probably have to hire someone else fairly soon. I thought of my business, my baby, my creation, what had been born out of acute depression and despair, but was now flowering. I thought of the article coming out written by my new friend Virginia, she of the smacking gum.

I thought of Reece.

"Give him the house."

Cherie whipped around to me. "What?"

"Give him the house."

Grayson was shocked, so was Walid.

"I'll sign the papers, Grayson and Walid, you itchy creeps. Cherie, draw them up."

"No, no, no—" Grayson started, bopping in his seat.

"No?" I wanted to throw another law book at him. "You wanted the house in Portland, you get it. That's what you said last time. You make no claims whatsoever on June's Lace and Flounces now or in the future and we'll call it good and this will be done. You keep all the money in the house."

"I—"

"You what, Grayson? You've ripped me off. You ripped me off in our marriage. You were a cold, deceitful, mechanical, thoughtless, critical husband and I temporarily lost my mind when I married you and I want out."

"I can't let you do that, sweets," Cherie said, and I knew she was playing my game. "You have a chunk of money coming to you from your half of that house."

"Let it go." June's Lace and Flounces was me. I am June.

Grayson and Walid had a whispered conversation and I muttered to Cherie, as low as possible, "I need this snake to slither on out of my life."

And there, in that office, I felt this surge of power.

I had, financially, nothing.

I had nothing but potential and possibility.

I had nothing but a pair of green eyes that laughed into mine.

"It's yes or no, El Monsters," Cherie said. "Right now. Give me an hour and I'll talk my client out of this and she'll take half the house."

"But I want part of the business—" Grayson whined. "She could make a mint."

"Actually, Grayson, I will close my business down if I have to share it with you and start over. Plus, I'll take half the money in the house and I'll take half the money you've made since we separated."

He twitched nervously. He made a lot of money, didn't want to lose it. "I'll make you sign a non compete so you can't open another business."

"You are odd and gooey and creepy," Cherie said. "She's not going to sign a noncompete. She didn't even have an official business before she separated from you, El Monster. Agree to the terms, slugs. If you refuse to sign these papers, I will accidentally let slip to my friend, a reporter at the newspaper, that you were arrested by police last weekend for indecent exposure. Now, why were you wearing red underwear in that parked car?"

Grayson paled. "I could sue you for that," he whispered.

"Red underwear?" I said, opening my eyes wide. "Oh, I remember those . . . the tight ones. The ones you wore when you were afraid of a judge."

"Stop it, June," Grayson said, so weak.

"Be my guest," Cherie said. "I'll make sure that my reporter friend knows exactly why you're suing me. Now, tell me. How did it go over with that executive's husband when he found out you were wrestling naked with his wife? Did she truly have on bunny ears when the police tapped on the window? Did you have the bunny tail on? Wasn't he a client of yours?"

Grayson slunk in his chair and I felt: nothing.

I had felt nothing for so long about Grayson. No jealousy, no regrets about leaving, no nostalgia. Nothing.

I laughed, free and freeing. Grayson turned bright red.

"Your face would have matched your red panties, Grayson." I laughed again. After today, I would never have to have that man in my life.

That was something to laugh about.

I drove out of Portland in my old truck. The paint was chipping. It was noisy. I was, officially, broke. I'd given Grayson half a house.

I rolled down the windows as I hit the road to the beach. I let the wind blow my hair around and cranked up the country music on the radio. I would get home in time for the sunset.

"Peppermint Lady," one of my favorite country songs of all time, filled the truck. It was about cowgirl boots, living life with peppermint sticks in your hand, and coming home. It always touched my heart.

It was written by Reece.

I sung along, picturing Reece out on his ranch, under an old oak tree, strumming that guitar in front of fields of wheat, stringing the words together.

I didn't have any money. I had a house that I rented that would be sold. I would not be able to buy it. I would have to move myself and my business to who knew where. I did have, thankfully, a lot of work and I had June's Lace and Flounces.

I felt . . . free.

Free and easy. It reminded me of honey and cream and applesauce.

I was going back to the beach. I was going back to watching sea otters, tossing bread to seagulls, and sewing faux pearls to ruffles while rocking in my rocking chair.

I was going back to Reece.

I was going home.

All I needed was the peppermint sticks.

"So, your sister August is getting married."

"Yes, she is, Reece. She is currently flipping out and hoping she survives the scary in-laws." I kept ironing a stubborn seam on a blue-black-yellow-white swirly-style bridesmaid dress.

The bride loved van Gogh, so the swirls were reminiscent of the sky in his painting *The Starry Night,* along with a sunflower on the left shoulder, to represent his Sunflower series. The bride herself was in traditional, lacy white, with a bouquet of sunflowers on her shoulder. She was an artist and had studied in Paris.

"What's the date?"

"July twenty-fourth."

Reece's eyebrows rose. "I didn't know it was so soon."

That's because I didn't tell you because I don't think I'm ready for you to meet my tartan-kilt-loving family who are out of this planetarium system in terms of uniqueness. "Yes, it's coming right up. That's why you see the lights on over here until the wee hours of the morning."

I didn't look up at his hard-jawed face for long, heavy seconds. He was waiting me out, I knew it. I spent hours every day with the man, sewing in the studio, strolling on the beach, dining in restaurants, and I knew him.

"Are you bringing a date to the wedding, June?"

"I don't have a date."

"Here's a date." He pointed at himself. "Date me." He leaned back against my red couch, his guitar propped up beside him.

"I don't think you'd want to be at the wedding." I knew I was stalling.

"Why not?"

"It's a typical MacKenzie family affair. It'll be loud, eccentric, edgy. Relatives will be rollicking around loose, uncaged, unguarded. They're looney. Looney but loving. There are strange traditions and family dances to be danced. Bagpipes. Possible gunshots. Ouija boards."

"I like bagpipes. Gunshots, as long as they're not aimed at me, get the blood pumping, and I find Ouija boards amusing."

"And Ben's family. They're proper, conservative, blue blooded. Who knows what will happen as the families unite and clash?"

"Who cares? It'll be fun." He picked up his guitar and

strummed a few chords. *"Woe is me, I'll miss it, though. Woe is me,"* he sang.

"Woe is you!" I threw a handful of satin at him.

He caught it, and caught my gaze. "I'd be a good date. I want to meet your parents."

"You mean the hippies?"

"The hippies and the rest of the gang."

"Even though many will be dressed as Scotsmen and women during the festivities?"

"I love Scotland, I've been twice."

"We have a watermelon-seed spitting contest."

"I have some talent in that particular area."

"We have a scavenger hunt. It gets competitive."

"I play to win."

"You need to know that I cannot predict my family and, most particularly, my Great-uncle Seamus, who says he's coming dressed as Abe Lincoln, my Great-aunt Lolly, who sings songs with swear words, and my twin cousins, Chuck and Duck. Those are their nicknames. Their given names are Cornell Brown Balashov and Harvard Yale Balashov. Their parents thought they were so brilliant they'd go to Ivy League schools. Didn't happen. They literally joined the circus and travel the world. Daredevil trapeze artists, they do tricks with this giant ring they run on top of, stand on each other's heads, et cetera. Anyhow, they'll be there. One cousin, Marci Shinola, recently was paroled. She shot her neighbor."

Reece's eyebrows rose again.

"The neighbor stole her dogs. He said they barked too much. She shot him in the knee."

"Oh," he mocked. "Only the knee. Did she get the dogs back?"

"Yes, she did." I put the iron down. "Reece, if you want...."

"Yes?" He strummed his guitar.

"If you have nothing else to do ..."

"Don't think I'm busy that day." *Strum, strum.*

"I'll be swamped with the bride and the bridesmaids ..."

"I'll find the groom and hang out."

"You might be asked to do ... crazy things."

"I'm good at crazy." *Strum, strum, strum.*

"I might be crazy, too. It's my sister's wedding."

"We're friends, June. I will bring you martinis and hugs for your craziness."

"You'd be alone."

"I won't be alone. I'll be with your relatives, including the shooter, the cousins who stand on each other's heads, and Abe Lincoln. Would you ask me?"

"Ask you?"

"Yes. Formally. Invite me."

I took a deep, deep breath. "Reece, this is going to be the bizarrest wedding ever, but if you are brave and want to come to August's wedding, I would be happy for you to be my date."

"Yes."

"Yes?"

"I'll be your date. I would love to be. I'm a date! June's date!" He smiled, blew me a kiss.

I could hardly resist that man. Some people might say I'm rebounding, but I'm not. It's been over two years since I left Grayson. My marriage was only two years long. The last year of the marriage was dead and I did my best to hide from it. I could fall into Reece's smile and stay there forever.

He stood up, towering over me, and I took a step closer. He wrapped an arm around my waist, pulling me in. I closed my eyes, shivered on the inside, and tilted my head back. I wanted to kiss that man so much I could hardly breathe. I felt myself relax into our sweet, hot passion . . .

The stairs shook as Estelle and Leoni clambered up, Morgan's laugh only somewhat muted by her astronaut's helmet.

Reece held my gaze, his chest rising up and down, up and down, and I knew that he was struggling as much as I was. He had such a nice chest and I wanted to wrap my arms around him, my legs around his hips . . .

I actually shuddered. What do you call a shudder like that? A lust shudder?

Oh, my friend Reece was irresistible, yes, he was.

The three burst through the door and Morgan shouted, "Four, three, two, one, liftoff!"

Estelle growled, "You can cut the passion in this studio with a pair of sewing scissors."

Leoni piped up, "We've interrupted the softness of the romantic moment. Sorry, June!"

There's a good reason for chaperones, you know.

Five Things I'm Worried About

1. August's wedding and the dresses. Will they all be done in time?

2. Reece. What's the point of falling in love only to be smashed by it?

3. What if a lightning storm crackles down on August's wedding?

4. Morgan. Her father is such a lout.

5. The article. What if people hate the dresses and I am laughed right off the beach?

I played online Scrabble. Again, I lost.

I spelled these words: "sexy," "loon," "songs."

I had a slice of the seven-layer chocolate cake that Reece had brought me the other day. Okay, two slices. I hoped I wouldn't eat the entire thing.

Over the next weeks I worked on high-speed fluster, spending maniacal hours in the studio, as did Estelle and Leoni.

I saw Reece, too, how could I resist? He was a magnetic pull yanking at me, and every single time I was with him, his strength and gentleness, his humor and wit, and his inherent goodness and honesty worked its way further into my soul. Not to mention that the barely restrained physical attraction I had for him about knocked me on my head.

He strummed his guitar and penned songs in my studio, I threw in words and phrases while I sewed at my machines or sewed by hand. We listened to classical, country, and hard rock music. We laughed as we jumped over waves, we built a sand castle, we buried each other in the sand and took photos. We walked hand in hand for miles along the shoreline and flew kites shaped like parrots.

We went searching for whole black butterfly shells, those green eyes smiling into mine like liquid emeralds.

He said, with all seriousness, "You are the most beautiful person I have ever met."

And, "June, I've never been happier. All my songs are happy ... I'm supposed to write songs about broken hearts." He winked at me. "Can't seem to do it right now."

And, "I love watching you sew. I think I could watch that for the rest of my life."

And, "When your divorce is final, June, we will have our first official date. I can't wait. You'll definitely be getting a kiss good night. Hopefully you'll be getting a good morning kiss, too. This has been torturous for me, waiting, trying to be patient, saintly. You know that, right?"

It'd been torture for me, too. I was so happy when I was with him, *he felt right,* we felt right, but I also felt skittish and totally unnerved. Worried, unsettled, a mite lost, as if I was being carried along on a frothing wave and had no control.

I told Estelle how I was feeling.

"That's because, June," she said, her voice more gentle than I'd ever heard it, "you don't know *you* yet. You don't trust yourself. You don't trust your own decisions. You've been hurt and battered about and you're still legally attached to someone else." She patted my shoulder. "Sometimes the only person we need to be with is ourselves. We need to be alone because that's the only time we can hear that teeny-tiny voice inside us talking."

"I can hear a teeny-tiny voice in my head, but I can't hear her loud enough. I lost June during all my years of incessant work chasing stupid stuff, and then she completely ran out the door when I was married and I haven't put the pieces back together yet. I'm unsteady, that's the word for it. I'm off-kilter. I'm not confident, not strong in myself. I feel like I'm half me, floundering about and scared and insecure."

Estelle tapped me with a ruler on the shoulder. "Be in your quiet, June. Think, but don't overthink. Don't be afraid of love. But remember that you can't be a healthy couple until you're emotionally healthy. He's not going to make you happy, *you* have to make yourself happy and whole. After that is when you can be a whole couple."

She is a ragingly smart lady. I gave her a hug.

"Fine then, we'll get mushy for a second if we must." Estelle kissed my cheek. "Lovey-dovey. Huggy-wuggy. Now get your butt back to work, June, we are crushed for time."

On a Thursday morning, at 6:00, not having slept at all, I packed my truck with August's wedding dress, the bridesmaids' dresses for September and me, and three flower girl dresses. Leoni had spent the night, along with Morgan. She and Estelle and I finished at three in the morning. August's dress had one stitch still not done, as was Scottish tradition. On her wedding morning, she'd sew it up.

I threw my suitcase into the truck with assorted other things I needed/August needed/my mom needed. I left a map taped to Reece's door, giving him directions to my parents' house in Eugene.

I stood at his door for long seconds, imagining him sleeping, that long body stretched out, eyes closed, blond hair over his forehead, vulnerable and soft, warm and cozy and strong.

I teared up, then turned to leave.

I waved to the beach as I passed.

I would miss it.

CHAPTER 9

My parents still have a VW bus. In fact, they have two. Neither is the one we puttered about in as kids wearing flowers and feathers in our hair and shark tooth necklaces, the sides painted with peace signs and flowers. No, these are newer.

Both VWs were painted by a friend of theirs, a professional, well-known artist. Across the "flower power" flowers on both sides, are the words "Hippie Chick."

They have a huge, Craftsman-style home in the country, along a river, outside Eugene, a liberal college town. The home has wraparound decks, an outdoor pool, and a hot tub that seats twelve.

None of us, August, September, March, nor I saw this placid domesticity coming.

"This world was made for existential experiences and a spiritual connection with nature," my mom had always said.

"To adventures I bow," my father vowed.

"Never stop seeking, chasing down your curiosity, believing in the wonders of life," my mom extolled to us.

"Challenge yourself to never, ever become boring, a life-killer," my father admonished. "Do not die during your lifetime from inertia."

We thought they would continue their traveling ways after the four of us fled the coop, or fled the VW bus, as it were, into college.

But as soon as March left for college, our parents were done traveling. Kaput. Boom. Quit.

The kids were gone, they wanted a home.

My father waxed eloquently, "We've traveled long and hard, rolling stones, stars shooting through the night, a family of land travelers on a quest for knowledge and enlightenment. We explored and pushed the boundaries."

"And now we want a full kitchen," my mom said, with impressive eagerness. "Where I can cook a proper turkey dinner, with the lace tablecloths and silver from my mother."

"And we want a big tub for two," my father said. "So nice on the back."

"Space so we can breathe, and shelves for our books. Books are your friends, you know. *Your friends.*"

"A deck for gazing at the Milky Way, but radiant heat on the floor so our feet don't get cold. *Brrrr!*"

"And air-conditioning. Anything over ninety degrees is too hot, hot, hot!"

"A gas fireplace, so when we're cold, we flick a switch, and voila. A fire, no rubbing sticks together anymore."

"Don't forget our dream appliances," my mom added. "All necessary for good health: our juicer, blender, water purifier, and espresso machine."

The four of us would have been less surprised if they'd plucked Venus out of the sky and ate it.

They wanted a home, so they went to work. My mom used her talents as a seamstress, my father as a painter and business organizer, and together those two developed a line of Hippie Chick clothes for girls and women. They sold them out of the back of their VW bus at various Saturday markets. My father set up a website. They worked long hours, they marketed and advertised in creative ways, and hired the right people: my brother, March, also a workaholic, who handled the marketing and PR and the charity donations, and my sister September, who has an MBA.

I did all the legal work. August did the accounting and number crunching. My parents eventually sold their clothes for a high price to a high-end department store. They hired more people and treated them well. No one in the Hippie Chick company, save a mother who became pregnant with triplets, has ever quit.

They made a bundle. And another bundle. More bundles after that.

Hippie Chick bought them their house, paid for with cash. "I will be beholden in debt to no one!" my father said, pointing his finger skyward.

"No one owns us!" my mom agreed. "We are free, free!"

Aligning with the rest of their values, they saved a bunch of money from the profits and gave it away to two different charities: one donated college scholarships to underprivileged children and one helped abused/sick/homeless horses.

"We've always found a friendship with horses, haven't we,

honey?" my father said to my mom. "A spectacular symbol of strength, endurance, physical magic."

"Don't you remember watching the wild horses run on our traveling, adventuring, rolling stones days? Don't you? Our first kiss was after horseback riding."

"Yes, it was. I remember every minute of it, to this day. It was spectacular. Never forgot it and the kisses have only gotten better." My father grabbed my mom and pulled her toward him.

"Love you, you old coot." She squeezed his butt, then kissed him back.

He put his hands up her shirt and rubbed her back.

"Get a hotel, both of you, old coots," I said.

They laughed.

But they weren't old. You start having kids when you're teenagers and as you get older, you realize your parents aren't that much older than you.

And, in my case, they were a lot more fun.

When I arrived, my parents were positively beaming and tranquil. My mom, blond and brown-eyed, like me, petite, not like me, was wearing a flowing pink pantsuit. On her lithe figure, it was fabulous. My father, dark-haired, dimples, was wearing jeans and a blue jean shirt with subtle swirls, and a peace sign on the pocket that Hippie Chick Man would soon be selling. They were the picture of Boomer youth. Both were carrying crystal wands.

"Give me a morning hug, June!" My father smiled, hugging me close. "I love you, baby. We're having the MacKenzie family Scottish breakfast, then the scavenger hunt will begin."

"Take your wand," my mom said, kissing me on the cheek again. "Don't drop it during the hunt, or you lose! It must be with you at all times. Oh, how I adore you, June. You are spectacular!"

"Thanks, Mom. I think I'll cast a spell on you now." I waved the wand.

She opened the door to the dining room. They have the largest dining room I've ever seen. My parents constructed a table to seat thirty. I hugged my brother, March. He wears his silky brown hair to his shoulders and resembles our father. Women go crazy for him. "Lookin' wonderful, sis."

September burst into tears and hugged me hard. "Sister! I have missed you!" September is blond-haired, like August and me, but she has blue streaks in her short wedge of hair and a tattoo on her left arm with our family's names shaping a heart.

"My Scottish clansmen and women," my father announced, deep voice carrying to each corner. "June has arrived!" He fisted his hands high into the air.

We are so into our Scottish heritage, our kilts and tartans and family crest, but the truth is we are a multicultural group. A United Nations Scottish-American family.

My cousin Earl picked up his bagpipes and blew. He is a champion bagpipe player. His father is from Zimbabwe. Great-uncle Seamus was, indeed, dressed as Abe Lincoln. He blew me a kiss. His mother's family is from Japan. Chuck and Duck, the circus performers, were there, too. Their father is Russian. They did handstands in greeting. Later they would put on a neat show with sticks set on fire. My cousin Marci Shinola, who shot her neighbor in the knee, grinned at me and waved. "I'm out of the slammer, June!" Her mother is from Venezuela. The twins who always dress in monster outfits have a father from Mexico. They growled at me.

My family cheered a hello.

Yes, I was home.

The MacKenzies have many traditions. One of them is that the women—*only women*—get together before every wedding and have a twenty-four-hour Salute to Our Heroine Geraldine. No, it is not a bachelorette party. That happens the night before the rehearsal dinner.

The Salute to Our Heroine Geraldine involves a real-life story straight from Scotland. It's all about Great-great-great-etc.-Grandma Geraldine who started the American branch of MacKenzies. Apparently she did not want to marry the man her father had chosen. She was sixteen, and you know how those rebellious teenagers are; it's so difficult to force them to marry someone they don't want to marry. So, Geraldine left her clan. She walked. And walked and walked. In fact, she walked so far away that on her wedding day, though her family hunted high and low, they couldn't find her.

There was no wedding.

Days after the wedding, she returned. Rested, refreshed, relaxed.

Family lore has it that she declared if she was forced to marry someone else, she'd leave for America. Well, in due time, her father corralled her into another marriage, but this time he had the relatives stand guard so she couldn't take off.

It didn't work. She managed to sneak off, this time with a bag in hand, and darned if she didn't land in America a year later, dead poor and sick from the trip. She later married Cormac MacKenzie and had eight children. She lived to be ninety-two years old. Her father forgave her. Her ex-fiancés did not.

So, in her honor, the Salute to Our Heroine Geraldine involves all of the women going on a hike early in the morning. A looong hike, to remember the long walk that Geraldine endured to escape her wedding. Then we volunteer our time to clean something, usually it's a women's shelter, a soup kitchen, et cetera, to show respect for the hard work that Geraldine did as a maid to earn passage to America. We take a boat ride, with a lot of wine, to memorialize her trip to America.

After that, we Americanize the journey: We all go to the spa. Many spas. They can't hold all of us.

"Geraldine would have wanted a spa trip if she'd had the opportunity to go to one," my mom always said. "She would know she well and truly deserved it after all she'd been through."

"In spirit, she's with us, getting a hot rock massage," Aunt Wilma declared.

"She's with us as we get oatmeal and chocolate treatments spread all over our bodies," my sister September said.

"At Myrna's wedding I had the lemongrass and vanilla massage," Cousin Darla said.

"I had the man masseuse," my great-aunt Kaitlin said, leaning on her cane. "I saw him trying to peep at my bust. I saw him!"

That morning, at my parents' house, we MacKenzie women met in the kitchen.

September yelled, pounding her chest, "Let me choose my own husband, or let me perish!"

"We will walk for your freedom, Geraldine, and for our own

womanly freedoms!" August shouted, holding hiking boots in the air.

"We work in sisterhood with you, Geraldine!" Aunt Tobias declared, holding up two huge sponges.

"We sail in harmony with your ocean's voyage!" Cousin Ally hollered, holding up a paddle.

"And," my mom said . . .

My mom's mother, white-haired, fiery, crackled out, "We go to the spa for you, Geraldine!"

Together we all yelled, "For Geraldine!" and held up our orange juice glasses.

We cheered! We laughed! We toasted Geraldine!

It was a fabulous day. I hardly stopped thinking of Reece once.

"Whooeee! He's on the front grass!" my aunt Belinda shouted from the deck the next afternoon. "Come and have a look-see, everyone. See! That's June's man! Is he a hunk or what?" She wore an Indian sari over one shoulder and a tartan over the other to respect both sets of her ancestors. "The other man was a wimp. Pimpy. Snobby . . . he was a tarantula."

Within seconds, the entire MacKenzie gang—at least a hundred of them—were out ogling Reece and me from the deck and front yard.

Most were dressed in Scottish tartans and kilts.

They held bows and arrows, swords and shields.

"This is my castle. I am the lairdette; you may enter!" my mom called, resplendent in the family tartan with blues, greens, and red.

My father held up a shield with the family crest on it. "You are welcome at our castle," he boomed out, his voice ringing off the trees and hills surrounding the home.

"Why?" a hundred voices shouted at once.

"Because we're the MacKenzie Scots!"

Then they burst into the family song, which started with, "Don't bust our butts, we won't bust yours," and described how we're the Clan MacKenzie, forever and ever we'll be, we love each other, fight to the death, our swords up, our shields a defense against all our enemies.

"What do we do?" my father railed, again raising his shield.

"We stick together!"

Next, they burst into the family dance, which can be best described as an Americanized Scottish version of rap/bounce/ Scottish dancing.

They hooted, they sang off key, they'd been downing whisky like true Scotsmen.

"You're in for an adventure," I told Reece, putting an arm around him.

"I can see that." He grinned. "Adventures are my specialty."

Soon Reece was wearing a kilt.

He was a mighty fine Scott. I flipped it up.

He'd kept his boxers on.

Later in the evening, amidst the hoopla, Reece and I snuck out to the river, away from a cacophony of noise and MacKenzie revelry. Some of the family had stayed in hotels in town, but most had spent the night at the house, and many had pitched tents and camper trailers. A line of fancy Porta-Potties out back had been strung with Christmas lights. The night was young, the parties would go late.

He reached for my hand, warm and sure.

"I missed you," he said.

"It was only three days," I laughed, feeling that sizzle between us, the electric current of unfulfilled desire.

"I still missed you."

"I missed you, too." I so had.

We strolled along the winding path by the river, chatting, as it splashed and played. We had a thousand things to say immediately, until he pulled me into his arms and hugged me close. We didn't kiss, but I wanted to, we didn't take off our clothes, but I wanted to, we didn't dive into the desire and the raging passion that zinged between us, but I wanted to.

"I'm trying my best to behave myself, June," he murmured into my hair.

"Me, too, Reece."

"It's killing me."

"Me, too."

I hugged him as my need to rip off his kilt razzed me straight up.

He pulled away, breathing hard, and said, "I need to jump in that river and cool off."

I took a shaky breath. "I'll follow you in."

We tiptoed, clothes and all, into that freezing water. I splashed him, he splashed back, we plunked ourselves down in the river, and he hugged me close, a deer watching us from twenty feet away, a crow cawing overhead in protest of our presence.

Later we snuck back into the house, or tried to.

My family laughed and chortled when they saw us, someone blared a bagpipe, another shook a tambourine. "A duet of love in the river!" my cousin Mimi shouted. Reece waved, I darted up the stairs to change. He winked at me.

I loved him. I knew it at that moment.

I loved Reece.

It scared me to death.

We ladies had our bachelorette party that night, which involved dancing outside in white dresses around the largest tree on my parents' property (for eternal freedom), eating a three-tiered cake decorated in the Clan MacKenzie colors at midnight (Go, MacKenzies!), and braiding a long, blue ribbon for August for "something blue" for her wedding.

The men had their bachelor party, which involved beer and football reruns.

There were no strippers, ever. Wasn't even a consideration.

"The MacKenzie men respect women, we will never debase them," my father said.

"The MacKenzie women respect men," my mom said. "We will never debase them, unless they *want* to get in their G-strings in front of us. Daughters, do you think that Hippie Chick should develop a G-string for men?"

I met Reece outside at one o'clock in the morning, the stars brilliant up in the blackness of the sky.

"June," he drawled to me. "This feels like family."

"Sure does, Reece, sure does."

Oh, how I wanted to lead that man down through the woods . . .

* * *

"I dressed conservatively for Benjamin's family," my mom declared the day before the wedding, as the entire clan stood restlessly on the porch waiting for Ben's family to arrive.

"Me, too," said my father.

They were both in dressy Hippie Chick wear. My mom had sparkles on her white gown, which was tied at the waist with a dangling white rope, her blond hair up in a loose ball under her crown of wildflowers. My father had a matching crown of wildflowers and a Hippie Chick Man blue suit jacket with a peace sign on the back.

"I feel very proper," my mom said.

"Me, too. Quite formal. But I do feel slick in the jacket." He rolled his shoulders. "Comfortable, but it makes a peaceful statement. Let's put on our tartans."

Some members of the clan/family wore Hippie Chick clothes, many wore kilts and tartans, and still others had donned bikini tops and shorts. The twins were, indeed, in their monster outfits. They gnashed their vampire teeth. My sisters were in Hippie Chick, March had a tartan over his shoulder.

On the porch, Reece put an arm around me and drew me close, which, as usual, took my breath away and gave me butterflies.

"Good afternoon, June," he murmured. "Good to see you're out of bed."

I laughed. "Dancing outside until the wee hours of the morning makes a woman sleepy."

"I can think of a few things that a woman can do until the wee hours of the morning that would make her even more sleepy."

How I sizzled, how I heated way, way up.

"Now I have a mental picture in my head, June." He sighed. "Can't seem to get rid of it."

I chuckled in a strangled sort of way, as my own graphic image popped up.

"It's a curvy image," he said, that voice low and gravelly. "I'm thinking of a king-size bed. White bedspread, white sheets. Hey! It's my bedroom at the beach house. Lights off, candles . . . chocolates in the shapes of butterflies. . . ."

I sighed.

"Yes, it makes me sigh, too, baby."

I wriggled as he pulled me close, his heat and mine meshing, flowing.

"It's a beachy image," he said. "I can hear the waves outside the doors, I know later we'll be down on the sand flying a kite, the sun shining, then we'll head back to the bed and the butterfly choco-lates—"

We were interrupted as my father shouted, "They have ar-rived!"

My family cheered as if greeting a victorious, returning army.

Hired limousines, one right after the other, turned down the long lane to my parents' home.

"Fancy schmancy," Great-uncle Tesh said, his Polish accent still heavy, even though he'd lived here for forty years. "Limousines. Money. Too much of it. Bah!"

The chauffeurs stepped out of the six limos. With military pre-ciseness they opened the door of each car, together. A high heel emerged, followed by an impeccably dressed woman. A black shoe emerged, shined and proper, followed by a man in a tailored suit. There were fancy hats, gloves, jewelry, designer dresses, more heels.

In a dignified, formal clump, they stared at us.

In a giant, jostling group, in tartans, kilts, bikinis, and monster outfits, we stared back. I reached for Reece's hand. August reached for mine, and whimpered, "Scary. Oh, they're so scary."

September moaned and pulled on a blue streak in her hair. "I don't think they're the groovy type that will want to get down to KC and the Sunshine Band's, 'Get Down Tonight,' the Clan MacKenzie's American wedding song."

I patted August's back as she made gasping sounds.

"I think they need a few shots of throat-burnin' whisky," Grandpa Stephen said, way too loud. His voice is never quiet. My father once said, about his thundering voice, "I am sure that Stephen's ancestors were the ones who led the charge on the battle-fields."

"Yep. Scottish whisky," Grandpa Stephen boomed once again, in case anyone within a mile couldn't hear him the first time. "Loosen 'em up. I'll go get it."

"You see, June," August stuttered, as her fiancé, Ben, a nice man totally in love with August, bopped down the steps to greet his family. "I don't fit in. I mean, do you see those suits! Suits! Women in suits. I can't wear a suit."

"They probably have more money than the entire Scottish empire," September said, her voice trembling.

"Are you sure you're going to be able to breathe in that family?" March asked, his brown hair sweeping his shoulders as he shook his head in concern. "You need air. Between the limos and the thousand-dollar suits, is there room to move and groove?"

Our parents were frozen beside us, which was so unusual, it made me freeze up, too.

"Is this a joke?" my mom whispered. "They're seriously not this uptight, are they?"

"My love, I don't know," my father said, back straight. He was a wanderer, but the man was a stud. Strong, brave, hyperprotective of his wife and us kids.

"I don't think they're going to understand the magic behind our wands," my cousin Harold said. He adjusted his flower crown over his mohawk.

"They'll probably be frightened when Bill Jr. and Mack shoot off their guns."

"Cousin Carrie, don't do the Ouija board with them!"

"Sal, no witchcraft!"

So there the Clan MacKenzie stood, watching, waiting. I leaned into Reece. My whole body trembled with that lust problem I have for him and concern for August with her future in-laws.

But one should never judge first impressions.

An older gentleman nodded at the chauffeurs, who then turned smartly on their heels to the limousines and brought out what looked to be packages. They handed the packages to each member of the family, then the older gentleman, clearly the patriarch, stepped forward to speak. He hobbled up, leaning on Ben's forearm, his hair white as a cloud.

He spoke in a thick Scottish brogue, his voice as loud as Grandpa Stephen's. "From the Clan Stewart to the Clan MacKenzie, we are united at last. From Scotland to America, I greet you now. This is a glorious day. May Ben and August be blessed with much laughter and many children, and a love for the homeland that never ends."

He straightened up, back tall, and recited a poem:

> *May the best you have ever seen*
> *Be the worst you will ever see.*
> *May the mouse never leave your grain store*
> *With a teardrop in its eye.*
> *May you always stay hale and hearty*
> *Until you are old enough to die.*
> *May you still be as happy*
> *As I always wish you to be.*

Struck dumb we all were. Struck dumb.

With that, the members of Ben's family unfolded their packages.

Out came their tartans. Their colors: Red, black, blue, green, white.

They whipped them over their shoulders, covering their proper, expensive suits.

"To America first, then to Scotland!" the old man declared, his fist in the air, and I swear his voice bounced off my parents' house, off the pine trees, off the mountains in the distance, and off the bubbly flow of the river. Clearly, his ancestors had led the charge on the battlefields, too.

My father stepped down, flicked his tartan over his shoulder, and shouted back, "To America first, then to Scotland!"

We MacKenzies woke up then, loud and hard, cheering and stomping our feet, waving our wands and flower crowns, adjusting tartans and kilts.

"The Clan MacKenzie welcomes the Clan Stewart! Welcome to our castle!"

And with that, members of the Clan MacKenzie and the Clan Stewart greeted one another, arms outstretched, long-lost family members from Scotland finally reuniting at a home in Oregon, near a rushing river, tucked between the hills

"Ah! To Scottish whisky!" Grandpa Stephen yelled. "To throat-burnin' Scottish whisky for all!"

CHAPTER 10

"Do you, August MacKenzie, take Ben Stewart to be your lawfully wedded husband?"

The minister, a cheery sort, had a low voice that carried over the rows of friends and family sitting outside in white chairs, a puff of wind meandering through.

"I sure do," August said, smiling up at Ben, who was in a kilt and a black tux jacket with a black bow tie. His groomsmen were in the same, as was my father, and many of the men on both sides of the family.

August was stunning, if I can brag a bit. Her wedding dress was exactly what she wanted, it was pure August. The dress was white lace, strapless, the bodice covered in pearls, and form-fitting to the top of her thighs, flaring out into a long train.

But she had asked me to Americanize hers and Ben's family tartans, and I had done so, combining both into one. The tartan looped over one shoulder, down to her waist, then flowed all the way down her lacy train, discreetly pinned. As is our Scottish tradition for good luck, August sewed the last stitch of her wedding gown with March, September, our parents, and I watching. Afterward, we did a MacKenzie family hug and cheer.

As bridesmaids, September and I wore red, much in the same style as August's, and we, too, wore the combined tartans. The flower girls' dresses were made of silky plaid, an exact replica of the colors in the Stewart or MacKenzie tartans. We all wore red heels.

Red heels are another family tradition. MacKenzies, or descendants of MacKenzies, have worn red heels for over one hundred years to symbolize that just because they're getting married, it doesn't mean they're giving up "hell-raisin' fun."

The wood stage for the wedding had been built by the river by Buddy. Yards of white silk hung across an arbor, the perfect backdrop to two enormous bouquets of wildflowers, August's favorite. On one side, a Stewart tartan hung; on the other, a MacKenzie tartan.

During the vows I snuck a peek out of the corner of my eye at

Reece. He was staring straight at me, a gentle, sweet, serious expression on his face. I tried to distract myself, I did, and focus on August, but those green eyes held me fast, and I felt my whole body melting, then turning fiery hot, then melting again. I had never been so physically attracted, and so emotionally attracted, to any man in my entire life. I didn't even know I could be that attracted to anyone . . .

"I now pronounce you man and wife!" the minister said, so cheery.

Oh, the kiss, the cheers, the smiles.

I was so happy for August, I had to wipe my tears.

"Now, in keeping with the MacKenzie family wedding tradition, let all married couples stand and face each other. . . ." The minister intoned.

August hugged September and me, then March, who was a groomsman, then went back to Ben, as it should be. September and I stood at the altar. Ben's best man and two groomsmen motioned for their wives to come up on stage. Other couples, including all married couples in the Stewart and MacKenzie families, stood and faced each other, holding hands.

That's when the problem started. A blistering problem. A walking problem. A terrible, wrecking ball of a problem.

"What the hell are you doing here?" I was furious to see Grayson. Yes, *Grayson.* My temper triggered instantly, searing through my shock, as he hopped up beside me on stage.

"I knew August was getting married, and I thought that you and I could renew our vows together, again." Grayson took my shaking hands in his.

"Get the hell off this stage." I kept my voice down so as not to cause a distraction.

"So many marriages," the minister proclaimed, quite jovially. "So much love."

"Why, June?" Grayson cocked an eyebrow. He was dressed in an expensive gray suit. "I think a renewal of our vows is what we need for a jump start." He squeezed my hands, then stepped closer. "To begin again. Reboot. Come on, June. One more chance."

My jaw dropped as for the first time, *the first time*, I heard sincerity in his voice.

"You're kidding."

"No. I miss you. I love you. I'll always love you. This has been the most miserable time in my whole life. Every day is worse than the day before. I'm in a pit, June. I have fought this divorce to ridiculousness because I don't want it."

The minister chirped, "What a blessing it is that all married couples can renew their vows together, as one family . . . eternal love and commitment . . ."

"I don't care," I hissed. "I want out."

"I know. But I want to try again. Once more. I'll do anything. You can do whatever you want. Make wedding dresses, we can turn the basement into your studio, we can travel more, I'll work less."

"No." I envisioned Reece in the audience, that blond hair, the man who loved lobster, loved talking about my wedding dresses, loved his ranch and songs, seeing this catastrophe, on stage, *at my sister's wedding.*

"Couples," the minister intoned, "hold the hands of your beloved and concentrate, for a moment, only on them, on your lives together, your love. Recapture that passion . . ."

"Go away now, Grayson." At that moment, I almost hated him. I ripped my hands from his.

"Please, June. See reason, be reasonable."

"Let us now," the minister sing-songed, "repeat our vows to one another, with love and forgiveness, humbleness and pride, grace and compassion, passion and fidelity."

"Last time, Grayson." I was trembling. Trembling with pulsating anger at him for invading my sister's wedding in front of Reece.

"Say the name of your beloved . . ." the minister said.

"Renew the vows, June—"

"Never—"

"I take thee . . ." the minister's voice rose.

"I take thee, June."

"Stop it, Grayson."

" . . . to have and to hold from this day forward . . ."

"I'm not letting go of you, June."

"You'll be forced to then, by law."

"For better or for worse, for richer, for poorer, in sickness and in health . . ."

"Listen to those vows. You took them, June. For better or worse, in sickness and in health."

"It was always 'worse,' Grayson, and you make me sick. Sick in the heart."

". . . to love and to hold, from this day until eternity . . ."

"You still care for me," he insisted, so arrogant. So delusional.

Well, that did it. *I still cared for him?* I wanted him to fly off the planet. I saw red. Grayson was red. All around him, red.

"Until death do us part. . . ."

I didn't even think about it. I wanted him gone. Gone for good. I could not have him in my life for another second. I stepped closer. I hooked my fun red heel around his ankle and pushed. He stumbled. I helped him fall backward when I slammed my fist into his face, and he flipped straight back, off the four-foot-tall stage, through the MacKenzie tartan. He landed on his back, a *poof* escaping his lips, the tartan covering his pinched face.

I whipped back around as if nothing had happened.

"I now pronounce, all of you," the minister said, delight and triumph running through his voice, "man and wife!"

When I could breathe I turned my gaze to Reece's, with the greatest fear I believe I have ever felt in my entire life. I couldn't find him, I couldn't see him. Without causing any more of a scene I searched the yard, and there he was, beside Grayson, picking him up by the shoulders and yanking him away, as if Grayson was a limp coyote.

Reece was livid.

"I can't be with you anymore."

"June, honey—"

"Reece, I can't." We were at the river, away from August and Ben's rollicking reception, in full swing after a bagpipe concert. Grayson had left. Ben's family had done well at the watermelon-seed spitting contest. His brother won. They were going to have another scavenger hunt, his mother wanted a crystal wand. Ben's sister was interested in Carrie's Ouija board. KC and the Sunshine Band's song, "Get Down Tonight," had been a huge boogie hit.

Next to me, so close, both of us on the grass beside the river, Reece said, his voice raw and frustrated, "You can't be serious, June."

"I'm sorry, I don't see this ending." I fought back hysteria that threatened to take over any rational part of my brain that was still left. "Grayson is not going to let go. I may have another year of this."

"Listen, June, I have money. I'll pay him off—"

"I would never accept that money." I started making a hiccupping sound as I tried to breathe.

"You wouldn't *accept* it?" He threw his hands in the air, his temper flaring. "I'm offering to go to him and give him a pile of money so he signs the damn divorce papers giving you full rights to June's Lace and Flounces, and *you won't accept it?*"

"No, Reece, I can't take money from you. I won't." I was still reeling from the scene with Grayson. He was stalking me, he would always stalk me. I felt a sense of desolation and despair fill my entire being. "And I won't allow you to pay him off, I can't live with that, I can't sleep with that. No."

"We could be together. It's only money to me, June, only money. And I want *us*. I want us and the beach walks, the butterfly shells, the sunsets. I want to hold you. I want to plan a future."

"I am not dealing with a normal person. Grayson has money, too. The money he makes as a partner in his firm, inherited money. His possessions, his things, his stuff, that's what he values. I'm a thing to him. A thing who he thinks is going to make more money for him."

"I know he doesn't want to let you go, June. I saw that. He's a dangerous, selfish man, but we can get this taken care of, we can."

"But when? It's been going on so long." It was sick. He was sick. Grayson made me feel trapped and suffocated. I had a right to my life, but he hung on like handcuffs.

"June, you and I can go on together. I'm tired of waiting. You're tired of waiting. You're divorced in every way possible except the final papers. I know how you feel about it, I know it feels dishonest to you, unethical, it doesn't feel right to me, either, but I don't see us putting *us* off anymore—"

"It's more than that, Reece." I thought my insides were going to chew me up and spit me out, I hurt so bad. I didn't want to say what I knew I had to say.

"What is it, then?" His eyes were worried, but he was angry, too.

"I'm not—" I felt faint. It would about kill me to say it, but I knew I was right. "Reece."

Our eyes locked, mine desperate, his dawning with devastating recognition.

"Oh no, June, please."

He knew, he knew me well enough to know.

I burst into tears. "I'm not ready, I can't do this."

He rubbed a hand across his eyes. "Honey—"

"I'm scared, Reece."

"Why? We're so great together, June. Give us a chance."

"You've been clear that you're looking for a wife. You want kids."

"I do. I've always wanted that. It's always been in the plan, but I hadn't met the person who made up the other half of the plan until now. Dammit, June." That temper was flaring again. "Did you think I was playing? A fun romance? A beach fling? Something to entertain me for a while? That's never what I wanted. It's not what I want now."

"I can't be a part of that plan." My hands shook, my whole body shook. "I want to be, but I'm not ready for a relationship that is that deep. I know you need, and you deserve, someone who can jump into this feet first with all her heart and mind. You don't need someone who is hesitating as I am, who doesn't trust herself, who still cries at odd moments, and rages with anger, too. Not only at Grayson, but at herself. I am so mad at myself sometimes, Reece, I could scream. We need time off, Reece. I need time. I can't be a couple when I'm so screwed up, not much confidence, so insecure ..."

"*No. No, June.*" Tears filled those green, frustrated eyes. "Please, no. For God's sakes. I don't want to be apart from you."

We went back and forth, ping-ponging, as the river rolled by, the music dim in the distance.

"Reece, give me some time. You have to. I have to get divorced, I have to figure things out...."

We argued, he left, running a hand through his hair in frustration, his kilt swaying.

I stayed, crying.

A minute later I heard Grandpa Bill, Bill Jr., and Mack shoot their guns off. A minute later I heard one more shot. Turns out it was Ben's Scottish grandpa's gun. "For Scottish luck, to the newlyweds!"

It made me cry more.

Over the next few days, at home in our beach houses, Reece tried to convince me to stay with him, stick it out, grow together. I couldn't. By the fourth day, I'd fallen apart and finally told him that his badgering was making me think of Grayson. "When you don't get your own way, Reece, it doesn't mean you can browbeat me until I give in. Don't do this to me. It reminds me of Grayson."

I could not have said anything worse.

He paled, he teared up, he hugged my trembling, lonely body close. The door shut, so quietly, behind him.

He left the next morning and took all the sunshine in my life with him.

Mr. Schone called again the next day.

"Put it up for sale, Mr. Schone. Please. I am so sorry. I will not be able to buy the house."

"It's definite then, dear?"

"It's definite. Did Mrs. Schone like the lace shawl I made her?"

"She adores it. We'll wait a little longer, June, I think your ship will come in."

"I hope so, Mr. Schone, I hope so."

I did not see any ship on my horizon at all. Only drowned seaweed.

I slumped quickly into emotional darkness. We were buried in work; I worked fourteen hours a day and walked for one hour on the beach where I continued my search for whole black butterfly shells. I never found any. I made Morgan and Leoni matching lace skirts and Estelle a lace shirt.

I dreamed of Reece running toward me and I was running away and he was swallowed by a wave.

As the weeks turned into months, he never left my thoughts. My mind was a morass of liquid, seeping pain.

And it seemed to get worse.

The *Couture Fashion* magazine article came out with a huge photo spread of my wedding dresses. "June's Lace and Flounces," was written, banner style, across the top. The article was about two thousand words, detailing my journey from being an unhappy lawyer in Portland to a happy wedding dress designer at the beach. There were photos of Estelle, Leoni, and me, and photos of my studio.

Virginia Bescotti, the reporter with the red-rimmed eyeglasses and the smacking gum, wrote exquisitely about each of twelve dresses. She had picked some of my favorites.

"If you insist on wearing a personal work of art for your wedding dress, June is your gal," Virginia wrote. "She will be the premiere wedding gown designer in this country . . ."

I was, overnight, overflowing with work, requests for interviews, and asked to be a guest on a couple of television shows. I would soon be able to buy the house. I would be able to give Leoni and Estelle a raise. We would have to hire a boatload of people. I had made it. I had made the business of my dreams.

I was so, so unutterably miserable. Loneliness sank into my bones.

"I'm not scared to be an astronaut," Morgan told us on a sunny day at the beach, the kite flyers out, along with three surfers and a bunch of kids. She pushed the black visor of her NASA helmet up. "I can do it. I know I can."

"I know you can, too," I told her.

"You're going to be the first person to Mars, you gutsy, fire-breathing girl," Estelle told her.

"Morgan," Leoni said, "tell Miss June and Miss Estelle your good news."

"I'm going to," Morgan said. "I was waiting until June stopped crying."

I wiped the tears off my cheeks. "Honey, I'm fine. Tell us the good news!" I smiled at her. I hadn't even known she knew I was quietly crying.

"Here goes, space astronaut friends," Morgan said, digging in her backpack. "It's not a letter from my dad, you probably thought it was."

We didn't say anything. I refuse to offer false hope to anyone, even a child. It's dishonest and wrong and only prolongs the harsh truth.

"Look what I got in the mail!" Morgan held up a large, white envelope. "Yep." She smiled. "NASA wrote me a letter and sent me a whole bunch of astronaut stuff."

"Wow!" I was quite impressed.

"Well, I'll be double damned," Estelle said. "Double or triple."

"They liked my pictures of the inside of the next shuttle and a new astronaut suit," Morgan read. She tilted her chin up, proud as can be. "Yessiree, I'm going to be Morgan Halls, astronaut, for the United States of America." She gave a toothy grin to the three of us as we applauded. "You three are going to be proud of me."

"We sure are, sugar." I hugged her close. "But we're already proud of you."

She took off her helmet. "This is what I get now. I'm different. I'm always gonna be different, but the kids at school don't bug me so much anymore. I think it's because they know I don't care. I know I'm not a freakoid, I'm just Morgan. And," she put her little fists in the air, "I won the spelling bee! I spelled 'aeronautics'!"

"What are you doing here?"

I wasn't even angry. I was exhausted to the bone, as if I was ill. My heart had cracked and I was so lonely I thought it would eat me alive and spit me out.

"I came to see you."

"Why, Grayson?"

"Can I come in?"

"No. You may not." I crossed my arms, sickened that I even had to look at him. I was in front of my garage, and I wasn't moving. His Porsche was in front of the house and I wanted to bomb it.

"I want to see where you're living, where June's Lace and Flounces is."

"I'm not going to show you it."

He stared off into the distance, at the ocean, before those cold eyes swung back to me. Only this time, in their depths, I could see something else. Was it ... *pain?* "You would rather shut down a company that you built from scratch rather than have me involved in any part of it, is that right?"

"That's right. June's Lace does not involve you."

He pondered that. "Who was the man at August's wedding who punched me, June?"

His face was tight and pinched. He resembled a muskrat chewing a lemon. I wondered how I ever could have been attracted to him in the first place. "It's no one to you, Grayson." Tears ripped along my eyes.

"It's someone to me. You're involved with him, we're still married—"

"I could have been divorced from you long ago, but you ..." I clenched my teeth tight. "All these months, all this misery, all this stress, all this money, out the door because you wouldn't let me go, you wouldn't sign the papers, you fought. And now," I took a deep, deep breath. I wondered if I was going to lose my mind, my grief over losing Reece about knocking me to my knees. I put a hand out and leaned against my blue cottage so I wouldn't fall over. "How much longer are you going to wait this out? To fight it? We are over. You win. I give up." I hated giving up. That's what I'd done in my marriage, but I couldn't fight any longer. Many things in life are much more important than money. Sanity, for one.

"Who is he?"

"He's who I want to be with. He's who I want to marry. He's the man that I love. I am so in love with him I can hardly think straight. Now, get off my property before I call the police." I turned and forced myself to wobble into the house, slammed my door, and reached for my phone to call the police.

Before I could dial, a blue folder slid under the door.

I heard Grayson's voice, broken. "Good-bye, June. I'm sorry."

There was a pause.

"I am sorry, June."

And there it was: my divorce. Signed, sealed, and shoved under the door.

He had also signed off on June's Lace and Flounces; he would make no claim to my business now or in the future. Inside was a check that would equal my half of the house.

For once in his life, Grayson had done the right thing.

I banged up the stairs and threw my arms in the air. "We're in business, ladies!"

"Yadala-hoo-hoo," Estelle said. "Being such a spry chicken myself, I love working twelve hours a day."

"I'm so happy!" Leoni said. "You should see the order that came in while you were outside. It's a zoologist getting married to a zookeeper! Animals all around."

"Cool," Morgan said to me, taking her helmet off. "Your business is almost as cool as being an astronaut."

Four Things I'm Worried About

1. I am worried that I have lost Reece forever.

2. I am worried that I will never be happy without Reece.

3. I am worried that I will be too emotionally whipped up and scared to try again with Reece.

4. Morgan. Still. I will give her more jobs to do and take her to tea.

I played online Scrabble for an hour that night. I spelled these words: "cattle," "love," "mine."

I lost.

Again.

I ate a chocolate doughnut with sprinkles. Okay. I had two.

CHAPTER 11

"That's a pretty song," Leoni murmured the next morning. She turned the radio up.

I listened with half an ear. I hadn't slept all night, my mind whirling. My divorce would be official soon. I could go to Reece if I had the guts. Would he still want me? Had I ruined things forever? Had he found someone else?

I heard the country singer croon about holding the hand of the woman he loved, in front of a bonfire at the beach, neither teenagers anymore, but they had wisdom and grace, and knew enough to know their love was enough to sail them around the moon.

Leoni's mouth gaped. "Didn't you have bonfires with Reece?"

My mouth gaped, too. "Nah, it's not about me."

"Check it out, June."

I darted to my computer with Leoni and Estelle breathing down my neck and clicked on the singer's website.

"Look, look," Leoni said. She pointed to a song and I clicked on it.

"Bonfire Beaches" written by Reece O'Brien.

She scrolled down. "Look, June."

Two other songs, written by Reece O'Brien.

We read the lyrics.

One was about a woman who sewed wedding dresses she would never wear, in blues and pinks and greens, she lived over a mountain in a house by the sea.

The other was about a runaway woman by the name of June, who ran as fast as she could away from love. He chased her, he could never catch up.

"You need to get your butt to eastern Oregon and hunt down that rancher singer," Estelle said. "You've found yourself, haven't you, and without using a slew of philosophical mumbo-jumbo junk words, you *know* June."

I did. I knew June again. And I knew that Reece was right for me. We were an *us*.

"I wouldn't turn down love, June," Leoni said. "This is the right kind of love from the right kind of man." She got teary and sniffled. "You've been so miserable since he left."

"It's like working with a jar full of depression, with two pinches of misery thrown in," Estelle said. "Socked in the gut, hit in the groin."

"Love, love, love," Leoni said. "Oh, it's all about love. Go get it, June. It's here. Don't lose it."

I ran for my suitcase.

The drive to eastern Oregon, from the beach, was going to be a long one. I drove for two hours, through the winding mountains, back onto a flat road, towering pine trees on either side, small towns . . . then I received a call and pulled off to the side of the road to answer it. I am so glad I did.

"June."

Oh, how that voice tingled me all over. "Reece."

"Where are you?"

"I'm . . ." Oh, how embarrassing. But still. I had nothing to lose. My pride would shortly be in shreds. "I'm driving to your place in eastern Oregon. I thought I'd try a little rodeoing."

I heard him laugh.

"What? What's so funny?" I felt a fog, a black and clingy fog, start to lift from my heart.

"You're going to my home in eastern Oregon?"

"Yes, Reece. I have to talk to you, to apologize, I am so sorry."

"Babe, I understand, I do."

"You do?"

"Yes. June," he said. "Come on home."

"What?"

"Come on home. I'm already at your beach house."

We met near the tide pools where we'd met the first time, when he'd yanked my tumbling body out of the wet claws of the ocean.

This was my favorite part of the beach. It was almost always deserted. The white-gold light was different here, as if it was specially made for only this corner of the Earth. The rays flowed down from the sun in columns. They sparkled, they shimmered, they glowed. I had spent a lot of time crying in that corner of the beach, a lot of time thinking, reflecting. Sometimes I brought my sketchbook, my colored pencils, my pens, and I wrote and I thought.

Today, though, I brought none of it. He was waiting when I arrived, standing tall, and smiling, the orange-and-red sunset framing him, his smile broad and welcoming.

When he held out his arms, I flew straight on in.

"I love you, Reece."

"I love you, June. From the first day I met you until forever, I will love you."

He laughed, and I laughed, our laughter floating around the waves, over the rocks, up to the sky where the sun was a dollop of gold and the sky was shooting flames of purple.

"Look at that cloud, June."

I tilted my head up. "Oh, my gosh," I breathed.

"It's a butterfly," Reece said.

Yep. It was. A cloud shaped like a butterfly.

I figured it was a sign to kiss that man silly. So I did.

EPILOGUE

Reece and I were married the next summer, in July, on the beach below my home, near the tide pools, at sunset.

My wedding dress was light blue, form-fitting, with a crisscross bodice that tied behind my neck and a long train that ruffled along the edges. I'd had yellow and red Scottish broom, foxglove, purple moth orchids, cherry blossoms, pink cyclamen, yellow witch hazel, all flowers grown in Scotland, painted—yes, *painted*—on the fabric of my dress by my father.

Later, the dress was featured in another magazine article. We have been bombarded with orders for the same dress ever since.

August and September wore dresses in an even lighter blue, with the same Scottish flowers. We wore red heels. I sewed the last stitch for good luck with March, September, August, and our parents watching. We did the MacKenzie hug and cheer afterward.

My bridal bouquet included all the flowers that were on my dress, but Reece had found two black butterfly shells, whole ones, and we'd stuck those in, too.

The reception was at a local bed-and-breakfast, with white tents and sparkling lights set up outside the Queen Anne home, the entire Clan MacKenzie present, the tables spread with our Scottish tartans. Estelle and Leoni attended and danced the night away. Morgan was my flower girl. She wore her NASA spacesuit. Instead of tossing rose petals, she spent hours making miniature space shuttles out of paper and flew those. She fit right in.

We celebrated our heroine Geraldine, we hiked early, boated, and enjoyed the spas, we had our bachelorette party under the moon in white dresses, and we had our rehearsal dinner where all of Reece's family came. Reece's family seemed to appreciate the wands and flower crowns. They loved the kilts and bagpipes.

I loved Reece. I loved him more than I thought it was possible to love anyone. I had been to his ranch and it was as compelling to me as the beach, only in a different way. The land undulates as the ocean does, only it's in gold and green and the silence is profound.

The afternoon before our wedding, out on the beach, he took both my hands in his and said, "June, when I take those vows tomorrow, I mean them. In sickness and in health, for richer, for poorer, forsaking all others, forever. I will always love you, there will not be a day in my life that I won't. You are the other half of my heart, the other half of my life, my future. I love you more than I will ever be able to say."

And I did what I seem to be doing best now: I cried. "I love you, too, Reece. And I'm so glad that sneaker wave knocked me over into your arms!"

For a wedding gift Reece gave me a diamond necklace in the shape of a butterfly and a quilt that he'd hired Leoni and Estelle to sew for me. All of mine and Reece's relatives had donated a cotton shirt to be cut into squares for the quilt. I had an uncle who donated a shirt with dancing fish on it. Another had palm trees. There were flowers, stripes, birdhouses, champagne glasses, flip-flops, and birds. The quilt was a compilation of our families, of us. In the middle was the Clan MacKenzie tartan.

It was stunning, it was family, it was love.

"You've resewn your life, June, that's why I wanted you to have the quilt." He pointed to a square with a monarch butterfly on it. "That one is me. And this one"—he pointed at the purple and blue butterfly next to it—"that's you." He pointed to five squares with smaller butterflies. "Those are for the kids. But don't feel limited by that number." He gave me a smackeroo on the cheek. "We could have more."

"That's a lot of kids!" I sputtered out, happy.

"Sure is, June." He kissed me thoroughly, without restraint, the passion flowing hot and heavy between us, no longer something we had to control and deny. Kissing Reece was kissing love. Eternal love. Forever love.

Later, we danced along the beach, into the waves, and when my family, and his family, saw us, they clambered down the stairs and we all danced together under the yellow-and-orange sunset, cranberry red slashes highlighting that golden orb, tartans flying.

Reece wrote a song about families later titled "The Wave Dancers."

A top country artist bought it. It was the number one country song for weeks.

Zero Things I'm Worried About

1.

2.

3.

I am winning in online Scrabble. The other night I spelled these words: "dream," "quest," and "Botox."

When I was done, I ate peppermint sticks with Reece.

Then we got naked.

SECOND CHANCE
SWEETHEARTS

By Holly Chamberlin

As always, for Stephen.
And this time, also for Margaret.

Acknowledgments

Thanks to John Scognamiglio for giving me the opportunity to write this piece. Thanks also to Kit and Carrie for inspiration on a variety of matters.

This is in memory of my beloved Jack. He was a very special and beautiful boy and will be remembered forever with great love. Ma-mow!

CHAPTER 1

Who so loves believes the impossible.

—Elizabeth Barrett Browning

The August light had not yet faded from the sky when thirty-four-year-old Thea Foss began to settle in for the night. It was quiet, as it always seemed to be at this time of the evening at this time of the year; birds and nonpredatory wildlife had long gone to bed. An occasional firefly flitted past the windows; Thea remembered catching them when she was a child, though as an adult she thought the practice a bit cruel. Later on in the night, a wakeful listener might expect to hear the melancholy hoot of an owl.

Though it was too early in the year for a fire, the night air was becoming progressively cooler as the month wore on. Thea went into the small bedroom and pulled from a drawer a heavy cotton sweater she had worn since college. The neckline was slightly frayed and what once had been a deep orange was now a rather faded melon color, but the sweater was roomy and comfortable. As she pulled it over her head she caught a glimpse of herself in the old cracked mirror over the painted wood dresser. Basically, she liked what she saw.

She was of average height, about five feet four when she wasn't slouching, which she tended to do when she was tired, just like her father. She had never been thin or fat, always what in an earlier day had been known as "pleasingly plump," and not much concerned about being any other way. Her eyes were a very pale blue and her hair a sort of red-gold now, though when she was little it was what her mother had called strawberry blond. She had worn glasses since the age of nine, contacts since the age of twenty-four or so, but only on certain occasions when it was easier, like on a really rainy day when glasses would spatter and then steam up when you went into a store or got onto a bus, or on really sunny days, when switching from sunglasses to regular glasses again and again could be annoying. She had never been a beach bunny so her skin was virtually flawless, though vaguely freckled. If asked, Thea would describe herself as a person who didn't stand out in a crowd, though, of course, a few people in her life would argue this. Like, for one, her mother, and, for another. . . . Well, he was long gone out of her life. Hugh Landry's opinions, though once so important, no longer mattered to her.

Thea went back to the living room and surveyed her surroundings. She had moved into the apartment about two weeks earlier, committing to a two-month stay, with an extension to be mutually decided upon after six weeks. She had paid her landlady, a friendly woman named Alice Moore, in cash and in full, mostly in order to avoid Alice's running a credit check. What Alice would find if she did might cause her to close the door against her new tenant.

The apartment was small and charming. It occupied the lower floor of a wood frame house built about thirty years earlier—Alice lived on the main floor—and opened out directly onto a small, rustic patio set with a tiny table, two narrow wooden chairs, and an old but serviceable grill Thea had no idea how to use. A birdfeeder was always occupied, sometimes by a marauding squirrel, but most often by a large variety of small and colorful birds. More feeders were attached to the back porch of the house, above Thea's apartment. Twelve Oak Street was one of the most popular sites among the local avian community.

The house had a spacious sunroom on its east side and a large, open deck on its west side, as well as a sleeping loft above the main floor. It was surrounded by a field that was the home of strutting wild turkeys, grazing deer, and an abundance of plants and wildflowers, many of which Thea could not name. An ancient, low stonewall, erected by some long-dead farmer, cut across the field in a slightly wavering line, providing a sort of Roman road for the neighboring cats and other small, furry animals to traverse. Just beyond the field began a dense wood, now a wall of thick, green leaves atop the massive gray and brown trunks of oaks and maples and the thinner trunks of the occasional white birches.

It was a quiet and peaceful place, close to idyllic, especially for someone who had been through what Thea had recently been through. She was finally beginning to feel comfortable, just a bit, after a period of immense trial. A two-week sojourn in this cozy little apartment in a pretty little vacation town, among people who knew nothing about her except what she wanted them to know, which was virtually nothing, was beginning to work wonders on her nerves.

Thea made a cup of Lipton tea, always reliable and less expensive than the fancy brands that she enjoyed but couldn't really afford, and began to scan the stacks of books that were piled on the floor against one wall. She had brought a large box of books with her from Massachusetts, and Alice had generously offered her full access to her own impressive library, some of which had overflowed into the lower apartment. Enticingly, Alice's library included several volumes of a very early twentieth-century collection of the complete works of Honoré de Balzac, in French. It was a bit of a dream come true for Thea, at least for now. So many books and for once, for a while, so much time in which to read them!

The difficulty, of course, was choosing a particular book to match her mood at a particular moment. Thea picked up a fairly recent biography of Margaret of Anjou, wife of Henry VI. She had been extremely lucky to find it at a secondhand bookstore for a really affordable price. No doubt it would be fascinating reading— the reviews were good—but at that moment . . .

Thea returned the biography to the box and chose instead something completely different, a Georgette Heyer detective novel, written in the late 1930s. She had read it before but found she never tired of Ms. Heyer's plodding but brilliant detectives, overly suave young gentlemen, madcap young women, and hysterical middle-aged matrons. Plus, the period slang was lots of fun. She settled into an old and very comfortable armchair upholstered in chintz. You might not like chintz all that much, Thea reflected, looking down at the massive pink cabbage roses pictured against a faded mint green background, but it was hard not to feel somewhat cheered by its presence in a room. All I need now, she thought, to make this moment perfect, is a cat on my lap. But a cat would come soon enough, she vowed. There was a shelter not far from her parents' house back in Massachusetts and—

Thea's brief reverie was blasted by the ringing of her cell phone. She shot to her feet and, after a moment's hesitation, stumbled over to the occasional table on which the phone sat, attached to its charger. Her heart was racing, as it always did when the phone rang. She peered down at the number displayed on the screen. It was a number she didn't recognize. She still hadn't touched the phone, as if by doing so she would unleash something bad or evil into the room.

The phone continued to ring. Her heart now began to pound uncomfortably hard. As far as she knew the only people who had this number were her parents and the people at the phone company. She let the call go to voice mail.

While only a moment before she had felt in a bit of an enchanted space, she now felt exposed. The large windows of the apartment's living room were no longer access to a natural paradise but portals through which a human being with malevolent intent might peer, a thing far worse than a goblin or even a hungry black bear.

The call had registered in voice mail. Carefully, Thea pushed the appropriate key and with her eyes squished shut, her lips pressed together, she listened. At the first note of the cheery feminine voice, she walked back to the chair and dropped into it with relief. It was nothing but a prerecorded courtesy call from her bank—of course they would have the number!—something about a new savings program she might want to explore. She sank back with a deep and trembling sigh.

Nothing important. Nobody of significance. She was safe for now.

But it didn't matter, Thea thought, pulling her sweater closer around her, her book forgotten, her cup of tea getting cold. It could have been Mark Marais. It could always, at any time, be Mark Marais.

CHAPTER 2

Tuesday morning found Thea sitting in Alice's kitchen, sipping very strong, very good coffee and eyeing a loaf of banana bread Alice was just taking out of the oven. Thea hadn't planned to spend her morning with her landlady, but Alice had pretty much forced the issue, and the smell of the bread baking in the oven upstairs had only added to Alice's argument. Besides, after that call the night before it had been a long time before Thea had managed to fall asleep, and when she finally had, her sleep had been restless, interrupted by anxious dreams. A big cup of good coffee might help hurtle her into the day ahead.

"We'll just let that cool for a few minutes and then it's every woman for herself." Alice placed the warm bread on a trivet and brought it to the kitchen counter. She was dressed in a pair of faded jeans, a white Oxford shirt rolled up at the sleeves, and navy sneakers. She was a tall woman, about six feet, and broad in the shoulder and hip, though not overweight. Her hair was thick and silvery gray and came to her shoulder. This morning it was pulled into a neat ponytail. Thea wondered what color it had been originally but thought that to ask might be impertinent. Alice's eyes were very bright blue and very keen. Her skin showed some damage, possibly caused by too many hours in the sun without a hat or long sleeves, but her smile was strong and overall, Thea found, Alice gave the impression of a woman much younger than her fifty-three years. Alice had told Thea her age on the day she had signed the lease. Thea still didn't know why; her landlady's personal information was of no concern to her. But some people seemed prone to sharing every little thing about themselves. Maybe Alice was one of those people.

"Everything all right downstairs?" Alice asked, pouring more coffee from a glass French press pot.

"Oh, yes," Thea said. "It's a lovely apartment." In spite, she added silently, of all those windows. What was I thinking when I agreed to move in? Oh, right. I wasn't thinking, at least not clearly.

"It helps pay the mortgage," Alice was saying. "Renting it out, I mean."

"Oh."

"And when I manage to get a tenant like you, someone nice and quiet, it makes it all the better. I think I told you that I work from home. Nothing worse than trying to write an article on shrinking coral reefs while some idiot's blaring one of those oversouling singers under your feet."

"Oversouling?" Thea questioned.

"Yeah, it's when those pop singers who all sound alike give every word about twenty-three syllables. I read the term somewhere online, 'oversouling.' Give me Frank Sinatra any day."

"Oh. But surely you interview the tenant first," Thea said. "To make sure he—or she—is, you know, mature?"

"Of course. But I've been fooled. Not often, but it's happened."

Alice, deeming the banana bread was ready for consumption, cut several slices, and slid one onto the plate set before Thea. "There's the butter, and that jam is boysenberry. I think. Some kind of berry other than straw. Never was a big fan."

Thea smiled and reached for the butter. Really, in the light of day, sitting in a cozy kitchen, slathering butter on homemade banana bread, the fears and anxieties of the night before seemed almost silly. Almost.

"Let me guess," Alice said suddenly. "You're running away from a bad relationship."

Thea almost choked. Had Alice been reading her mind? "How did you know?" she asked a bit warily.

"Why else does a young, single woman move to a small town where she knows nobody and rents an apartment from another single woman in a house on a dead-end road, miles from the center of town?"

Thea took another sip of her coffee. It really was very good. She probably owed her hostess some sort of an answer, if only in thanks for the breakfast.

"I was married," she said finally, not meeting Alice's eye. "It didn't work out."

Alice nodded briskly. "That's too bad. I was married, too. Twice. Both husbands died before their time. A shame."

"Oh, I'm sorry," Thea said sincerely.

"Yeah. Me, too. They were good men and the relationships were good, too. If I'm at all lucky, and I seem not to be, I'll meet another good man and marry him. I'm not that old. I don't flatter myself, but I still look pretty appealing seen from a certain angle in a certain sort of dim light."

"You would get married again," Thea asked, "after being widowed twice? I don't know, that seems so . . . risky."

"Sure, I'd get married again," Alice said robustly. "The relationships didn't suck, it was the husbands dying part that sucked."

"But you'd be taking such a chance of being hurt again . . ."

Alice shook her head and reached for another slice of banana bread. "Better than being alone for the next twenty or thirty years. Some people aren't cut out for the solitary life. I'm one of them."

"But you seem so . . ."

"Self-sufficient? Reasonably happy? That doesn't mean I'm not lonely."

No, Thea thought, she supposed that it didn't. "Well, I'll never get married again," she said emphatically. "Or move in with someone or even date someone seriously. I'm done with relationships. I'm just fine on my own. I always have been."

"Then why did you get married in the first place?"

Was that question a challenge, Thea wondered, or was Alice simply curious? Either way, how to explain—and to a virtual stranger, at that—why she had married Mark Marais? It wasn't something she could fully explain to herself.

"I made a mistake," she said after a moment. It wasn't a lie.

"Ah. Well, we all make mistakes on occasion, as I've admitted."

Thea felt that she had revealed enough about her personal life for one morning. "Well," she said, rising from her seat, "I should get going. Thanks for the coffee, Alice, and the breakfast. It was very good. I'm afraid I can't make a decent cup of coffee at all, let alone bake."

"You're welcome," Alice said. "Thanks for the chat. As I said, I'm not one for the solitary life. It helps to have someone around every once in a while. But don't worry. I'm not going to interfere with your seclusion."

Thea, already at the front door, turned back. "Oh. I wasn't worried," she said.

"Yes, you were."

Thea smiled in spite of herself. "Maybe a little."

CHAPTER 3

Thea was scheduled to work from 11:00 to 3:00 at Maggie's diner. At 10:40, she parked her car in a small lot reserved for employees of the diner and a few of the other businesses in the heart of town and waded through vacationers on their way to the beach or the shops.

She had waited tables back in college and then in graduate school and she still generally enjoyed the work. It was mindless enough to be left in the restaurant at the end of the workday, and yet required enough attention and social skill to keep her interested. Sure, there were the occasional difficult customers to contend with, the sort who were never, ever pleased, and the overly permissive parents who seemed to think that it was okay for their precious kiddies to throw food and fits without check, but compared to some of the other part-time jobs she had held—babysitting a truly incorrigible three-year-old and working the deep fryer at a local fast-food joint, for example—waiting tables was a pleasure.

At the end of the shift, which had been busy but largely uneventful, a young waitress named Kathy invited Thea to go out for a drink that evening with some of her friends. It wasn't the first time Kathy had asked Thea to socialize and it wasn't the first time Thea had politely declined. It was true that she didn't want to get too close to anyone as she planned to leave Ogunquit before the winter, but the primary reason she preferred to keep to herself was the fear of exposure. What if she did let someone know about the disaster her life had been for the past few years, and what if, crazily, that someone knew Mark Marais and told him where she could be found . . .

Yes, Thea knew she was being dramatic, maybe even overly cautious, but sometimes drama and caution were called for. Interestingly, she didn't feel so worried about being found out when she was with Alice, though she still had no intention of telling her the gory details of her spectacularly bad marriage and divorce.

After waving good-bye to the other staff, Thea left the diner and joined the crowd of vacationers making their way from the beach to an ice cream shop, from a long lunch in the Cove to a motel for a nap, from Bread and Roses bakery on Main Street to the antique store a few doors down from the post office. At the corner of Beach and Main Streets, Thea stopped to wait for a lull in the traffic before risking her life crossing. It was a notoriously busy corner and one with no traffic lights or crossing guard or police personnel to bring order to chaos.

A loud male voice boomed through the throng gathered with her on the sidewalk. Thea startled and a small cry escaped her lips. The two teenage girls standing next to her giggled.

"Yo! Dude, it is you!"

It was only an enthusiastic teenage boy, now pushing his way through the crowd to slap the upraised hand of a buddy. Thea felt foolish. At the same time she wanted to shake those girls who had laughed at her. She wanted to tell them that life might just test them the way she had been tested and that someday they, too, might jump at the ringing of a phone or a raised male voice.

But of course, she did no such thing. She just stood there like every other solid citizen and waited for a break in the traffic. She had read somewhere that the town's population swelled to around twenty thousand in the summer. It was easy to believe, especially if you were silly or crazy enough to attempt to drive through the heart of downtown Ogunquit anytime between five in the afternoon and eight at night and actually expect to make your dinner reservation.

In spite of the crowding, Ogunquit certainly had its share of charm. The town's library was housed in a beautiful stone building set on a perfectly manicured lawn. Harbor Candy, a family-owned shop on Main Street, had been handcrafting its chocolates and other treats since 1956. A fleet of brightly painted trolleys carried visitors through Ogunquit and down into Wells.

And, as with any vacation destination, there was plenty of shopping to be had. There were low-end gift shops, the kind that sold inflatable beach toys, T-shirts with silly slogans involving lobsters, and novelty gifts like snow globes filled with sand instead of artificial snow, and there were high-end shops, like Abacus, which was more of an art gallery than anything else. You could buy a baseball cap at one end of town for a few dollars and a one-of-a-kind gold-and-diamond necklace at the other end of town for a small fortune. With little if any disposable income, Thea avoided all the shops except for the Hannaford in York, the huge grocery store that sold everything from fresh and prepared foods to pharmaceuticals to kitchen utensils to pet carriers.

The same held for the restaurants. Thea ate her meals at home, though she was entitled to a reasonable meal after her shifts at the diner, and sometimes she took advantage of that offer. Not for her the high-end places like MC Perkins Cove or 98 P.R.O.V.E.N.C.E., or even Barnacle Billy's. But that was okay. She wasn't in Ogunquit to see and be seen. She was there to lay low and recover a bit of her sanity. Besides, she had never been fussy about food. As long as it was served in a copious amount, she was pretty much satisfied. Alice seemed to have sensed that about her.

Thea reached the employee parking lot and got into her car, a 1987 Clunker. She had bought it for next to nothing because it was worth next to nothing. To help pay for the divorce she had had to sell her almost brand-new car, and finding herself momentarily desperate for a mode of transportation, she had jumped at the dubious deal offered by the Clunker's owner. She doubted this "gently used" vehicle would last the winter; the power steering was squealing, the shock absorbers were chunking, and the brakes were grinding, but she hadn't bought it with an eye to an investment. Just before she had left home for Ogunquit her father had offered to help her with the cost of a good secondhand car. The last thing Thea wanted to do was turn to her parents for support after all that had happened, but she was afraid she was going to have to swallow her pride and accept some financial support in the form of a loan.

Thea pulled out into the summer traffic and headed back to her apartment in Alice's remotely situated house. Another day was coming to an end, another day of refuge in a town largely populated by seasonal transients, people she would never come to know. And another long evening lay ahead, during which, Thea promised herself, she would try very hard not to have a minor nervous breakdown if the phone rang. She stopped to let a strolling, cuddling couple cross the road. The sight made her stomach clench. Maybe, she thought, my therapist was right after all. Maybe I should never have come here.

CHAPTER 4

After a dinner of a baked potato (easy to cook in the microwave), frozen broccoli (ditto), and a muffin (a day-old she had picked up at the diner for half price), Thea poured a glass of red wine and placed it on the small table next to the chintz-covered chair. She would attempt to begin the Georgette Heyer book she had intended to read last evening, before that call had made her such a nervous wreck. Well, the call hadn't made her a nervous wreck; Thea had done that to herself. It wasn't what happened to you, her therapist had told her repeatedly as she struggled through the worst of the divorce and its immediate aftermath. It was how you decided to react to what happened that mattered. It was good advice, but difficult to put into action.

Before Thea could settle into the comfortable chair with her wine and book, an impulse sent her into the bedroom. She hadn't brought much with her to Ogunquit—an adequate supply of clothing; a bathing suit, though she had no real plan to use it as she didn't like the idea of spending time on the beach by herself; a selection of favorite books, of course; and one precious piece of her long-distant past.

Thea opened the second drawer of the painted wood dresser and removed a square, purple velvet box. Inside was a painted miniature of Napoleon, with the emperor's authenticated signature on the back. Hugh Landry, her first and greatest love, had given it to her for her sixteenth birthday. He had found it at an antique shop on Beacon Hill in Boston. Thea's parents had urged her to return the gift; they thought it was "too much." But Thea had refused. It was the most special, thoughtful thing anyone had ever given her. Once she had begun to suspect Mark of double-dealing, she had put the miniature in a private safety deposit box in a bank different from the one where they had their joint accounts. To imagine Hugh Landry's gift being callously sold for someone else's profit was a horror.

In light of what had happened later in her brief marriage, Thea was glad that she had hidden the miniature away. Now, it was with her again, nestled in its velvet box and tucked into a pile of underwear and T-shirts when it wasn't in her hand, being gazed upon. Though selling it would help her immediate financial situation, Thea knew she could never bring herself to part with it. The engagement and wedding rings Mark had given her had gone long ago, as had her car and her condo. The miniature was here to stay.

Thea carefully closed the lid of the purple velvet box and returned it to its hiding place. She went back to the living room and its comfortable chintz-covered chair. She opened the Georgette Heyer novel but only a few pages in she realized she was still too distracted to read. Her mind seemed determined to reminisce about the giver of that special gift.

Hugh Landry was everything a young girl could have wanted in a boyfriend—handsome, friendly, popular, and smart. More importantly, he had been everything Thea herself could have wanted in a soul mate. He understood and appreciated her for who she was, not for who he wanted her to be. That, alone, in a teenage boy, was a remarkable thing. Though he was a star on the football team, he never pressured her to go to his games like the other players expected their girlfriends to. He knew she wasn't interested in sports; he liked the fact that she was her own person and chose to stay at home and read books about European history or "cozy" mysteries set in English manor houses rather than cheer in the stands.

Thea was suddenly aware of Alice's footfalls upstairs, moving from her living room to her kitchen. She wondered about her own future; she wondered if she would be living alone in her fifties, like Alice was. The prospect didn't seem so awful, certainly a lot better than living with an abuser, a liar, and a cheat. And if she could be like Alice, self-sufficient and, as Alice had said, reasonably happy, a solitary life might be just fine. Even though Alice had admitted she would like to be in a relationship, her life still had great value and she seemed to know that.

Alice must have settled down somewhere because her footsteps ceased. Thea looked at the book in her lap. That was the problem, she thought. Learning how to become self-sufficient and relatively happy, both of which she had been back when she had been dating Hugh Landry, and both of which she had been for all of the years before her marriage.

Which didn't mean that several times during those self-sufficient and relatively happy years she hadn't considered contacting Hugh, but for a variety of reasons—the fear of rejection being one of them; another being the promise she had made to him in her final letter—she had dismissed the idea. Besides, it was unlikely a new reality could ever equal the perfection of an old memory. Distortions were normal; maybe the Hugh of her memory didn't really exist; maybe he never really had. Besides, there was every chance that a man like Hugh Landry was either married or engaged or soon to be. And there was every chance that he was a father, responsible to his family, and not interested in being bothered by a long-ago girlfriend. Thea wasn't sure she could handle seeing a happy family picture posted on Facebook or wherever she would find Hugh Landry. Especially not now, in her vulnerable state. She didn't begrudge Hugh whatever happiness he had found, but she wasn't sure she wanted to be confronted with that happiness.

Thea took an appreciative sip of the wine that had been sitting untouched. She suspected the only reason she was thinking so much about Hugh these days was because she was in this unique situation—divorced, virtually friendless, somewhat estranged from her parents, who were her entire family, and on hiatus from what had become a fraught career, through no fault of her own. Well, that could be debated. She had quit her job as a high school French teacher, if not happily, at Mark's request. He hadn't put a gun to her head; not literally, at least.

Thea took another sip of wine and then another and firmly put all thoughts of Hugh Landry and of Mark Marais to the side. With only a few false starts, she finally managed to engage in *No Wind of Blame.* Former chorus girl and wealthy widow Ermyntrude Carter was a vastly amusing character, with her flamboyant but good-natured behavior, as was her daughter, Vicky, a pretty and determinedly theatrical young woman who changed costumes and personas as the mood struck her, which could be several times a day. Knowing in advance "who done it" was no obstacle to the fun of following the investigation through to the remarkable conclusion. Halfway through the novel and all thoughts not associated with the murder of the charming loser Wally Carter had flown far, far away.

CHAPTER 5

Shortly after a breakfast of bad coffee and cold cereal Wednesday morning, Thea left the house to tramp through the fields surrounding Alice's house. Not far into her ramble she encountered Alice's calico cat, a large, ill-tempered beast named Henrietta, who ostentatiously ignored Thea in spite of her attempts to coax the kitty for some stroking. With a flash of her white-tipped tail, Henrietta was over the old stonewall that snaked across the backfield and out of sight. Probably chasing chipmunks, Thea surmised. The area was full of them, chipmunks and squirrels and roly-poly hedgehogs and more varieties of birds than she could possibly name. There was a bird identification book in the apartment and Thea had made good use of it in the short time she had been in residence, but she still had a lot to learn.

She breathed in the air that smelled ever so slightly of the sea.

The best thing about being "in Nature" was that there was no way she would ever run into Mark Marais. She smiled at the thought of his twisting an ankle on a rotted tree root or frantically swatting away nonexistent bugs. Compared to Mark, Thea was Mountain Girl and Grizzly Adams rolled into one. One time, early in their courtship, Thea had suggested a walk through a popular suburban park. Still playing the obliging suitor, Mark had readily agreed. But in spite of the wide, flat, and well-cared for trail, Mark had managed to fall twice, tearing the knee of his chinos; be struck with a sneezing attack in the vicinity of a stand of pine trees; and come down later that afternoon with a particularly ugly-looking rash on his hands and arms. At the time, Thea had thought Mark's willingness to endure such trials for her sake gallant. Only much later did she see that "willingness" for what it really was: calculation.

What had begun as a restorative morning ramble suddenly morphed into a sinister episode as Thea was startled by a powerful mental image. Mark's face slammed its way into her consciousness, obliterating the velvety moss-covered boulders and the delicate sprays of Queen Anne's lace, blocking out the stands of lush, green ferns and the rough sculptures made by fallen branches. Mark's sneering face, his expression one of superiority and deep disdain. Mark mocking her stupidity. And then, as suddenly as it had come, the image was gone.

Thea stumbled to a halt, physically affected by the vision. She no longer felt safe all alone and out of earshot of Alice's few distant neighbors. She turned and half ran back to the house, small rocks flying up under her heels, tiny wildflowers crushed underfoot. The sudden scream of a blue jay almost sent her to her knees. Once inside her apartment, she carefully locked the door behind her and went to the kitchen sink for a glass of cool water. The past, at least her recent past, was a menace. She wondered if she would ever be done with it.

Now it was a little after noon and Thea was headed into town to pick up her check at the diner. The task could have waited until her next shift, but the nasty image of her former husband had decided her against staying alone in the house; Alice had driven off before Thea had gone out to walk and she had no idea of when Alice would be back. Not that town was necessarily any safer should Mark decide to make an actual appearance outside of her imagination, but there were more people she could call to for help. She knew it was ridiculous to be living her life this way, in fear and trembling, but she clung to the hope that time would do what it was supposed to do and heal her wounds. For the moment she would keep her head down, scrape together what living she could, and keep fantasies of Mark's revenge at bay.

Once inside the diner, she greeted her colleague Louise, a single mother of two. Louise also worked part-time for a local woman who made exquisite floral arrangements for weddings and other special occasions.

"I came by for my check," Thea told Louise. "I'm sorry to come at such a busy time. I don't know what I was thinking."

"Not a problem," Louise said, her usual imperturbable self. "I'll get your check for you, honey."

Louise hurried off to the office behind the kitchen and Thea scanned the diner. Really, it was thoughtless of her to have come by at lunchtime, chased out of her own home by what amounted to a ghost. Every stool at the counter was occupied, as was every table up front. Thea glanced to the back of the diner. Yes, every booth, too, was occupied, including the very back booth, though it was occupied by only one person. A man . . .

It couldn't be. Thea blinked, shook her head, did all the ridiculous things a person did automatically when she saw or thought she saw the impossible, or at least, the improbable. But it wasn't a hallucination. It was Hugh Landry, in the flesh, sipping from a thick, white china cup.

Thea knew she could be a bit superstitious; she also knew that it wasn't one of her best character traits. But still, how odd was it that just last night she had sat reminiscing about her first great love and now Hugh was here, as if summoned by her memories . . .

That's ridiculous, Thea told herself, clutching the straps of her brown leather bag more tightly. But . . . really, what were the odds of Hugh Landry being in this little town, at this little diner, at the very moment she was coming by for her paycheck?

Thea had a strong urge to turn and run out of the diner, paycheck be damned. But she found that she couldn't move a muscle.

And then Hugh lifted the cup in front of him again, took a sip, and over the thick, white rim, his eyes found Thea. She might have smiled; she wasn't sure. Hugh put down the cup with a bit of a clatter and definitely did smile. She found herself walking back to his table and just standing there, looking down at him.

Neither made a move to touch, to kiss, to hug, or even to shake hands. Thea felt just like she had the day Hugh had come to sit by her in history class. Overwhelmed. Slightly dizzy. Disbelieving. Could this be, she thought, my mind playing a trick on me?

Hugh found his voice first. "Thea. Wow. Sit down, please."

She slid into the booth as if in a trance. "I can't believe this," she said finally, her voice sounding a bit weak in her ears. "I can't believe it's you. That's such a clichéd thing to say. I'm sorry."

"Clichés are what's called for in a moment like this," Hugh said, shaking his head. "I feel the same way. Stunned. Well, I'll be a monkey's uncle. You could knock me over with a feather."

Thea laughed and hoped she didn't sound as slightly hysterical as she felt. "What are you doing here?" she asked. "I mean, what are you doing in Ogunquit? Are you on vacation?"

"First things first," he said. "I just ordered lunch. Are you hungry?"

Thea was suddenly aware of being ravenous—no Alice-made breakfast that morning—and asked Louise, who had appeared as if on cue, an inquisitive grin on her face and paycheck in hand, for a tuna salad sandwich on white toast and a cup of tea. When Louise had gone off, Thea had a sudden vivid memory of sharing nachos with Hugh during the summer before college at a chain restaurant in their town. Every Tuesday night, without fail, they would order a large plate of nachos, extra jalapeños on the side for her, followed by a brownie sundae. She wondered if Hugh remembered that magical, bittersweet summer . . .

"Now, to answer your question," Hugh said, "I was visiting friends in Boston, and I just thought, why not drive north for a few days before heading back home to New York. I've lived in the city since graduate school at Columbia."

"Oh," Thea said. "But why did you choose Ogunquit and not someplace else?" Why, she thought, the place that I just happen to be hiding out from my life?

Hugh shrugged. "I'd been here about a million years ago and remembered it as being really beautiful. Seriously, I'm staying in a bed-and-breakfast right out of a picture book. If it was any more charming I'd choke on the sweetness."

"Charming isn't too hard to find here. Is your . . . I mean, are you traveling alone?"

"Yeah," Hugh said. "I'm single at the moment. I've been divorced for almost nine years. I came close to getting married again a few years back, but—" Hugh smiled a bit and shook his head. "It doesn't matter. Nothing came of it."

"I'm sorry," Thea said, and she was. And she wasn't.

"No need to be. So, what are you doing here in Ogunquit?"

Thea hesitated and concentrated on folding the edge of her white paper napkin, over and under. "There's kind of a long and complicated answer to that question," she said finally, looking back to Hugh.

"Short, uncomplicated version?"

"I guess you could say I'm taking a break from things after my divorce."

"Oh. I'm sorry," Hugh said feelingly. "I mean, divorce is never pleasant, but I hope it was for the best."

"Unquestionably."

"Good."

Their sandwiches arrived. Hugh had ordered a turkey club; Thea remembered it had been one of his favorites back in high school. While they ate, they exchanged more basic information. Hugh told her about his career; he was the CEO of a company that designed and manufactured sets for theaters around the world. Thea told him about her career as a high school French teacher; she chose not to mention the very different job she eventually had taken on Mark's demand. Neither had children. Yes, both had read about the death due to cancer of a former classmate a few years back. No, neither had gone to the last reunion of their high school. Although the content of the conversation was mundane, Thea felt herself to be in a sort of dream state. In spite of the evidence to the contrary, she still could not entirely believe that she was sitting across a table from her first love.

But at the same time she felt disoriented, she felt oddly comfortable. It was almost as if nothing had changed since they had last seen each other. Hugh had hardly aged at all. His hair was as thick and dark as ever, a brown that was almost black. His eyes—oh, how she had always loved his eyes!—were still so very, very brown and the little lines around them somehow only added to their beauty. His hands—well, aside from a small scar on the left hand—were still strong and nicely manicured. His shoulders were still broad, his smile still big.

"I guess we should let someone else take this table, now that we're done." Hugh nodded toward the diner's entrance. "There's a line of people forming up front."

"Oh, right!" Thea shook off her momentary reverie and reached for her bag, but Hugh shook his head and placed enough money on the table to cover both their meals and a generous tip.

Thea slid out of her seat at the booth. Hugh followed, but much more slowly, one hand braced on the Formica-topped table, the other, clutching a dark wooden cane.

He saw the look of surprise, even shock, on Thea's face; he would have had to be blind not to. "I'm sorry," he said with a kind smile. "I forget that if someone first sees me sitting down they can't necessarily know. I was in a bad car accident a few years back. Shattered the left leg. I should have said something earlier."

"Oh, Hugh, don't apologize! I'm so sorry." Thea felt as if she might cry and absolutely did not want to, not in front of all these happy, hungry vacationers.

"Hey," he said, touching her arm briefly with his free hand. "I'm alive. A little slower than I used to be, but still here."

She smiled feebly and headed for the front of the diner. Hugh followed her out to the busy sidewalk. They stood facing each other, impeding the flow of young families in beachwear, teenage girls in tiny shorts, middle-aged couples in bright, neatly pressed, and often disturbingly matching day-trip attire.

"I'm so happy we ran into each other, Thea," Hugh said, slipping on a pair of sunglasses. "Would you like to get together again, talk about old times? You can tell me what you've been doing for all these years. I haven't even asked about your work. Or about your family."

"Yes," she said promptly. "I would."

"How about dinner tonight?"

They agreed to meet at Jonathan's at 6:30 that evening.

"She gets too hungry for dinner at eight," Hugh said with a smile.

"That much will never change," Thea admitted, touched by his remembering. Again, she felt tears threaten and willed them away.

With a wave, Hugh headed down Beach Street to the parking lot where he had left his car. Thea stood on the corner and watched him for a moment. Her heart felt as if it were going to break. She had a sudden, vivid image of him in his football uniform, charging down the field. She had gone to a few of his games, of course, though seeing him in action had made her incredibly nervous. Whenever the players had—well, tackled each other, she supposed it was called—she had covered her face with her hands.

But in the end it wasn't football that had hurt him. It was an accident, Hugh had said, and accidents weren't sought after or asked for; lots of times they simply could not be avoided.

Nothing in this world is sure or certain, Thea mused as she walked to the lot where she had parked her own car. The only thing you can count on is not being able to count on anything. The only thing you can count on is—surprise.

CHAPTER 6

Thea's hands were shaking as she let herself into her apartment fifteen minutes later. She felt a little sick to her stomach, but in that good way that happens when you're so excited you think you're just going to burst wide open.

She desperately wanted to tell someone about running into Hugh but didn't know whom to tell. She had isolated herself to a great extent ever since she had met Mark, who had never cared for her few friends. And she had isolated herself even more so since the divorce. She could, she supposed, share her news with Alice, but then she would have to explain the whole history of her relationship with Hugh and she wasn't at all sure she was ready to do that. She and Alice had shared one meal. That hardly made them confidantes.

Thea took her cell phone from her bag and looked down at it. She could, she supposed, call her former colleague Peggy, but Peggy had recently had her second baby and Thea hadn't seen her since the shower. It wouldn't be right to call with a story that wasn't really a story. Yet. Why would Peggy care?

She could call her mother, but . . . no. Thea still wasn't feeling very charitable toward her mother, or her father. And she certainly wasn't at all sure she could trust them, ever again. Not really. Especially after what her mother had told her in one of their unprecedented heart-to-heart conversations after the divorce. It was as if the proverbial floodgates had been opened and Gabrielle Foss, in need of atonement, had not only admitted her part in urging Thea's disastrous marriage, but also had confessed to being pleased and relieved when her daughter had finally split from Hugh Landry all those years ago.

Thea had been shocked, bewildered. But why, she had asked. And Gabrielle Foss had explained, hesitatingly and with some embarrassment, that she and Thea's father had feared losing their daughter, their only child, to a world in which the Fosses might be unwelcome—a world in which Thea herself might find herself miserable. Certainly, the Landrys had never invited the Fosses to dinner at their grand home nor to their elegant country club for drinks. Certainly, the families were socioeconomically incompatible. Wouldn't it be nice, the Fosses had thought, if Thea met someone closer to her own kind, someone they might understand and recognize as one of their own.

It was a bold and courageous confession for Gabrielle Foss to have made, and she had shed many tears during the telling. But the confession had enraged Thea, who saw in her parents' attitude a lack of respect for and belief in their daughter's abilities. In short, she took her parents' "fear" of the Landrys as a sign of pitiable weakness and selfishness. Months later, she was still not ready to forgive the part they had played in her romantic failures, though she wasn't stupid or immature enough to blame what had happened with Hugh or with Mark entirely on her parents.

Thea placed the cell phone on the occasional table. There was no one to call. She would have to hug this moment to herself. What do I feel? she asked herself. "Happy" was her heart's prompt reply. "Sad" was its next admission. She felt sad for Hugh, who had suffered a car accident that had left him needing the use of a cane.

And maybe—yes, maybe she also felt sad for herself. For what could come of her brief meeting with Hugh? They were at very different places in their lives from the places they were when they had first met. They were no longer young—not really—and they certainly were no longer innocent. They had each been through a divorce and Hugh had endured that awful car accident. Life had changed them, and maybe not for the better. To think, to hope that a new relationship would blossom at this point was absurd.

Nothing will happen between us, Thea told herself. Nothing can happen. I don't want anything to happen; haven't I vowed to spend the rest of my life on my own? Besides, Hugh will go back to New York in a few days and I'll . . .

Thea was caught short. She had no real answer for that question. She wondered if she would be able to stay on hiding and healing in Ogunquit if Hugh Landry left as suddenly as he had appeared. What had become a welcome near-solitude might then be a tortuous ordeal . . .

Thea shook her head as if to steer it away from the ridiculous path of thought it had taken. She had shared one meal, a sandwich and a cup of tea, with Hugh, and here she was leaping ahead to disappointment and heartache.

Still, she thought, sinking into the chintz-covered armchair, if dreaming was ridiculous, certainly indulging in a walk down memory lane was normal at a time like this. Even her therapist would agree. Maybe.

During the summer before Thea's sophomore year in high school, the Foss family had moved to a new town in order to take care of Thea's ageing maternal grandmother. They bought a modest house with a small but full apartment in the basement, where Mrs. Wallis would reside. Thea was a nice girl but she was young and self-centered, as the young are and need to be. She remembered being so angry with her do-gooder parents for uprooting her from her old school where she had been happy. She remembered being so angry with her rotten old grandmother for not having oodles of money so she could hire someone to take care of her, instead of burdening her family and ruining her granddaughter's entire life. She remembered being terrified to start at another school. All the other sophomores would know one another. She was sure she would be the despised new kid. She was sure she would never make friends, ever again.

But by the second or third week of school, Thea had to admit that things were not turning out half as badly as she thought they would. A few of the girls in her class had asked her to sit with them at lunch. The teachers were pretty okay, except maybe for the gym teacher, but Thea hated the whole idea of gym class, so Mr. Nelson never had had much of a chance. And then . . .

She had noticed him—how could she not have?—the very first day of the semester. He was in her history class. It didn't take a genius to see that he was one of the superpopular boys, maybe even the most popular of the entire sophomore class. He was in really good shape and he had the most beautiful brown eyes she had ever seen. He played on the football team; at the time, Thea wasn't sure what position he played, but she sensed it was something important. Someone had whispered that he had gotten the highest overall grades in freshman year. He laughed a lot, and it was a nice sound, not mocking or harsh like the laughter of so many of the other boys. The history teacher liked him. Supposedly, he was a tutor to a troubled kid in the local grammar school.

Thea figured there was no way in the world that Hugh Landry would ever notice, let alone talk to, a girl like her. She knew she was sort of shy. She knew she had no flair for clothes like some of the other girls in the class. She had never had a boyfriend, or even a boy who was a friend. Boys were still a big mystery to her; the only example of the male sex she had ever really known was her father, and he didn't count because he was old and part of her family. Her mother routinely told her that she was pretty, but Thea had never really believed that. Her grandmother, back when she made sense, had insisted that Thea's eyes were "lovely" and that her hair was her "shining glory," but grandparents were supposed to say those things, whether they were true or not. Anyway, Thea was absolutely certain that Hugh Landry was not the sort of guy who would like a girl who preferred to watch the PBS stations rather than MTV. No. Way.

The adult Thea smiled to herself. She would never, ever forget the day when Hugh first spoke to her. Mr. Black was running a bit late, so kids were wandering around the classroom, talking, laughing. All except for Thea, who was reading ahead in her textbook. She remembered suddenly becoming conscious of someone standing by the desk to her right. A boy.

"Hi," the boy said, sliding into the desk's chair. "I'm Hugh."

Looking up from the open book was one of the hardest things Thea had ever done and even at the time she was amazed she had the courage to do it.

"Hi," she had somehow managed. Her heart was fluttering. That excited, nauseous feeling overcame her. It was the first time she had ever felt anything like it.

"You're Thea Foss, right?" he asked.

How, how, how did the most popular boy in class know her name? Thea could only nod.

"Must be tough being the new kid. Are you adjusting okay?" Hugh was looking intently at her, an expression of kindness and sympathy on his face. It looked very real.

"Yes," Thea had said. "Thanks."

"Good. Hey, I was wondering if you want to grab some pizza after school today. I mean, if you don't have to get right home or anything . . ."

Thea tensed. For one sick moment she thought that this was a cruel joke, cooked up by some of the cool girls in the class, a joke meant to humiliate her. "Oh . . ." she said. "Uh . . ."

Hugh immediately began to slide out of the chair. "It's okay if you can't. It's just that . . . I thought that maybe . . ."

"Sure," she blurted, pained by the look of disappointment on his face. That look could not be faked. She believed that he really wanted to get pizza with her. "Okay."

Hugh's smile returned in megawatts and he got up from the chair next to hers. "Great. Meet you out front after school, okay?"

And that, Thea reflected, had been that. The beginning of a relationship that still ranked as the most important one in her life to date.
Her marriage had been a farce; that much was clear. Thea still couldn't
give herself an adequate reason for having married Mark Marais. Her
poor judgment didn't excuse him for his sins, but still . . .

Thea pushed herself out of the chair. No, she told herself firmly.
She would not think about Mark tonight, not when such a potentially wonderful time awaited her with the man who had been the
love of her life. Even if this dinner marked the end of their brief reunion, she would enjoy it for the time it lasted. At least, she would
try.

CHAPTER 7

Hugh was already at the restaurant when Thea arrived. Hugh had
always been punctual, she remembered, and sometimes less than
perfectly patient when she made them late for a movie. She had had
a tendency to dawdle when it was least appropriate. It was a bad
habit that age and effort had corrected.

They greeted each other a bit shyly. Hugh was wearing a dark
blue Oxford shirt rolled up at the sleeves and tucked into slightly
worn black jeans. You couldn't say that Hugh cared much for fashion, which was only one of the many things he and Thea shared in
common, but he had an instinct for dressing well and for the occasion. Nothing flashy, nothing nerdy, just basic male attire that
somehow managed to make him stand out against the more
trendily dressed guys and all those men who seemed to think that a
baseball cap was a necessary accessory at all times.

Thea had not expected she would be enjoying a social life in
Ogunquit so she hadn't packed any clothing that could remotely be
considered, as her mother would say, "dressy." A pair of taupe
linen pants left over from her days of working in an office and a

much-worn navy linen blouse would suffice tonight because they had to. She carried the only bag she had with her, the old brown leather one with worn shoulder straps. Her low-heeled sandals were black. Even Thea knew that with few exceptions one shouldn't attempt to mix brown and black leather in one ensemble, but she just didn't care.

The hostess led them to one of the smaller dining rooms. In spite of her resolve not to waste a thought on her ex-husband, Thea automatically scanned the room for his all-too-familiar face. When, she wondered, would she lose the habit of watchfulness and surveillance? Probably not until she forcibly broke the habit.

They were seated at a corner table. Thea was glad for the relative privacy. Hugh propped his cane against the wall behind his chair so as not to be in the waiter's way and they ordered without much delay.

"Do you remember when my brother found out we were a couple?" Hugh asked when the waiter had gone off to place their orders. "Piers totally thought we were putting him on."

"I guess we did seem like an odd pairing," Thea said. "Opposites attracting. Mr. Popularity and Miss . . ."

Hugh laughed. "Miss what?"

"I don't know. Miss Shy and Studious."

"I was studious, too," Hugh pointed out. "And you weren't really shy. Just—quiet."

"More of an observer than a doer."

"You did plenty. Just not on the football field or on the stage."

"Yeah," Thea said with a laugh, "my arena was the library. I rocked the card catalogue! Remember how the local library still kept an old card catalogue even after the collection went online?"

"And you were probably the only one who continued to use it."

"Thanks to Mrs. Rabinowitz, the head librarian," Thea said. "I guess she saw in me a final member of the old guard. Someone who actually liked using those tiny pencils to note down the call number of a book on a scrap of paper. So, how is Piers these days?"

"He's doing really well," Hugh said promptly. "He's a partner in an important law firm. His wife's pregnant with their third child."

"Your parents must be so proud of the both of you."

"Tell me about your parents," he said, ignoring Thea's comment. "Are they well?"

"Fine," Thea said. "Nothing's changed." She was aware her response to his question had been dismissive, but it was all she could think of to say.

"Your grandmother was so sweet. I know she wasn't quite all there when I knew her, but I could tell she really doted on you."

"Yes," Thea agreed. "I'm afraid I probably wasn't the most doting granddaughter in return."

"You were good to her. But you were young. Of course you had your own life to lead."

"And you were so good to me when she died. Coming to the wake and the funeral and the cemetery. And then that awful reception back at my house. Everybody talking in hushed voices and people saying the most inane things. 'Such a shock, Maryanne dying like that.' She was eighty-five!"

Hugh shrugged. "Grief is puzzling to most people; nobody really knows what to say in the face of a death. Anyway, you were my girlfriend. Of course I would be there. I loved . . ." He smiled a bit shyly. "I loved you."

Loved. Past tense. Well, Thea thought, of course. "My parents appreciated it, too," she said. "You being there."

My parents had known Hugh was a good person, Thea reflected. They had gotten to know him as an individual, as someone apart from his family. And yet, they had hoped for the breakdown of her relationship with him for their own selfish reasons. Thea felt the anger rise in her yet again and, with some difficulty, pushed it back down.

"I thought about something when we were in the diner this afternoon," she said. "Do you remember nacho night?"

Hugh laughed. "The summer before college, every Tuesday. Why did we pick Tuesdays?"

"I can't remember. And I'd get extra jalapeños on the side."

"I never knew how you could eat so many of those things and not have your head explode. Or your intestines, for that matter."

"I'm an industrial-strength eater, as you know. And there was dessert, of course. Remember the brownie sundae?" she asked.

"Ah, youth," Hugh said with a theatrical sigh. "The amount of calories I could put away back then and still lose weight."

"I'm afraid I still eat like I did when I was a teen. Though I have cut down on the hot peppers."

"Probably a good idea. Hey, do you remember that awful Halloween party we went to, I think it was junior year? Remember those costumes we rented? Sylvester and Tweetie?"

Thea shivered for effect. "How could I forget! I had a rash for over a week. And why I ever let you be Sylvester, I'll never understand. I fell over those big yellow bird feet about a thousand times that night."

Hugh laughed. "Yeah, that experience cured me of Halloween forever. It was such a big-deal holiday in college, but I always managed to avoid the parties. Besides, they were just out of control drunk fests."

"Are there other kinds of drunk fests?"

"Not that I'm aware of!"

They talked about *The X-Files,* which had been Hugh's favorite television show back in high school; it had scared Thea silly whenever she gamely tried to watch an episode with him. Hugh admitted to owning the entire series on DVD. They reminisced about the time they had gone to the aquarium in downtown Boston and then for dinner at the Union Oyster House. Thea wondered where Hugh had been when he heard the news of the World Trade Center bombing. The answer was that he was in class at Columbia, uptown. News of the disaster came from another professor and classes were immediately dismissed. Hugh wanted to know what Thea had been doing on New Year's Eve, 1999. The answer was that she had spent it alone and at home. "You know I hate New Year's Eve parties," she said. What she didn't say was that she spent the night miserable and depressed and oozing self-pity because no one had even offered an invitation that she could reject. Hugh's family and a few select friends had been ringing in the new millennium in high style in a grand New York City hotel.

At one point they ordered coffee and dessert and lingered over both. Thea glanced surreptitiously at her watch when Hugh asked the waiter for the check. It was after 10:00. Hours had simply flown by.

When the waiter returned with the check, Hugh snatched it up before Thea could reach for it. "Please," he said, "let me pay. I've been through the aftermath of a divorce. Unless you're as rich as Croesus, money will be tight, at least for a while. I've been back on my feet for a long time now."

Thea had never had false pride or an overly sensitive attitude to money—unlike her parents—and she graciously accepted Hugh's offer.

When the bill had been paid they walked out to the parking lot. It was a beautiful night; the air had a slight chill to it, a minor foretaste of fall, and the moon was distinctly visible in all its halved glory. Hugh walked with Thea to her car. She hoped he wouldn't comment on the state of her vehicle. He didn't.

"Good night, Thea," Hugh said when she had unlocked the driver's-side door. "This has been . . . well, it's been quite a day."

"Yes," she agreed. "It certainly has."

"Are you busy tomorrow? Well, I'm sure you must be, at least for some of the day, but I wondered if—"

"Let's go to the beach," Thea blurted.

Hugh laughed. "It's a plan. And I happen to have my bathing suit with me."

"Me, too, though I hadn't really expected to use it."

Hugh then leaned down and kissed Thea's left cheek. "Till tomorrow," he said.

Thea was suddenly aware that if she spoke she would cry and only nodded. Hugh watched as she drove out of the parking lot, only getting into his car when Thea's was out of sight.

CHAPTER 8

Thea saw Alice coming around the side of the house. Before her landlady could knock, Thea opened the door for her. Henrietta appeared from somewhere under the house and began to circle Alice's ankles. The cat's purr was deafening.

"Good morning, Alice," Thea shouted over the noise. "How does she do that?"

As if knowing she was the topic of conversation and not caring to be, Henrietta darted off into Alice's small vegetable garden to wreak havoc on the worms and bugs.

"Henrietta was on the stage in her younger days," Alice said, raising the plate she held in one hand. "I made these muffins earlier this morning and if I don't get some out of my house I will eat them all by lunchtime. Here."

"Oh, corn muffins!" Thea exclaimed, taking the offering. "They're my favorite. I waited tables at this little diner by my college. They made the best corn muffins. I pretty much ate one a day for four years."

"Good. They're best with butter, but then again you probably know that."

Alice made no move to leave. "Um," Thea said, "do you want to . . ."

"I'll just stay for a minute, thanks."

Thea put the plate of muffins on the kitchen counter. When she turned back around, she found the door closed and Alice standing in the living room.

"If I'm not mistaken," Alice said, "you went out last night."

"What? How did you know I went out?"

Alice waved her hand dismissively. "Don't be alarmed. I'm not stalking you. But it's a bit impossible not to hear a car pull out of a gravel drive, especially at night when it's otherwise dead quiet. Except for the occasional owl or coyote whooping it up over dinner."

"Oh," Thea said. She felt embarrassed, caught out. She felt guilty, but of what, she couldn't say. She was also dying to blurt the truth about Hugh, and, equally, to keep him a secret all to herself. "Of course," she said finally. "I ran into an old friend yesterday. He's on vacation."

Alice nodded. "So, you guys went out for dinner?"

"Yes. Just dinner. Then I came home. He didn't come with me. I drove myself."

Thea thought she saw a twinge of a smile on her landlady's face, but maybe she had imagined it. "That's nice," Alice said casually. She shoved her hands into the back pockets of her jeans. "Say, what was it about this ex-husband of yours that was so bad? Mind you, I'm not implying he wasn't guilty of all sorts of crimes. I'm just curious as to what they were."

"He lied," Thea blurted, taken aback by the bluntness of the question, and by the bluntness of her answer.

"Everyone lies."

"These were big lies. And he spent all of our money. My money, really. And he . . ." Thea felt herself blush, whether in shame or in anger, she didn't know.

"Ah." Alice removed her hands from her back pockets and let them fall to her side. "Enough said. You were smart to throw the bum out."

"He sued for divorce, not me. Though I was working up the nerve to."

"Sounds like a real tool."

Thea laughed, the tension the conversation had caused suddenly gone. "Well, that's not a word I would have chosen, but yeah, he is."

"They're out there, no doubt about it."

"How do some people turn out to be so awful?" Thea said. "That's a rhetorical question."

"Blame the parents. Blame society. Chalk it up to mental damage, something wrong with the brain's wiring. It almost doesn't matter, not to the victims, anyway."

"No," Thea agreed. "It doesn't."

Abruptly, Alice turned toward the door. "Well," she said, without looking back, "I'd better get down to work. Articles don't write themselves." She left the apartment and a few minutes later Thea heard her footsteps overhead, retreating into the sunny alcove where she worked at a small, old rolltop desk.

And then, the phone rang. Daylight, and knowing that Alice was only a shout away, made Thea's reaction to the call close to calm. She picked up the phone and recognized the number as her parents'. It would be her mother calling; her father didn't do too well on the phone. His conversation ran to about three sentences: "Hello, it's your father." "So, how's the weather there?" and "Okay, let me put your mother on."

Thea put the phone down again on the occasional table. The call could go to voice mail. She really had nothing to say to her parents. And if they had anything of significance to say to her, well, then they could call again. And maybe she would take that call. Or not.

Right now Thea had a more pressing matter with which to deal: What to use as a blanket when she met Hugh at the beach later on. And she would deal with that matter right after she ate one of Alice's corn muffins.

CHAPTER 9

When Thea had suggested the beach as their destination, she hadn't really considered the fact that it would be so very crowded on a sunny afternoon in mid-August. She and Hugh walked for almost a mile toward Wells before they found enough space on which to lay down the blanket Thea had borrowed from Alice. If Hugh found walking on shifting sand difficult, he didn't say. Thea resisted the urge to take his arm, to offer assistance that he might not need and might even resent. She was relieved and sweaty when they settled on the blanket, looking out at the receding tide sparkling in the sun.

Hugh sat with his damaged left leg stretched out in front of him. He wore a bright blue T-shirt and a bathing suit that came down to the knees. On the damaged leg, two long scars ran from his ankle up past his knee. The calf was slightly misshapen. "I'm not sure you want to see the thigh," he said with a bit of a laugh. "Doctors do wonders with reconstruction these days, but in my case there's a gnarly factor . . ."

"Oh, Hugh, don't joke about it," Thea cried. "I just feel so terrible this happened to you. Your poor leg."

"Actually," he said, "in some ways the leg wasn't the worst of it. I had to have an emergency splenectomy when the paramedics got me to the hospital."

"Oh." Thea wasn't quite sure what the spleen did, but she assumed it had some importance. "Um, what does that mean in terms of . . ."

"Well," Hugh said, "it increases my risk of sepsis, so I'm vigilant about cuts not getting infected. It might also increase my risk of developing diabetes at some point. Or not. I don't dwell on it."

"Oh," Thea said, deciding that if she were the one with no spleen she would be thinking about it an awful lot. "Do you want to tell me what happened, exactly? With the accident, I mean. Of course, you don't—"

"No," Hugh said, "it's okay. I don't remember much of it, but I pieced together the story afterward. There were witnesses. A truck, one of those huge eighteen-wheelers, went out of control. I tried to avoid it and wound up flipping over the guardrail and tumbling down an embankment. Somehow I managed to get myself out of the wreck before it caught fire. I was incredibly lucky. Not everyone was. The truck hit a woman in another car head-on. She never had a chance. The driver of the truck didn't make it, either."

Thea gasped. "Oh, Hugh," she said. "I'm sorry I asked you to talk about it."

Hugh reached over, took Thea's hand, and squeezed it briefly. His touch made her feel dizzy; she didn't think it was merely the oppressive heat or her growing hunger. The restorative effects of the corn muffin were rapidly wearing off. No, Hugh's touch was still electric.

"Actually," Hugh was saying, "talking about the accident helps make it less of a trauma and more of just 'one of those things' that happen."

"If you say so . . ."

"I do. Anyway, after the surgeries I was in the hospital for some time, unconscious for the first few days. Then I was released to rehab for the leg. I continued to go to physical therapy for almost a year after I moved back home. Fortunately, I was in good shape to begin with so the whole thing wasn't as bad as it might have been."

Thea handed Hugh a bottle of water from the canvas bag she had also borrowed from Alice. She opened a bottle for herself before commenting, "You always did try to see the bright side of things."

" 'Try' is the operative word. There were some bad moments during the ordeal. My fiancée at the time was an avid skier—an all-around athlete, really—and she didn't exactly relish the idea of saddling herself with a husband who wasn't going to be roaring down the slopes with her. So, she ended the engagement and took up with one of the guys we used to ski with on weekends."

"She doesn't sound like a very nice person!" Thea cried. "I'm sorry, Hugh. I had no right to say that."

"Oh, she was nice enough," he said mildly, "just kind of limited. I'll say this much for her. She knew what she wanted and what she didn't want. That's got to stand for something."

Thea smiled. "And you always did try to say something nice about a person, even someone not at all nice. Do you remember that kid in our homeroom junior year? The one who bullied some of the quieter kids? I thought he was just awful, but you really tried to find the good in him. You tried to understand why he did what he did. You tried to forgive him."

"If he had bullied you, I wouldn't have been so forgiving, or so understanding."

"The only reason he didn't mess around with me was because I was dating you!"

Hugh looked surprised. "You can't tell me I actually scared anyone. I've never been in a fight in my life."

"No," Thea explained, "I think it was that people knew that if Hugh Landry didn't approve of them, they were toast, socially speaking. No one wanted you on his bad side."

"Interesting. I didn't know I had such—authority."

"You could easily have been class president," Thea said. "If you had ever bothered to run."

"You know that politics has never been my thing, beyond voting, I mean."

"I know. And I always liked that about you."

"Well, you're about the only one," Hugh said with a small, uncharacteristically bitter laugh. "My father and my former wife saw my lack of interest in a political future as a sign of laziness. Dad doesn't bring up the topic anymore, thank God. He's focused all of his unfulfilled political ambition on Piers now."

"Is Piers planning on running for office?" Thea asked.

"I'm not sure. We haven't talked about anything personal in a long time. But I wouldn't be surprised."

"Yes," Thea said musingly. "I can see Piers as a politician. There's something—well, something a bit ruthless about him."

"Yeah," Hugh agreed. "I stick to volunteer work. There's a lot less of an ego requirement."

"Where do you volunteer?" Thea asked.

"For the past year I've been working at a center for grieving children. There was an awful lot of training involved. It's tough work, but worthwhile. At least, I like to think we help some of the kids who come in."

"I used to volunteer a fair amount," Thea said. "But then, when I got married... Well, my husband didn't like my spending time with anyone but him. So I cut back..." Thea felt herself blush. "Eventually, I stopped altogether. I'm afraid that since the divorce I've been pretty useless to anyone. Even to myself."

"Thea." Hugh's tone was entirely sympathetic. "You shouldn't be so hard on yourself. It seems to me this is the time for you to concentrate on your own well-being. The time will come to focus on others again. You know what I'm saying is true."

"Sorry!"

A boy about ten or eleven years old waved with both arms to accompany his shout. The Frisbee he had been tossing around with some friends had gone wild and landed a few feet from Thea and Hugh's blanket.

Hugh got up, left his cane on the blanket, and limped over to the Frisbee. With a smooth throw, he sent it flying back to the boy, who waved his thanks. Thea watched nervously as Hugh came back to the blanket. "You can walk without the cane," she said, knowing it was an inane thing to say.

"Of course. It's just not as safe. Speaking of safety, I'm pretty sure I saw a sign forbidding Frisbee and ball games this far down on the beach. The parents of those kids should be on that."

Parents. Back when they had been but kids themselves, Thea remembered, she and Hugh had talked about having a family. She both wanted and didn't want to ask Hugh why he and his wife hadn't had children. And Hugh, Thea surmised, might be wondering why she hadn't had children, either. In Thea's case, the answer was simple, if not easy. The notion of having children with anyone other than Hugh had always seemed wrong. It had seemed an impossibility.

She was about to venture what might have been another inane comment when Hugh spoke. "The only reason I feel badly about not being close to my brother," he said, "is that I miss out on spending time with his children. I mean, I'm at as many birthday parties and holiday functions as I can be, but other than that, well, let's just say the invitations to hang out on a Saturday afternoon aren't exactly forthcoming. He was my best man at the wedding, but that was more because it was expected of me to ask him than the fact that he was a real friend."

"That's too bad," Thea said. "How old are Piers's children?"

Hugh dug his phone out of his bathing suit pocket and found photos of his niece and nephew. "Five and three, Amelia and Arthur."

"Nice names," Thea said. "And they're adorable children. Arthur has your eyes!"

"They're good children, too. Whatever my opinion of Piers, I have to admit that he and Patricia are doing an excellent job of raising their children."

"Maybe when Amelia and Arthur get older," Thea said, "you can spirit them away for magical weekends in New York. You can be the glamorous uncle, the one they go to when they're mad at their parents for being, well, parents."

"Yeah," Hugh said, "I guess. It would be better than nothing. Look, are you hungry?"

"Starved," Thea admitted.

Hugh got to his feet, this time with the aid of his cane. "Me, too. Why don't I go get us some hot dogs or something?"

Thea began to rise from the blanket. "Oh, I could go," she said.

"No." Hugh smiled down at her. "You stay here and watch for stray Frisbees."

"Okay." Thea smiled back at him. "If you happen to find some cookies or something . . ."

"I'm on it."

Thea tucked her knees up under her chin and wrapped her arms around her legs. And she watched as Hugh Landry, the man who was undoubtedly the love of her life, the man who should have been the father of her children, made his careful way amid prone sunbathers and toddling children and boys illegally playing ball. Tears had been threatening yet again since Hugh had told her more about his horrible accident and now they began to roll down Thea's cheeks. She let them.

CHAPTER 10

They met again for dinner that night, after going back to their respective rooms for showers to remove all traces of irritating sand and greasy sunscreen. Again, they talked easily and laughed often. When Hugh suggested getting together again the following day, Thea said yes before he had quite finished speaking. Briefly, she wondered if he felt an obligation to spend time with her. And then she reminded herself that Hugh was an honest person. While he was the kind of person to perform a social duty without complaint, he was not the kind of person to act falsely when it really mattered.

So on Thursday, after Thea's early shift at the diner, they found themselves prowling through one of the many antique stores on Route 1. While Hugh examined a cache of old catcher's mitts, leather football helmets, and other sports memorabilia, Thea wandered over to a glass case in which was displayed a collection of antique jewelry. Immediately, her attention was drawn to an

Edwardian-style diamond ring. The price, scribbled on a small card next to the ring, was prohibitive—at least, it was for Thea—and, she guessed, for most of the people she knew. But the ring was lovely, just the sort of piece she would feel comfortable wearing. If, that is, one day . . .

Thea turned deliberately away from the display case and walked over to a rack of dresses from the 1950s. Mindlessly, she fingered through them. She thought of the engagement ring Mark had given her. It had not been at all her style—the stone was set in a sleek, modern setting—but she had convinced herself that she loved it. After the divorce, in need of ready cash, she had taken the ring to a jeweler in Boston's downtown diamond district, someone who had been recommended by a colleague. She had hoped to sell it for a substantial sum. What she had learned was that the stone was a not so very good fake; it wasn't even cubic zirconia or Diamonique. The metal turned out to be sterling silver, not white gold, as Mark had claimed. Shamefaced and furious, and all too aware of the jeweler's pitying looks, Thea had left the store with the meager check in hand and cashed it immediately.

Thea felt a tap on her shoulder. She turned and screamed, "Oh my God, it's Mr. Marbles!"

"Who?" Hugh asked. In his arms sat a seedy-looking ventriloquist dummy with a ratty yellow wig and a striped shirt.

"From *Seinfeld*. Kramer's dummy. Remember?"

Hugh laughed. "Oh, right, the Kenny Rogers episode! Yeah, this thing is pretty creepy, huh?"

"It's the stuff of nightmares. Put it away!"

Hugh laughed again and stashed the dummy behind a pile of old magazines. "Let's get out of here," he said. "It's a shame to waste a gorgeous day inside, even if some of this stuff is pretty interesting."

Thea followed Hugh out into the midday sunshine. "What do you suggest we do?" she asked.

"How about a couple of rounds of miniature golf?"

"Oh, Hugh," Thea cried. "You know I'm awful at miniature golf!"

"I know. It's part of your charm."

"Being awful at sports is part of my charm?"

"Yup."

"Okay, I'll play," Thea said, "if you agree to let me win at least one round."

"Deal."

Hugh did let her win one round, which took considerable skill on his part. Thea managed to lose a ball entirely, and to almost get her head struck off by the rotating arms of the windmill feature. After miniature golf, they went to Billy's Chowder House for lobster rolls and steamers and then they stopped at a farmstand for the farmer's wife's homemade whoopie pies.

"I feel like a kid again," Hugh admitted as they ate the traditional Maine dessert while leaning against his car just off the side of the road. "Seriously, Thea, I haven't had this much fun with someone in . . . well, since you and I last spent time together just—being together."

Thea smiled. She agreed with Hugh wholeheartedly but didn't trust herself to speak without crying. *All I seem capable of doing since rediscovering Hugh is crying,* she thought. It actually didn't feel like such a bad thing.

"Hey," he said, "remember we talked about backpacking through Europe when we graduated college."

"*You* talked about backpacking. *I* talked about taking the train."

Hugh laughed. "That's right. Well, did you ever get to Europe?"

Thea swallowed the last bite of her whoopie pie before answering. "Unfortunately, no," she said. "I'd been saving up for an extended visit to France. Then I met the man who was to be my husband and he pretended to be as interested in French history and culture as I was. We agreed to go to France for our honeymoon but to postpone the trip until we'd saved more money. But then, well, let's just say that never happened, the saving part or the honeymoon."

"You'll get to France someday, Thea," Hugh said earnestly. "Your life hit a rough patch but the road will be smoother ahead. You really have to believe that."

Thea smiled. "I try. Mostly."

Hugh pushed off the car with the aid of his cane. "I have an idea," he said. "Let's go to the Nubble Lighthouse."

If there was ever a romantic spot it was the Nubble Lighthouse, Thea mused as she got back into Hugh's car. Which, of course, didn't mean that Hugh had any romantic intentions in mind when he'd suggested it as their next destination. She knew that. They were not on a date. They were just hanging out. They were just old friends spending time together.

The point of land from which one viewed the lighthouse was known as Sohier Park. In truth, the park was little more than a parking lot and a gift shop. Oddly, for such a popular attraction, it was relatively empty when Hugh and Thea arrived. They got out of the car and once again leaned side by side against it, looking out at the red-roofed keeper's house, the white tower with its beacon on top and the two small outbuildings. It was almost seven o'clock and there was a chill in the breeze coming off the water. Thea was glad she had brought a sweater with her. In a little over two weeks she had learned the truth of a popular saying: If you don't like the weather in Maine, wait three minutes.

"I read somewhere," Hugh said, "that this is the most photographed lighthouse in all of Maine. It really does define 'picturesque,' doesn't it?"

Thea nodded. She was acutely aware of her left arm being a mere inch or two from Hugh's right arm. She wanted to lean ever so slightly against him; she wanted him to put his arm around her shoulder. She wanted . . .

"Hey." Hugh bumped his elbow into hers in a gesture that was unmistakably unromantic. "Penny for your thoughts." His eyes, still hidden behind sunglasses, were unreadable, but the tone of his voice was easy and natural, without any hint of flirtation.

Thea forced a smile to her lips and shrugged. "I'm not thinking anything in particular," she said. And she shifted ever so slightly away from him.

CHAPTER 11

The plastic alarm clock on her bedside table read 2:43 a.m. Thea had been checking it at intervals since getting into bed at 11:00. Sleep, it seemed, might not be on the agenda this night. With a sigh, she sat up and turned on the small shaded lamp on the table. It was less trying to admit defeat than it was to battle on hopelessly.

The day she had spent with Hugh had been as near to perfect as anything she could imagine. The one thing that would have made the day entirely perfect, of course, was if he had kissed her in Sohier Park. Maybe. Because if Hugh was going to wave good-bye in a few days, a kiss would only have made his leaving that much more painful.

Thea thumped her fists against the mattress in frustration. She had so many questions, both for Hugh and for herself. For example, they had talked about all sorts of things—from nachos to former classmates, from Hugh's relationship with his brother to costumes they had worn to a Halloween party in high school—but the one thing neither of them had mentioned was the breakup. If they were going to part in a day or two never to meet again, maybe there was no need to explore the causes that had led to the end of the relationship. It might be best just to let the past, especially the sad parts, go the way of forgetfulness. Without one of them introducing the topic—"Let's talk about what went wrong"—there would be no way to know. And Thea felt certain that unless Hugh was brave enough to introduce that topic, it would go unexplored. Bravery was not something Thea felt she could easily lay her hands on at the moment.

Besides, she had to admit that what had happened in the past really didn't interest her half as much as what was happening in the present—and what might happen in the future. She rubbed her temples and sighed. It was hard for her to believe—because she didn't want to—that she and Hugh were really only passing the time together as old friends. It was hard for her to imagine that they would part in a few days with only an exchange of "contact information" and a promise to "keep in touch." Was it really possible that in a year or two she might open her mailbox—wherever she was living—to find an invitation to Hugh's wedding to an incredibly successful, outstandingly beautiful woman with a heart of gold? Because of course Hugh would marry someone like that, now that he was truly independent, now that he was no longer shackled by an overdeveloped sense of duty to his parents.

Or, by some miraculous twist of fate, would they . . . what? Fall into each other's arms? Declare their undying love? Run off and elope? Buy a crumbling château in Provence and spend their days lovingly restoring it? Thea shifted uncomfortably in the bed. She felt a little disgusted by her melodramatic thoughts. The future—her future with or without Hugh—would happen entirely without reference to her middle-of-the-night agonies.

Thea sighed and looked at the alarm clock: 3:30 a.m. She turned off the lamp and scooted back down onto the pillow. Just try to accept each day as it happens, she counseled her troubled self. Just try. And after a moment or two, she finally fell off to sleep, worn-out by her own confusion. She dreamed of windmills refusing to turn and lighthouses going dark and planes crashing into the sea. And behind or beneath these images of destruction was the image of a ventriloquist's dummy with the vaguely sinister features of Mark Marais.

CHAPTER 12

Thea and Hugh passed the day being tourists. First, they had breakfast at the Maine Diner in Wells. Then they drove down to Portsmouth and poked around in the craft and jewelry shops. They had lunch back in Perkins Cove, after which they visited the Ogunquit Museum of American Art. In the late afternoon Hugh dropped Thea at her apartment and went back to his room at the bed-and-breakfast to do some work. At 6:30 they met at the Old

Village Inn on Main Street. It was now close to nine o'clock and neither felt in a hurry to part.

"I want to show you something," Thea said when she had finished her dessert, a slice of the ubiquitous blueberry pie.

Hugh nodded. "All right."

All day long, after her almost sleepless night, Thea had debated showing Hugh the miniature portrait of Napoleon. It would, she thought, be forcing a memory of intimacy. It would be reminding them both in a highly visual, tangible way of the love they had once shared. But maybe, she had decided, a tangible reminder was necessary at this juncture. Maybe, just maybe, it would prompt a talk about that topic neither of them had mentioned—the breakup. And maybe, just maybe, it would help clarify the current state of their relationship. Thea could only hope.

She reached into her bag and took from it the purple velvet box. She was aware of her fingers trembling ever so slightly. She opened the box and turned it to face Hugh. "My sixteenth birthday present," she said.

Thea couldn't be entirely sure, but she thought she saw tears come to Hugh's eyes. Certainly, the sight of the tiny painting had stolen his words. He gazed down at it for some time and finally looked back to her and smiled.

"I'm so glad you kept this, Thea," he said. "The minute I saw it in that antique store on Charles Street I knew it was meant for you."

Thea smiled back. She closed the box and returned it to her bag. "I never told you this," she said, "but my parents wanted me to give it back. They said it was 'too much.' But I just couldn't. I knew you really wanted me to have it."

"I did want you to have it, very much." Hugh paused before adding, "And I guess it can't matter at this late date if you know that my parents were furious with me for having spent so much money on a gift for you."

"Because it was for me, Thea Foss?" she asked. "Or would they have been angry about your spending money on any sixteen-year-old girl?"

Hugh looked uncomfortable and Thea regretted having spoken

aloud a question with such a potentially awkward answer. "I'm sorry," she said. "I shouldn't have said that."

"No, it's okay. Honestly, Thea, I never thought about it. Like I said, it doesn't matter now. Hey, I kept something special from you, too. Do you remember that monogrammed keychain you gave me, back in freshman year of college?"

"Of course."

"Well, I keep it in my desk at home. It's been broken for some time but it's always had sentimental value for me."

Thea smiled. "You know it's worth next to nothing, monetarily speaking. I wanted to get you something nicer but it was all I could afford. Most of the money I made babysitting and working at the college's bookstore and waiting tables went toward school expenses."

"It was the thought that counted," Hugh said firmly. "You know I believe that. That was another bone of contention in my marriage. Susanne had been raised by an extremely doting daddy whose idea of showering his daughter with love meant showering her with expensive gifts. Not that I didn't do my duty to her in that regard, but it seems I was totally off base when I tried showing my love with more lowly gifts like driving her mother to the grocery store or cooking an anniversary dinner instead of taking her out to a popular restaurant."

"People's idea of money," Thea said, "and the meanings they attach to it, can tear a relationship apart. Of course," she added ruefully, "in my case it was less our conflicting ideas about money and more my husband's criminal habit of theft that broke us up."

"Ouch. At least Susanne is an honest person. I heard through the grapevine that she's remarried and I really hope it works out for her."

"I can't say the same about my ex-husband," Thea admitted. "I think if I heard that he was remarried I'd send a rescue squad to spirit his new wife to safety."

They talked for close to another hour, and though Thea hoped the conversation might naturally progress to something definitive, it did not. Hugh's having kept a broken keychain, she realized gloomily as the conversation turned to politics, that most unromantic of topics, might signify nothing more than mere nostalgia.

Finally, Hugh excused himself and went off to the men's room. Thea watched him stop to chat with their waiter, who had gone off shift and was sitting at the bar.

Thea sat alone in the emptying restaurant. She could no longer tell herself that Hugh was just a friend. She had fallen in love with him all over again, though she didn't dare to presume that he had fallen in love again with her. She hadn't planned for such a potentially disastrous thing to happen.

She became aware of a sudden pounding in her temples. She felt more miserable than she had felt before she had shown Hugh the miniature, a gesture that seemed to have accomplished nothing. Her irrational, superstitious self wondered if this reunion with her first love was a sick joke staged by the universe, some punishment perhaps for a crime she didn't even know she had committed, retribution for her own stupidity in having made such a lousy marriage. Her rational self, though weakened, denied such a possibility. Of course, their reunion wasn't some divinely orchestrated happening. It might just be pure bad luck, a natural disaster.

Hugh appeared from the direction of the men's room. Thea watched him with longing as he approached their table. She so wanted to pull him close against her. She wanted to kiss him, to hold his face in her hands. But she didn't dare. She didn't think she could survive the results of humiliating herself in such a way.

"Ready to go?" Hugh asked.

Thea smiled gamely up at him and hoped that her face betrayed nothing of the yearning in her heart.

CHAPTER 13

"Am I too early?" Thea asked, peering into Alice's living room through the open front door Sunday morning around 9:00.

"Not at all," came a voice from the kitchen. "Come on in."

Alice had left a note under Thea's door the evening before, inviting her to brunch. By this time in her Ogunquit sojourn, Thea was smart enough to accept any and all invitations from Alice, especially those involving food, which, as a matter of fact, they all did.

Alice had made eggs Florentine with a side of maple-smoked bacon, and a salad with crumbled blue cheese, walnuts, orange chunks, and local greens. There was also a basket of warm biscuits, a plate of butter, and two varieties of jam. And, of course, there was a pot of Alice's signature good, strong coffee.

"I'm in heaven," Thea said, taking a seat at Alice's kitchen counter. "At least, the breakfast version of it."

"Glad to hear it. Every cook needs an appreciative stomach nearby. So, where's your old friend this morning?"

"He's working. He's got his phone and computer with him, of course. Where's your furry sidekick?"

"Off chasing poor innocent wildlife, I suppose. Well, she had a slice of bacon before she left the house, so maybe the wildlife is safe for the moment."

Alice made sure that everything was in reach of her guest before digging in to her own meal. After she had gobbled up the egg dish and a biscuit, she laid her fork against her plate. "Need a little break," she said. "So, kiddo, what are you holding back from me?"

Thea coughed on a bite of salad.

"It's a small town," Alice went on. "People have seen you hanging around with the handsome guy with a cane. Naturally, they've been coming to me, as if I would know anything more than he's the 'old friend' you ran into."

Thea finished chewing and took a gulp of coffee before answering her curious landlady. "Well," she said, "I suppose there's nothing to hide. His name is Hugh Landry. We were a couple in high school and for most of college."

"So, what happened?" Alice asked, picking up her fork again and applying it to her salad.

"It's hard to say, really. He went to school in California. Things just . . . fell apart. I made one last effort—plea, really—for us to try again, but . . ."

"And you hadn't seen each other since college?"

Thea shook her head. "Nope. No communication at all. And then, he just showed up in Ogunquit."

Alice slapped the counter with her open palm. "Fate. The relationship is meant to be."

"Oh, I don't know about that . . ."

"It sounds ordained to me. But then again, I'm a romantic. I want people to be happy. I believe they can be."

"But we're just friends, really," Thea protested. "I . . ."

Alice eyed her young guest with interest. "Yes?"

"I'm afraid that if we . . ."

"Do you still love him?"

"I don't know. Well, of course I do, but maybe I'm just remembering that I loved him. Maybe—"

"Have you kissed yet?"

"No!" Thea cried.

"Well, Jeez Louise, grab him and kiss him already!"

"I can't do that! What if he . . ." Thea felt herself blush as she remembered how badly she had wanted to kiss him and to be kissed by him two nights before. "Besides, he's going back to New York soon," she added, though in truth she had no idea what Hugh's immediate plans were. After that first meeting in the diner, neither of them had even mentioned their immediate, daily lives back home in Massachusetts and New York. It was as if they had been living in the moment and the moment was all.

"Seize the day. Carpe diem, if you prefer the Latin. He who hesitates is lost."

"I . . ."

"Okay, okay," Alice said. "I'll let you finish your meal in peace."

Thea did finish her meal and took a deep breath afterward to help digestion. "Alice, how long have you been in Ogunquit?" she asked finally.

"Oh, for about four years now," Alice replied, "since right after my second husband passed. We used to come here for a week each spring and fall. I suppose that like you, I came to Ogunquit to— recuperate. I fell in love with the house and got it for a song. As far as I can see, I'm staying put."

"Where are your husbands, uh, buried? That's an odd question. I'm sorry."

Alice waved her hand in a gesture of dismissal. "No worries." She nodded toward the fireplace. "Gabe is in that yellow ceramic jar on the mantel. He's number two. Ted, my first husband, wanted to be buried in his family's plot in Oregon. Bit inconvenient for me, in terms of visiting, but he understands."

"Oh." Did Alice really talk to her dead husbands? Well, if she did communicate with the spirit world, Thea supposed there was nothing wrong with it. She herself was fairly obsessed with dead people and times gone by. "Do you have—do you have any living family?" she asked.

Alice laughed. "Guess it's only fair that I answer some personal questions after I've been badgering you for information about your love life."

"I'm sorry."

"You need to stop apologizing," Alice said briskly. "I have a sister in Michigan. Terry and I are close but life deposited us an airplane ride away from each other, so we keep in touch as best we can on the phone and via e-mail. Her son lives in Boston. He finds his way up here about once or twice a year and I return the favor about the same. John's a nice young man, in his second year of medical school. I'm hoping that when I get old and violently out of sorts he'll help me depart this weary world."

"You mean . . ."

"Better not say it aloud," Alice said in a stage whisper. "Of course, I haven't broached the subject with him yet, but there's still time."

Thea laughed. "Alice, you're incorrigible. But on the subject that must not be named, I do agree with you. About . . ."

"Yes. Well. So, do you have siblings? Cousins? Aunts and uncles?"

"No to all. Both of my parents were only children. So am I. My last surviving grandparent died when I was in high school. Hugh knew her. He was so nice to her. He used to bring her flowers and she used to flirt with him a bit. It was kind of sad but also kind of cute. It made her happy."

"So, this old paramour is a nice guy?"

Thea felt herself blush. "Yes," she said. "He's very nice. In truth, he's probably the nicest person I've ever known." Much nicer than I am, she added silently.

"I always thought that niceness was underrated," Alice proclaimed. "More coffee?"

Thea declined. She offered to help Alice clean up but Alice refused, claiming she enjoyed the washing up after a meal as much as she enjoyed the preparation of the meal. "All part of the entertainment process," she explained. "It works for me."

Thea went downstairs to her apartment a few minutes later to find her cell phone ringing. It was her mother. Thea, feeling relaxed and emboldened by her talk with Alice, took the call.

"We were worried," Gabrielle said reproachfully. "You didn't call us back. We left two messages this week."

"Sorry," Thea lied.

"Are you all right, Thea?"

"I'm fine, Mom." She paused, hoping to maximize the shock value of her next words. "You'll never guess who I ran into in town. Hugh Landry."

Gabrielle was silent for a moment. Then she said, "Oh. My. I don't know what to say."

"How about, 'That's nice.' Or, "How is he?'" Or, Thea thought, enjoying her mother's discomfiture, how about, At least it wasn't Mark Marais.

"Oh. Of course. How is Hugh?"

"Great," Thea said defiantly. "Fantastic." She would offer her mother no more than that.

"Well, that's good," Gabrielle said. "Please give him our . . . I mean, please tell him that we said hello."

"Sure. Look, Mom, I have to go. Thanks for calling."

Before Gabrielle could protest, Thea ended the call. She felt a bit guilty for having been less than pleasant to her mother. She might even have been downright rude. She knew that to act so was childish and unworthy of her better self. She hadn't even asked about her father. Thea looked down at the phone sitting in its usual place on the occasional table and then went to find a book with which to spend the afternoon.

CHAPTER 14

"Is everything okay at your office?" Thea asked. It was evening and she and Hugh were having dinner at the Cape Neddick Lobster Pound.

"As okay as it ever is," he said. "I realize that's not much of an answer."

"I'm sorry you had to work all day."

Hugh just shrugged.

Since they had sat down to eat, Thea had been aware of a strain between them, an element of uneasiness in their conversation. Or maybe, she thought, she was imagining it. She knew that her own dissatisfaction with the progress of their reunion might be coloring what was in reality an ordinary and companionable chat between two old friends. Since when, she wondered, had everything become so awfully complicated?

"I guess you'll have to be getting back to New York soon," she ventured.

"I still have a few vacation days," Hugh said, "but, yeah, I can't be away forever. Even though right now I'm feeling frighteningly content right where I am."

"Me, too," Thea admitted. Her dissatisfied but expectant heart made a tiny little leap.

"Being out of the city is always refreshing."

"Oh," Thea said flatly. "Yes."

"What will you do when you go back to Massachusetts?" Hugh asked.

"I'm not quite sure," she admitted. "My career . . . during the last year of my marriage it kind of went off track. I haven't told you that I gave up my teaching position for a more lucrative path at my former husband's request. It was a disaster from the start."

"Oh. I'm so sorry I brought up a painful subject."

"No, I don't mind. It's just that . . . it's frightening. I kind of have to rebuild my life. Part of me knows I can do it because I have no other choice. But another part of me is . . . is very scared."

Hugh took her hand in what Thea could only call a brotherly

way. "You were always far more resilient than you gave yourself credit for, Thea," he said. "And maybe it's time you learned how to feel some compassion for yourself."

Thea managed a smile.

Hugh released her hand and patted it. "I know I sound kind of parental or paternal. It's one of the results of all the therapy I had after the divorce and then the accident. My friends tell me I can drive people crazy when I'm in counselor mode."

"Oh," she said. "That's okay."

There was a moment or two of what Thea was certain anyone, even her own counselor, even Alice, would judge to be awkward silence.

"I don't know why," Hugh said suddenly, "but I'm feeling kind of tired. Do you mind if we call it a night?"

Thea felt his words like a blow. "Of course not," she lied. Her appetite had fled anyway; her dinner stirred uneasily in her stomach.

They drove back to Thea's apartment in silence. When Hugh pulled into the driveway, Thea assured him that he didn't have to walk her around to her door.

"I'll wait until I see your lights come on," he promised.

When the last sound of Hugh's tires on the gravel driveway had faded, Thea fell into the chintz-covered chair and buried her face in her hands. Only days before she had sworn to Alice that she would never marry again. Since then, she had been reunited with Hugh and though nothing at all had been said to make her believe there was a shared future in store, it was exactly the thing she wanted—a shared future with Hugh Landry. She wanted to be married to him. She wanted to have children with him.

Thea lifted her head and sighed magnificently. "You're an idiot, Thea," she whispered to the empty apartment. If she had followed the advice of her therapist she would never have run away to Ogunquit. She would never have stumbled upon Hugh. In short, she never would have gotten herself into such a glorious, heartbreaking mess.

CHAPTER 15

The next morning Thea drove to the Hannaford in York to stock up on a few basics—deodorant, toothpaste, milk, and coffee. Alice had suggested that maybe if she bought a better brand of coffee she might make a better cup of coffee. It was worth a try.

Red plastic basket over her right arm, Thea joined the line at one of the express checkout stations. The woman in front of her was positively ancient and moved with a slowness that was very close to stillness. The cashier, a teenage boy with one of those huge earplugs in his left earlobe, seemed to know or at least to recognize her, and chatted amiably while with trembling fingers the woman extricated coins from her cracked leather purse.

While she waited patiently, Thea scanned the impulse purchases—candy, horoscope scrolls, and of course magazines. Cooking, health and exercise, fashion, gossip . . . The glossy at the end of the row caught her attention. Rather, the words printed along the right side of the cover did: "Reuniting with an Old Flame—Is It Worth It?"

Thea reached for the magazine and then let her hand fall. How much real, sound advice could you get from an article in a magazine that featured makeup tips, the latest fad diets, and a feature on a gaggle of sisters staggeringly popular for nothing more than being public? To waste money on something so ephemeral and . . .

The ancient woman in front of her finally moved off and Thea tossed the magazine onto the counter, along with her other purchases. Five minutes later, she was sitting behind the wheel of her car in the parking lot, rapidly scanning the article.

Phrases, sentences leapt out at her. "An early relationship that the parents had belittled or in some ways actively hindered." "A split that had occurred for largely situational reasons." Being separated by three thousand miles could count as a "situation," Thea decided. And certainly her own parents hadn't been supportive of her dating Hugh.

Her eyes darted to the final few paragraphs of the article. If the two people now reunited had been each other's first loves, if their relationship had been criticized and cut short, the writer told her, then their chances of romantic success the second time around were close to eighty percent.

Thea's heart began to race. If this article could be believed, then she and Hugh stood a very good chance of making it again as a couple. They wouldn't part in a few days, Hugh for New York and Thea to rot away in her rented apartment. She thought about their conversation at dinner the night before, how she had sensed that there were so many important things being left unsaid. Well, maybe not on Hugh's part, but certainly on hers. But if Hugh really didn't have anything to say to her, anything like, "Thea, I love you," then . . . then, she was imagining a future that existed only in her own fantasies.

Thea looked down at the glossy cover of the magazine, at its bright purple and pink lettering, sensational headlines, and ridiculously airbrushed model. The article could all be lies, she thought, the studies faked, the results a joke perpetrated by the sneering editors on an unsuspecting, gullible, magazine-reading public. There would most likely be no future with Hugh, no romantic reunion, certainly no marriage, and the sooner she accepted that strong possibility, the better.

Thea tossed the magazine into the backseat of the car and started the engine. Her therapist, she thought, would be proud. How Alice would judge her determination to reject the hope of love, she decided, she would rather not know.

CHAPTER 16

"I don't think I've ever seen so many dragonflies in one place."

"Hmm."

Thea shot a look at Hugh. That sort of noncommittal, unengaged answer was not usual for him at all.

"The Marginal Way is so lovely, isn't it," she said.

They walked at least another two yards before Hugh said, "Uh-huh."

Thea felt the icy hand of dread on her neck. "Are you okay?" she asked, though she was afraid of what Hugh's answer might be. She herself did not feel okay. She felt sick. The other night, things between them had been strained, and then that stupid article she had read that morning had given her false hope, if only for a moment, that life might actually turn out to be lovely.

"No, actually," Hugh blurted, "I'm not okay. I've been wanting to say something to you almost since that first day in the diner."

The icy hand of dread tightened. Hugh was going to tell her that nothing could come of this reunion, that it was simply too late for them. Of course, he was. "Okay," she whispered, completely unsure of how she would handle hearing the devastating words from his mouth.

Hugh took her arm and led them off the path and out of the way of the other strollers. He took off his sunglasses, took both of her hands in his, and looked down at her intently.

"I love you, Thea Foss," he said. "Maybe I've always loved you, maybe I never really stopped loving you. Maybe I just let other people's plans for me get in the way. I'm sorry if this is hard for you to hear. I'm making no presumptions about your feelings and I'm asking you for nothing. But I just had to speak up."

Thea sagged forward and felt Hugh's grip on her hands tighten in response. "Oh, Hugh," she cried. "Hugh, I love you, too. I really do! I thought you were going to—Never mind what I thought. I—"

Hugh cut off her words with his mouth on hers. Their kiss, the first one in so many years, was passionate and heartfelt and almost as wonderful as the long and tight hug they engaged in right after. I could die a happy woman at this very moment, Thea thought. But I so don't want to.

"Get a room," someone called, not unkindly. Someone else laughed in appreciation.

Hugh and Thea pulled apart. "Let's sit somewhere," Hugh suggested. "We'll be less of an attraction with our backs to the audience." They took a seat on a bench a yard closer to the cliff. Hugh held her left hand with both of his.

"Well," he said with a grin, "that was a big relief. A guy's never sure he's going to get the answer he's hoping for."

"You mean you really didn't know how I felt, how I feel?" Thea asked. "I'm stunned. I thought I was being very transparent. I was afraid I was throwing myself at you. Well, as much as someone like me does that sort of thing."

Hugh laughed. "Women are mysterious creatures for us, Thea. Even a woman you've known for a long time can be impossible to understand. It's a flaw in the masculine design, I guess."

"Well, then, I'll try to be very clear in the future. That is, when I get over the shock of our being here together. Honestly, after you didn't respond to that letter I sent you the Christmas of our senior year, I thought I'd never see you again, let alone be declaring my love for you."

"Wait," Hugh said, "what letter? I don't remember getting a letter from you that Christmas. If I remember correctly, we hadn't been in touch at all for months."

"Yes, you know, the one in which I said I wanted us to try again. I said I thought we had what it took to be a really good couple for the long run. And I promised that if I didn't hear from you by the end of January, I'd never contact you again."

Hugh's expression was troubled. "Thea, I swear I never got that letter. Believe me, that's something I'd remember."

"I do believe you," Thea said. "Oh my God. What could have happened?"

"I don't know." Hugh shrugged. "Maybe it got lost in the holiday mail. Maybe—Well, I suppose my parents could have intercepted it . . . I'm sorry to say that sort of behavior isn't beneath either of them. But there's no way to know for sure. It's hardly something they would admit to after all this time."

Thea was stunned. She had never considered the possibility of the Landrys having interfered with her life in such a blatant way. But before she could process the enormity of that possibility, Hugh asked:

"What made you reach out to me again that winter?"

"Mrs. Tolliver."

"Who?"

"I was volunteering at a retirement home," Thea explained. "Mrs. Tolliver was one of the residents. She'd been there for almost ten years by the time I met her. We got along really well. She told me she'd been married for almost fifty years to the boy who had been her first love. It was a real-life love story, Hugh. Seriously, every time she talked about her husband and their life together, she—glowed. It made me think that maybe you and I could have that special life together, too. I know we hadn't been getting along all that well, but . . . I still had feelings for you so, I wrote you that letter."

"Wow. That was brave."

"Would you have called me?" Thea asked. "If you'd gotten the letter?"

Hugh didn't answer right away. "Well," he said after a long moment, "I don't know."

"Oh," she said, her voice a bit wobbly.

Hugh squeezed her hand. "No, let me explain. I want to be honest about everything. And from what I can remember about who I was in senior year of college and where I seemed to be going . . . remember, I was pretty heavily influenced by my parents . . . I just can't say for sure that I would have been able to listen to what you had to tell me with an open mind."

Thea nodded. "Okay. I have to admit I'm disappointed. I was hoping you'd say you would have jumped the first flight back east to be with me. But at the same time, I know that your being honest with me is better than lying to protect my feelings."

"That's what we should be about, especially now, Thea, after all that's happened to us. Honesty."

"That's not something I've had much experience with lately," she said ruefully. "Let me ask you another question. Were there times over the years when you thought about me?" she asked.

"Of course I thought about you. Especially, I have to admit, when my marriage began to fail so spectacularly. I couldn't help but compare Susanne to you, which was ridiculous because—well, because of all sorts of reasons. It was unfair of me."

Thea tried to remember if she had ever consciously compared Mark Marais to her memories of Hugh Landry. Oddly, she couldn't remember if she had. "Did you ever think about contacting me?" she asked.

"Sure," Hugh said promptly. "But I didn't want to make a messier situation even messier. And I was afraid that if I did contact you I'd find you wanted nothing to do with me. And maybe I'd find that you weren't at all who I remembered you to be, or who I needed you to be for me at that lousy time. All in all, I made the right decision to—well, to leave you alone."

But if he hadn't left me alone, Thea wondered, maybe I would never have married Mark. But that was gross speculation. "And then . . ." she prompted.

"Then," Hugh went on, "after the divorce, I threw myself into work even more than I had before. After a time, when I began to burn out, I met this woman, Raina, at my gym. I've told you a bit about her already. We had absolutely nothing in common but a love of sports. Seriously, I don't think we ever talked about politics or the arts or anything remotely important. Instead, we went skiing and scuba diving and hiking and rode our bikes fifty miles each weekend. My parents were horrified with the match. Which is probably why I eventually asked Raina to marry me. Childish, huh?"

Thea smiled ruefully. "I'm not one to judge."

"And then the accident happened. Suddenly, like I told you, I was no longer a suitable playmate for Raina. Better I found out when I did than years into a marriage. So, it doesn't say much for my track record, two spectacular fails."

"Don't be so hard on yourself, Hugh."

"I could tell you the same thing," he replied with a smile. "So, do you want to tell me a bit about your marriage? You know you've never even mentioned your ex-husband's name."

"Yes," Thea said, surprising herself a bit, "I think that I do want to tell you. I probably should say that I didn't date much in my twenties, hardly at all, in fact. And I never considered getting married. Really. I felt I was doing just fine on my own. I liked my work; I was a good teacher. I bought a condo when I was only thirty. I had some nice friends, nobody very close, but there were people I could go to the movies with, even travel with if I wanted to."

Thea paused and looked out at the Atlantic glistening in the August sun. She had never spoken this narrative before, not to anyone but her therapist, and that had been at times an excruciating process. To tell it now to someone she knew so well, someone with whom she had shared so much, both good and bad, should, she thought, be easier. But as she went on, she found that in some ways revealing her past was even more painful when the listener was a person whose respect she so desired to maintain.

"And then?" Hugh prompted.

Thea sighed. "And then, I met Mark. Mark Marais. It was at the MFA in Boston. There was an exhibit of medieval illuminated prayer books on loan from some small museum in Belgium. I was studying a particular book in a glass wall case when this person, this man, suddenly spoke to me. I forget what exactly he said, something about the piece I was looking at. Next thing you know, we were chatting and having lunch in the restaurant upstairs, the expensive one. He paid. He was older then me, by ten years, I found out later. He was dressed nicely, kind of a mix between preppy and, I don't know, a European elegance. Oh," Thea cried suddenly, "this is so embarrassing!"

"Thea . . ."

"He seemed so nice," she went on. "He spoke French, though not very well, but he laughed at himself for it. It all happened so fast. The next thing you know I was introducing him to my parents and he was charming them with a story about how his father was a self-made man and how he'd followed in his father's footsteps and was now an entrepreneur but had never lost his feel for the 'common man.' " Thea winced. "Yes, he actually used that term. And we fell for it, all three of us."

Hugh whistled. "Oh, boy. A classic con artist. Let me guess. You eventually found out he'd scammed other women before you."

"Not until much later. But yes, I found out about the other women he'd duped, and about his arrest record. I should have known things weren't what they seemed. There were so many signs, but I just didn't see them. Or, if I did see them, I ignored them, like the fact that he had no friends, none at all. When we got married some guy showed up at the church to be his best man. He left before the reception was over and I never saw him again. And Mark never talked specifically about his work. He claimed client confidentiality. He said because he was entrusted with so much of his clients' money he had to be ultradiscreet. I believed him."

"People like this guy Marais are good, Thea," Hugh said grimly. "They're professionals. You weren't taken in because you were stupid. You were taken in because this Mark person knew what he was doing."

"I know that now," she admitted. "But it still . . . it still hurts. And my parents were so thrilled that I was finally getting married! My mother started dropping broad hints about becoming a grandparent before we were even on the honeymoon."

Hugh shook his head. "It's amazing how unsubtle parents can be about that topic."

"Yes, well, it wasn't long after the wedding that I started to doubt Mark's—honesty. We were living in the condo I'd bought on my own. I put him on the deed as co-owner, but in spite of all his talk about the big money he handled, he rarely made his share of the mortgage payments, let alone of the utility bills. And odd sums of money began to disappear from our bank accounts. Stupidly, I'd agreed to put all of our money together. We'd get into terrible fights about that. He'd say he needed some capital to put back into his business, that it was all an investment in our future. He'd promise to let me know in advance when he would need to withdraw money, and then, he'd break that promise. Bills started to go unpaid. Checks started to bounce."

"Not a good situation."

"No, not good," Thea agreed. "Until then I'd had perfect credit. And then he even convinced me to quit my job teaching, which I really loved, to enroll in a corporate training program at one of the big marketing firms downtown. Getting into the program was exhausting, but I made the cut. The pressure was enormous, but so was the money, and that's all Mark cared about. I was absolutely miserable but as money at home was always tight, I stayed on. I had no choice. But when I had to work late at the office, which was often, Mark would get so angry . . . I felt I was losing my mind. I felt so alone. The marriage, everything, was a nightmare."

"What about friends?" Hugh asked gently. "Did you talk to your friends about what was going on?"

Thea shook her head. "Oh, no. Peggy, the woman who'd been my maid of honor, she'd just had her first baby and the last thing I wanted to do was bother her with my woes. Besides, Peggy was doing everything right. She had a good husband, she was starting a family, and she was working at a job she enjoyed. I felt like such a big failure compared to her. And Mark, well, he'd pretty much driven my few other friends away, though I know I was partly to blame for not standing up to him."

Hugh's expression had tightened into the closest resemblance of anger Thea had ever seen on his face. "But what about your parents?" he said. "You were so close with them in high school. You must have turned to them for help?"

"My parents were useless," Thea said vehemently. "They thought I was just being dramatic. They thought I was worrying for nothing. All they saw—all they wanted to see—was a picture-perfect son-in-law. He kept up a fine act with them."

"That must have been horrible for you," Hugh said. "I hope they eventually came around?"

"Oh, finally. One morning my mother stopped by our house unannounced. I'd stayed home from work because . . . because of my black eye. Which wasn't the first black eye I'd had. She was just going to slip something through the mail slot, some magazine article or other she thought I'd like. The last thing she expected to see was my sneaking out the front door with the garbage, wearing a big floppy hat and an enormous pair of sunglasses, neither of which was enough to cover the damage."

Hugh hugged Thea tightly. "I'm so sorry," he whispered.

"Me, too. After that, of course, I had their support. But it was kind of too little, too late."

"What happened then?"

Thea sighed. "I'll spare you the details, but I got a restraining order on Mark. He was the one who sued for divorce. And he wanted spousal support. Needless to say, that was not granted. And here I am. No condo, no nice car, no good job. I quit the job Mark had convinced me to take, of course; I had to. And I had to get away from my parents so I came here to ..." Thea looked up at Hugh. "Well, to hide out for a while and lick my wounds until I was ready to go back and rebuild my life."

"And instead," he said, "you found me."

Tears sprang to Thea's eyes. "Yes," she whispered. "Instead, I found you."

Their lips met in another kiss and it was some time before they headed back to the Cove.

CHAPTER 17

"This is the most beautiful day ever. I don't think I'm exaggerating."

"I don't think you are, either," Hugh said. It was the following afternoon and they were at the beach again, and it was true that the sun was bright and the water was glittering and what few clouds there were in the sky were definitely the happy kind. Thea had borrowed Alice's blanket and beach bag again. Hugh had bought two small folding beach chairs at one of the shops in town. It was less painful for his leg, he explained, when his back had some support.

"And less painful for my back, period," Thea said. "Though I'm not complaining. I'm sure any back pain I have is due to inactivity, which is something completely in my control."

"The older you get, the harder it is to maintain flexibility and strength."

"Ugh. Let's not talk about getting old! Let's enjoy this moment."

"Deal."

They had each spent the night before in their own beds. Thea would have been more than happy—ecstatic, in fact—to have spent the night with Hugh, but he had—in his usual thoughtful way, Thea noted—suggested they hold off a bit before having sex.

"There's a lot at stake for us, Thea," he had argued. "For each of us as an individual, as well as for our future as a couple. I don't want to risk ruining things by forcing an intimacy we might not be ready for. I don't mean physically," he'd added quickly, with a grin. "I mean emotionally. We've both been through a lot of bad stuff."

"I know," Thea had agreed. "I agree. But you know I'm at my sexual peak, right?" she teased.

"All the more reason to build up to spending the night together, or the afternoon, or the morning, or all three. Expectation," he pointed out, kissing her forehead, "can be very exciting."

"Okay, but let's not wait too long."

"Patience is a virtue."

Thea had laughed. "Well, then, I'm not very virtuous!"

Now, stretched out in the warm sun, Thea felt calm and satisfied. Patience, she recalled, was said to have its rewards.

"I brought lunch today," Thea said, taking two sandwiches, two bags of chips, and two bottles of water from the bag. "I can put two slices of bread together. Anything more complicated and I need a manual."

"You made me a birthday cake in high school. I don't remember getting sick."

Thea blushed. "That's because my mother was standing over me the entire time, making sure I didn't add salt instead of sugar."

Hugh looked over at her and smiled. "This is the most important moment in our life together, Thea. I'd say it's even more important than the first time we talked. Remember, before history class that day?"

"You asked me to go for pizza. I thought it was a prank devised by some mean girls."

Hugh's eyes widened. "Then what made you say yes?"

"You looked so disappointed, I had to take the risk that you really wanted to go out with me."

"Very courageous!"

They ate in companionable silence for a while, save for Hugh once commenting on how good his roast beef and Swiss cheese sandwich tasted. The beach was crowded but Thea was enjoying watching others enjoy themselves. A teenage couple to their right was lying side by side on beach towels, holding hands. A much older couple, browned almost beyond belief and glistening with oil, sat in chairs complete with cup holders, side trays, and padded foot rests. She smiled as a tiny toddler in a bright pink bathing suit made her way determinedly, if crookedly, toward the water, her daddy a nervous inch or two behind. Life can be okay, she thought. People are often nice.

Thea looked over to Hugh. "I feel I have to apologize," she said. "I was so mad at you by junior year. It never really occurred to me to be mad at your parents for whisking you away every Christmas season. I was just mad that you agreed to go to Vienna or wherever they were jetting off to and not to come home to see me."

"I'm sorry," Hugh said, reaching for her hand. "I mean it, Thea."

"Oh, it's all right now. Were you ever mad at me?" she asked. "Did you blame me for the breakup?"

"Well," Hugh said, "only a little, and only in my more immature moments. And you know me, Thea. I'm not one to hold a grudge. I try to be as fair as I possibly can. Deep down I always knew I was partially—maybe mostly—to blame for letting things happen the way they did. I guess I just wasn't strong enough to say no to my parents. It was easier to find ways to be disappointed with you. I'm sorry."

"Oh, me, too. What a waste."

"We ended with a whimper," Hugh said, "not a bang."

"Not that I wanted us to end at all, but I know what you mean. A whimper is somehow sadder than a bang."

"You know, I'm still embarrassed to admit that I actually allowed my parents to manipulate my life to such a degree. Sometimes a devotion to duty becomes badly destructive. Sometimes it becomes an excuse not to live your own life, to make your own choices, good or bad. I mean, my parents chose my wife for me, and I let them. It sounds pathetic, doesn't it? It sounds medieval."

"Closer to home than medieval," Thea said. "Arranged marriages happen in all sorts of societies. Sometimes it works out. But when it's a union made for dynastic purposes, chances are pretty strong the couple will be unhappy as a couple, though maybe successful as politicians of a sort."

"Or when it's a union made for money," Hugh said, "plain and simple. Like my marriage pretty much turned out to be. Susanne was a nice enough person. She was very social; she loved giving parties; she was the ultimate hostess. She had absolutely no career ambition other than marrying the right sort of man. Apparently, I was that right sort of man, and all the parents thought so, too. I convinced myself I was in love with her. But in the end I was just being a good son, which was unfair to Susanne and unfair to me. My parents were furious with me when I filed for divorce. Thank God there were no children. And then after getting engaged to Raina and then the accident . . . well, let's just say I've proved a big disappointment to them."

Thea felt a surge of anger toward the Landrys. She didn't see how Hugh could prove a disappointment to anyone with half an ounce of sense. And if his parents had indeed intercepted her letter all those years ago, it was evidence of a deep dislike of Thea for no good reason at all; worse, it was an indication of a deep disregard for the emotional welfare of their child.

"We were manipulated," she said forcefully.

"Yes," Hugh agreed. "But parents often manipulate their children. Mostly, I think, parents aren't even aware they're being puppet masters, or trying to be."

"I think our parents knew exactly what they were encouraging when you went off to college in California and I stayed home. What were your parents afraid of, that I was pretending to love you for their money?"

"Even if they did consciously manipulate us—and, okay, I do think that they did—it was a long time ago. And look, we're here together again now. That's all that matters."

"But the lost time . . ."

"You can't think like that, Thea," Hugh said forcefully. "At least we found each other again."

Thea smiled. "Always trying to see the positive in a messy situation."

"The alternative is not a choice for me. It never was."

"An eternal optimist?"

"Maybe," Hugh admitted, "but one with limits. I like to think I don't foolishly put faith in something or someone not worthy of that faith. Sometimes, often, it's a hard call."

Thea nodded. She certainly had learned all about putting her faith in a worthless person. "You know," she said, "we can't pick up again where we left off because where we left off wasn't in a good place. I want us to start again from when we were parted, from those last days of summer vacation before you went off to college, when we spent every moment possible together. Do you think that's possible?"

"I have to believe it's possible," Hugh said. "So do you."

"I know. But our breakup wasn't entirely our parents' fault. Why did we stop trying, Hugh? Why did we allow ourselves to drift apart?"

Hugh shrugged. "We were young."

"But isn't youth the time for great romance," Thea argued, "for making lifelong promises? Youth is when you believe that anything is possible."

"In storybooks, maybe. Maybe sometimes in real life. Honestly, Thea, I'm not sure it would have been a great idea for us to have stayed together back then. It's impossible to know what might have happened if we had, of course, but I can't help but think, given all that's happened to both of us since then, that we're stronger people for having been apart. Okay, for having been torn apart, if you want to be dramatic about it."

"I do want to be dramatic about it," Thea insisted. "Our love was rudely interrupted."

"But maybe it was a good thing that it was. Look, if I was so easily persuaded by my parents to not come home during the holidays and eventually to marry a girl they practically threw at me, what sort of husband would I have made to you? I wasn't half as tough as I am now. I'm guessing you weren't, either."

Thea wondered about that for a moment. "Yes," she said then. "Maybe you're right. We were—maybe I still am—parent pleasers. It certainly didn't hurt Mark's cause that my parents adored him and that by marrying him I knew I would be giving them a gift of sorts."

"Being a people pleaser isn't all it's cracked up to be, is it?"

"No," Thea agreed. "It isn't. I know now that I had no real idea what marriage was or what it involved. Mark is a bum, but in some ways I do blame myself for having gone into that marriage for such—feeble reasons. I'm not even sure I was ever actually in love with Mark. Maybe I was using him in some way, like he was using me. The bottom line is that I never should have married him."

"Do you remember how we talked about running off to city hall to get married?" Hugh asked.

"Maybe we should have done it. Everything could have been so different for us!"

"Maybe different in a bad way. My parents probably would have cut me off. Maybe I didn't care so much at the time, but from the perspective of a thirty-five-year-old, the idea of being eighteen and entirely on my own—with a wife to support—seems insane. Which is not to say people don't risk such things all the time, but what about college? Our careers? It wouldn't have been smart. It probably would have destroyed us."

"Yes," Thea said reluctantly. "I can't imagine running into you after all these years and being so happy about it if we'd been through a messy divorce. We might have come to resent each other, even to hate each other."

"Let's not think about the what-ifs anymore, okay? We need to keep talking and learning about each other all over again. We need to face forward."

"Were you born mature?"

Hugh laughed. "I wish! You in the mood for ice cream?"

"Have I ever said no to that question?"

Hugh reached for his cane and got to his feet. "I'm on it."

Chapter 18

Thea was up not long after dawn. She had slept incredibly well, deeply and dreamlessly. Now she was ravenous. She made a small pot of coffee with the brand Alice had suggested she try. It still didn't taste as good as the stuff Alice brewed, but it was a major improvement on her own previous efforts. And then she managed to scramble two eggs without them becoming pasteboard and toasted two slices of bread without burning them. It was going to be a fantastic day.

Thea felt that she hadn't stopped smiling, not since that magical moment on Marginal Way when Hugh had declared his love for her. Okay, they hadn't slept together yet and he hadn't asked her to marry him, but she felt sure that both sex and a proposal would come in the not-so-distant future. Hugh, always Mr. Responsible, wanted to pace things for a while. Fine, Thea thought. She could handle that. Maybe.

After breakfast, Thea opened her laptop with the intention of checking her e-mail, though she expected to find nothing of importance. Then she would check the local weather. The air felt slightly damp and the sky was overcast. She wondered if it was going to rain. She hoped not as she and Hugh had planned to go blueberry picking that afternoon.

There were only three e-mails, one from her college's alumni association; she would read that at some other time. There was an e-mail from Peggy; the attached photo showed her two small children in their plastic wading pool with Daddy. Thea smiled. She didn't recognize the address of the third e-mail. Without the caution that had become her constant companion, she opened it.

There was no subject line. The message had been typed in caps. There were only three lines and even if Thea had slammed the computer shut or hit the delete key, her eyes would have seen and her mind would have read the words before they could disappear from view.

JUST WHEN YOU THOUGHT IT WAS SAFE TO . . . HOW'S THE NEW VENTURE GOING? YOU'LL HAVE TO TELL ME ALL WHEN WE MEET.

Now she did hit the delete key and slammed the screen down over the keyboard. She was furious and she was frightened. Her heart thumped painfully and her stomach roiled. How had he gotten her contact information? She had changed her e-mail address after the divorce and closed out her Facebook account. Who would have given her new e-mail address to her ex-husband? Could her parents have betrayed her—again?

Thea took a deep breath. It need not have been a betrayal. The culture was obscenely public; there was no real privacy unless you went entirely off the grid. She had gotten a restraining order on Mark after he had moved out of her condo and filed for divorce, but that was long outdated. And a restraining order did not prevent him from using a search engine or even a phonebook to find her.

Thea got unsteadily to her feet and fearfully scanned the fields surrounding Alice's house. No standing male figure, watching her. But he could be lurking . . .

The nightmare had come true. Mark had returned. He could very well be in Ogunquit, as she had feared, watching her. What did he want from her? He had already taken her money, her peace of mind, her dignity. What else was there for him to plunder!

The fury she had initially felt upon reading Mark's e-mail was now entirely replaced by the fear. The e-mail had been jaunty and vaguely threatening. Hadn't it? For a moment, Thea wished she hadn't deleted it. She thought it had implied that he would be in touch again . . . and what had he meant about her "new venture"? Her life postdivorce? Or her relationship with . . .

She would call Hugh. She would be totally honest with him, like in the old days. Hugh was all for being totally honest with each other; he had said so. Thea dashed over to the occasional table, reached for her phone, and then snatched her hand away from it as if it were on fire.

No. No, she couldn't tell Hugh that the man who had terrorized her had returned. She couldn't admit to him just how terrified she felt, how one brief e-mail had made her feel completely vulnerable, how it had sapped every bit of strength she thought she had recovered since the divorce. A feeling of deep mortification engulfed her and she stumbled into the kitchen. She barely reached the sink before the meager contents of her stomach came roaring up.

With shaking hands, Thea pulled a paper towel from the standing roll, wet it, and wiped her face. No. She simply could not ask

Hugh for his protection. She would not involve him in her sordid past. She would leave all the lights on that night; she would remain vigilant. No doubt Alice would see the lights from her bedroom and comment. Thea would make up an excuse—a bout of insomnia—but what about the next night, and the one after that? Mark had made her a prisoner again . . .

Her cell phone rang and Thea cried out. She stumbled back to the occasional table and peered at the bit of machinery warily. It was Hugh. She let it ring twice, three, four times before answering.

"Hi," she managed.

"Hi, back. Guess where I am?"

"Where?"

"On my way to the emergency room. Now, don't panic. I'm just taking a precaution, though some people would have you believe the place you don't want to be if you're afraid of infection is the hospital."

Thea's grip on the phone tightened. Had Mark gotten to Hugh? Had he hurt him? "Oh my God, Hugh," she cried, "what happened?"

"I was shaving and the razor slipped and I cut my hand. Clumsy of me. The cut's pretty deep, but I cleaned it immediately and I'm wearing a bandage and antibiotic cream, so it should be okay, but I figured I'd have a doctor check it out, just to be safe."

"Do you want me to meet you at the ER?" Thea asked automatically, her sense of duty momentarily overriding her terror.

"No need. I probably won't be able to use a cell phone there and I'm not sure how long I'll be, so don't worry. I'll call as soon as I get out. Okay?"

"Okay." Thea's tongue felt thick and heavy in her mouth.

"I'm sorry I won't be able to make our date to go blueberry picking this afternoon. I'll make it up to you, I promise."

"Okay, yes."

"Thea? You sound—upset. Please don't worry about me. I'll be just fine."

Thea nodded, though there was no one there to see. "Just . . . be careful, Hugh," she said. "Be careful."

* * *

Thea spent the endless afternoon on the move. She drove down to the outlets in Kittery through a steady drizzle of rain, watching as best she could to be sure she wasn't being followed. Blindly, she went into Old Navy and walked up and down the aisles seeing nothing, watching over her shoulder for Mark. She got back into her car and drove the winding, picturesque roads of Kittery Point, and then turned back north, all the time vigilant. She worried about Hugh. She tried to figure out how best to avoid Alice and her keen questioning when she got home. Not that she wanted to go back to her apartment in Alice's house. Everything that had become commonplace and comforting—the field, the woods, the old stonewall—had been tainted by the reappearance of Mark. Everything that had come to feel welcoming in her world of refuge now seemed sinister and threatening.

But eventually, exhausted and enervated, she turned the car toward—no, not toward "home" because no place was home now. She turned the car toward what had been her temporary shelter. She would have to leave Alice's apartment, soon; she would have to move somewhere else, maybe someplace even more remote, someplace where Mark would have trouble tracking her down. But how would she live? She needed money. . . . Thea's grip on the steering wheel tightened so that her knuckles were dead white.

It would be so simple, a tiny part of her mind said, so natural, to tell Hugh what had happened and to ask him to stay with her that night. But Hugh might be spending the night, and the next night, in the hospital. He might have a dangerous infection. She couldn't burden him with her troubles; he had enough of his own.

Thea turned the car onto Oak Street. She was amazed she had made it back to the apartment without having gone off the road, distracted as she was. She peered intently at the driveway, at the house itself, at what was visible of the surrounding fields and the far-off tree line. Nothing obviously foreign leapt out at her. Alice's car, she was relieved to see, was there; Alice was home. Not that she would trouble her landlady with her woes.

Thea parked the car and hurried around back and into the apartment. Quickly, she locked the door and leaned against it, her eyes closed. No. No one had come to her rescue before and yet she had survived. She was damaged, but she was alive. She would survive again, even if she had no one to rely on but herself. And if I don't survive, she thought, well ... she wasn't so sure that she cared.

CHAPTER 19

"I'm sorry we had to miss out on blueberry picking," Hugh said, wiping his mouth with his napkin. "But if it doesn't rain tomorrow, and if you don't have to work an afternoon shift, we could go then."

Thea nodded.

Hugh had called Thea as soon as he had been released from the hospital earlier that evening. Professional opinion was that the wound was going to heal nicely. He was starved, having missed breakfast and lunch. Could he come by and pick her up for dinner? Thea, who felt completely sapped of strength and rational thought, had seen no way out of saying yes. Now, they were at a lobster shack, sitting across from each other at a picnic table set with plastic salt and pepper shakers, plastic silverware, and paper napkins. Hugh was devouring a boiled lobster, two ears of corn, a basket of garlic bread, and a salad. Thea was picking at her crab roll, uncharacteristically uninterested in food.

"Is the crab roll okay?" Hugh asked, dipping a piece of lobster in butter. The bandage on his right hand didn't appear to be a hindrance to movement.

Again, Thea nodded. "It's fine," she said with a poor attempt at a smile.

Hugh called to the waiter for another beer. Thea watched him enjoying his meal and felt her heart breaking with every moment. Every decision she had ever made regarding love had been wrong. She had let Hugh slip away back when they were in college; she hadn't fought hard enough to keep him; she hadn't known how. She was a weak person. She had succumbed to Mark's lies, not once, but over and over again. She had allowed herself to become a victim. There was no way she would be anything but a burden to Hugh in the future.

"Thea," Hugh said, breaking into her morbid thoughts. "What's wrong? Are you feeling okay? You've hardly eaten a thing."

"Nothing's wrong," she said. "I'm fine."

"Did you hear anything of what I was just saying? About the nurse in the ER, the one with the tattoo of Elvis?"

Thea colored violently. She shook her head.

"You're not still worried about my hand, are you? I was probably being overly cautious going to the emergency room but—"

"No, no," she protested. "I'm fine, really." As if to prove it, she took a bite of the crab roll and chewed. It was tasteless in her mouth. She saw the concern on Hugh's face—of course, he knew something was worrying her; of course, he didn't believe that she was fine—and it saddened her beyond words. But there was nothing she could say to assure him that nothing had changed between them, that everything was all right. She couldn't even tell him that she loved him. She did love him, but it was no longer right for her to . . . her duty now was to protect him.

Finally, Hugh piled his dirty napkins on his plate, sat back, and sighed. "Wow. I hadn't felt that ravenous in years." He looked at Thea's half-eaten dinner. "Why don't I ask the waiter to wrap up your leftovers," he suggested.

Thea shrugged. "It doesn't matter. Okay."

They drove back to Alice's house in silence. Hugh walked Thea around to the back of the house, to the door of her apartment. Thea scanned the shadows for the figure of a man, someone watching, someone waiting, but saw no one.

"Good night, Thea," Hugh said. He put his hands on her shoulders and leaned in to kiss her. She turned her head slightly so that his lips didn't quite meet hers.

"Did I have too much garlic at dinner?" he asked with a smile that didn't quite reach his eyes.

"No, no," she said, "it's just that . . . I have a bit of a headache. I just need to go to sleep."

"Okay." Thea thought she heard an awful mix of concern, sadness, even suspicion in his voice. "Take some ibuprofen if you have it. Good night, Thea. I'll talk to you tomorrow."

She nodded, opened the door, and quickly closed and locked it behind her. Hugh stood where he was for a moment before slowly walking toward the front of the house and his car. Once he looked over his shoulder to see the lights in Thea's apartment coming on one by one. The sight unaccountably saddened him.

CHAPTER 20

The sound of knocking on the apartment door the next morning caused Thea to crash her mug against her front teeth and spill hot coffee down her chin. Hastily, she wiped her face with a napkin and called out, loudly but with a tremulous voice, "Who is it?"

"Alice," came the loud and not-at-all tremulous reply.

Thea opened the door for her landlady and, it turned out, Henrietta, too. "Sorry," she said. "I didn't see you coming around back."

Alice followed Henrietta inside. The cat leapt easily onto the high back of the chintz-covered chair, from where she watched her human companions intently.

"The lights were on all last night," Alice said without preamble. "All of them. I know you're paying your share of the electric bill, Thea. That's not what I'm worried about."

Thea looked down at her feet in their old slippers. She said nothing. She flinched at the cry of a bird.

"You won't meet my eye, you're as jumpy as a cat—sorry, Henrietta—and the bags under your eyes could hold a sandwich each. What's going on?"

Thea looked back to Alice's keen, inquiring, and concerned eyes and then to Henrietta's wide, unblinking stare and didn't know which female intimidated her more.

"I'm sorry," she managed. "I hope the lights didn't bother you. I couldn't sleep, that's all."

"That was obvious. Something's bothering you, Thea. Now, don't lie to me. You look like a completely different person than the one you were a day ago."

Thea had absolutely no intention of telling Alice anything, but then the words were spilling out.

"Hugh told me he loves me."

"Well, that's wonderful," Alice said with a nod. "I'm happy for you, kiddo. And why is this making you look like a refugee from hell?"

"He cut his hand yesterday. He went to the emergency room. There was a terrible accident a few years ago. He lost his spleen, which makes him susceptible to infection. That's why he went to the ER. His left leg was also badly broken, 'shattered' is the word he used."

Alice squinted as if somehow that would help her to understand what it was Thea was trying, and failing, to say. Squinting didn't work. "So," she said, after a moment, "let me see if I get this. You're reunited with someone you loved passionately when you were young, someone you still love now, and you're freaking out because he's got a bum leg and no spleen?"

"No, no," Thea cried, shaking her head. "That's not what I mean!"

"Then you'd better start over."

"He could get really sick. He could die before me. I could lose him all over again."

"And the world could end tomorrow."

"I have to be careful. I have to protect myself. I have to protect him."

Alice shook her head. "I don't understand. Protect him from what?"

Thea turned away from Alice and walked a few mindless feet in the direction of the kitchen. She couldn't tell Alice about her ex-husband's e-mail and how frightened and vulnerable it had made her feel. A small part of her mind knew that by leaving out that vital piece of information she was preventing Alice from knowing the entire truth and maybe, just maybe, preventing Alice from helping her. But telling Alice about Mark might put her in the line of danger, too . . . and it might make Alice despise her.

"Hugh was always so strong," Thea said, almost to herself. "He was always so strong and competent. I'm not like that at all. He can survive without me." Her last words were whispered to the sink.

"Thea? What did you say?"

Thea turned around to face Alice. "His parents never liked me," she said, her voice trembling. "They thought I wasn't good enough for Hugh, and they were right. I see that now."

A small, odd noise came from Henrietta's throat, a sound of distress but also a noise that to Alice's ears sounded like one of impatience.

"Thea," Alice said, "you're frightening me. You're not making much sense, if any. You didn't take anything, did you? Pills?"

"What? No, no, never."

There was a long beat of extremely uncomfortable silence. When Alice spoke again, her tone was gentle. "Hey, kiddo, I think there's something you're not telling me. Something else is behind all this sudden craziness."

"No," Thea said vehemently. "No, there's nothing else."

Alice didn't believe Thea's protestations for a minute, but she was smart enough to know that badgering her was not going to produce any good results. She considered what she might say now; it was difficult, given such little and such conflicting information. Finally, she decided she would address the fear that hung so thickly and so obviously around her young tenant. "Do you really want to be living all alone in my basement for the rest of your life?" she asked, careful to keep her tone neutral.

"It's not a basement," Thea mumbled.

"You know what I mean."

This time, Thea did not reply.

Alice sighed. She suddenly felt terribly old. That tended to happen when she found herself in the presence of despair.

"Come on, Henrietta," she said. "I'm afraid there's nothing we can do here."

With one smooth leap, Henrietta was off the back of the chair and at the door. Alice closed the door behind them. A half second later, she heard the lock click into place.

CHAPTER 21

"Why did you want me to come here?" Thea asked. She stood just inside the door of Hugh's room at the bed-and-breakfast. Hugh was half leaning against, half perched on the small desk between the room's two windows.

"Privacy," he answered. "But if you stand all the way over there, I'll have to shout to be heard and that kind of blows the privacy idea."

Thea reluctantly came farther into the room. She felt as if she had been summoned before a judge for a crime she had indeed committed. She noticed that Hugh's laptop was open on the desk. Next to it was his phone, a manila file folder, and a Cross pen. Hugh, Thea remembered, had always liked good pens.

"I was hoping to put off my return to New York for a while longer," Hugh went on, "but it looks like I have to get back to the office in the next few days."

"Oh."

"And I'm not at all happy about leaving when it's clear that something's gone wrong between us, Thea. What's happened since yesterday?"

"Nothing's happened." The lie came automatically. She hated herself for telling it.

Hugh stood away from the desk. His cane was within reach but he ignored it. "Don't lie to me, Thea," he said. "It's unworthy of you and it insults me."

Thea clasped her hands before her in a vain effort to stop their trembling. She lowered her eyes. "I'm sorry."

"Apology accepted. Now, talk to me."

She stood silent and motionless for what seemed like a very long time. Hugh said nothing more. When she began to speak, she was surprised at the sound of her own voice. She still did not raise her eyes to look at Hugh.

"It's just that since the divorce, I've . . . I've felt so stupid, and afraid, and alone. And then you came along."

If she had been looking at him, Thea would have seen the small smile on Hugh's face. "I thought my coming along was a good thing," he said.

"It was. It's just that . . ."

"It's just that what?"

Finally, Thea looked up. "My ex-husband," she blurted. "He sent me an e-mail yesterday. I got it right before you called to tell me you were on your way to the emergency room. I don't know how he got the address, but I suppose there are all sorts of ways . . . It frightened me. It . . . it made me feel like I felt before you and I found each other again . . ."

"Did you save the e-mail?" Hugh demanded. "Did you answer it?"

Thea shook her head. "No, no, of course I didn't answer it. I was so upset I just deleted it without thinking."

Hugh took a step closer to Thea. "Why didn't you tell me that creep was bothering you again?" he demanded. "You don't have to deal with him alone, Thea. You don't have to deal with him at all!"

"I . . ."

"Did he threaten you?"

"It felt like he was threatening me. I don't know . . . he said something that made me think he was going to be in touch again. But I can't remember, exactly . . ."

"My God, Thea. This can't go on. I'll—"

"Wait!" Thea cried. Her hands were clasped so tightly now that her fingers hurt. "It's not all Mark's fault, the way I've been acting. It's my fault, too."

"What do you mean?"

"I don't know if I can explain."

"Try."

Thea finally unclasped her hands and sank onto the edge of the neatly made bed. She looked up at Hugh, silently pleading with him to understand something she herself didn't entirely understand. "When you had to go to the hospital yesterday," she said, "all I could think about was, what if you died? I'm just so afraid to—to risk anything, my heart, my peace of mind."

Hugh sat down on the edge of the bed next to Thea. Gently, he touched her arm. "Oh, but Thea, that's normal, to be afraid, especially after all you've been through!"

Thea moved her arm away from his hand. "And your parents . . ."

"What about my parents?" His voice sounded puzzled and frustrated. "What could they possibly have to do with us now?"

"They were mad at you for buying me the miniature. There's a possibility they stole my last letter to you. They never liked me, Hugh. They never thought I was good enough for you. There's a real chance that if we're together now they'll make my life miserable. And that would make your life miserable and . . ."

"Oh, Thea." Hugh tried to take her hand, but she pulled it away. "I can't believe you've talked yourself into this state of—"

"And if you were in my life, Mark could hurt you, too. Neither of us would be safe."

"That's ridic—" Hugh took a deep breath. "That's not possible, Thea. You have to trust me."

They were quiet for a long moment, Thea studying her lap and Hugh studying Thea. When she spoke again, her voice was a mere whisper. "I'm ashamed of myself," she said. "I'm sorry, Hugh. I'm not the person you thought I was. I'm just a bundle of fear and panic and lame excuses. I would be such a burden to you. You would regret every minute of our life together."

"This is not the Thea Foss I knew." Hugh's voice broke as he spoke the words.

"It's who I am now. It's who I've become."

"I don't believe you're stuck being 'a bundle of fear and panic and lame excuses.' I won't believe it."

"But what if I am, Hugh?" Thea cried, jumping to her feet and looking down at him, tears streaming across her cheeks. "What if this is all I'll ever be?"

"You can't talk like that!"

"I am talking like this. This is my reality now, Hugh. This— mess!"

Hugh sat rigidly. He felt furious with the creature who had destroyed the woman he had always loved, the creature who had transformed a once beloved person into this . . . into this stranger.

He also felt suddenly and utterly exhausted.

"We should both try to get some sleep," he said quietly. "We'll talk again tomorrow. Okay?"

Thea nodded dumbly.

"Do you want me to drive you home? You can get your car tomorrow."

"No," she whispered. "I'm fine." And she left his room, closing the door quietly behind her.

CHAPTER 22

Alice was sitting in a rocking chair on the narrow front porch when Thea pulled into the driveway a short time later. Thea got out of her car and stumbled on the loose gravel. Before she knew what was happening, Alice had taken her arm and was guiding her behind the house to the door of her apartment. She opened the door with her own key and half dragged Thea inside. Thea was vaguely aware of a blur of brown, black, and white slipping in beside them.

"I'm fine," Thea said nonsensically.

"And I'm the Queen of Sheba." Alice lowered her into the chintz-covered armchair and sat herself on the love seat close by. Henrietta was now nowhere in sight. "Are you going to tell me what's going on," she demanded, "or am I going to have to torture it out of you? Look, I know I'm not your mother, but I do have a certain responsibility as your landlady not to allow my tenant to go completely insane on the premises."

In spite of the deep depression, despair, and fear that hung around her like a heavy, wet blanket, Thea felt a very small smile come to her lips. "All right," she said, her throat dry. "I'll tell you."

And she did tell Alice, about her abusive marriage to Mark, her months in therapy trying to heal, and then about her escape to Ogunquit against her therapist's advice. She told her about how absolutely wonderful and happy and hopeful she had begun to feel with Hugh. And then she told her about the vaguely threatening e-mail Mark had sent just the day before and how it had reminded her that, in the end, she was a victim and would always be a victim.

Alice was silent for the duration of Thea's tale. When it was over, she let out a long, low whistle. "I think I'm speechless, kiddo," she said finally. "Or near to speechless. I'm sorry. Were you just with Hugh?"

Thea nodded. "At his bed-and-breakfast, the Hartley House. And I'm afraid it's all over. I told him how I felt, how messed up I am. But now I'm so scared that Hugh won't want to be with me and I couldn't even blame him if he did tell me to go away. He should go away. I'm not worthy of him. I'm not strong enough to be a good partner to him. I've always loved him but I've never been good—"

Alice stood abruptly. "You need to stop talking and to stop thinking," she commanded. "Not that you're doing either at all clearly. Come on. You're going to bed."

"I couldn't sleep a wink," Thea protested.

Alice pulled Thea to her feet. "You'll sleep more than a wink," she promised, directing Thea along to the bedroom. "I'm making you a stiff drink, pulling the covers up to your neck, and singing you a lullaby if I have to. Now," she said, "I'll be right back."

Alice left the bedroom and went upstairs to her kitchen. Wearily, Thea got into the bed and pulled the covers up over her shoulders. A few moments later, Alice returned, a tumbler of amber-colored liquid in her hand.

"I couldn't drink all that," Thea protested.

"Do your best." Alice sat on the edge of the bed while Thea sipped as much as she could of the whiskey. "All right," Alice said, taking the half-empty glass from her hand. "Now, lie down."

Thea slid down and adjusted a pillow beneath her head. She gasped as Henrietta jumped up on the bed, settled against her left leg, yawned, and closed her green eyes. Thea's own eyes widened in alarm.

"Don't worry," Alice said. "She won't bite. At least, I don't think she will."

"Why is she doing this?" Thea whispered.

"She knows you need her. And trust me. Things will look brighter in the morning. They always do."

Thea didn't hear Alice's car pull slowly out of the driveway fifteen minutes later. Against her conviction, she was already deeply asleep, and any unhappy dreams she might have had were kept in abeyance by the watchful, protective presence of Henrietta.

Chapter 23

"Sorry if I woke you or interrupted something important." Alice stood up from a plush, rose-colored velvet armchair. The front parlor of Hugh's bed-and-breakfast was furnished in a rather successful if improbable mix of dense Victorian detail and lighter, seaside inn chic.

Hugh walked farther into the room. "No, that's okay," he said. "I was just reading. Well, trying to read. So, you're Alice Moore."

"Yes." Alice stuck out her hand. "It's good to meet you, though I wish it were under a more pleasant circumstance. I need to talk to you about Thea."

Hugh shook her hand. "Look, I don't really think—"

"Would you rather talk in your room?"

Hugh glanced around the empty parlor. "No, we're fine here," he said. "But—"

"I know I have no right to speak for Thea," Alice interrupted. "I've only known her for a few weeks, but I like her. And she's been badly, badly hurt. And she's acted like a ninny in the past day, sure, but I also know this. She loves you. She always has."

Hugh gestured with his cane to an overstuffed couch strewn with overstuffed pillows. "Do you mind if we sit?" Alice sank back into the pink chair and Hugh perched on the couch. "She told you that she's always loved me?" he asked.

"Yeah. But she didn't have to. It's obvious to anyone with eyes. She also told me about that louse of an ex-husband. She's scarred from her experience with that idiot, but not beaten. You should believe that. She's got inner resources she doesn't even know she has."

Hugh chose his words carefully. "I'd like to believe that she hasn't given up."

"You can help her find those resources."

"Can I?"

Alice sat forward. "Look, from what I hear, you two have had some seriously bad luck. But now, you've got the chance to change that for the good. Seems like a no-brainer to me, but hey, I'm a romantic, what can I say? Just a big softie."

Hugh sat with his thoughts for several minutes before speaking. "I don't know why I'm telling you this," he said, "but before I found Thea again, I felt pretty much alone in the world. I didn't like it. I don't think a person is meant to be alone. Certainly, I'm not. And then . . . then she told me she loved me and I allowed myself to hope, just a bit, that everything would be better. That my life would be richer, fuller."

"And now?" Alice prompted.

Hugh sighed. "Look, a day or two ago, Thea asked me if I considered myself an eternal optimist. I said no. I said I tried not to be stupid when putting my faith in a person. And I meant it."

"And you're worried she can't live up to your expectations of her."

"Not expectations," Hugh corrected. "I only want Thea to be Thea. But maybe who Thea has become isn't someone right for me, after all."

"She's just scared," Alice insisted. "Fear can be conquered."

"I'm scared, too, all right," Hugh replied forcefully. "I'm not getting any younger. I really don't want to make another major mistake. I know there's no guarantee that a relationship will be forever. But there is such a thing as making a good choice in the first place. And so far, I've got a lousy track record. If Thea's telling me straight out that she's in no place to be with me, why should I doubt her? Why shouldn't I run for the hills?"

"Because you love her."

Hugh blinked away the sudden tears. "Yes."

"Just promise me you'll be the hero she thinks you are."

Hugh shook his head and wiped his eyes with the back of his

hand. "I can only promise that I'll think long and hard about this conversation. And about what I'd be losing if I'm not brave enough to trust her."

"Thank you." Alice stood abruptly. "Well," she said, "I've said what I came to say. The rest is up to you and Thea."

Hugh walked Alice to the door of the Hartley House and watched as she got into her car and drove off. That, he thought, is a remarkable woman.

CHAPTER 24

In spite of her protestations to Alice the night before, Thea had slept and deeply at that. If she dreamt, she had no memory of having done so. When she woke at 6:30 that morning, Henrietta was gone not only from Thea's bed, but from the apartment itself.

She went into the kitchen to make coffee; she was due at the diner at 8:00 for the busy breakfast shift. She felt better than she had the night before. Not perfect, not happy or strong, but somehow less anxious, less scared, a little bit more calm, a little bit more receptive. Yes, that was the word. Odd. Briefly, she wondered if Henrietta had some sort of magical healing power or if Alice was indeed a witch and had slipped some healing concoction into that glass of whiskey last night. She smiled at the thought.

A knock on the door chased the smile from her lips. Her heart sped up but she managed to call out, "Who is it?"

"It's Hugh."

Thea hesitated. She considered telling him to go away. But she couldn't. That odd little feeling of receptivity she had woken with led her to the door. She let him in and locked the door behind him.

"I didn't expect to see you here," she said.

"What did you expect?" he asked. He looked determined. Tired, too, but determined.

Thea blushed. "I don't know," she admitted. "Hugh, I don't really have much time to talk right now. I have to work the breakfast shift."

"Call in sick."

"But I'm due—"

"Thea," he said, "if you ever cared for me at all, please, call in sick. What I have to say can't wait."

She did. When she had ended the call, Hugh reached for her hand—she did not protest his touch as she had done the night before—and led her to the chintz-covered armchair. He dragged a ladderback chair from against a wall and lowered himself onto it. Their knees were almost touching. He laid his cane on the floor.

"I need you to listen to me, okay?" he said. "Just listen. And don't look away."

Thea nodded. She felt strangely calm, as if time were suddenly suspended.

"I need you, Thea," Hugh said simply. "I need you to be in my life if my life is going to be worth anything."

He paused, as if expecting Thea to protest, but she said nothing. She nodded for him to go on.

"We were," he said, "we *are* a good team. Thea, I don't want to tackle life alone or with someone else. I want to tackle it with you. I want to face down the challenges and enjoy the good stuff together. I'm willing to take a chance on us. Are you? No prevarication, Thea. Yes or no. You owe a real answer to the both of us."

Thea felt her body relax until she wasn't quite sure where it left off and the chair began. It was like falling asleep. It was like waking up. A feline shape darted past the part of the window visible behind Hugh and then was gone. "Henrietta," Thea murmured.

"What?"

"You know what I've been through."

"Yes," Hugh said. "I do. But that's the past. I'm not discounting your experiences, or mine, good or bad. But the past can't dictate the future. It can't. We can't allow it to. We can help each other in that. I need your help, Thea, maybe more than you need mine."

Thea looked deeply into Hugh's dark brown eyes for some moments. And then, something clicked. Why, she wondered, had she not understood that Hugh was simply a fellow human being, wounded, vulnerable, desirous, and in need of an equal companion? How, she wondered, could she have been so wrapped up in her own pain that she could ignore the pain of a fellow human being so dear to her?

She leaned forward and put her hands lightly on Hugh's knees. "Okay," she whispered, and then she kissed him.

"To hell with waiting," Hugh muttered, standing and pulling Thea to her feet with him.

"Are you sure you—" she began, but Hugh cut her off with a kiss.

Thea wrapped her arms around him and wanted more than anything she had ever wanted to be with him again. Her mind and body were flooded by sense memories of their youthful lovemaking, potent memories that had lived so deep inside her she had forgotten their presence—until now.

Somehow, they found themselves in the bedroom. Thea allowed Hugh to undress her—he was the only man she had ever allowed this sensual rite—and lay back on the bed, watching as this man, her first and her only true love, undressed and then joined her.

"Do you remember our first time?" she whispered, as Hugh pressed the length of his body against hers.

"I was a nervous wreck," he whispered back.

"And now?"

"No."

And when they came together, Thea felt exalted. Being with Hugh again, now, after all they had endured both together and apart, felt more perfect than she could have imagined.

Eventually, they lay sweaty and exhausted and deeply satisfied among the tossed and tangled sheets. Thea realized she was grinning like the proverbial Cheshire cat and laughed out loud.

"So," Hugh said, still slightly out of breath, "this means you'll marry me, right?"

Thea turned on her side to stare at him. "You still weren't sure?"

"Humor me."

"Then, yes, I will marry you."

"Good. I was hoping you'd say that." Hugh got up from the bed and walked over to where his clothes had landed an hour earlier, in a pile by the dresser. (In spite of what he had implied about his injured thigh, Thea, looking through the eyes of love, didn't think it looked "gnarly" at all.) From the pocket of the wrinkled jacket, he withdrew a small, black box. "This," he said, "is for you."

Thea could say nothing. Her fingers clutched the damp sheet now wrapped around her. Grinning, Hugh came back to the bed and sat on its edge. He loosened the fingers of her right hand and put the box in her open palm. "Do you want me to open it for you?" he asked. "You seem a little stunned."

Thea gulped. "Yes, please."

Hugh opened the box and fell back as Thea screamed in his ear.

"This . . . I know this ring!" she cried. "I saw it in that antique store, the one with that scary old ventriloquist dummy . . ."

"I know. I saw you looking at it. I can be pretty sneaky. I went back to the store later and bought it. And I think you just punctured my eardrum."

Thea winced. "Oh. Sorry. But . . . but you didn't even know if we . . ."

"I was hoping really hard."

"Thank you for hoping." Hugh slipped the ring onto Thea's finger and she sank back against the pillows. "We'll start our lives over again," she said. "We'll reclaim the lives we were supposed to have had, with each other. Hugh, I'm so sorry for what happened yesterday, and the day before. I guess I had a bit of a breakdown."

"There's no need to apologize," he said. "Look, what I said before about the two of us helping each other put the past to rest? We'll do that for each other, of course, but I do think you might consider going back into therapy. At least until you believe in yourself again. At least until you feel as strong as I know you are. So that if the past does rear its ugly head again you can confront it."

Thea sighed. "I know, you're right. The enemy isn't without; it's within. No more running away to hide, because you can't ever hide from yourself."

"And another thing."

"Is this you being all bossy and parental again?"

"Yes. No city hall wedding. How about . . . how about we get married in Paris, or in the south of France? We could find some beautiful old stone church with gorgeous stained-glass windows.

You could wear the Napoleon portrait as a brooch. What do you think?"

"I think it's a wonderful idea. But Napoleon might become a pendant on a necklace."

Hugh laughed. "And then a honeymoon in Europe. We'll go to England, of course. If I can pry you out of France."

"Oh, I can be pried!"

"How do you feel about living in New York? My apartment is big enough for the two of us, but we'll find a new place together, something we both choose."

"My parents won't be happy that I'll be living so far away from them. For my entire life I've either lived with them or within a five-mile radius."

"They'll adjust," Hugh said firmly. "There's Amtrak. And if you're not happy living in Manhattan, we'll move out of the city and I'll commute to work. As long as we're together."

Thea laughed. "Oh, I think I'll like living in the city. The museums!"

"And it should be relatively easy to find a teaching position. At least, I hope it will be. I can help you. I know a lot of people whose kids go to private school. I'm sure I could get you an introduction. You could even go to graduate school for another degree, if you wanted to."

"Now, that would be a fantasy! Maybe I'll get a degree in art history..."

Thea's cell phone rang, interrupting the conversation. She reached over to the night table for the phone.

"It's my mother."

"Let it go to voice mail," Hugh suggested.

Thea looked down at the lovely ring on her finger and took a deep breath. "No," she said. "I want to take this call."

Hugh slipped out of the bed. "I'll give you some privacy."

Thea didn't wait for Hugh to leave the bedroom before taking the call. "Hi, Mom," she said.

"Thea," Gabrielle replied with an audible sigh of genuine relief. "I'm so glad you answered. I was afraid I'd have to leave another message and worry about—"

"Mom," Thea interrupted, "Hugh and I are getting married. Just like we should have done all those years ago."

There was a long beat of silence and Thea was half-convinced that her mother had been stunned into dumb disappointment, when suddenly a sob on the other end of the line made her jump.

"Oh, Thea! I'm so, so happy for you!" Gabrielle's meaning was distinct, if her words were not entirely clear. "Oh, I'm so sorry I ever doubted your love for each other!"

Tears sprang to Thea's eyes. "Thank you, Mom," she choked out, reaching for a tissue on the night table.

"When will you be home? You'll bring Hugh, of course. Your father and I . . . well, we'll want to celebrate with you."

Thea wiped her eyes and blew her nose before answering. "I'm not exactly sure when we'll be . . ." Not "home." she thought. Home was with Hugh now. "I'll let you know as soon as I can when we can visit."

After uttering a few additional sobbing sentiments, the women ended the call. As if on cue, Hugh returned from the bathroom, showered, his wet hair sticking up at odd angles.

"She's thrilled," Thea said. "I think my father will be, too."

"Good. Really, I'm glad they approve of us, not that we need anyone's approval."

"When will you tell your parents?" Thea asked, watching Hugh work his hair into a semblance of order with his fingers.

Hugh shrugged. "I'll tell them when they get back from their cruise. There's no rush. They've long since given up trying to manipulate or control me and I've long since stopped allowing them to do it." Hugh finished dressing and then looked seriously at Thea. "There's one more thing I think we should talk about," he said.

"Okay."

"We used to talk about having children. We're not too old, you know."

Thea grinned. "Still, we should start right away."

"Oh, absolutely. And Ogunquit is a nice place for kids, isn't it? We could make it our summer destination. In homage to our incredible reunion."

"That sounds very, very nice."

"I'll head back to my B-and-B now and check in with my office. We can leave Ogunquit as soon as you've wrapped things up at the diner and with Alice, tomorrow, the next day. And by the way, I'd like us to treat Alice to dinner tonight, someplace really special."

"Alice?" Thea said. "Sure, but why?"

"Let's just say she's my—our—fairy godmother. I—we—owe her big-time."

CHAPTER 25

When Hugh had left, Thea immediately called her boss at Maggie's diner and apologized again for missing work that morning. And then, she gave her notice, offering to stay for a week or two if necessary. But Jimmy had just laughed.

"No worries, Thea. I've got a list a mile long of kids wanting that job. I'll have hired one by this evening."

Satisfied she had done no great harm to Jimmy's business, Thea set to cleaning the apartment with the intention of leaving it even more spotless than she had found it when she had moved in. After almost two hours of dusting, scrubbing, and vacuuming, she decided to take a break and went into the bedroom with the intention of a brief nap or a stroll through one of the magazines Alice had thoughtfully provided for her tenant. No sooner had she plopped down on the bed but there was a knock on the door. Without hesitation, Thea hurried from the bedroom and threw open the door.

She found Mark standing there.

Thea's hand tightened on the doorknob. She began to think. She had heard Alice drive off about a half hour earlier, there was no one to hear her if she screamed, she had no weapon at hand . . .

"Aren't you going to invite me in?" Mark's voice, with its affectations of class and education, was all too sickeningly familiar.

"No," Thea said, with more force than she had thought she was capable of mustering. She had no weapon at hand but her own intelligence . . .

Mark shrugged. "Fine. How've you been, Thea?"

Thea slammed the door shut and locked it. She ran upstairs into Alice's part of the house and out the front door to the yard where she might possibly be seen by a car passing down the road, where she might possibly be heard if she did shout for help.

A moment later, Mark came sauntering around the side of the house, hands in the pockets of jeans even Thea recognized as expensive—who paid for those, she wondered; certainly not her ex-husband—a grin on his carefully shaven face.

"There's no need to run away, Thea," he said, slowly moving ever closer to where she stood with her back to the house, her eyes darting to the road for signs of human life. "We were husband and wife. I'm hardly some stranger. I know you."

And something about that smug grin and those ridiculously expensive jeans and that affected voice insinuating intimate knowledge served to infuriate Thea—and to make her want to burst out into crazy laughter. In that very moment, it had finally dawned on her that she was no longer the young woman Mark Marais had fooled into a travesty of a marriage.

Thea's desire to laugh passed as quickly as it had come, but the anger remained, and with it came disdain. Mark was a lot shorter than she remembered him to be, thinner, too. His French was abysmal. He had no friends. He was frightened by bugs. Over time, Thea realized, she had made him into a powerful opponent, when in reality all he really was was a less-than-average example of a seriously flawed human being.

"You don't know anything about me," she said steadily.

"Oh, I think I know a few things," he shot back with a wink.

"You disgust me. You need to leave right now."

Mark laughed. "Or what? I'm not doing anything illegal, am I?"

"You're trespassing. And I want you to leave. Now."

"Going to call the cops on me again?"

"I don't need to call anyone," she said. "I can handle a pathetic little worm like you. Stealing money from innocent women. Beating them up. You're not a worthy adversary for a baby, Mark. You're not a man. A man doesn't posture and threaten and lie and—"

Thea's words died away as Mark made a rapid move toward her. She stood absolutely still, braced for an assault if one came, ready, if necessary, to fight.

But in the next half second, before Mark could strike, if that was indeed his intention, a blur of flying color passed before Thea's eyes. It was Henrietta, moaning and shrieking, her fur standing up away from her body, making her look three times her actual size and her tail as big around as the thigh of a professional wrestler. Thea jumped back, her hands flying up to cover her ears against the violent aural assault. But she kept her eyes open as Henrietta launched herself onto Mark's stomach and dug in. He roared and pushed at the cat but Henrietta wasn't so easily dismissed. She sunk her teeth into Mark's hands, first one, then the other, before twisting around and launching her body back onto the ground, where she crouched, snarling and hissing, her eyes slits of green fury.

Thea stood rooted to the ground, hands still over her ears, as Mark, blood dripping from beneath his torn shirt and from the jagged cuts on the backs of his hands, limped to his rental car, muttering what were probably vile, uninventive curses. With a spew of gravel, he tore out of the driveway, narrowly missing Alice, who was just returning home from wherever she had been.

Thea dropped her hands as Alice got out of her car and stared in the direction of Mark's fleeing vehicle. Henrietta, her fur settling down by degrees, loped over and began to encircle Alice's ankles, purring as if nothing nasty had just taken place.

"Who the hell was that?" Alice demanded.

Thea put her hand against her racing heart. "Just some old piece of trash I needed to get rid of," she said. And then she began to laugh, a tiny bit hysterically.

Alice grinned. "Ah! Well, good for you."

"You should have seen Henrietta. Are you sure she's not part Satan? Or a lioness in disguise?"

"She might be either. I'm not saying."

"Well, whatever you are, thank you, Henrietta. You came to my rescue twice today."

The cat stopped her winding road around Alice's ankles, gave Thea a thoughtful, assessing look, and shot off in the direction of the woods.

"You okay, kiddo?" Alice joined Thea and gave her shoulders a one-arm squeeze.

"I will be once my heart stops pounding. Alice, please tell me you have something really nice to wear out to dinner. I've never seen you in anything but jeans."

"I've got nice stuff," Alice answered, a bit defensively. "Why am I going out to dinner?"

Thea held out her left hand. "To celebrate my engagement to Hugh."

Alice raised her arms over her head and whooped. "Hot damn, Thea, you did it!"

"So did he. And Alice? Thanks. For everything."

"No problem. I'm a sucker for a happy ending." She smiled down at Thea. "You're going to be okay, you know."

"I know. It's going to take more work, but I've got my partner now."

"Good. Hey, I think I'll go put rollers in my hair!"

Thea smiled. "How about a snack before we get all dolled up?"

Alice led the way into the house. "Kiddo," she said, "you read my mind. Hey, does Hugh have a single brother? I'll take a cousin if he's got one."

EPILOGUE

"I'm in the mood for some steamers. A big bucket of them."

Hugh glanced briefly over at his wife sitting in the passenger seat. "I thought pregnant women weren't supposed to eat seafood. Shellfish in particular."

"That myth has been debunked. At least I think it has."

"Are you sure you want to take a risk?"

Thea sighed, pretending annoyance, but what she really felt was deep gratitude for life having given her such a caring, if sometimes overly cautious, husband. "Okay," she said, "if it makes you feel better, I'll call my doctor and check before I order anything that came from the ocean."

"Yes," Hugh said with a smile, "thanks, it would make me feel better."

It was the summer after that momentous one, the summer after the one in which Thea Foss and Hugh Landry found each other after far too many years apart. It was the first summer of their married life and Thea's first summer—first any season!—of being pregnant. She was about four months along and due in late November. She was kind of hoping the baby would be born on Thanksgiving, which was her favorite holiday, but the only thing that really mattered was that he, or she, was healthy. Neither Hugh nor Thea wanted to know the baby's sex beforehand. At least, each had declared as much. Thea had a sneaking suspicion that they were both going to break down before long and have a nice chat with Dr. Mathis.

"It was really nice of Alice to have us stay with her for the week," Thea said as they drove past a crop of new summer cottage communities along Route 1 in Wells.

"She might not feel as generous with her home when the baby comes."

"She likes babies. I think."

"Liking babies is one thing," Hugh said. "Graciously putting up with someone else's baby screaming all night is something else entirely."

"Our baby won't be a screamer. He—or she—will be very polite."

"You're being delusional."

"I know."

Thea watched as the summer cottage communities gave way to picturesque bed-and-breakfast establishments and expensive hotels and resorts as they left Wells and entered Ogunquit. And she thought back to last summer and realized how vastly different—

and better—her life had become in the space of about a week. First, she was alone and depressed and frightened of her own shadow. And then, she was not alone and no longer depressed and if not entirely courageous, then well on her way to being so.

She and Hugh had left Ogunquit together last August and within the space of a month they had planned a wedding. Though Hugh had suggested they marry in France, in the end they both agreed that it would be much more fair, i.e., affordable, to the most important guests—particularly the Fosses and Alice, who was to be Thea's witness—if they married in New York. Which they did, at a lovely chapel in the Hudson River Valley. Thea wore the Napoleon miniature portrait Hugh had given her for her sixteenth birthday on a chain her mother had given her for the event. A honeymoon in Europe followed, taking the pair from Rome to Paris and then on to London. Only the demands of careers brought them home after almost a month abroad. Hugh returned to his office and when the spring semester opened, Thea began teaching at a small, academically rigorous high school in the upper reaches of Manhattan.

And then, Thea learned that she was pregnant and life really did seem magical, wondrous, amazing. After a brief run of morning sickness, her body seemed to settle down comfortably in its new job of building a new life.

"Anyway," Hugh was saying, "I thought we wanted to buy a summer place of our own in Ogunquit. We can't inflict a growing family on Alice forever. And your parents will want to spend some time with us, right?"

"And your parents . . ."

"Most likely will not. Which is fine by me."

As Hugh had predicted, the Landrys had voiced no objection to their elder son's marriage to his high school girlfriend. Neither had they rejoiced. It seemed that what Hugh had told Thea was true—they had lost any real interest in Hugh's life sometime before. All of their dynastic concerns had been transferred onto Hugh's younger brother, Piers, who, it was rumored, was gearing up for a career in politics, something in which Hugh had never had the least interest.

"Did you bring the gifts for Henrietta?" Hugh asked.

"Of course. How could I ever forget my guardian angel? A bag of organic catnip, though I suspect Henrietta won't care about the organic part, and a bag of pom-poms with bells inside. Though honestly, I never saw her playing with anything other than live creatures."

"It's the thought that counts."

Yes, Thea thought, and I hope Henrietta knows just how thankful I am to her. The last Thea had seen or heard of her rotten ex-husband Mark Marais was the moment after Henrietta's spectacular flying attack. Thea grinned at the memory of a bloody Mark racing for escape.

"Almost there," Hugh said when they had passed through the heart of town and turned onto a smaller road that, after some twists and turns, would take them to Oak Street.

"Good, because I'm starved. Alice is bound to welcome us with a snack."

She did. When Hugh and Thea pulled into the gravel driveway in front of Alice's timber-framed house, the smell of freshly baked bread greeted them. As did Alice, who had been waiting on the tiny front porch for their arrival.

"The drive was okay, I hope," she said after greetings and hugs were exchanged.

Hugh shrugged. "No worries. Except for Thea's alarming hunger pains."

"Ha ha. But before I eat, I'd love to say hello to Henrietta."

As if on cue, the large, irascible calico strode from around the back of the house and made directly for Thea. She arched her back and wound herself around Thea's right leg and then her left, and strode back the way she had come.

"That was unusually obliging of her," Alice noted. "Now, come inside you two."

Thea smiled. "Please tell me that's cinnamon-raisin bread I smell."

Alice put an arm around Hugh and one around Thea and ushered them up onto the porch. "And there's plenty of butter to go with it," she said.

CAROLINA SUMMER

ROSALIND NOONAN

*"I have this theory
that if one person can go out of their way
to show compassion
then it will start a chain reaction."*

—Rachel Scott

In memory of Rachel Scott,
who started a chain reaction
of love and compassion.
We never met, but you've touched my heart.

CHAPTER 1

Standing at the floor-to-ceiling window, Jane Doyle quietly said her good-byes to the city below—the grid of streets, the park, the rooftops, cars, and tiny pedestrians—as she scooped cereal into her mouth. Not so long ago she would have eaten her breakfast out on the little balcony beyond the kitchen, but not anymore. These days, she tried to stay out of sight, behind doors and tinted glass.

At this time of the morning, with the sun a golden glow over the green patch of Madison Square Park, Manhattan seemed more like a gentle giant than the beast that could make or break a person with a single blow.

One deal . . . one appointment on your calendar, and the whole world could turn upside down.

She swiped at a drop of milk on her chin and turned away from the window. It was time to go.

Heading south.

Everybody tries to get out of town for the summer, she told herself. Her customers were looking at cottages on the Cape and mansions in the Hamptons. Come Labor Day, business would pick up again here in Manhattan. *Until then, think of yourself as one of the lucky ones who gets to escape this concrete oven.*

She rinsed her bowl and took a swig of milk right from the container before pouring the rest down the drain. She wouldn't be back for more than a month. She'd already tossed the other perishables from the fridge and packed her favorite casual clothes into a duffel bag and a backpack. If someone came nosing around, they'd find the two large suitcases and rule out a long trip. At least, that was the general idea.

"Ms. Doyle, can I help you with that?" Alvin Garcia cocked his head toward the green canvas duffel.

"I'm good, thanks, Al."

"I almost didn't recognize you without your briefcase and business attire. You look like you're going hiking. Or camping, is it?"

She nodded . . . the vague nonanswer. "Up north," she lied. "I'm meeting some friends."

"Good for you. I wish I was getting away this weekend. They say the mercury is going to hit ninety."

"Really? Well, I'll be glad to cool off . . . in the river," she added, hoping that sounded like something a camper would say. The closest she'd come to nature in the past few years was sitting on a blanket for a concert in Central Park, and she hadn't been smitten with the feel of clotted dirt under her palms. She'd come to accept that she was a "city slicker," just like her brother TJ called her. Didn't bother her in the least, though he hated it when she called him a surfer dude. "It's windsurfing that I do," he always said. "There's a difference."

Jane smiled at the thought of her brother as the doorman helped her into a cab. She'd see TJ soon enough.

"Have a good trip, Ms. Doyle." Alvin patted the yellow roof of the cab and she was on her way.

Forty minutes later she made it to the front of the line at the small rental car office. Unfortunately, they were short on vehicles.

"I don't have an economy car for you," remarked the young man behind the rental car counter. He was as squat as a football tackle, though his hair was as coifed and gelled as a Madison Avenue model. "Everyone wants to get out of town this weekend. I don't know what's going on."

"It's freakin' hot, man!" called the guy lined up behind Jane.

The good news: They would honor Jane's reservation and upgrade her to a small SUV. A Jeep.

Jane signed and initialed the contract, then wrapped her fingers around the keys, liking the pressure of metal and plastic in her hand.

Escape was easier than she'd expected.

For the next half hour, she was so caught up in inching her way through traffic and trying to squeeze her way through the Holland Tunnel that she didn't have time to think about the fact that she was leaving the city she'd called home for the past ten years. Soon enough, she was cruising on the Jersey Turnpike, the Manhattan skyline a gray cluster receding to her left.

I'll be back, she thought, settling into the seat as miles began to separate her from her troubles.

The navigation system directed her to take Interstate 95 straight through to Florida, and when traffic stayed at an even pace, the miles clicked off quickly. In two hours, she was leaving Jersey for Delaware, then suddenly she was in Maryland and it was afternoon—a safe time to call TJ, who was an itinerant night owl unless he was chasing the tide.

She pulled on her headset and made the call. "Hey, guess where I am? Maryland already."

"Sounds like you're making good time. And I haven't even finished cleaning the boards out of the guest room."

"You'd better get cracking, bro. I'm not sleeping with your windsurfing equipment."

"You always were a picky one. Where are you planning to stop?"

"I don't know." She raked her dark hair back, glad to be so far on her way. "I'm thinking of driving through the night. The thought of some fleabag hotel along the way doesn't have a lot of appeal right now."

"No, no, no way, sis. That's too long a drive for one shot. Stop in Virginia."

"I'm almost there, and I'm too wired to stop."

"You have to stop. You'll fall asleep at the wheel."

"If I feel sleepy, I can pull over and sleep in the car."

"Right. I can see the headlines. 'Twenty-eight-year-old hottie found parked on the side of the expressway.' A pitch-black night in the swamps of Georgia. What is wrong with this picture?"

Jane groaned as she slowed to let a car merge ahead of her. She hated when her brother was right. "Fine. I'll look for a hotel when I get tired."

"Wait! I've got a better idea. Stop in North Carolina and stay with my buddy Axel. He runs a little motel in Buxton. That's right near the water. I'll get him to hook you up with a room for the night. It's a detour, but you'll love it. It'll get you off the interstate and driving through the Outer Banks, smack between the ocean and bay. You'll love it."

The fight went out of her when he mentioned driving near the water. It would beat the monotony of the long stretches of hills and trees she'd been passing.

"Okay." He told her to program her navigation system for Buxton, North Carolina. "I'll call Axel and let him know you're on your way. Let me call him now."

"Talk to you later."

"Drive safe," TJ said before disconnecting.

That was TJ, always looking out for her. He'd always been a caring, sometimes bossy big brother, but his role had expanded when they'd lost their parents young. Jane had been a sophomore in high school, Thomas James a senior, when their parents' car had slid on an icy road and hit a tree. With no other relatives living in the Buffalo area, their great-aunt Minnie had moved into the old house on Sycamore. An aging Broadway actress, Minnie had brought more drama to their lives than the high school prom, and though they enjoyed her, TJ and Jane knew that, from that point on, they would have to parent each other.

"Why don't you come stay with me?" Minnie had said last week when Jane had called her to say she'd be leaving New York City for the summer. "It gets lonely, knocking around in this big old house."

"You've got the studio to run," Jane had pointed out, not wanting to mention that a summer with Aunt Minnie was not what she had in mind for a vacation. Besides, she would feel safe with TJ, even if Florida was not the best place to be in June. "And I haven't seen TJ's new condo in West Palm."

"I heard he has an ocean view," Aunt Minnie had said. "That's hard to compete with," she admitted. "All I can promise is Lydia Lehman's tush when she's bending over her primroses."

They had shared a good laugh over that, but now, with the air conditioner blowing and the compass on South, Jane was glad about her decision to visit her brother in Florida. She felt like she was heading forward, not back.

Somewhere in Virginia, the navigational system steered her off I-95, and Jane was surprised to see pockets of traffic that slowed cars to a standstill in what seemed like rural areas. At last, she made it to Virginia Beach and the first signs of the sea, a choppy blue bay beyond the string of bridges and tunnels.

Even with the windows rolled up she could smell the salt in the air, and she smiled as she imagined her car rimming down the coast of Virginia on the map.

There was something calming about the sea. Living on the shores of Lake Erie, she had grown up testing the moods of the water. Even in a storm, the cresting swells and spray reminded her of the perpetual motion of the earth. Gotta move forward, TJ always said. She understood that, though she'd never faced anything in her life that had made her stop dead in her tracks.

Until this summer.

The scenic route got even more interesting as the expressway turned into a highway and she began to see old-fashioned signs along the way for hammocks and diners, crabs and Christmas shops, roadside markets and surf shops. TRY MY NUTS! was a brand that advertised every few miles, making her smile. The farmland gave way to water on both sides, and suddenly she was crossing the bridge to the land of summer. Sunlight streamed around the opaque clouds, casting a sparkle on water and sand. Small boats coursed through the inlet and wave runners looped playfully as seabirds floated overhead.

Maybe summer in Florida won't be so bad, she thought. She would have a chance to spend a block of time with her brother, right on the beach.

In Kitty Hawk, she stopped for gas. The gas cap in the Jeep was tight, and it hurt her hand to turn it. Then there was the smell of gasoline on her hands . . . so alien to her pampered life in the city. She restrained herself from wiping her hands on her flouncy skirt and went inside to use the restroom. After so many hours in the car, she felt as if she were moving underwater, all in slow motion.

When she was done, she went outside and bought a Diet Coke,

pretzels, and a map that would show the Outer Banks. She'd worked with clients who had vacationed in the barrier islands that fringed the Carolina coast, but she'd never been here herself.

"You lost?" asked the woman behind the counter. She had weather-worn skin and wore square turquoise glasses that brought out the silver in her short, curly hair.

"I'm just wondering how far it is to Buxton," Jane asked, propping her sunglasses on her head.

"It's just down the road. Fifty miles, I'd say. Take you an hour and a half, but it's a straight shot." She reached over the counter to point the way on the map. "You see here? You're in Kitty Hawk now. You'll stay on the main highway all the way. Through Kill Devil Hills and Nags Head. After that the road gets real narrow and you'll hit a few more little towns. I think Avon is the last one before Buxton."

Jane thanked the woman, paid for her purchases, and stepped out into the balmy air. The sun had been dancing in and out, and the thick humidity hinted of rain, but the cars and travelers around her hinted of laid-back summer with kids in swimsuits, trucks towing boats, and minivans packed to the windows with coolers, duffel bags, and Styrofoam boards.

The smile on her face didn't fade as she climbed into the Jeep. Vacation time.

As she drove south, the highway did winnow down to two lanes and the towns got smaller. Rodanthe seemed like not much more than a gas station and pizza place surrounded by huge cottages lining the ocean to her left and the bay to her right.

The town gave way to marshland that took her to Salvo, and then more grasses blowing in the warm wind for miles and miles. The eerie darkness of an afternoon storm settled in as she reached the outskirts of Avon. The splattering rain took her by surprise, and she slowed as her fingers fished to find the rental car's wipers.

The fast-thrashing wipers barely cleared away the downpour, but Jane slowed her speed and eased ahead, focusing on the red taillights in front of her. When the lights glowed bright, she pressed the brake, gripping the wheel tightly as the Jeep pulled to a stop.

Long-term driving did drain your energy, she thought, feeling the weariness.

The blast that rocked her car came out of nowhere. The wrenching jolt came with a *boom* that smacked the air around her.

A bomb? A gunshot?

A gasp escaped her lungs as she closed her eyes and braced herself against the steering wheel as the car slid beyond her control.

Adrenaline thrummed in her blood, her heartbeat a thundering noise. *Escape. Get away. Now!*

They had come for her.

She took a desperate breath, hoping it wouldn't be her last.

CHAPTER 2

Cooper Locklear was the only person inside the post office when the sky turned black and began to pour. Good. He wasn't really up for having anyone around to watch him suffer through Leah's letter.

Not that everyone in town didn't know she'd been writing him. A letter might be privileged and confidential, but anyone could look at the return address and the postmark. Bruce, Avon's postmaster, had a tighter network than Facebook.

"Got something from Leah again," Bruce had told him yesterday when they'd both been getting haircuts at Clive's.

"She still live in Charlotte?" Clive had asked, pulling the apron away as Bruce rose from the chair.

"That's what the postmark says." Bruce turned toward the mirror, examining his haircut. Although he had quite a head of hair for a man his age, it was silver through and through.

"That's the thing with the young people these days," Clive said. "They leave with the summer people and never come back. Not you, Cooper. You're the exception to the rule, and Avon's lucky to have you as sheriff."

"That's the truth," Bruce agreed, swinging around to face

Cooper. "But it's slim pickins here for a young man like you. Don't you get lonely?"

The question made Coop want to squirm right out of his shoes. Instead, he rubbed the back of his neck, grateful for the drone of Clive's vacuum as he cleaned up the fallen hair.

The vacuum shut off, and Clive gestured toward the chair. "You ever regret not going off to live in the city, Coop?"

"I've done all that," Coop said, settling back into the leather chair. "West Point and Fort Drum. North Korea and Afghanistan. How far does a man have to go to satisfy the wanderlust?"

"You did get to travel with the army," Clive agreed.

"Gone seven years." Bruce peeled a twenty from his wallet and handed it to Clive. "Maybe that was Leah's problem."

"Seven years is long for anyone to wait," Clive agreed.

Cooper hadn't asked her to wait. And as rumor had it, Leah hadn't always waited alone. He rubbed his chin. "You know, Clive, I came here for a haircut, not advice on women."

"The advice is free," Clive said. "It's just the haircut that'll cost you."

"In that case, I'd like a little off the top, and a little less advice."

"It's hard not to say anything when we both know you and Leah so well," Bruce said. "And to my eye, it looks like Leah's still waiting for you." Bruce paused at the door to put on his sunglasses. "Only she's waiting over in Charlotte, and you won't see her coming back here." He pointed to Cooper. "But she keeps sending those letters."

Only because I changed my cell phone number and refused to answer her e-mails, Cooper thought as he turned the key and removed the mail from the box. Three flyers from a junk removal service and coupons for the local grocery store. And then there was the letter, big and square and bold, with her swirly girl writing.

He tossed it onto the sorting table, tempted to rip it into shreds and stuff it under the other trash without reading it. But then, that seemed downright mean after she'd gone to the effort.

Thunder boomed in the distance as he took a breath and tore the envelope open. A card, with a cute little puppy on the outside. That just showed how little she knew him.

He felt his lips tug in a grimace as he deciphered the girly loops of her handwriting.

I still think of you a lot, and I know we'll always be friends. That's why I wanted you to be the first to hear my news. I'm getting married, Coop! I met a wonderful guy and we're . . .

Married? After all her declarations of undying love? He wasn't sure whether he felt more relieved or betrayed.

"Well, I'll be . . ."

Just then the radio on his collar crackled. "All available units, we have a car accident on Highway Twelve. Two cars involved and injuries reported. Got an ambulance rolling."

Cooper swiped the mail into the recycle bin, saving only the card. "This is Coop. You got a location, Brenda?"

Brenda gave him the mile marker, just north of the Quickstop.

"I'm on my way." He stepped out into the rain, which had slowed to a steady patter. Inside the police cruiser, Cooper stuffed Leah's card deep into the crevice between seat cushions, flipped on the lights and sirens, and peeled out of the post office parking lot onto Highway 12.

The post office wasn't far from the scene, and within minutes he was coming up on the two vehicles, one with its hood creased in two. Behind them, other vehicles had been pulled onto the shoulder while someone with a flashlight directed the backup of vehicles to move around the accident.

"Hey, Coop," called the man with the flashlight. The bill of an L.A. Dodgers cap peaked out from beneath the hood of a yellow raincoat.

Cooper recognized Rusty Mallory, owner of the nearby Quickstop, beneath the rain slicker. "Rusty. Looks like you're making my job easy."

"You got to get out and help when it happens on your doorstep."

"How are the injured?" Cooper asked.

"Nothing life-threatening. Older couple got scraped up, probably from the air bags. Kailani has them inside the Quickstop, sitting down." Rusty's wife, Kailani, was a nurturing soul who handed out free candy to kids and could predict the changing weather better than anyone Coop knew. "The other driver looks fine. A lady," Rusty went on. "She's probably in shock, though."

"And where is she?" Cooper asked as he lit a flare and tossed it onto the roadbed a few feet away.

"Still in the Jeep. No one could coax her out of it."

"Thanks for your help." Cooper handed Rusty two warning triangles and hurried toward the Jeep, the only vehicle still blocking the southbound lane. Why hadn't the driver pulled off to the side?

Not wanting to stand in the line of moving traffic, Coop went to the passenger's side of the vehicle and tried the door. Locked. He tapped the window and a moment later it opened a sliver.

"Ma'am? Are you all right?"

"Go away," came a hoarse female voice.

"We've got paramedics on the way, but I'd appreciate it if you'd unlock the car so we can speak more personably." *And so I can assess what's really going on with you.*

There was a pause, then she said: "Show me your ID."

He pulled it from his pocket, thinking she was a suspicious old lady. "Name's Locklear. Cooper Locklear," he said as he held his badge and ID card up to the slit in the window.

He saw the shadow of her leaning over to inspect his ID. Then the door lock clicked and he pulled it open. He was relieved that she seemed okay, at least physically. In her purple tank top and black-and-white skirt, she looked girly and sophisticated . . . except for the fact that she was shaking all over.

"Ma'am, I think you're in shock," he said. "I'm just going to shut this engine off, for our safety." He reached over and turned the key in the ignition.

She stared at his hands, confused. "Officer, I need your help." The quaver in her voice had made her sound older, but now he saw that she was only a girl in her twenties, with polished nails and skin as smooth as silk. Her long dark hair framed a face of fear: blue eyes as round as quarters and shiny with tears. "I need to get out of here."

"That's a good idea," he said slowly. "How about I come around to your side and we'll get you into the Quickstop for some coffee?"

"No, I need to leave, now. With this Jeep. Please, help me . . ." she begged.

Something in those dark blue eyes tugged at his heart, and he leaned across the passenger seat, trying to get through to her with firm but gentle persistence. "I am going to help you, ma'am. What's your name?"

"Jane."

"Okay, Miss Jane. We're going to get you out of this car, out of harm's way. There's a spot where you can sit in the Quickstop, and Kailani will take real good care of you."

"No!" She cowered against the window, trembling hands covering her face. "I can't do that."

"I'll help you," he said, realizing she was in a bad way. "You just hold tight and I'll come around and get you."

He was about to close the door when he noticed a pair of sunglasses on the floor. Bronzelines. A coveted brand, some going for a thousand dollars a pair. He put them on the seat, then stepped away from the Jeep, closing the passenger door behind him.

The rain had slowed to a drizzle, and though the sky was still gray, two rainbows jutted right out of Pamlico Bay in the distance. Within seconds he was around the car, easing open her door.

She stared at him accusingly, her hands still pressed to her face.

"Don't you worry, Miss Jane. You were in an accident, and that can be very traumatic. But we're going to take care of you."

A little sob escaped her throat, but she pressed her fists to her mouth, as if to hold it all back.

"Come on, now. You just step on out here and I promise you, everything's going to be all right."

He put a hand on her left arm, gentle but firm, and stepped back to give her room.

She sobbed, then rubbed her fists over her eyes. "Okay." Turning toward him, she slid from the car and fell against him.

Oh, Lord. The perfume of her hair struck him as his arms closed over her, small bones and warm flesh collapsing against him.

She was heaven in his arms, but this was not the time to let his body think for him. He had a job to do and she was a victim.

He propped her up against the car, seeing the surrender in her face. "Do you think you can walk?" he asked.

She nodded, and he slid his right arm around her waist, holding her body against his to support her. He'd promised to take care of her, and he was a man of his word.

With Kailani in the office tending to the beautiful Miss Jane, Cooper checked on the passengers of the other car. The Rosendahls were seated in the seating area of the Quickstop's eatery, being checked over by Roman, one of the paramedics.

"How's the other driver doing?" asked the tall, gaunt man, Douglas Rosendahl.

"She's looking better than you two," Cooper said, looking at the older man's license. "This says you're eighty. Is that right?"

"Indeed, I am. Eighty years and not a single strike on my driving record. Then today, in one big downpour, it's all out the window."

"Eighty years is a pretty good record," Coop said, handing back Douglas's license. "And that was a blinding downpour. But at eighty, you really want to be driving all up and down the East Coast?"

"Next time, we're riding with my daughter and son-in-law," Lila Rosendahl said as two paramedics wheeled her in. They'd been outside, using saline to flush away the chemical residue from the car's airbags.

"It could have happened to anyone," Doug said defensively. "When the sky opened up, I couldn't see two inches in front of me. How's the damage on her car?"

"Relatively unscathed," Cooper said, "but I can't say the same for your car."

"All for the best," Rosendahl said. "Cars can be replaced; people are another story."

"Words of wisdom," Coop said as he finished the accident report and peeled off a copy for Rosendahl.

"The good news is, it didn't happen along one of those stretches of marshland. We'd probably still be out there, waiting."

Coop glanced out the plate-glass window to the highway. Outside, the storm had passed and brash sunshine cast its silver sheen over the wet pavement and cars. That was the weather in the Outer Banks; summer storms came and went faster than a family of jackrabbits.

As he was watching, a neon green Volkswagen Beetle pulled off the highway and parked by the door. Good. "The doc's here."

"That's lucky," Mrs. Rosendahl said, "because I'm not going all the way back to Nags Head to get checked out. As it is, we're already late for dinner."

"Better to be late for dinner than never get there at all," Roman told her, slipping the blood pressure cuff from her arm.

Coop had called Ruthann Pope, more to have a look at the girl, Miss Jane, than the couple. The girl had been so out of it, Cooper worried that she might have sustained some head trauma, and he was always relieved to turn health care decisions over to a professional like Ruthann. "Doc . . . thanks for stopping by."

"Sheriff. Fortunately, I was on my way to the grocery store." She placed her medical bag on a table as she looked down at Lila Rosendahl and introduced herself. "Air bag injuries?"

"I was covered with a white powder, and it burned," Lila said.

Ruthann nodded. "Yes, the talc can burn. But it's better than the alternative. Looks like you were wearing your seat belts?"

As Ruthann examined the couple, Cooper headed into the office to check on Miss Jane Doyle from New York City. He'd gotten her name and address from her driver's license, and the registration showed that the Jeep was a rental car. But that was about all the information he'd managed to get.

Although the office door was cracked open, he knocked twice, remembering how she'd seemed like a frightened animal when he'd brought her in.

Kailani motioned him in. "She's tired," she said, nodding at Jane, who was sitting in the leather chair, her head resting in the shelter of her arms on the desk, next to an empty paper cup.

Kailani, a petite but round woman who'd moved here from the South Pacific when she met Rusty, sat nursing her own cup of hot tea. "Poor thing's been driving for hours, from up north."

"Vacationing here?"

"Just passing through. She's headed to Florida."

238 • *Rosalind Noonan*

Passing through . . . that was probably a good thing, considering the way something in his gut went off-kilter when he was near her.

"The Outer Banks is not the most direct route to Florida."

"She was planning to stay with her brother's friend in Buxton."

"She's got a friend here?" Coop folded his arms. "Then we need to call him. Maybe he can come get her, help her out."

"I already called." The voice came from the desk. A moment later, Jane lifted her head and he was face-to-face with her amazing blue eyes—eyes that cut right through a man. "He doesn't live there anymore." She squinted up at Coop. "How far is Myrtle Beach from here?"

"Myrtle Beach?" Coop raked back his hair with one hand.

"That's where her friend moved," explained Kailani.

"Myrtle Beach is too far to travel right now. Especially after an accident like that. The doc is coming in to take a look at you, but chances are, you're going to be staying in Avon for the night."

"No . . . I need to keep moving." There was a wistfulness in her voice that made Cooper wonder what this girl was running from. Her panic in the car had made it clear that she was trying to escape someone or something, but at least her voice has lost the raw desperation of a deer fleeing a hunter.

"Everyone needs to rest." Kailani's mellifluous voice seemed to calm Jane. "We can get you a room at the motel. I'll call Marvin and make sure he saves something for you."

"I . . . I don't know . . ." Jane pressed her fingers to her temples, her face a play of confusion and anxiety.

As she spoke, Ruthann came in, her dark eyes assessing as she moved.

"She's staying at the motel," Kailani told the doctor, then stepped out.

"Lucky girl," Ruthann said. "It's not everyone who can get into Avon-by-the-Sea without a reservation."

Jane winced. "I don't have the money for a resort hotel."

That surprised Coop, as everything he'd seen about this woman, from her strappy sandals to her designer sunglasses to her monogrammed duffel bag, said otherwise.

"Don't let the name fool you," Ruthann said. "It's bare bones, but it's tidy and friendly." She turned to Coop. "If you'll step outside, I'll take a look at Miss Jane and make sure everything checks out."

"Will do." He turned to the door and paused. "And Rusty is out there checking out your car, making sure it's good to go."

"Oh . . ." Jane frowned. "I didn't even think of that. How much will it cost me?"

"I'm sure it's just an act of goodwill," Coop said as it occurred to him that this would be a way to make sure she stayed the night. "But . . . chances are it won't be ready till morning."

As Jane nodded absently, and Ruthann shooed him out, Coop let out the breath he didn't realize he'd been holding. Jane seemed resigned to stay the night, and that was one obstacle conquered.

It was a start.

CHAPTER 3

It wasn't until she began to sob in the warm company of the kind stranger named Kailani that Jane realized how traumatized she'd been by the collision.

She'd thought it was an attack.

She'd thought Canby's men had come to kill her.

But no . . . it had been a genuine accident, a rear-end collision caused by the onslaught of rain and darkness. Just a brief glance at the older couple in the car that had hit her was enough to convince her that they were not hired guns. The poor woman, who reminded her of Aunt Minnie, had been burned by chemicals from the exploding airbag, and the inside of the man's arms had been scraped raw.

A simple accident, and Jane's composure had crumpled like the hood of the other car.

But these people—strangers—had helped her.

Kailani had sat with her, both of them sipping tea, while Jane had spilled out some of the details of her trip, telling her mostly that she had been traveling all day from Philadelphia, she'd said in a quick lie, trying to get to Buxton.

"You're close," Kailani had said. "Buxton is just down the road." When she had suggested that Jane contact her friend in Buxton, Jane had looked at her phone and discovered that she had a message from TJ, telling her that it wouldn't work out in Buxton. His buddy Axel had picked up and moved to Myrtle Beach. Could she make it there tonight?

That had brought a fresh wave of tears, and Kailani had told her no worries, she could rest here. Jane didn't mean to take her at her word, but she'd closed her eyes and dozed off.

Awakened by the low, bearish voice of the sheriff. And suddenly, it had all come back to her . . .

The rumble of his voice. The broad expanse of his chest in that white uniform shirt. The feel of his hands, sure and firm on her sinking body as he'd rescued her from the Jeep. She remembered kind eyes in a rare shade of blue, and that voice, like a friendly bear.

She'd opened her eyes and there he was, standing before her, arranging things and covering details. Between the two of them, he and Kailani seemed to have figured out where she was staying and when her car would be ready, which was awfully kind of them, though her city instincts made her suspect anyone who extended themselves when there was nothing in it for them.

Now, as the gray-haired doctor in a T-shirt and khaki shorts examined her, she felt a mixture of exhaustion from the shock and wariness of this place she'd been forced to stop in. Avon.

"Follow my fingers without turning your head," the doctor instructed, and Jane followed her instructions. There was a variety of drills, as well as questions about pain.

In the end, Ruthann pronounced her good to go tomorrow, after a night of sleep. "Sounds like you were in shock, but Kailani fixed you up just fine. And it doesn't seem like you hit your head at all, so that's good. But call me if anything starts to bother you tonight." She handed Jane her card. "Any questions?"

Jane looked at the card: Ruthann Pope, MD. "If you're a doctor, why do people call you Ruthann?"

"Because that's my name, and we don't stand much on formality here. Manners, yes. Some people call me 'Miss Ruthann,' if that makes you feel any better, but 'Dr. Pope' sounds a bit pompous, and I didn't much fancy being called 'Doctor Ruth.'" The doctor's serious demeanor gave way to a grin.

Jane felt herself smiling in response, the dark feeling lifting. "That didn't occur to me."

Ruthann handed her two sample packets of ibuprofen. "Take one or two of these if you start feeling achy later."

"Thank you." Jane looked down at her hands, which, thankfully, weren't shaking anymore. "I'm a little short on cash." And she didn't want to use a credit card, which would track where she'd been. "Can you send me a bill?"

"For ten minutes of my time, I'm willing to make this a freebie. Just as long as you follow my instructions and rest up. Stay off the road for the rest of the day."

"That's a deal," Jane said, thinking that her rented Jeep was going to be out of commission until the morning anyway. "Thank you."

When she followed the doctor out of the office, it was her first real chance to get a look at the Quickstop, a large space that sold everything from groceries to swimsuits. There were big displays of sunscreen and beach gear, sunglasses, souvenir shells, and miniature lighthouses and postcards. There was a newsstand with a large rack of paperback books, a pharmacy aisle, and a lunch counter with a lit glass case of warm fried chicken that made her mouth water. The line at the counter was three people deep, but Kailani and another young woman at the register moved customers through quickly.

"Jane, I'll be with you in a minute," Kailani said as she closed the drawer of her register.

Jane ventured to the book display by the window, amazed that the day had turned sunny again and the pavement was nearly dry except for a few puddles.

"You can carry this for your mother," Kailani told a young boy in a baseball cap as she handed him a plastic grocery bag. "Don't smash the bread, now."

Across from the gas pumps, Jane's Jeep was parked outside one of the garage bays. How had it gotten there? Someone must have moved it for her—probably the sheriff. The man with gentle hands and the voice of a bear.

"I'll give you a ride to the motel," Kailani said, coming up from behind her. "It's only half a mile down the road, but you've got bags and maybe you're too tired to walk."

"I'd appreciate a lift."

"I knew that. Rusty already put your bags in the back of our truck."

"Rusty?" The name didn't ring a bell.

"My husband. He's the one checking over your car."

Jane nodded as the picture began to take shape. "So you guys run the Quickstop?"

"Yeah. We run it. We own it, too."

It was a straight shot down Highway 12 in Kailani's pickup, and suddenly they were pulling into a little motel on the right side of the road. The turquoise trim and shutters on the white, two-story building reminded Jane of the tropics, and the grounds were tidy, with a garden-size pool and flower boxes.

"I'll take you in to meet Marvin," Kailani said, pointing Jane toward the door.

Jane liked the looks of the place, and relief washed over her at the prospect of not having to drive again until tomorrow. "I really appreciate you helping me out," she said. "The accident really rattled me and . . . thank you."

"You're welcome." Kailani smiled as she held the screen door open for Jane.

They rang the bell on the desk, and eventually an older man in jeans and a golf shirt came out of the office.

"This is Marvin," Kailani said. "He builds things." She turned to Jane. "This is the lady who got caught in the car crash."

"Sorry to hear that, but I'm glad to meet you," Marvin said. "It's lucky that I have a room, high season and all."

"Thank you," Jane said.

"You're welcome, but no one around here has the gumption to say no to Kailani. I'm happy to help out, and I always appreciate the business. Just got to tell you it can only be for one night. Need the room back tomorrow for a weeklong reservation."

"That's perfect." Jane signed the rate card and gave him seventy dollars cash. "I have to be on my way in the morning."

"Unit twelve." Marvin handed her the keys, then held the door as the women went out. When he insisted on carrying Jane's luggage, Jane decided she was beginning to like these people with kind actions and polite manners.

Kailani told her that the beach was a short walk just across the highway and the Pamlico Sound, not so good for walking but beautiful at sunset, was just behind the motel. They had passed a shopping center with takeout food and a small theater. "And you can always walk back to the Quickstop," she added.

"Best ice cream in town," Marvin said as he stowed her duffel bag in her room.

"Thank you. You've been very helpful."

If she had to be stuck somewhere, there were many worse places than Avon, North Carolina.

The sun poked out from behind a cloud as Kailani bid her good-bye. Yes, she was lucky to have landed in the lap of southern hospitality.

Inside the small, tidy room there wasn't much unpacking to be done since she was only staying one night, but she placed her travel case on the vanity by the sink and washed up. How heavenly it felt to press her face into a warm washcloth, steaming away the grime and sweat, the tension and lingering fear. Although the accident wasn't caused by Canby, she knew she couldn't let her guard down, but it was a relief to think that his men weren't onto her disappearance from New York just yet.

Once she was cleaned up, she pulled down the covers and closed the curtains. She needed rest—maybe just a nap. She tucked her feet under the sheets and let her head sink into the pillows. The bed was comfortable, the right combination of firm and cushy. She turned to her right, then her left, and she found her eyes following the glow of sunlight peeking in at the edge of the curtains.

The beach was just across the street, and it was still broad daylight. Why was she in bed?

She'd been so tired after the accident—utterly exhausted—but now, with sunlight nipping at her and the ocean calling, sleep wasn't going to come.

She switched her sandals to flip-flops, plunked on her floppy sun hat, and headed out. Two or three blocks, straight ahead, Kailani had said.

As she waited to cross Highway 12, she admired a nearby one-story house with arched windows and a white picket fence. There was a gravel parking lot and a charming sign out front that said it was Blue Water Realty.

A local realtor.

She was tempted to stop in, just out of curiosity, to see what some of these beach cottages went for, but she wouldn't be able to identify herself as a New York realtor. Besides, she reminded herself that the less contact she had with people, the better.

The side street on the beach side was chockful of cottages. Large and small buildings with wooden balconies, some with hot tubs. The larger cottages were surrounded by privacy fences, and as Jane passed, the unmistakable hum of a filter let her know they had their own swimming pools.

As she reached the end of the street, the path to the beach turned into a short boardwalk over the dunes. The two houses bordering the path were wedding cake mansions—huge, four-story buildings rimmed with balconies and sparkling with floor-to-ceiling windows. The massive buildings were on stilts, with room to park ten cars or more in the shade underneath.

Wow. As a high-end realtor, she'd seen some amazing structures, but these were grand cottages.

As she rose over the dunes and took in the expanse of blue ocean, thoughts of real estate faded. With its white sand and gently cresting waves, this was a beautiful stretch of beach.

"Better than the Hamptons," she said, thinking of her colleagues who bragged about summering in the pricey beach towns on Long Island. This beach was a true gem.

She kicked off her flip-flops and sighed as her feet sank into the warm sand.

If you ever feel lost, let the ocean be your point of reference, her mother used to say. *You always know where you are when you're standing on a shoreline.*

Mom had loved being near the water. It had been one of the reasons they'd lived on the shore of Lake Erie, and nearly every summer she'd dragged the whole family to Cape Cod, where they'd rented cottages in the same town so that they could meet at the beach by day and share dinners together at night.

Out on the water, three surfers bobbed on their boards, waiting for the perfect wave. It reminded her of TJ. She needed to call him back, but had wanted to wait until she was in a better place emotionally. Walking down the beach, with the warm ocean breeze lifting her hair and skirt, she realized she was getting to that place.

Since it was the dinner hour—after six—there was activity to the right on the poolfront decks and balconies of homes, but Jane mostly had the beach to herself as she walked along, cold water sweeping in and out around her ankles. She passed a young couple walking and a gaggle of kids fortifying their castle, which stood on the precipice of attack from the incoming tide.

There were a few handfuls of people out in chairs, reading or sleeping or sharing cold drinks. Most people smiled and nodded as she passed.

When she approached a bearded fisherman who stood in the surf tending a line with a bobber on it, she tossed out a question. "What are you fishing for?"

"This time of year, mostly croakers," he said. "Not too big, but they're good eating."

"Nothing like them. Are you using bloodworm bait?" she asked.

One side of his lips lifted in a subtle grin. "That's what they like."

"Yesterday, around this time, he caught a baby shark," called the woman from the chair. "About yay big." She held her hands out a yard or so.

"A shark?" Jane winced. "Really?"

"This is the time of day. Dusk and dawn," said the man with the beard. "That's when the sharks come in close to feed."

"Ooh." Jane danced away from the surf, smiling. "I think I'll walk a little closer to the land, then."

The woman's laugh carried on the breeze. "You have a good day now, sugar."

About a mile down, the beach turned inland and she followed

its jagged line to three abandoned cottages with boarded windows. The surf lapped at the support pylons. One of the homes had lost its front wall to the water. In a few hours, she suspected that the surf would be slapping at the front doors.

Jane stopped before she got too close, wary of broken glass and boards embedded in the sand near the damaged cottages. She suspected these were the ruins of the hurricane that had roared through this area last fall. She recalled news reports of how the main road had been washed out in five places, but she hadn't seen any sign of the remaining damage until now.

It was time to turn around.

As she rounded the point, she saw that the fisherman and his wife were still there, and the thought of fresh fish made her mouth water. She was hungry, and it was no wonder. Breakfast had been a long time ago.

"Did you enjoy your walk, sugar?" the woman called out to her.

"It's a beautiful stretch of beach, but I was sorry to see those houses lost to the sea. Was that from the hurricane?"

"Yes, ma'am, it was." The woman called her "ma'am," though she easily had twenty years on Jane. "It's sad, but when you live in these parts you get used to it. Every year the dunes shift a little. Then you get one of those hurricanes blowing through, and the ocean takes back some of the land and a few houses are lost to the sea. It happens every few years."

"Why don't the owners take the buildings down?" Jane asked.

"Who's got the money when you lose your house and the land it's sitting on? People just take what they can from the house and walk away."

Jane looked up the beach at the grand cottages. All this could be gone with one storm. Yes, things could change in a heartbeat; she'd seen how that worked. She turned back to the woman. "I take it you're a local?"

"All my life. I'm Carol Hawkins. That proud fisherman's my husband, Jimmy. We run Cappy's Fish and Tackle, over at the marina, but that's an early-morning business. Gives us the evenings to get Jimmy out here fishing."

"I'm Jane."

"And you're not from around here," the woman said with a sly smile.

"Just visiting, but I know a thing or two about storms. I grew up on Lake Erie."

"I've never been there," Carol said.

"How's the fishing?" Jimmy asked.

"Great for walleye or perch. My mom used to sauté them in flour and butter and they would melt in your mouth."

"You're making me hungry, Jane."

"I'm doing that to myself. Where's a good place to eat around here? Within walking distance."

Carol and Jimmy directed her toward the shopping center near her motel, telling her Bubba's Barbecue couldn't be beat. She thanked them and headed back down the beach with a new mission.

The sun sank low over the beach houses, a ball of red fringed by orange and pink clouds. *Red sky at night, sailor's delight,* Mom used to say. It boded well for good weather tomorrow. No more storms for her. This time tomorrow, she would be planning dinner with her brother in West Palm.

CHAPTER 4

"Bummer!" TJ's disappointment was clear. She had decided to place the call while waiting for her sandwich at Bubba's, a small storefront shop that smelled heavenly. Taking a seat at a window table, she switched the phone to her left ear. "But you're okay, right? And your rental?"

"A mechanic is looking it over, but it seems fine. I'll be back on the road early tomorrow morning."

"I'm sorry. This wouldn't have happened if I didn't steer you down to Axel in the Outer Banks."

"No worries. It's a beautiful place and the people here have been very helpful. Have you ever seen the beach here?"

"Many times. Pamlico Sound makes for great windsurfing. Kite surfing, too. There's a spot there called the Canadian Hole that's awesome for windsurfing. It's a destination."

"It really broke up that monotonous drive, but I'll be glad to finish the trip tomorrow. How's the cleanup going?"

"Don't worry; your room will be ready when you get here. Laura is at the store right now, getting a new bedspread. She didn't think the old moth-eaten blanket I've had since college was going to work for you."

"God bless Laura." She'd only met TJ's girlfriend once before, but she had liked her immediately. "Did you clear your gear out of the guest room?"

"That's what took me all day. Once we got to moving things . . ."

Though his voice was crystal clear, Jane lost focus when she turned toward the parking lot and noticed the police cruiser headed this way. Was it the sheriff? In a town this size, was Cooper Locklear the entire police force?

Please let it be him, she thought, then chastised herself for being so silly. The sheriff had seen her in shock, a definite low point. She should be embarrassed by that, but somehow she felt bonded to him, like a victim to a rescuer.

"Hello, hello?" came her brother's voice over the phone. "You still connected?"

"I'm going to go. My dinner's ready, so I'll call you later."

They said good-bye, her eyes never leaving the patrol car as it waited for a mother to cross with two little kids before it pulled into a spot.

When Cooper Locklear stepped out of the cruiser, she felt a little glow inside. It was him. Sheriff Locklear, on patrol, and stopping for a sandwich. Just like any other summer night in Avon, only the girl he had helped out earlier that day just happened to be in the sandwich shop.

She pressed a hand to her suddenly warm cheek. Would he remember her? Should she nod and say hi, or pretend to be digging for something in her purse?

Why was she thinking like a kid in junior high?

And then the door was open and before she could pull her thoughts together, he strolled in and looked her way.

"Well, hey, Miss Jane." His lips curved in a grin as he studied her. "You must have gotten a tip from a local, because you've found the best barbecue in North Carolina."

"I did."

"Excuse me one moment." He stepped up to the counter. "Hey, Andrew."

"Sheriff. The usual?"

"That sounds good. Except I might not want it to go today." Cooper turned toward her. "Are you dining here, Miss Jane?"

There was something surprising and charming about being called that. "I am."

"What I mean to say is, would you mind if I join you?"

"Sure. That'd be great."

She watched as he paid for his meal, taking a bottle of iced tea from the case. Earlier in the day she'd been too rattled to notice, but now she observed the way he filled out his uniform, solid, but probably not an ounce of fat on him. As he sat in the chair across from her, she wondered how one man could fill the room with so much energy and warmth.

"I hope I'm not imposing," he said as he sat down.

"No worries. I was just sitting here people watching."

"Then this works out for the both of us. No one should have to eat alone."

"Don't you have dinner with the deputies and other cops?" she asked.

"Our department is small, and we have to take our meal breaks one at a time."

"Do you ever go home for dinner?" she asked, wishing she could add, *And is there a wife waiting there?*

"As I said, no one should have to eat alone."

So . . . there was no wife at home. That was good to know, but surprising. How was it that a man as attractive as Cooper Locklear was still not hooked up with anyone?

Just then Andrew came over with two plastic baskets filled with fat sandwiches, chips, and slaw. "Orders are up."

"I thank you, Andrew." Cooper reached for the bottle of hot sauce.

"And I'm glad you brought a fork," Jane said, admiring the sandwich bun piled high with pulled pork.

"Enjoy." Andrew went back to take the order of a large family that was streaming in the door.

Jane's first petite forkful of pork truly melted in her mouth in a symphony of barbecue sauce and tender meat.

Cooper sighed over a mouthful, then swallowed. "Good eats."

"Delicious." And she hadn't eaten all day. Jane abandoned her fork, picked up the fat sandwich, and dug in.

"I'm glad to see you looking in the pink," the sheriff said. "How are you feeling?"

"Much better. I took a walk on the beach. You've got a beautiful stretch of ocean here."

"Our claim to fame. Though this stretch of land has come close to being wiped out a few times over the past two centuries."

"Hurricanes?"

"That and deforestation. This area originally was thick with forest—live oaks and cedars. In precolonial times, this town was the hub of the island because of its central location and all the lumber used for boat building. Back then the town was called Kinnakeet. Comes from the Algonquian word for 'that which is mixed.'" He paused to take a bite and wipe his mouth with a napkin. "Just stop me if I'm boring you."

"No, go on. I love the history of a place." It was one of the pluses of her job—to learn the history of old buildings in New York City. Places that had once been used to manufacture cigars or wool. Penthouses that had received gilded crown moldings from a wealthy resident. Apartments that had once been homes to famous composers, actors, or scholars. "So, what happened to the forests here?"

"Back in the 1800s, the commercial harvest stripped the land of trees. I guess that's what happens when you're the center of an industry at a time when eastern sea exploration is big. Once the trees were gone, the other vegetation died out within years. A massive sand dune formed to the west, pulling land mass from this area and shrinking it down to the skinny strip of land that it is today."

"I can see how erosion is a problem." She pressed a napkin to her mouth, energized and mellowed from the hearty meal. "Walking down the beach today, I saw a few houses that have been lost to the sea."

"Water is not a homeowner's friend." His blue eyes were thoughtful. "Still, there's nothing like an ocean view. When I look out over that surf, I know this is where I belong. It's like the waves call out to me, telling me that I'm in the right place."

"A point of reference." She stabbed the air with a pickle spear. "That's what my mother used to say."

"Exactly." He picked up the last of his chips and she wondered how he'd eaten his entire meal while talking. "But you're not here to vacation, like most people. Where are you headed?"

"Florida. I'm going to visit my brother," she answered, grappling for a way to turn the conversation away from her. She didn't want to give up any more personal details; as it was, the accident would leave enough of a paper trail here.

"Florida's going to be awfully hot this time of year. Sticky, too."

"It will. Thank God for AC."

"Are you going to take the ferry to Ocracoke, or drive back inland?"

"I haven't decided. But enough about me. You've done the paperwork. You've got my info. I think it's my turn to ask the questions." *Before you start digging too deep.*

"Okay. Knock yourself out."

"You're from around here?" she asked.

"Homegrown. I went to high school with Rusty, the owner of the Quickstop. We both had summer jobs in Nags Head."

"But there's something different about you." She narrowed her eyes, trying to pinpoint it. "Your accent; it's not as strong."

"I left for a while. Went to college at West Point. Six years in the service as an Army Ranger."

"So, you did leave home. Did you travel in the military?"

"My first assignment was North Korea. Then Afghanistan."

"Oh . . . wow." Jane had never met anyone who'd served in that difficult situation. "That must have been intense."

"You don't think about it much while you're in the thick of it. That's a big part of the problem. Your mind just shuts down. Then when it's all over, once you get home, all the horrors and tension come barreling toward you like a runaway train."

She paused, studying the tiny lines that fanned out at the outside corners of his eyes. So this was where he'd gained his wisdom; this was why Cooper Locklear was an old soul in a young man's body.

And yet, he didn't seem lost anymore, thank God.

"I can't imagine the pressure ... and all the difficult memories that you had to process." Had he dealt with post-traumatic stress? Had the military given him therapy—any assistance at all? She would have liked to know more, but didn't want to probe. "It's no wonder you decided not to make a career of the army."

"I did my time, but being under someone else's command wasn't for me in the long run. Someone tells you where to live, when you can see your family ... I couldn't abide by that for the rest of my life. I'm glad I served, but I couldn't wait to get home. I missed the sunshine and the ocean. I missed surfing and steamed crab and good barbecue like this. And boy, did I miss the people. Decent folk who care about their neighbors."

"Back in New York, most people don't even know their neighbors."

Amusement flickered in his eyes. "Then I guess that's one of the things that make Avon a little gold mine."

"So ... you came back here. And they just happened to have an opening for the sheriff's job, and you were a perfect match."

"I like the part about the perfect match, but there was a little nepotism involved. My old man used to be sheriff. He retired with the intention of handing the reins over to me."

"Oh, really? So law enforcement runs in the family."

"I like to think of it as public service," he said with a slow grin.

She smiled over her iced tea. "I'll give you that. You certainly saved my skin today. But it says a lot about this town that after traveling all around you chose to make it your home."

"I saw enough of the world to show me that Oz isn't what it seems." He took a draw of the tea, the lump on his neck working as he swallowed. "As Dorothy learned, there's no place like home."

Jane sensed that there was one hell of a story under his blithe paradigm, but it wasn't the sort of thing you'd spill to a stranger at Bubba's Barbecue.

"Words of wisdom." She looked down at the empty baskets on the table, wishing that she could go home. But really, she had no safe haven. Her apartment was luxurious, but it had served mostly as a showplace and a venue for entertaining clients. She had clearly outgrown the old house in Buffalo with Aunt Minnie, and she hadn't lived with TJ since he'd left for college. That was the problem with independence like hers. When you wanted to return to the nest, you turned around and found that it had been knocked out of its tree.

Cooper stacked their baskets and rose, and she was sorry that their time together was ending. "I thank you for the company, Miss Jane."

"You know, we've broken bread together, you can call me 'Jane.'"

He grinned and his whole face warmed. "Old habits die hard, but I'll try. Let me give you a ride home, Jane. It's getting dark out there."

She glanced out at the fading light, despite the indigo glow in the sky. "It's not far. I can walk."

"I wouldn't hear of it."

Secretly, she was glad, and it wasn't just the security of being accompanied by the local sheriff. Something about Cooper Locklear made her feel alive again, restored to her old self before terror had spilled into her life.

It was nice having doors opened and closed for her, being reminded to buckle her seat belt. It made her feel safe . . . even precious.

Sneaking a glance at him while he drove, Jane imagined that they were a couple on their way home after a quiet dinner out. How sweet that would be! Maybe they even had kids . . . and a dog.

Her throat knotted with emotion over the imaginary scenario. So simple, and yet so far from the reality of her day-to-day life.

Cooper's Oz imagery stuck in her mind.

There's no place like home . . .

All these years she'd been reaching for the next star, stirring up excitement, when the missing puzzle pieces weren't colored by any of those things. She'd been missing stability. A home on solid ground. A love that would last.

Settling into the seat of the police cruiser, she studied Cooper's handsome silhouette and allowed the dream to ease her heart . . . just for a moment.

CHAPTER 5

What a difference a few hours could make.

The smart, lovely lady beside him was nothing like the stunned, jittery mouse he'd pulled from the car late that afternoon. It was a marvelous twist of fate that had him walk into Bubba's that night, allowing him the reassurance of knowing that Jane Doyle would be just fine.

And now, just having her beside him in the car brought a new excitement to the evening. It was an effort to keep his eyes on the road when she was invading his psyche, her perfume softening the edges of the patrol car, her soft sigh easing his tension as she settled into the seat.

Too soon, he was turning into the parking lot of the motel, pulling up near the unit she pointed out. He put the car in park and turned to her.

"Thank you for . . . for everything," she said. The glow of the dashboard lights lit the smooth planes and curves of her face, and he had a crazy desire to run his fingertips over the creamy skin along her jawline. "I don't know what I would've done without your help today."

"No need for thanks." It would be so easy to reach over and touch her, but he restrained himself, his hands gripping the steering wheel. "I'm glad I ran into you tonight, Miss Jane. A lot of time in my line of work I see people at their worst. People in accidents.

Evacuating hurricanes. Folks all beat-up from barroom brawls or domestic disputes. It's good to see a happy ending for a change."

"I don't know about a happy ending," she said wistfully, "but I'm glad we ran into each other, too. It looks like my luck is changing."

"That, or you're good at turning lemons into lemonade."

"I don't know about that, either. But thanks and . . ."

She turned to him, her face tipping up toward his, and suddenly he wondered if she meant for him to kiss her. Was that possible?

The breath stalled in his lungs and the air between them warmed as he considered taking her in his arms, pulling her close, pressing his lips to hers . . .

In a patrol car? Kissing the victim of an accident? What the hell happened to his ethics and his sanity? Reality seeped back into the edges of his consciousness and he turned away.

"Okay." She sighed. "I have to ask you a favor."

"Sure thing." He dropped his right hand from the steering wheel, then turned back toward her, and his fingers caught the edge of Leah's card sticking out from between their seats. Damn, but it wasn't the first time Leah Pope had come between him and another woman. The reminder of his ex-girlfriend dampened his spirits like the cold glass of water that was Leah. Suddenly the temperature in the car seemed cooler, the air thick with regret.

"You know, I hate to do this. I feel like a total wimp, but . . ." She looked out the window, her focus intent on the little room she was renting for the night. "Would you mind checking out my room?"

He cocked his head. "You want me to come inside?"

"If you don't mind. There's this . . . this fear I have of finding someone else in there. Walking in on a robber or just some creep. It will only take a second."

"Of course. I'm happy to do it." In a second, he was out of the car, moving around to get Jane's door for her. "You got the key?"

She handed over a key on a large plastic disk with the motel name. Without a thought, he opened the door and stepped in. No real need for caution; he knew that Marvin ran a pretty tight ship.

Inside, the room was nicer than he remembered. A robin's egg blue on the walls. A double bed with a dark wood headboard and printed quilt. All tidy and clean and smelling of lemon. The bathroom window was locked tight. Front windows, too.

"Looks fine to me," he told Jane, who had crossed the threshold gingerly. "But hold on and I'll check the closet." The small space was empty but for a small safe and a rack of hangers. "It's all clear."

"Thank you." She threw up her hands. "I seem to be doing a lot of that."

"It's my job to help. My pleasure, too." He went straight to the door, not wanting to tangle ethics and emotions again. "I enjoyed talking with you, Miss Jane." He paused on the patio, just beyond the threshold. Safe outside. "Next time you head down this way, you'll have to stay a while."

"I'd like that." She leaned on the doorjamb, a sheen on her dark hair from the yellow outdoor lights.

He put two fingers to his forehead in a sort of salute. "Safe travels. You take care now."

"Good night," she said. Then the door closed behind her.

Talk about a long, torturous good-bye. He kept his eyes on the ground as he got into the cruiser. He drove off without looking back.

Cooper's shift was nearly over when he got a call from Brenda, the night dispatcher.

"Dale would like you to meet him at the Quickstop. He's having trouble with his cruiser. Might need a lift."

"Ten-four." The cruiser's lights swept the parking lot as he turned into the Quickstop. The three garage bays were closed up tight for the night, but the Avon police car was parked in front of the center garage. Rusty and Deputy Dale Martin stood beside the unit.

Cooper stepped into the dark, humid night and joined them. "What's up?"

"Car keeps stalling on me," he said. "I jumped it a few times, but now it won't turn over. Rusty came and gave me a tow."

"The battery is good," Rusty said. "Looks like the alternator. I'll take a closer look in the morning, but I was about to head home for the night. Unless you need to have the car."

"Nah. That's okay. You can use mine, Dale." He fished the car keys from his pocket and tossed them to Dale, one of two cops working the night shift.

"I was just hoping for a loaner from Rusty," Dale said, swinging the keys in one hand. "I never expected to be riding around in the sheriff's car."

"It works like any other cruiser," Cooper said. "Just keep it clean inside. I got no tolerance for old coffee cups. And no smoking."

"Got it." Dale tipped two fingers toward them, then strode toward the car.

"Pretty finicky about your car, Coop." Rusty tipped back the brim of his Rangers baseball cap. "You sound like my wife."

Cooper bumped him on the shoulder. "You aren't allowed to make wisecracks about Kailani. You're lucky she puts up with you."

"I know that. Too bad we never found a girl with the grit to put up with you."

They were laughing when Dale approached, back from the cruiser. "Sheriff? In the name of keeping the vehicle clean, I just thought you might want to hold on to this." He held out the card with the puppy on it—the note from Leah.

"Crap." Trying to ignore the sting of embarrassment, Cooper took the card. "Thanks, Dale. You know I want to take this home and, uh . . . put it into my puppy scrapbook."

"I had a feeling, sir."

The three men looked at one another, then burst out laughing.

"All right." Cooper shook his head. "That's the last time I check my mail while on duty."

Dale sighed, wiping tears from his eyes. "It's great to start the shift with a good laugh. Thanks, Coop."

As Dale drove off, Rusty gestured toward the card. "What the hell is that? A birthday card from your little nieces?"

With a growl, Cooper waved him off. "You don't want to know."

When Rusty scowled, Cooper answered, "It's a Dear John letter from Leah, just a few years too late."

"Gimme." Rusty grabbed the card and opened it up. "From Leah." He read silently. "Oh. Oh. She's getting married."

"So she says."

"And how do you feel about that, tough guy?"

"Relieved that she won't be stalking me anymore. Sorry for the poor sucker she's latched on to."

"Now, now, let's be charitable. That girl did wait for you the whole time you were in West Point."

"All four years. Then when the going got tough, when I was freezing my nuts off in North Korea, she hightailed it to Charlotte and took a job working in a girly bar. Can you imagine how it feels to hear that your girlfriend is working in a place like that?"

"I heard she was working on the modeling career," Rusty said.

"Whatever. The point is, I ended it then, and once I said it was over she refused to let go."

"She always had a stubborn streak."

"Like a mule. I always wonder how Ruthann deals with her. Daughter of a doctor who goes off track like that. At least Ruthann never held my part against me," Coop said.

"Ruthann knows it's not your fault. Folks say that she and Leah had a screaming match one day at the go-karts in Rodanthe. After that, they didn't talk for years, but that's probably not hard with Leah living over in Charlotte."

Coop lifted a hand. "I kept out of their business and tried to stay away from Leah. I never wanted to be downright mean to her, but it was coming to that. This is all for the best. I hope the wedding is real soon."

Rusty looked over the card once more and handed it back to Cooper. "This is good, Coop. Good that she's moving on. Good to get it off your chest. We haven't talked about Leah in years. I always wondered when she came in town. Thought maybe you two were friends with benefits."

"You kidding me?" Coop scowled. "That's not my speed. Nah, I've kept my distance."

"Saint Cooper." Rusty clapped him on the shoulder. "We gotta get you a woman, man. I'm going to keep my eyes open for you."

"Don't do me any favors."

"That's what friends are for," Rusty said earnestly, making Cooper feel like a total loser.

Rusty dropped him at home so that he could pick up his car for the last half hour of the shift. Cooper could have cut it short and stayed home, but he didn't like taking liberties, figuring that the head of the department needed to model good behavior and all that.

He had just clocked out when a call came from the Salty Dog, a bar/billiards hall next door to Golden Pizza. Brenda told him someone needed a ride home.

It was the bartender's way of asking to have someone removed before they became a problem.

The parking lot was crowded with shiny SUVs and sports cars. One look inside the bar, and he understood the crowd.

Frat boys.

Cooper wove through the room, chatting as he passed the tables. "Hey. How's it going? Nice night." He kept low-key, testing the waters, getting a read on the situation, the players, the potential for danger.

When he reached the bar, Cracker, the bartender, came right over.

"Evening, Sheriff. Can I get you a water?"

"That'd be great. With a lot of ice, please." Cooper spoke to the old-timer sitting beside him at the bar. "Frank. How's everything?"

Frank lifted his head, but couldn't seem to come up with an answer.

"Got a lot of Greeks here tonight," Cooper said when Cracker handed him the water. "University crowd?"

"Newland College," Cracker said. It was a private school, closer to Avon than the U in Columbia. Cracker leaned closer. "Some of the kids had a little brawl a few minutes ago. Bloody nose. I was ready to toss them all, but the troublemaker's buddies hauled him out of here fast enough."

Cooper looked around the room. "Seems pretty tame now."

"I think this crowd is going to be okay." Cracker plucked two empties from down the bar. "But Frank here needs a ride home."

"I got my car!" Frank sputtered suddenly.

"I know you do," Cracker said.

"But nobody wants you using it," Cooper said. He didn't fancy having to lock Frank up for the night. "You can come pick your car up in the morning. I'll give you a lift for now. You ready?"

Frank lifted his head and gestured toward the door. His eyes were bloodshot, his face unnaturally red.

"Okay. Let's go, then."

With his head down, Frank managed to motor along on his feet, at least until they got to the parking lot. Instead of following Cooper, he paused on the wood walkway, staring. "Where's er pllleese car?" he muttered.

"Got a car in the shop, Frank. You get to ride in the luxury of my private wheels." Cooper went back to the walkway to guide Frank to his car. "Come on, now. Slow and easy."

Frank lunged to the left, stumbling in an odd diagonal from car to car until he made it to Cooper's Ford Escape. "Are you on duty, Sheriffff? Or just being a good S'maritan?"

"Whatever works to get you into the car, buddy." He was off the clock, but he didn't mind taking Frank home. Some weeks he did a bar run every night. It wasn't the prettiest form of philanthropy, but it kept Cooper out of the bars himself, and he figured it was all payback for the people who had helped him out of the black hole he'd been sucked into when he got home from Afghanistan.

Cooper opened the door for him, but Frank paused to announce, "I think I had one too many."

"You got that right." Cooper buckled the older man in, then closed the door securely.

As he started the car, he turned to Frank, who was staring blindly ahead. "You still living on Cross Way, beyond the foot-bridge?"

"Till my wife throws me out," Frank answered.

Cooper laughed. A drunk with a sense of humor. "Okay, Frank. Let's get you home."

As they cruised down Highway 12, he slowed near the motel, checking the windows of the units.

Jane's lights were still on.

Was she still up, reading or watching TV? He mulled it over, wishing he could stop in on his way home. But that was crazy. He barely knew the girl.

Besides, she probably left the light on while she was sleeping. Anyone who has someone else check the closets is definitely a bit of a chicken. A scaredy cat, his sisters used to say.

She'd be gone in the morning, but he had to admit, Jane Doyle was a good example of the kind of girl he'd go for these days. Smart and heartachingly pretty with that dark hair and eyes as blue as the ocean. A girl who thought about things before she blurted them out of her mouth. And her size—so small and petite. When she'd fallen out of the Jeep and into his arms, she felt so light, he could've lifted her with one hand.

We gotta get you a woman, Rusty had said.

It was embarrassing to think that way once you hit your thirties. Still, if Cooper was seriously looking, he'd be after a girl like Jane Doyle. A girl just like Jane.

CHAPTER 6

Gulls cried overhead as a wave slapped the sand, sending a fine mist in Jane's direction. She breathed in the salty spray, reveled in it as she kept running.

When she'd awoken that morning to the distant roar of the ocean, she had pulled her running gear out of her duffel bag. Of course, there was time for a run before she left, and it would be the perfect way for one last journey down this beautiful stretch of beach.

Now, as she slowed her pace for the final stretch back to the path, she was sorry she had to go. This beach held a distinct serenity that spoke to her heart with its endless miles of pale sand and rhythmically curling waves. Maybe it was its distant location on this thin barrier island; maybe it was the kind people she'd met here yesterday. It was a special place.

You'll see plenty of beaches down in Florida, she told herself. But wouldn't it be fun to return here? She could bring TJ and Laura, too. He could go windsurfing at that spot that he'd mentioned. Under different circumstances, it would be a fun vacation.

She decided to shower and pack up, then walk down to the Quickstop for breakfast and her Jeep. A breeze cooled her walk, though the sun promised a hot day ahead. It was a relief to step into the coolness of the Quickstop, where Kailani greeted her from behind the register.

"Aloha. You look healthy today."

"I feel much better," Jane said.

"Rusty has your car ready."

"Perfect. I'm going to grab a quick bite before I go."

"It doesn't have to be so quick," Kailani said, looking over at the luncheonette counter. "You'll get indigestion."

Becca, the girl over at the counter, told her that the fruit salad had just been cut up, the cinnamon rolls baked that morning. Jane wasn't a huge fan of sweets, but the warm cinnamon bun melted in her mouth.

As Kailani handed her the Jeep keys and gave her a hug goodbye, Jane felt a twinge of regret. "I hope we meet again sometime," she said.

Kailani patted her hand. "We will."

If I make it through the summer and the trial in September, I will definitely come back, Jane promised herself as she inspected the rear bumper of her Jeep—barely a scratch!—and climbed inside.

It was a straight shot down the road to pick up her things. She had just made the turn into the motel lot when her cell phone jangled. She grabbed the phone and slowed for the parking lot. It was TJ.

"Hey, hi! I am just about to head off. I got the ferry schedule for Ocracoke, and—"

"Hold on a minute," he said. "Are you in a safe place?"

Something in his voice scared her. She put the Jeep in park and cut the engine. "Sure. What's up?"

"I got a weird phone call last night. Someone looking for you."

That familiar sick feeling seeped into her chest. "Are you sure it wasn't someone from Tia's family?" she asked.

"This was no friend of yours."

"Or someone from work? My boss, Murray, is hardly warm and fuzzy, and we have some real vipers in the office." Murray Diamond, owner of the agency, was notorious for his aggressive approach to colleagues and clients.

"Jane, no. I don't want to scare you, but . . . no. This was one of Canby's guys. He didn't say that, but he was menacing. He made threats."

As if an alarm had sounded, Jane was on alert. "What did he say—his actual words?"

TJ's sigh was nearly a growl. "At first he was acting like a business associate. Asking if I was your brother. When I said yeah, he wanted to know where you were. But it wasn't like he sounded worried about you. When I told him that you live in New York, he got nasty. Said he knew that, but where were you *now*? Of course, he said it in more vivid language."

"Oh, no." Her heart was beating so fast, it seemed to rattle in her chest.

She had suspected that Canby would send someone after her, but knowing that it was true just ratcheted everything up a notch.

"When I asked for his name, told him I was going to call the police, he just laughed," TJ said. "But before he hung up, he told me to give you a message. He said to tell you that you can run, but you can't hide."

She shivered, despite the warm sun beating down on the car.

She had been right to flee her home.

She was safer on the run.

But now that they knew about TJ . . .

"This changes everything," she said quietly. "Do you think they know that I'm on my way to stay with you?"

"I don't know, but I don't really think it's a good idea anymore. You know you're always welcome here, but this condo unit is hardly a fortress. What if they come here looking for you?"

"I didn't think they'd go that far."

"I didn't either, but now, after talking to that guy? I wouldn't put it past him."

"You're right. I mean, how hard is it to hop on a plane, rent a car?" She hadn't flown to Florida because she didn't want to leave a paper trail, but for someone else, someone who made it their business to hunt people down, having their name on an airline roster really wouldn't matter.

"I'm sorry, Janey. I should have thought of this."

"It's not your fault."

"And now, you're stuck in the middle of nowhere."

Fear hardened in her heart and she smacked the steering wheel. "Dammit. I should have gotten more money out of the bank before I left. But they don't make it easy. Do you know there's a three-hundred-dollar-per-day limit on withdrawals from an ATM?"

"Are you short on cash?"

"Not yet, but the money I took out isn't going to last me all summer."

"We'll figure that out down the road. I can wire you cash or something. Right now, you need a place to stay for a while. A place with a decent law enforcement community."

Immediately, she thought of Sheriff Cooper Locklear.

"Let me get on the Crackberry and see what comes up when I Google 'top ten witness protection cities,'" TJ said with his characteristic dry wit.

"You do that." She took a breath, thinking back over how careful she'd been since she'd left New York. She had paid cash for everything. She had told people she was going camping up north. She hadn't left a paper trail—and she was going to keep it that way. "And I'll think about my next stop . . . a place to spend the night. Taking it one day at a time."

Since she was in the motel parking lot, she started in the office of Avon-by-the-Sea.

"I'm right sorry, Miss Jane." Marvin squinted as he leafed through his calendar. "I wish I could help you out, but I'm full up for the next three weeks."

"Are there other motels in town?" she asked.

"We got a couple of motels and B-and-Bs here, but they're going to be booked, too, what with today being Friday and most schools ending just this week."

It was Friday? Somehow she'd lost track of what day of the week it was.

"I need a place for tonight," she said, "but I wouldn't mind committing to a week or two. Would that help?"

He scratched his scruffy chin with the tip of the pen. "Could be. I'll give you the numbers for the other motels so you don't have to drive all over town. If that doesn't work out, you can try the realtor right out here. Blue Water. They might have something you could rent for a week or so."

She thanked him, then went outside to call the other motels. It soon became clear that there was no room at any of the inns.

"Time for Plan B," she said as she gathered her belongings from the small motel room and loaded them into the Jeep. If she couldn't rent a small condo from Blue Water Realty, she would have to move on. Once she got inland, she knew she'd have a better shot at finding a room.

But in her heart, she felt destined to stay here for a while, near the beach that spoke to her, close to kind, caring neighbors, under the watch of an honest, kind sheriff.

She decided to leave the Jeep in the motel lot and walk down to Blue Water. The office was quiet, the reception desk empty, but she heard someone talking in an office to the right of a small fountain.

"Hello?" Jane moved toward the office, catching the eye of the woman behind the desk.

"Oh, sorry! I didn't know someone was out there." She popped out of her desk chair and came out of the office. "Look, I gotta go. Call you back in a bit," she murmured, then pressed a button on her headset. "I forgot—Liz stepped out. What can I help you with?"

"I was talking with Marvin over at the motel," Jane said, deciding to do some name dropping for leverage. "He thought you might have something small in Avon that I can rent for a week or two?"

"Something small . . . let's take a look." She motioned Jane into the office. "I'm Jolene Revels." She had dark hair that was cut to fall gently around her face, round dark eyes, and high cheekbones that gave the impression of a smile.

"Jane Doyle."

"Nice to meet you, Jane." Jolene reached across the desk to shake hands, then plopped into the chair and tapped a few keys on the keyboard. "Is it just you or do you need room for friends and family?"

"It'll be just me. I'm ... taking a sabbatical from work."

"That sounds wonderful!" Jolene said, her eyes on the computer monitor. "And what's your price range?"

"On the low end." Jane wrung her hands under the desk. How strange to be on this side of a real estate transaction. Jolene knew her stuff, but Jane felt a strong urge to push her out of the way, take her seat, and key in the data to hone in on exactly what she was looking for.

Jolene showed her photos of a two-bedroom house on the sound that had its own hot tub. It was beautiful, but too pricey for Jane.

Then there were photos of a cottage that looked as if it had been built in the 1800s. Between the knotty pine on the walls and the stains that showed even in photos of the carpeting, Jane had to decline. "It's a little too rustic for me."

"Rustic!" Jolene laughed. "I'll say, but that's a nice way of putting it. Maybe we should put that word in the online description."

Next, Jolene showed her the downstairs apartment of a two-story home. "It's a one-bedroom. You've got the property owner on the second story. Your unit would have total privacy unless you want to use the hot tub, which is on the upper deck. That you would have to share with the landlord."

"That would work," Jane said, thinking that she could do without the hot tub to maintain her privacy. Jolene swiveled the monitor so that Jane could have a look. It struck her as clean and streamlined, with bleached wood floors, a fireplace, a shiny kitchen with granite counters, and tall windows. "It looks nice."

"This is a good one," Jolene agreed. "And I know the property owner personally. He's a sweetheart."

In one photo, the sun was setting over the water in the distance. "Does it really have a view of the ocean?" Jane asked.

"That's Pamlico Sound. Pretty, isn't it? It's available now. Do you want to go take a look?"

At this point, Jane was ready to put her money down, but she didn't want to appear too eager. "Let's go check it out."

The exterior of the house on Sea Breeze Road was similar to most others on the block, covered with wood shingles and propped open with windows and skylights. The trim had been painted robin's egg blue, as if in an homage to the sea a few yards down the road.

"The downstairs deck is part of the rental," Jolene said, looking at her listing. "We had a renter here for Memorial Day, but it's been empty since then." She turned the key and opened the door. "Oh! Well. That's not good."

Curious, Jane stepped in behind her to find a shrink-wrapped cube of clean linens sitting on the pale wood floor. A few cups and cans were scattered on the kitchen counter. Remnants of the last occupants.

"This property was supposed to be cleaned weeks ago." Jolene frowned at the printout of the listing. "That's annoying, and it's not the first time. I'd fire the cleaning service, but at this time of year, we can't survive without them."

"Do you work exclusively with one service?" Jane asked.

"We have some ladies who have their own businesses, too. It's mostly summer work, but when it's busy, it's hopping. Most of these rentals turn around on Saturday or Sunday, so we've got crews whipping through between tenants on the weekends."

As they talked, Jane surveyed the apartment, which, despite the mess, had a good feel to it. The pale wood floors gave it a beachy feel and the windows opened the rooms up to air and light.

They peeked into the bedroom. "Kind of small," Jolene said.

"But cozy. And the living space is so wide open." Jane gave it another look as hope bubbled up inside her. This would actually be a lovely place to spend the summer.

"Do you want to check out the shared hot tub?" Jolene asked. "The landlord's a really nice guy. Salt of the earth. You'd have nothing to worry about with him."

Jane shook her head. "That's okay. I'm sold on it." The price was reasonable, but her budget was limited. "Do you need a week in advance?"

"One week up front. The balance by next Saturday. Unless you just want a week? Or if you want longer, there's a discount on the monthly rental rate. This one's a little hard to rent, since it really only suits one or two people."

"I'll take it for a month." The words were out before Jane processed the ramifications. Her cash would be depleted, and what if she had to move on?

To hell with the what-ifs, she thought, running her hand over the cool granite counter and watching a yellow-and-red–striped kite make its way down the sound. She needed a place and this was perfect.

"I'll get someone in here to clean for you," Jolene said, "hopefully by this afternoon."

"Can I get a discount if I clean it myself?" Jane asked, surprising herself yet again. "The work would be therapeutic and I could use the money."

Jolene folded the listing and patted Jane's shoulder. "Really? Aren't you the enterprising tenant. Darlin', I can cut the cleaning fee off your rent, for sure."

"And you can come back and check it out when I'm done." Jane's mind was spinning ahead. "If you like what you see, you can add my name to your list of house cleaners."

"Jane Doyle, you are the most industrious Yankee vacationer I've ever met." Jolene's face lit in an enthusiastic grin. "But you know, I think we can help each other. If you're willing to scrub your little behind off, I'll give you as much summer work as you can handle."

"I'd appreciate that."

"Oh, honey." Jolene laughed. "Come back and tell me that after you've cleaned one of those nine-bedroom castles on the beach."

"I can handle it," Jane said. After all, she had cleaned rooms in a hotel during her summer breaks from college. She was no stranger to hard work. "Trust me, I'll get the job done."

"I've no doubt you will."

"About the landlord . . ." Jane paused. She wasn't completely thrilled with having her landlord overhead, but Jolene had assured her that he was a good guy. "Will he want to screen me first? I mean, it is his home."

"Oh, no. He'll trust me on this one. But truthfully, I can't wait for him to meet you. He's going to love you." Jolene's smile faded abruptly. "I mean, in a platonic way, of course. And you can feel real safe here. Our town sheriff lives upstairs. He's the owner of the property."

"The sheriff?" Jane laughed in disbelief. What were the chances of that?

"Yep. The owner of the house is our very own sheriff, Cooper Locklear. Oh, we forgot the balcony! Come on out and I'll just point out the hot tub to you."

Jane couldn't deny feeling pleased at the thought of Cooper Locklear living one floor above her. As she stepped out into the sunshine of the balcony, she couldn't help but feel that fate had put Cooper in her path once again. Maybe he was meant to be her protector. Maybe God was shining down on her again. What was that saying her mother always used? When God closes a door on you, he always opens a window.

Leaning against the balcony rail, she looked up at Cooper Locklear's house and smiled.

So many windows.

CHAPTER 7

"You got a minute?" Jolene asked Cooper when he pulled over in the cinema parking lot to take her call.

"Sure. What's up?"

"You know that lady I told you about—the new tenant for your downstairs apartment?"

Jolene had called him earlier that day to say that she'd found a renter, probably for the summer. "Right. Is there a problem?"

"No problem. I just want you to see this with your own eyes. Meet me at your place."

Cooper shifted in his seat, concerned. "Okay . . . but I hope it's not one of those bad surprises like she ran her car through the garage door or poisoned my dog."

"Just meet me there," Jolene said quickly before she ended the call.

When he pulled up, Jolene's car was in the driveway and she was waving to him from the back deck. Knowing her, she'd probably broken the speed limit to get here. Coop had known Jolene and her husband, Mitch, for a few years now, since they'd moved here from Philly with their two young sons. They were good people, but sometimes Jolene was a little pushy for his taste.

"Hey, Coop! Come on and step inside here and take a look. Nice and clean, isn't it?"

Even from the threshold, he could see the luster of the floor. The granite counters were so shiny you could see your reflection in them and the stainless appliances were burnished smooth, without a single smudge. "I've never seen this apartment so spic and span."

Jolene shrugged, hiding a giggle. "Told you." She shot a look over her shoulder. "Your new tenant did it. I think she's a find."

He hadn't seen surfaces gleam so bright since his time in the army.

"Pretty good, right?" Jolene asked. "I'm going to hire her to do some of the big beach houses. And Coop, you should get her to do your place, too." She nodded toward the upstairs. "Scary to think that a man and a dog are living up there with no one cleaning up."

"I'm a tidy guy," he said defensively. Right now the last thing he wanted was some old lady meddling in his stuff, picking up his dirty boxers and rooting through his fridge.

"Oh, there you are! Honey, I hope you don't mind, but I brought your landlord over to take a look at your handiwork," Jolene called down the hall toward the bedroom.

Coop turned away from the kitchen to meet the new tenant, but there was no old lady. It was Jane coming down the hall demurely. She wore thin spandex shorts that showed off shapely legs, yellow rubber gloves, and an oversized gray T-shirt. Her hair was pulled back in a ponytail . . . and she looked gorgeous.

"Miss Jane?"

"Hi, Sheriff." She held her gloved hands away from her and wiped her chin with the sleeve of her shirt. "I didn't know you were stopping by."

"That was my doing," Jolene said proudly. "I thought you two should meet since you'll be sharing the same house."

"I didn't know you were still in town." Cooper tried to get his mind to fast-forward, process the details more quickly. "And you're renting my apartment?"

"If that's okay."

"Of course it's okay," Jolene said. "Coop's been telling me he wanted to rent for the summer instead of week to week. You're exactly what Coop has been looking for."

Isn't that the truth, Coop thought. Jolene sure did have a knack for stripping away the trimmings and getting to the heart of the matter. Though this time, she probably didn't realize how her words had hit home.

"I was just telling Cooper how he ought to hire you to clean up his place upstairs, too." Jolene went on as if the air wasn't as volatile as gunpowder. "We're both way impressed with your work."

"Thank you, but it's not brain surgery." Jane wiggled off the rubber gloves and dropped them in the sink. "Not that I'm not happy to have the work. There's just no art to it."

"If you're reliable and consistent, you'll make more than any artist in the Outer Banks," Jolene said, looking from Coop to Jane and back to Coop again. "And why didn't you two tell me you already knew each other?"

"How was I to know Miss Jane was the lady you were talking about?" Coop pointed out. "And we don't know each other well."

"The sheriff handled a motor vehicle accident yesterday, and I was one of the drivers."

"And I thought Miss Jane was moving on this morning." In fact, she'd been emphatic about it. Going down to visit her brother in Florida. He studied her, wanting to ask why she had changed her mind, but not wanting to open a can of worms in front of Jolene, who could spread a story faster than Facebook.

"Well, Miss Jane is staying right here, and you two are going to have a chance to get to know each other much better." There was a touch of mischief in Jolene's smile that made Cooper uncomfortable.

Or was it the whole setup—having an attractive, single girl living in his downstairs apartment? Normally he'd consider that a recipe for scandal and disaster, but there was something different about Miss Jane. Call it integrity. Call it backbone. Either way, his instincts told him he wouldn't have problems renting to her.

The radio speaker on his shoulder crackled and his hands automatically went to the button there. "Sector one-two."

"We've got a middle-age man down in the parking lot at the Safeway," Brenda said. "ETA for the paramedics is eighteen minutes."

"Copy." He turned to the women. "I have to go. But thank you, ladies. I'm glad to have the place rented, and to a real tidy person. And welcome, Miss Jane."

A chorus of good-byes followed him out the door as he slid into his cruiser, wondering how women did that. They got into your house and your life and changed things around, setting the planet spinning on a different axis.

It wasn't a bad thing; just distinctly female.

After work when he pulled into the driveway, Miss Jane's Jeep was parked in front of the house. Good. He'd bought steaks for two, figuring that it was a fit welcome for a new renter and neighbor.

There was no answer when he knocked on the front door. Maybe Miss Jane wanted her privacy. He would respect that. But she might change her mind when she got a whiff of these steaks grilling.

He set to his usual routine, drinking two tall glasses of water, changing into shorts, listening to the evening news on television. When he opened up the sliding glass door to turn on the grill, there she was in the distance, walking along the path by the water.

Behind her, the sky was awash with color. It was going to be another amazing sunset. He stood there a moment, taking it all in. Though he'd lived in this town most of his life, he still stopped to marvel over a beautiful sunset. Life was short; you only got one sunset a day. You just couldn't waste something like that. But today there was the double wonder of a beautiful sky and a lovely young woman moving amid the tall grass, graceful as a sea fairy.

He threw skewers of vegetables on the hot grill, stepping back from the heat as footsteps sounded on the steps.

"Hey, Miss Jane," he called. "I'm grilling some steaks and you're welcome to join me."

He went to the rail and saw her peering up from the landing. Her hair was still in that cute ponytail and her cheeks had gotten some healthy color in the sun.

"That's nice of you, but I don't want to impose."

"It's a tradition around here. You get a new neighbor, you'd better make sure they're well fed and on your side."

She laughed. "I doubt you make too many enemies, Sheriff."

"Please, call me 'Coop.' And I try to keep it friendly with most folks. But really, can you smell those peppers? And the roasted onion. I leave it on the grill till it gets nice and tender. Goes great with steak."

Jane put a hand up to block the sun, as if she needed to get a better read on his expression. "Okay. I accept your invitation, but only if you let me bring something. Some wine? Or are you a beer drinker?"

"These days I stay away from that stuff, but I don't mind if you imbibe."

"I don't need to. How about dessert? Ice cream?"

"Now you're talking."

"I'll grab it from the freezer and be right up."

As Cooper tended the grill, Jane set two places at the outdoor table and poured two tall glasses of lemon water. She found the steak knives and brought the salt and pepper shakers out. In a few minutes, they were sitting down to a meal that made his mouth water, and sitting down to a real nice table at that.

"We work well together," he said.

"We do." She handed him a glass of water. "To teamwork," she said.

They clinked glasses and he took a long drink. "I know I didn't have any lemons in my fridge."

She laughed. "I like to keep them in a bowl. The color is so cheerful. Though you don't really need that out here, with this." She gestured toward the sky, the water, the encroaching night.

"Yeah, it's a beautiful place we live in." And not everyone appreciated it. The image of Leah popped into his mind as he recalled how she had sat right here at this same table, telling him she had to get out of this "backwards town." That was two or three years ago, in his darker days.

Pretty pathetic to think that the last woman he'd had dinner with, if you didn't count his sister, had been Leah Pope. And years ago, he'd promised himself that he would never get involved in a woman's drama. Never again.

And now here he was, sharing dinner and a sunset with a girl with cheeks pink from the sun and eyes as blue as the ocean. He was coming close to breaking his promise. Granted, Miss Jane was not another Leah, but he sensed that she had her own drama to play out—something mysterious that she tried to keep tamped down.

The fear that had gripped her after the car accident—that was more than shock. He didn't know what or who had wounded her, but Jane Doyle was definitely afraid of someone.

Someone had put that wounded look in her eyes.

Cooper wasn't going to let anyone hurt her here, not on his watch. Sure, he was a sworn peacekeeper, but his protective instincts ran much deeper than any occupation would allow. She trusted him, he could see that. And maybe she thought of him only as a friend. If that was true, he would have to deal with it.

But either way, he was going to look out for her.

I got your back, Miss Jane, he thought as she made a production of scooping ice cream for him. *I got your back.*

CHAPTER 8

Placing her empty buckets outside the house called Sea Sprite, Jane sighed with the deep-felt satisfaction of a job well done. Despite its name, Sea Sprite was hardly pixie-size, with its ten bedrooms and two full living areas. It had taken her six hours to clean the sand, grime, mold, and mildew from the house, but now the mansion sparkled, clean and fresh for its next lucky inhabitants. With a feeling of pride, she stepped outside, buffed the entry tiles to a shine, and locked the door behind her.

Since she'd arrived in Avon five days ago, she had cleaned seven palatial beach homes, all containing numerous bedrooms with en suite bathrooms that had required a good amount of scrubbing.

Kailani had questioned her about the interiors of the houses. The other store clerks had wandered over to listen in, and even Ruthann had expressed curiosity.

"Just because we're islanders, doesn't mean we've ever been able to go inside," Kailani had explained during one of Jane's many visits to the Quickstop.

So Jane had told them about the house with the swimming pool built like a pirate's ship. "Walk the plank and you end up going down a waterslide," Jane had explained.

"I know that house!" Becca, one of the younger clerks, had been to a party there once.

Jane had told them about the house on the sound with a pseudo-lighthouse. "There's an observatory and a game room at the top, with felt tables for poker and bridge."

They had grinned as she'd told them of another house with a more impressive game room with Ping-Pong and foosball tables, as well as two pinball machines.

Even Jane had to admit, these houses were built for fun and recreation. Nearly every house had a home theater, hot tub, private swimming pool, and pool table. Some had elevators, which came in handy when it was time to lug the vacuum from one floor to another. Double dishwashers, washers, dryers . . . the property owners made it easy for large families to converge in one dwelling for a deluxe beach vacation.

As a realtor, Jane appreciated the amenities like en suite bathrooms, marble flooring, granite kitchen islands, and gas fireplaces with charming mantels. But in every house she cleaned, it was the view that grabbed her heart and never let go.

The water dance beyond each cottage's windows was an ever-changing phenomenon. From diamonds on the water to striations in every shade of blue, the sea was a reminder that life was constantly changing, day by day, minute by minute. She'd had her share of misfortune in the past few months, but it had forced her to adapt.

These days she was learning how to change plans and how to appreciate the small things, like a run on the beach or the delighted squeal of a child easing into the surf for the first time.

Simple pleasures.

Like her evening chats with Cooper.

Since her arrival at the house on Sea Breeze Road, she had spent nearly every evening sitting on the upper deck and watching the sun set with Coop. The first day he had convinced her that it would be neighborly to join him. After that, she had begun to look forward to stealing up to his deck for that magical hour of sunset as he filled her in on different neighbors and people in the town, and she told him about the insides of the posh beach mansions she had spent the day cleaning.

"We're getting to be good friends," she had told TJ on the phone. She didn't tell her brother about the sexual tension that occasionally lit the air between her and Coop.

"Just friends?" TJ had probed.

"There's been no stripping down to jump into the hot tub . . . or into bed."

"Too bad."

"You have such a boy brain. Right now I think Cooper just likes blending up some virgin daiquiris and having some company."

That was one of the things that kept her going; Cooper seemed eager for her company and spending time with him restored her spirits in a surprising way. For the first time in months, she could look to the next day with a feeling of hope and optimism.

She drove to the Quickstop for a sandwich and a bit of spying. Last night Coop had mentioned that today was his day off, and she was curious as to how he might be spending it.

"Seen Coop around?" she asked as Kailani rang up her sandwich.

"Not today." Kailani folded a napkin and tucked it in the bag. "I don't think he's working."

"He's off." Jane looked around to see if anyone was eavesdropping. "Any idea what he does on his days off?"

"I don't know. Coop stays under the radar. Now that he's better, he keeps to himself."

"Was he sick?"

"Post-traumatic stress. He had it bad. After he came home from Afghanistan, he fell apart."

"He mentioned that." Jane thought of how he'd compared it to a runaway train coming at him.

"Rusty said it was the war. That and his high school sweetheart had been cheating on him. She left town for Charlotte, but I heard she wanted him back."

A girlfriend? Jane hadn't thought of that. "Do you think they'll get back together?"

Kailani shook her head. "Leah couldn't wait to get away from Avon. And Cooper, he won't ever leave again."

"How do you know that for sure?"

"I just know." Kailani shrugged. "Some things I know. He loves this place, and Cooper is the backbone of this town. He's going to stay."

It was just after 2:00 when Jane drove up to the house. The driveway was empty, and again she wondered how Cooper spent his days off. Did he have family in the area? Did he go out on fishing charters?

She unlocked the door and stepped inside, pausing to bend down and check the loose bit of fishing line that she'd stretched out across the edge of the entryway.

Still in place.

It was her personal alarm system, rudimentary, but enough to reassure her that no one had come through this door and slipped into the house while she was gone.

After a quick shower and another look at the diamonds of sunlight on the sound, she decided that today would be the day she would take TJ's advice and check out that surfing spot he adored. Although she'd never been on a board—wind, kite, or surf—she knew TJ wouldn't let her rest until she visited his mothership.

Like many windsurfing spots, the Canadian Hole wasn't marked, but most of the locals knew how to find it.

"Just drive south until you see signs for Ego Beach," Kailani had told her. "You'll turn right into the parking lot, and the Hole is there on Pamlico Sound."

Jane followed her friend's directions and turned into the paved lot across from Ego Beach. The narrow strip of sand and dunes was hardly impressive, though from the dozen or so windsurfers picking up speed on the steady breeze, she realized it was all about wind.

Although there were restrooms at the site, there was no concession stand or place for a board, so Jane drove back a mile to a sprawling, wood-shingled house on the sound that boasted rentals with a dozen or so hand-painted signs.

Various-size boards leaned against sawhorses in the yard. The French doors of the house were open, revealing tables of clothing and gear in the front room.

"Hey, how's it going?"

Jane started at the voice from the side yard, alarm ringing in her ears. The man's smile was friendly enough, but she stepped back cautiously.

"Did I just creep up out of nowhere?" He tipped his baseball cap back, and she noticed concern in his dark eyes. "Sorry, ma'am. I was just down by the water, trying to get some windsurfers set up. I'm Newt. This is my place. What can I help you with today?"

"I was wondering about renting windsurfing equipment."

"You're a windsurfer?"

"My brother is. I would need a lesson."

"Your brother won't teach you?"

"He's not here at the moment."

"Well, where is he?"

"He lives in Florida." She tested the weight of a long board as apprehension rose, a knot in her throat. Was he digging for information, or just being chatty?

He nodded. "Plenty of opportunity to windsurf there. And where are you from? You don't look like Florida."

Jane swallowed back fear. "Pennsylvania," she said, thinking of the plate on her Jeep. "So . . . how about those lessons?"

"I'd like to help you out." He took off his cap, revealing a shaved head with a pink sheen at the top. "But I'm booked up today."

They made arrangements for a rental and lesson in a few days. He told her it was important to have the right size equipment and promised to reserve a board her size. As Newt hurried back down to his customers in the shallow water, Jane felt ashamed at her cool response to him. He'd only been trying to help.

All the people she had met here had been kind, and most had extended themselves well beyond the usual boundaries of strangers.

If only she didn't have to be on guard all the time . . .

Her feet scraped the warm sand as she tipped the water bottle back. If lessons were out, she figured she could at least spend an hour or two observing windsurfers at the Hole. Half of learning was study, and as she watched the figures course over the water, many of them picking up a good amount of speed, she had a feeling she was watching some of the best in the world.

TJ would go crazy here. She pulled out her cell phone and snapped some shots of the cove, the windsurfers, the kite boarders with their colorful puffed kites just off the point to the north.

Toward the northern edge of the cove, a surfer leaped from the water, made a sharp turn, and landed on the board. Spectacular. "Don't think I'll be doing moves like that anytime soon."

"Miss Jane?"

The sand beside her shifted as a large canvas bag of equipment was dropped down. She followed the line of one spectacular male body up . . . up to Coop's handsome face. She pointed to the bag. "You know how to do this?"

"Sure. Got my board in the car. How come you're not out there?"

"I've got some lessons scheduled for later in the week."

"Lessons with Newt?"

"You know him?"

"He's as good as it gets."

So Newt was legit; maybe she was getting paranoid.

Coop knelt down in the sand so that his eyes were level with hers. "So, you're a newbie?" When she nodded, he grinned. "Well, I can show you a few of the basics."

"That'd be great. Though watching some of the guys out there . . . I'm a little worried about holding on to the sail at that speed."

"Let's see." He wrapped his fingers around her biceps and gave a little squeeze. "Not bad, Miss Jane. You must have gone to a gym back in New York City."

She had, but now that she ran on the beach and scrubbed houses to a shine, a scheduled workout seemed sort of lame. "Want to see the photos I sent to my brother?" she asked to change the subject. "He's the one who's been insisting that I see the Canadian Hole."

"Very nice." Coop smiled and reached for her cell phone. "Why don't you stand by the water and I'll get some shots with you in them?"

She posed for a few shots, then thanked him.

"No worries. Look at this gorgeous day we got."

"They seem to like it." She gestured toward the cove, now bursting with colored sails. "I don't understand why everyone crowds into the same spot. What's the magic of this cove?"

"It's a whole combination of things. You got the land mass off the island blocking off the rough water from the ocean. But the low landscape doesn't block the Atlantic winds. That means steady conditions. Smooth water, strong winds. Gives you the chance to pick up some real speed."

"Which was my first concern."

"What are you worried about, Miss Jane? I'd never let anything bad happen to you."

It was such a sweet thing to say, but Jane knew there was substance behind his words. He meant to protect her.

She met his eyes, seeing the commitment there. "I just don't see myself doing one of those curlicue flips anytime soon."

He smiled, that grin that warmed her down to her toes. "We'll save the curlicue for a later lesson. And you'll be happy to know the water here is thigh-high, which makes for easy in-and-out. There's a nice sandy bottom and the temperature is just right. You can't beat the warm Carolina water."

There was such warmth in his words; his love for Carolina came through. "Well, then, I'd be honored if you could give me a few pointers."

"Sure. Just hold on while I get my boards from the truck."

She turned her phone off and tucked it away in her bag before stripping down to her one-piece print swimsuit. Enthusiasm warred with nerves as she thought about the lesson. Kind of strange, getting so close to Coop with so little on.

Cooper returned with two boards, one that was just her size. He told her he'd bought it for "a friend," though he said his nieces now used it when they visited.

Jane studied the board as if it would reveal something about his ex-girlfriend. But no, it was just a board . . . and Leah was miles away, in Charlotte.

Her loss.

The water was warm but refreshing, and shallow, as Coop had promised.

"Now, just watch me for a minute." Cooper got up on the board and showed her "neutral position," which meant standing on the board in the water, feeling right and left of the mast, and holding the mast upright.

"Neutral position is important to learn," he said. "Got that?"

"Mm-hm." But mostly Jane loved the excuse to stare up and down his body as he demonstrated. Maybe it was his military training, but Cooper was ripped. His stomach was flat with slight ripples of muscles and he had the legs of a runner, muscled yet lean.

"Now, eyes on me."

She wouldn't think of looking anywhere else.

"See how I start in neutral? Then I grab the uphaul line and crouch down to bring the sail up. See? Easy."

"Piece of cake," she agreed, though Coop's body was a huge distraction from the lesson. "So show me the rest."

He stepped behind the mast, knees bent, butt tucked and body square to the board. At once, the wind caught his sail, and he adjusted his body slightly as his board was propelled forward.

"The wind pushes the sail and the sail controls the board," he had told her. "It's real wind power."

Waiting in the shallows with the smaller board floating beside her, she was content just watching Coop catch the wind from this cool, blue haven.

He was good. He sped across the flat water, leaning back to get maximum wind. He made it look so easy.

And he looked damn good doing it.

CHAPTER 9

With Coop giving her a personal lesson, the afternoon went by quickly. After a few hours of wobbling and crashing into the shallow water, Jane had earned a fondness for Coop's limitless patience and sense of humor.

He was a tireless teacher, though she had to admit, the body could be distracting. Who knew his crisp, white uniform shirt and loose Hawaiian shirts covered the body of a perfect man?

It made her wonder about her insistence that they were just friends. A niggling voice in the back of her mind kept saying: "You know you want it to be more."

What she needed was some good girl talk to sort out her feelings. But no . . . that wasn't going to happen. She hadn't been able to spend much time with any of her friends since the shooting, and now that she was on the run, they were safer if she kept her distance.

"Back to neutral position," Coop kept telling her. "Say it with me: 'neutral position is my friend.' "

"Neutral position is my favorite thing in the world," she teased.

"Well. Let's not go crazy."

By the time they called it a day, Jane had gotten a few fun rides, and Coop had even managed to snap a few photos of her catching the wind.

"More proof for your brother," Coop said. "When they see that you're here at the Hole, you'll be the envy of all his friends."

I doubt that, Jane thought. No one would want to be in her precarious situation. But, thankfully, Coop didn't know her whole story.

Dinner that night was carryout from Bubba's, shared on Coop's deck. It was Jane's favorite time of the day, watching the sun set with Cooper.

"I think I've earned myself some ibuprofen and a hot bath tonight," she said as she bit into a wedge of watermelon, sending juice dripping down her chin. Something about making a fool of yourself in front of a person broke down all kinds of barriers.

"You'll definitely want to soak those muscles," Coop said. "But we can use the hot tub. It's ready to go."

Their day at the Hole had shifted things to a new playing field. Now Jane felt comfortable hanging out on Cooper's deck in her swimsuit. Barefoot, too. Pretty soon, people around here were going to mistake her for a local girl.

"Thanks for the lessons." She popped a chunk of pork into her mouth and sighed. "And this . . . dining al fresco. It's wonderful. But I hope I'm not keeping you from doing other things. I mean, it's your day off."

"Sunset on the deck is my ritual," he said. "If you haven't noticed, I'm not a real flashy guy. I keep a low profile."

"Really. I'm surprised you're not beating the beach bunnies back with a strand of seaweed."

Coop laughed. "Funny, but I don't have that problem. Maybe it's because I was 'attached' for so long."

"Your girlfriend Leah?"

"So you've heard. You really are settling in around here, Miss Jane."

"Gossip isn't that discriminating. Besides, I didn't get any juicy details. Just her name."

"Leah was my childhood sweetheart. We had talked about getting married one day, after I finished with West Point and the army, but she got restless while I was gone. Can't say I blame her."

"So she broke it off while you were off serving your country?" She frowned.

"Yeah. It happens to a lot of guys over there. You feel like that one person is your tie to the good world. You're hanging on by one tether. And then, snap . . . she cuts the cord and leaves you drifting in space. Alone."

"That must have been rough."

"I got over it. But after I got home, things really got dicey. I was broken, and Leah was only a small part of it. I was reeling from post-traumatic stress. All the killing and the smoke, the suicide attacks and ambushes . . . I couldn't process the things I'd seen in the war. But at the same time, my life here seemed wrong. It was flat and dull, compared to the adrenaline rush of combat."

His voice was low and steady but laced with an anguish that made her heart ache for him. She sensed that he still needed to keep some of the memories in check.

"Where were you stationed in Afghanistan?"

"The Kunar Province."

A deadly area known for its notoriously violent ambushes. "I've read some news stories about Afghanistan, but I never knew anyone who was assigned there."

"Your friends are probably a hell of a lot more functional than that," he said darkly.

"I'm sorry. I pushed you to talk about something that still hurts."

He shrugged. "Not your fault. When I first got back, everyone wanted to know what it was like over there. Now . . . not so much. Probably because you can see it on the news these days."

"Maybe we should go back to a safer topic . . . like Leah."

He laughed. "I wouldn't describe Leah as safe."

"Do you miss her?"

"Not at all. In fact, Leah wanted me back, only on her terms. She wanted me to move to the city with her. She's done with Avon."

"So, you couldn't leave here?" she asked. "Even for love?"

"I guess I wasn't so much in love anymore. And the more I said no, the more persistent she got. Started hounding me." He shook his head. "Saw an ugly side of that girl. But all's well that ends well. She's getting married soon and I'm relieved to be done with her."

Thank God the giddy smile on her face was masked by darkness.

It was over between Leah and him. For some reason, that made her heart dance.

"And how about the skeletons in your closet?" he asked, catching her with her guard down.

She looked down at the table, not wanting to lie. She trusted him. Oh, how she'd love to tell him everything.

But she couldn't.

"Would you believe that my closet is clean?"

"Everyone has something. It's part of our past, part of who we are. Personal history."

She swallowed a delicious morsel, thinking of a way around revealing too much. If she went back past the last few months, she could be totally honest.

"I was sixteen when I lost my parents," she said. "Maybe that's not a skeleton, but it spun my life in a one-eighty. TJ, too. My brother and I were lucky to have each other."

The grooves at the edges of his eyes softened. "Sixteen is young."

"At the time I thought I had it all together, but I was a mess. We didn't have a close family. Somehow it was decided that our widowed aunt would move in to take care of us. Our great-aunt Minnie." She smiled. "She turned out to be quite a character. A Broadway actress."

"Is that right?"

"Small parts. But her life is full of drama. She moved into our house in Buffalo and took good care of us. She's still there, giving acting lessons in the parlor."

"But you and TJ moved on?"

"For me, that house will always be haunted by my parents. I was glad to leave it behind for college. I've visited since then, but I could never move back."

"Because you love New York City?"

New York . . .

Was she still in love with the city?

"When I first arrived there, it seemed loaded with opportunity and character. It was such an exciting place to be."

"And then . . . ?" he prodded.

And then someone I trusted showed me the ugly side of the city.

As she struggled to find a safe answer, she heard the rising song of frogs in the nearby marshes. The sky overhead was a sheet of stars, and the fresh, salty smell of the sea blew in on the soft breeze.

It was the antithesis of the city she loved and yet . . . this town spoke to her heart.

"Miss Jane, you falling asleep on me?"

She slapped at a mosquito and laughed. "Could be, Sheriff. I think I need to get into the hot tub and rest these aching muscles. Escape the mosquitoes, too."

"Yeah, they're starting to bite." He removed the hot tub cover while she brought the remains of their dinner into his kitchen.

He was lighting torches as she slipped into the bubbling water and sighed as warmth pervaded her soul.

When he joined her, he didn't bother with the stairs, but vaulted over the side. Such a man.

"Your muscles sore?" Coop asked.

"Just my shoulders."

"Let me see." He shifted in the water, moving behind her.

A moment later, his fingers pressed into her shoulders and she moaned at that sweet dichotomy of pain and pleasure as he probed the sore areas.

"You will let me know if I'm crossing the respectful boundary between landlord and tenant," he said.

She laughed. "Shut up and keep massaging."

"I can do that. I could do this all night."

"That's such a guy thing to say."

"But I mean it." His hands cupped her shoulders, then slid down to work her upper arms.

Lost in exquisite sensation, Jane still had the presence of mind to know they were at a crucial moment. She could thank him for the fun day and the massage and escape downstairs.

She could.

She should.

But every fiber in her being cried out for her to stay. She wanted to stay right here and be with him, pleasure him, love him.

Reaching her right arm across her body, she took one of his hands and tugged it down to cup her breast. He moaned at the feel of her softness. And suddenly he was pulling her against him, encasing her in his strength.

I'd never let anything bad happen to you. His words brought tears to her eyes now, tears of relief and love and passion. The feel of his hands on her breasts, massaging her nipples to pleasure, sent a stream of warmth coursing through her, and she drew a deep breath, knowing she had never before felt so secure, so delicate, so loved.

She covered his hands with hers to draw them away, then swirled around in the water, turning to face him.

His eyes sparked with wanting her. His body confirmed it when she pressed against him and lifted her lips to his.

The heat of contact ignited feelings deep inside her, yearnings she had tamped down for years, thinking that she had way too many things to invest in before she could get emotionally or physically involved with a man. Her job, her friends, her condo—those things had been her life.

And now, suddenly, those things were part of her past.

And her present was this man holding her in his arms, their bodies buoyed and buffeted by warm gentle waters.

The kiss deepened, and she moaned, losing herself in the sensation of his body against hers as bubbles effervesced around them. His fingertips trailed along the line of her jaw, touching her shoulders as he ended the kiss.

She nuzzled his wet neck, pressing her lips to the spot just under one ear.

He groaned. "That feels so good. Right now I want nothing more than to take you into my bed and make love to you . . . every blessed inch of you."

She lifted her head, studying his handsome face. "Me, too," she said. "Do you have . . . protection?"

"I do. But I don't think tonight is going to be our night, Miss Jane."

She squinted. Had she heard him right?

"Don't be mad at me. You know I'm disappointed, too."

She sank back in the warm water, drifting away from him. She had never been rejected by a man before and it stung. "So, tell me. What's wrong, Coop?"

"I want you in the worst way, but when it happens for us, I want to know that I've got you, here and here." He pointed to her chest, then to her forehead. "Heart and soul, sugar."

"Heart and soul," she murmured. She couldn't argue with his reasoning, but that didn't take away the sting. "I have to admit, I've never heard that from a man before."

"Because I'm no ordinary man, I'm sure."

"I'll give you that." Crouching on a seat in the tub, she closed her eyes and considered his proposal. "How do you know you don't already have me, heart and soul?"

"I just know. Call it instinct."

"And how do you know that my soul is in my head?" she asked, pointing to her forehead.

He laughed. "You got me on that one. But my overall impression is on the money. You're not a hundred percent in this. Am I right?" His expression was so stern she had to look away. She swished her hands on the surface of the water to create a distraction.

"I'm crazy about you, Coop. That's the truth. It's just that . . . I've got some other things on my mind, too. But they have nothing to do with you."

He held up a hand to stop her. "Say no more, and please don't apologize for where you're at right now." He settled in the opposite corner of the hot tub, irresistibly handsome now that she couldn't have him. "I have faith in you, Miss Jane. It may take a while, but I do believe you'll come around."

She frowned. He wouldn't be saying that if he knew the terror that was looming over her.

She switched to the seat by the hot tub stairs. Time for the graceful exit.

"I get what you're saying," she said as she perched on the top step. "Personally, I think we should strike while the iron is hot, so to speak. Life is short, and there are so many things in the world that we can't control. When you run into something that you can act on, I say go for it."

"I get your point," he said. "But my mind is made up. I stand firm. So to speak."

She had to laugh. "You are no ordinary man," she said as she climbed out of the tub, water coursing down her bare legs. She grabbed one of the towels he'd left on the chair and wrapped herself up like an egg roll. "I'll bring the towel back tomorrow," she said.

"No worries."

Oh, I've got plenty of worries, and now some of them include you, she thought as she climbed down the stairs and went into her apartment. Closing and locking the slider behind her, she rolled her eyes.

With all the guys she'd dated in the past few years, she had to make a pass at the one man who stood on solid principles.

Still, Jane had to respect the purity of his desires.

Heart and soul . . .

Wouldn't that be nice?

CHAPTER 10

"You need to have a party," Jane told him one rainy evening when they were staring at the fire in his living room.

"What do you mean? I just had a party a few weeks ago."

Cooper's annual Fourth of July potluck, usually a gesture of thanks to the town he served, had felt more like a celebration this year with every aspect enhanced by Jane's touch. Her homemade coleslaw and sugar cookies decorated with red, white, and blue frosting. The small vases of flowers and candles decorating the tables.

Yeah, he was still hearing about how great that July Fourth party had been, and he knew it was because of Jane. Good Lord, the folks around here really did love her.

The way she managed to get people talking to each other, even estranged friends like Rusty and Bubba or Cappy and Clive. By the end of the night, Bubba was no longer sore at Rusty for setting up a sandwich counter at the Quickstop that competed with his barbecue, and Cappy was promising that he'd come see Clive for a haircut after all these years.

"I'm talking about a party for Rusty and Kailani," Jane said, tucking her feet under her on the couch. "To celebrate their great news about the baby."

After four years of trying, Rusty and Kailani were expecting a baby, and it was tough deciding which one of them was more excited. Kailani had taken up crocheting to make baby blankets. During a lull at the Quickstop you could find her behind the counter on her stool, working that yarn. Rusty, his good friend and a guy's guy, had decided to research all the right things to do to prepare for a baby. Cooper had helped Rusty paint the spare bedroom, and the whole time Rusty had talked about the importance of paint with zero VOC—volatile organic compounds. Cooper had never heard of VOC before, but he figured it was all good for the baby. Still, it was a little weird to see all of Rusty's library books open on the coffee table.

"Are you talking about a baby shower?" Coop asked, thinking how Jane looked so cute curled up in her usual spot on the couch. "Guys don't do that girly stuff."

"Not a shower. Just a meeting of friends to celebrate their good news."

"I am happy for them," Coop said. "They've wanted a kid since they got married." He was normally not a party guy, but with Jane around, he was beginning to see how a get-together bonded a community. "I guess we could do that. But I'd keep the guest list small. Just friends of Rusty and Kailani."

"Which is pretty much everyone in Avon," she said with a glint in her blue eyes.

"True." And Jane would know. In little more than a month, she had gotten to know this town well. The surprising thing was her attitude—not the snooty city slicker at all. Jane stopped to talk with people, and once she met someone she always remembered his or her name.

When he was on patrol, it wasn't unusual to see Jane walking through town, taking photos of the ice cream stand at the Quick-stop or the display in front of Sara's flower shop. He'd taken shots of her in a goofy pose in front of a movie poster at the Cineplex. And she'd thought TJ would love the photo of her shaking hands with Bubba.

You'd think the girl was running for mayor. And if she was, he'd be the first in line to vote for her.

She looked like she belonged on that couch. Sitting across from her, half listening as she debated the merits of a crab feast versus burgers and dogs, he thought about the dysfunctional aspect of their relationship. The sad lack of sex.

That had been his call, and he was paying for it, big-time. At the time, he thought that laying it out that way might make her see that she could trust him with her secret.

But no, the plan had backfired in his face.

Five weeks later, she had become an integral part of his life, like morning coffee or the setting sun.

The answer to the question was Jane. Jane in his heart; Jane in his soul.

But no Jane in his bed.

He was falling for her . . . he *had* fallen for her, hard. And still, they were ending their nights with kissy-face sessions on the sofa that left him aroused and wondering about his sanity to make such a stupid ultimatum.

Still . . . he knew she was holding back. She was hiding something, and damn, didn't she realize at this point that she could trust him with her darkest secret?

Lately he'd come that close to taking it all back, retracting everything he'd said so that he could make long, lingering love to Jane.

He was the one who had pulled away, laid out the requirements for a relationship. He had set the rules.

But man, he was sorely tempted to break his own rules.

Jane was looking at the calendar on her cell phone, trying to pick a date for the baby party, when her cell rang.

"TJ," she said, staring at the caller ID. She hopped up from the couch and strode toward the sliding glass door. "I'll be right back."

She always did that; Coop had noticed how she moved out of earshot whenever she needed to talk to TJ. Apparently, the brother was in on the secret.

He rolled to his feet and grabbed their empty soda cans. On his way to the kitchen, he saw Jane pace toward him, her face stricken and frantic.

He shoved the cans on the counter and opened the slider. "What's wrong?" he asked.

"TJ—they've got him. Oh, God!" She pressed a shaky fist to her mouth.

"Jane, what's going on?"

"I think they kidnapped him! What if they—"

"Who? Who kidnapped TJ?"

Her eyes flared a moment, then she took a quick breath and answered: "The people who are trying to kill me."

CHAPTER 11

Using the approach that got him through police work, Cooper placed his hands on Jane's shoulders to calm her. "You need to tell me what just happened."

She gulped in a breath, showing him her cell phone. "The call . . .

it was TJ's number that came up. The call came from his phone, but he wasn't there."

"Maybe it was a mistake. A pocket dial."

"But there was someone on the line. He . . . I could hear him breathing."

Coop studied her frazzled expression. "And you're thinking this is no ordinary cell phone thief. You think someone stole TJ's phone to call you. These people who are trying to kill you?"

She nodded. "I know it's Canby's men." She clenched her fists, her face strained. "They've got my brother now, and there's no telling what they'll do to him."

"Hold on a second. Even if these criminals have his cell phone, TJ might still be okay. Think of how we can reach him—who he might be with. A girlfriend or a friend. Do you have contact information for any of his friends?"

"I have a number for his girlfriend, Laura."

"That'll work. Dial her up."

As he waited for the phone to connect, he wondered about their next plan of action if they couldn't reach TJ. They would have to call the Florida police. The FBI, too.

"Laura, hi, it's Jane Doyle. Is TJ with you?" The hope on Jane's face faded as she looked up at him. "No? I'm trying to reach him. It's an emergency." After a pause, she told Coop, "He's at a Marlins game."

"Ask her if he went with a friend," he told her. "Get a number."

Jane quickly determined that TJ was with his friend Max, and yes, Laura had Max's cell phone number. She jotted it down quickly and called as soon as she got off with Laura.

"Please, please, pick up," Jane said. He was thinking the same thing. Lots of guys turned their cell phones off at baseball games. They didn't want to be bothered.

"Hello? Oh, Max, is TJ with you? This is his sister, Jane." Her face lit with relief and she paced nervously. "Oh, thank God."

Cooper smiled, echoing her relief as she told him her brother was there. A second later, she was talking to TJ, explaining about a strange call that had come from his cell phone.

From listening to Jane's side of the conversation, Cooper deciphered that TJ had left his cell phone at home. Didn't have a pocket in his shorts.

"Then this is a heads-up," Jane said. "I think your cell's been stolen and they may have gone through your apartment, too."

Jane made him promise that he would take caution when he returned to his apartment. "If there's any sign of a break-in, call the police," she warned him as Cooper nodded in the background.

She ended the call, pressed her phone to her heart, and closed her eyes. "Thank you. Thank you, God."

"I'm glad he's okay," Cooper said.

"He's fine, and he's going to be careful." Her eyes flashed open and suddenly she was blinking back tears. "I can't believe they're going after him."

"These guys on your case sound like some pretty bad dudes."

She snorted. "They're bad dudes, all right. Cold-blooded killers."

He nodded. "Are you ready to tell me about them? Fill me in here, Jane, because I don't much care for swinging in the dark."

Her eyes met his and she nodded. "I'll tell you, Coop. I didn't want to burden you with it—that didn't seem fair—but now that I've pulled you in with me, you need to be armed with the truth."

"Yeah, I'd like that ammunition. But just for the record, you didn't pull me in. I've been in with you from the start, Jane. Just for the record."

She paced to the couch and sank down. "It started in the spring. April second. I used to think that was the last day of my life in New York."

Coop stood behind his chair, watching the shadows on her face cast by the firelight.

"I was out with another realtor, my friend Tia, and we were showing a property to a wealthy Manhattan importer, Arthur Canby. Tia and I were excited because we had just shown Mr. Canby a five-million-dollar property and he seemed very interested."

Coop tried to imagine the scene: a spring day in Manhattan, Jane and her friend both dressed to the nines, coming out of a fancy apartment building in Manhattan.

"We were just walking Mr. Canby to his limo outside the building when a car with dark-tinted windows pulled up. It all happened so fast, but I replay the scene in my mind every day. Suddenly a man jumped out of the car. He called to our client and Mr. Canby paused. 'Say your prayers, Arturo,' the man said. He reached into his belt and suddenly he had a gun pointed at our client, Mr. Canby.

"It seemed fake to me, like a joke or a prank. Maybe because Mr. Canby didn't seem scared. He told the man it wasn't going to work because there were witnesses. That sort of threw the man off, but he said it wasn't a problem.

"Then he turned his gun on Tia and me." The air felt heavy around them as she paused.

Suddenly the fire was too hot, but Coop had to hear her out. How long had he waited for the truth? He would commit her story to memory, etch every detail in his mind until he could figure a way out of her predicament.

"Tia and I knew the man was going to fire on us, but suddenly there was a loud scatter of noise and the man was knocked back. He fell to the ground, covered in blood, shot by Canby."

Coop let out the breath he'd been holding. "What a nightmare."

"At first, Tia and I thought we were safe. But then Canby turned his gun on us." She pressed her hands to her temples. "Tia was hit first. I lunged behind the car and crawled under a big truck that was parked behind it. I saw Canby's footsteps as he came back looking for me. His shoes, they were buffed to a perfect shine. Weird, the things you remember. His driver was calling him, saying they had to get out of there, and I could hear the wail of sirens. Canby's shoes moved out of my sight, and a minute later, the limo squealed out of there." She raked back her hair, taking a deep breath. "When I crawled out from under the truck and saw Tia and all that blood...that man was dead. And Tia..." She shook her head, her eyes welling up with tears.

Cooper couldn't remain separate and objective anymore. He sat beside her on the couch and put his arms around her. She felt so fragile in his arms, such a small, quivering bundle. Delicate and precious.

"I thank God that you got away," he said, rocking her gently. She heaved a sob, but then relaxed against him.

"Sometimes I still think it was a miracle that Tia and I are still alive."

"How's she doing now?"

"She's recovering, going through physical therapy. I hear that it's painful work, but the doctors think she'll eventually be able to walk again."

"Have you two ever talked about what happened that day?"

"No. She doesn't remember leaving the building. It's frustrating for her, but really, her blank memory is a blessing." She sniffed and leaned back to swipe the back of her hand over her face. "She doesn't have to testify."

The final puzzle piece fell into place as he held her close.

The trial.

"You're the only one who can testify against Canby," he said. "The only people who saw the killing are you and Canby's driver."

"That's right. The DA tried to plea bargain with the driver, who was charged with homicide, too, but so far he's backing up Canby's ridiculous alibi."

"So, who is this guy? What's his real story?"

"It turned out that our wealthy importer, Arthur Canby, was involved in a ring that 'imported' drugs into this country. It took the police less than twenty-four hours to track Canby down. When they searched his warehouses, they found a large shipment of heroin in one of them."

"And I suspect the man he shot is from a rival cartel?"

"Something like that. His name was Joe Muldanado, and he worked for a rival drug runner. The Manhattan DA has a solid case against Canby for the drug charges, but they need me to identify him as the killer in court to make a case for homicide."

"And Canby doesn't want to spend so much time in the big house," he said.

Jane nodded. "He wants the murder charges to go away and he's working from inside jail to let me know that. As soon as Canby was arraigned, I began receiving threats. Anonymous notes in the mail. Text messages and voice mails. They were scripted in different ways, but they all warned me to back down. Eat my words. One note said I should develop amnesia, just like Tia."

"Like I said, bad dudes."

"That's the tip of the iceberg. I started getting a creepy feeling, like I was being watched, but I figured it was paranoia. You know, trauma from the shooting. Then one night, it was after midnight, I was waiting for a train down in the subway. The station was quiet, nearly empty, and suddenly I saw this man coming toward me. I think . . . I think he was planning to push me on the tracks. I ran up the stairs and lunged for the exit, but he followed me all the way. He even chased me on the street until I ducked into a twenty-four-hour convenience store. I made the manager call nine-one-one and the cops came, but they never found him."

"So, Canby has hired a hit man to silence your testimony?"

"I know he did, but again, it's hard to prove he's the one behind it all. I don't think the police took it too seriously until someone took a shot at me. One day early in the summer, I was eating break-fast on the balcony of my apartment—I used to love eating out there—and suddenly the glass door behind me exploded. I didn't know what had happened, but the police found a bullet embedded in the kitchen floor."

"A sniper shot?" He shook his head; someone wanted her dead. They wanted it real bad.

"So now the police are on board?" he asked.

She nodded. "They think a hit man has been hired by Canby's people—his gang or his family. The DA's office tried to get me some protection, but the cops don't have the resources to provide twenty-four/seven protection until the trial in September. So . . . I was starting to feel like a big bull's-eye in New York. I had to get away. I rented a car and headed down to see my brother, and then the accident. When I was about to leave the next day, TJ called to tell me someone had called him, asking about me. We decided it was too dangerous for me to stay with him. You know the rest."

"I do. And I'm sorry I didn't know the first part a long time ago. I would have helped you, you know. We could have gotten you a job at the realty office instead of cleaning houses. You could have used an alias here, just to make it harder if anyone did come snoop-ing around."

"Coop, I appreciate your help, but you didn't know me when I first arrived here. It would have been a hell of a story to lay on you, and I'm not even sure you would have believed it back then."

"You underestimate your powers of persuasion." He pushed back a strand of her silken hair so that he could see her face, track her emotions. "But my hat is off to you, Miss Jane. I'm proud of you. It's a courageous thing you're doing, testifying and tangling with the likes of a man like that Canby."

"Well . . . thanks, but it's not like I had a lot of choices. I have to testify, for my own sanity and for Tia, and I'm committed to getting Canby off the streets for good."

"And it's your good fortune that you landed here," he said. "If you hadn't had that accident, you would have driven down to Florida, right where this hit man is looking for you."

She shivered, and he cradled her in his arms, placing a kiss on her forehead. "Don't worry, Miss Jane. I'll take care of you. Now that I know, I promise, I'll protect you."

"I believe you," she said, her gaze locking on his. "I'm sorry to heap this on your shoulders, but there's no one else in the world I would trust telling right now."

He touched her chin, letting his fingers trail along her jawline to her right ear. "Bring it on, sugar. I got wide shoulders."

"Wide enough for the skeleton in my closet?" She reached over to him, cupped his shoulders, and gave a squeeze. "Yeah, I think you do. So . . . that's the worst of it. You know everything now. That's me, heart and soul."

"Mm-hmm." He was focused on her ear, the little channels and ridges, as perfect as a seashell. As perfect as the rest of her.

"Coop?" In a sudden move, she got up on her knees, then rose to straddle him on the couch. "Doesn't this mean we can make love now?"

He smiled, his body already responding to her weight on him.

"I believe it does," he said. "I believe—" The rest was cut off by her lips descending on his, soft, luscious, and thick with hunger.

Such a perfect match, as he'd been hungry, too. Starving. And oh, man, Jane tasted so good.

CHAPTER 12

Hours later, as they lay in bed talking and snuggling by candlelight, Jane's phone sounded on the nightstand.

Cooper reached a long arm out and reeled it in. "Laura," he announced.

"It must be TJ. I'll take it." She propped herself on one shoulder and answered. "Hello?"

"Jane? I hope I didn't wake you, but this couldn't wait." There was a bristle of alarm in her brother's voice.

"They did steal your cell," she said.

"Yeah, and they rifled through the apartment. Took my laptop, too."

"Oh, TJ. Your laptop, too? I'm sorry. Is the apartment a mess?"

"Nothing we can't clean up in the morning. And don't be sorry. This is so not your fault. The police just left, but there's not much that they can do. They don't even fingerprint for a break-in. I told them about your situation, but they said, short of getting the FBI involved, their hands are tied."

Jane raked hair away from her face. "I'm not surprised. Everyone's resources have been cut down. But you and Laura are okay, right?"

"Yeah. We're staying at her place tonight."

"You're safe," she said with a heartfelt sigh. "That's what matters most."

"I know, but I'm worried about what's on my phone. Besides your new cell number, I saved all those pictures you sent. The photos of you at the Canadian Hole?"

The digital images . . .

Jane smoothed the sheet over her breasts. "Right. That was really stupid of me to send them." Stupid, stupid, stupid.

Cooper turned toward her, mouthed "What?" but she waved him off.

"It's not your fault," TJ said. "How could you know they'd steal my phone? You had no idea . . . neither did I. But that phone contains a lot of photos from Avon. You with ice cream outside the

Quickstop. Bubba's Barbecue. The movie theater...even the flower shop. Jane, those pictures mark where you are. These skells might not know the Outer Banks as well as I do, but eventually they'll figure out where those photos were taken. My advice is that you get out of there, fast."

Leave, now?

Jane looked over at Cooper, his beautiful body splayed comfortably atop the sheets. One quick look and she wanted him again. She wanted to lock her lips to his and move her body against his and make enough noise between them to drown out the rest of the world.

"Jane?" TJ's voice drew her back to reality.

"I...I need some time to process this," she said as Cooper gave a playful tug on the sheet, sliding it down to reveal her breasts.

"I gotta go," she said. "We'll talk more in the morning."

"For now, use Laura's cell to reach me. I'll replace my phone tomorrow."

"Okay. 'Bye." She barely had the words out when Cooper took the phone from her hand, ended the call, and tossed it to the far corner of the bed. "It's bad," she said as he rose to his knees and pulled her up to meet him. "They broke into TJ's apartment and stole his computer, too."

"I heard." He pressed his lips to hers, pulling her into the deep, secret place where they had so recently ventured together.

Jane sighed, melting against him.

"We can't do anything about that now," he said gently. "But we can do this."

Cupping her ass, he pressed his hips into hers, a hint of the pleasure in store. "Tomorrow will come soon enough."

He was right. Gripping his shoulders, she held on for dear life and kissed him, long, hard, and deep.

As if it were the last kiss of her life.

Sunlight peeked through the blinds as if to announce that the storm had passed. Jane stretched, her bare body moving against the sheets a reminder of the glorious night with Cooper.

Not that she needed reminding with the naked man asleep beside her, his body shifting gently with each breath. He was facing the windows, affording her a view of his broad shoulders and muscular back tanned bronze from time in the sun.

She scooted closer, cupping his shoulder and pressing her lips to one shoulder blade. The contact was still somewhat electrifying, even after a night of lovemaking that had left her feeling more than satisfied. But then, rain was never so delicious as after a drought.

"Mmm." His chest rumbled with sound, and a hand reached back and cupped her ass. "Is that my morning wakeup call?"

"You can sleep," she said. "I have to go clean Beach Bliss. Jolene has some renters coming in early this week."

He rolled over to face her and she felt sure that the creases in his brow had eased over their night together. "I could use a little off-the-beach bliss."

"Really? The novelty of new sex hasn't worn off?"

"I have a theory about that." He let a hand trail down her shoulder, tracing the line of her rib cage and waist over the sheet. His fingers tantalized, leaving heat in their path. "After the first time, the learning curve goes up and it gets better and better."

She smiled, running her palm down over his pectoral. "I like your theory." When he pulled her against him and she felt him hard against her, desire flared again. It was a new surge of wanting, a raw need for him. "But I do have to work today."

"I'm on duty, too. How about we make this one short and sweet?"

She peeled the sheet down so that there would be no barriers between them. "Okay, Sheriff. Here's one to remember me by when you're out there cruising the beach of bikini-clad vacationers."

Afterward, their bodies still warm from sex, she snuggled into his protective arms for one last moment of security.

"Thank you," she said softly. "You've made me feel safe again."

"The safety thing is my job. You can consider the sex a little personal bonus."

"Well, I hope it's not something you share with the general public."

He tipped her chin up so that she was looking directly into his eyes. "It's just for you. Only you, Miss Jane."

She smiled. This guy knew how to steal a heart.

"In fact, I'm wondering about you cleaning houses alone, now that we know someone is out there trying to hunt you down."

"It's my job," she said. "I've got to work."

"But now Canby's guy has TJ's cell phone, with all those photos from here. If they come looking for you here in Avon, I don't want you to be an easy mark. Maybe Jolene can find another cleaner you can partner with for a while. Just to be on the safe side."

"Maybe," she agreed, sick at the thought of losing the little bit of freedom she'd found here in Avon.

"And you should move your stuff up here, stay with me."

Move in with him? "I can't do that, Coop. Yes, I feel really safe when I'm with you, but I can't use you as a bodyguard."

"Why not, sugar? Use me, please."

She laughed. "You know what I mean. I don't want to ruin our relationship over this. We both have jobs to do, and yours doesn't include inviting stalker victims into your bed."

He grinned lazily. "That would be a perk, though."

She pinged his shoulder. "Really, Coop. So far there's been no sign that someone is looking for me here. I don't want to give up my independence."

"But you do need to stay safe," he said. "Think about it. And how hard would it be for you to move your toothbrush up here? I'll be a perfect gentleman if you decide you want to sleep in bed instead of all this."

"Oh, I'm in for all this," she said.

"Then come on up. You can go visit your apartment whenever you want."

That afternoon, Jane was mopping the kitchen floor of Beach Bliss when she heard a noise downstairs.

Was that the door?

Another noise—footsteps—and she dropped the mop and went scurrying for cover.

But where could she go?

The closet? Under a bed?

Adrenaline kicked in and she lunged for the sofa as the footsteps drew nearer.

"Hello?" a gruff voice called up the stairs. "Jane?"

Huddled behind the sofa, she thought she recognized the voice. It certainly sounded friendly.

"Who's there?" she called.

"Isaiah Dunner. I'm here to service the hot tub."

Her fear gave way to relief as she hurried over to meet him at the top of the stairs. She'd met Isaiah before; he took care of the hot tubs in most of the rental houses. He told her the tub needed draining and refilling and asked if she could unlock the supply closet downstairs.

"That sunscreen always leaves a nasty scum on the edge of the tub. Got to scrub it off by hand."

As soon as Jane finished helping him out, she reached for her cell phone and dialed Jolene's number with trembling hands.

Coop was right; better safe than sorry.

CHAPTER 13

"Why do you always use pink yarn?" Jane asked one morning as Kailani put her crocheting aside to ring up a purchase.

"Because I'm having a girl," Kailani said.

"Really?" Jane smiled. "Did you have amnio?"

"No." Kailani adjusted the ponytail of silky dark hair behind her neck. "I just know."

"It's her psychic sense." Becca, who was refilling the chewing gum display, now made it a point to join in the conversation when Jane stopped in. They had been working together to arrange the baby party in secret, but now Jane wondered if Kailani had a sixth sense about that, too.

"Now that I think about it, you knew I'd be coming back to Avon, back on the day I got in that fender bender here," Jane said. "So, if you really do have a psychic sense, can you see the future?"

Kailani shrugged and continued her crocheting. "Sometimes."

"Can you see my future?" Jane asked.

Kailani looked up at her, then frowned and returned to her handiwork. "I don't know. I see danger."

Danger? Fear glimmered in Jane's chest.

It had been four days since TJ's phone had been stolen, and so far, everything was fine. Jolene had hooked her up with a cleaner named Adele, and it was no problem as they conquered twice as many houses working together.

"So . . . my middle name is danger." Jane raked her hair out of her eyes. "I was looking for something more along the lines of eternal sunshine or a windfall at Vegas."

Becca's eyes were as wide as quarters. "Really? What kind of danger?"

Kailani shrugged. "I don't know. I've always seen danger for you, Jane, and you're always fine. So maybe I'm wrong."

"Wow," Becca said. "I was going to ask what you saw for me, but I think I'll just finish up here and get to pulling the outdated milk from the case."

"That'd be good," Kailani said. Her hands worked steadily as Becca grabbed the empty box and ducked into the back of the store. "I don't mean to scare you," she told Jane when they were alone. "But it's the truth."

"I appreciate your honesty. Can you be more specific?"

"There's a man and a gun." Kailani shrugged. "That's all."

Jane nodded. Maybe Kailani was seeing the trial ahead: the days of testifying, the gun submitted as evidence, the despicable man, Canby, sitting at the defendant's table.

"You know, considering where I've been and where I'm headed, what you're seeing makes sense," Jane said, looking at the clock. "So, Coop's picking me up here in twenty and we're headed out windsurfing. What looks good for a picnic lunch today?"

"Grilled chicken. Rusty made it himself, with his secret marinade."

"Then grilled chicken it is." Jane went to the lunch counter to get the chicken, while Kailani cashed out a few more customers.

Kailani is right; there's danger in my life, Jane said to herself as she waited for April to bag the chicken. How she dreaded returning to New York for the trial in September. She felt sick at the thought of facing Canby in court. She couldn't even imagine staying in her own apartment again. No, September was not going to be a good time for her.

Coop arrived with his truck loaded up with boards and sails, and they headed out to Dragon's Point, a spectacular but tricky cove, as the high tides often washed over the peninsula, turning the cove into a temporary island. High tide was around 3:00 p.m. today, so they would windsurf for a few hours, then head in and take their picnic lunch inland.

Music played on the radio as they drove. Warm air blew through the cab of the truck, tossing Jane's hair around. How long had it been since she'd seen her stylist? She didn't know and she really didn't care. Down here, she didn't need the gelled, precision haircut that was crucial to a woman in her profession. Here at the beach, no one seemed to fuss too much with hair and makeup. One of the things she loved about the place.

"You're in a quiet mood," Coop told her.

"I was just thinking how I don't miss New York as much as I thought I would," she said. "And right now, I dread going back. Oh, by the way, Kailani saw danger in my future."

"What?"

She explained about Kailani's penchant for prediction, adding in the vision of the man and a gun.

"Well, did anyone stop to think that could be me?" Coop asked. "I'm your man. And I'm a sheriff, so I'm always packing."

Jane looked at him and burst out laughing.

"Why is that so funny?"

"Because it's true." She clapped a hand on his shoulder and gave him a shake. "I guess I'm just relieved that something that seemed so bad a few minutes ago might actually be a positive omen for the future."

"Well, good."

When they arrived at the cove, Jane helped tote the boards and equipment to the narrow strip of beach. In the past few weeks she had mastered the basics of windsurfing, but setting up all the equipment to build a mast, sail, and dagger board was still a bit of a chore.

With Coop's help she was soon out in the water, coasting along. *The wind moves the sail.* She heard Coop's voice, reminding her not to try and manipulate the board. *Leave it to the wind.* It was hard for her to let go and trust; she liked to have her ducks in a row. But she was learning to leave it to the wind.

Beyond the cove, a few kite surfers moved steadily along. Other than that, she and Coop had Dragon's Point to themselves and she marveled at the color and serenity here.

Blue sky.

Dark blue water lit by diamonds.

Pale, sandy beach.

Green marsh grass.

Danger may have driven her to this place, but here in Avon, with Coop by her side, she was on safe, solid ground.

CHAPTER 14

The next morning Jane had a good, long laugh for the first time in months. She and Coop were having coffee in bed, trading childhood stories about learning to ride a bike, and Coop had her laughing so hard she nearly spilled her hot drink.

"Easy there," Coop said. "No hot liquids on the family jewels."

She was laughing again when Coop's cell phone jangled.

"It's dispatch," he said, putting the phone to his ear. "What's up?"

Jane took a breath and shook her head as he walked away from her, sunlight casting shadows over his bare, muscular body. *What a gorgeous man.*

"Contact the Coast Guard," he said. "They'll bring out a helicopter to search by air."

As he talked, Jane grabbed one of his slightly worn T-shirts from the floor and slipped it over her head. It smelled of Coop—clean and a little salty. Although she'd been sleeping up here every night, she still hadn't moved any of her belongings up. Wasn't it healthy to keep a little distance in a new relationship?

From the way he slipped his uniform on while he handled the call, Jane could tell it was a serious incident. By the time he hung up, he was dressed in pants, shirt, and a belt.

"What's going on?" she asked.

"We need to stage a search and rescue operation for a missing toddler. Wandered away from the parents at the beach."

"That's scary." Jane couldn't imagine the panic of a parent in that situation.

"We need to act fast."

"Where do you think the kid went?"

"Back to the cottage. To play in the dunes. Down the beach. Kids wander off a few times every summer, but I've got an excellent record of return. A hundred percent."

"Good. Keep it up." She bent down to straighten his collar, thinking how fun it would be to seduce him in uniform. Hmm. Some other time.

He finished tying his shoes. "Okay. I'll see you later."

She returned his kiss, walking him to the door as if she had lived here forever.

Like a wife . . .

Her toothbrush might be in the apartment downstairs, but she slept in his bed every night and she had a set of his keys hooked onto hers. That sounded pretty damn settled, and she didn't mind it at all.

Watching his truck pull out, she wished him luck and said a little prayer for the safe return of the toddler.

Since it was midweek, there were no houses to clean, but Marvin had asked Jane to help clean a few rooms at the motel—an easy gig compared to the rambling cottages. She worked methodically, and by one o'clock she was stowing her buckets and gloves and heading over to the Quickstop to pick up some lunch.

The muted noise of the Coast Guard helicopter overhead let her know that the search for the missing child was probably still going on. Up ahead, she saw that one of the side streets leading to the ocean was closed, blocked off by orange traffic cones and a police cruiser with flashing lights.

At the Quickstop, Kailani was noticeably absent from her stool behind the counter.

"Where's the crochet champion of OBX?" Jane asked Becca.

"She's a little under the weather." Becca bagged a purchase for a customer, wished him a nice day, then turned to Jane. "So, did he find you?"

Jane squinted. "Who?"

"Your brother. He was just in here looking for you. Said he wanted to surprise you."

Jane braced herself as a sick feeling seeped into her belly. TJ, here? He would love a few days at the Canadian Hole, but after all they'd been through in the past few days . . . "What did he look like?"

"You know. A big guy," Becca said casually. "Solid build, dark hair. Nice smile."

Jane's worry hardened to dull panic. TJ was thin—a beanpole with sandy blond hair.

Someone was in town, looking for her.

Canby's hired gun.

"How long ago was he here?"

Becca shrugged. "I don't know. Maybe an hour ago?"

An hour . . . she might have passed him on the road. Maybe he was even staying at the motel where she'd spent the morning.

Suddenly, Jane felt conspicuous . . . a walking target.

"He said he'd been looking around town for your Jeep, and I told him you had a job cleaning houses, so you probably weren't around this morning."

"Oh, really?" Jane swallowed, a strain with the knot of fear in her throat. "Did you . . . did you tell him where I live?"

"Oh, no." Becca laughed. "I don't even know where you live."

Thank God for that, Jane thought.

"Excuse me a second," she told Becca, looking around the store for a private place. The office. She knocked on the door and it fell open. The light was on, but it was empty. She stepped inside and she fumbled with trembling hands to call Coop.

It rang four times when she realized he was still on the search and rescue operation. She hung up, then called a second time. "Please pick up," she whispered.

The line clicked, then his voice. "Miss Jane? I can't really talk . . ."

"I know, but I've got a problem." Trying not to babble, she spilled the details of the strange man who had come into the Quickstop looking for her.

"Okay, Miss Jane, first thing is to stay calm, okay? I can't get away right now, but . . . how about I send a car over? Dale can come get you."

"Did you find the missing child? I don't want to pull your cops off the search."

"Haven't found him yet, but we're following up on a lead. But put that aside for now. You need to stay away from your usual places. And you can't be driving the Jeep around if he's looking for it. Where are you now?"

"In the office of the Quickstop." She ran her hand over the old desktop, eyeing the dark kneehole underneath, wishing she could duck down into the shadows and stay in the cool obscurity there. "I don't know where to go." Her voice sounded thin and frail and she hated herself for being so weak.

"Don't go to the house, and don't go cleaning any cottages, especially now that Becca's tipped him off to what you do."

She rested her cheek on the cool desk. Her skin felt hot from the fire of panic as she considered where she could hide. "I'm scared, Coop."

"I know, sugar. Damn, I wish . . . look, I'm going to come get you, okay?"

"No, no! You've got something important to do. I . . . I'll figure something out."

"Hold on! I know. You can go to the precinct. Brenda is there. She's not armed, but you can sit with her. No criminal type would have the nerve to go strolling into a station house."

She took a halting breath. "I can do that. I'll just leave my Jeep in the parking lot here and walk."

"Now you're thinking smart. You go to the station house and call me or text me when you get there. You hear?"

"Okay."

The blood seemed to be drained from her body as she left the store, a walking zombie headed over to the police station. She deliberated about walking along Highway 12—the shorter route—but decided on a backstreet that ran parallel. It was more deserted, but there was a lot less traffic, and she didn't want to chance the hit man driving by and recognizing her.

The hit man.

The hunter.

Knowing he was here, she felt tears sting her eyes as she passed familiar spots in Avon. The pizza place. The cinemas.

The little gray-haired lady who sold kites from her Cape Cod–style home was tinkering around on the porch as Jane passed, and Jane swallowed the lump in her throat to exchange a greeting.

Avon was supposed to be her protected haven—her escape.

How dare he track her here!

She was angry, furious for all she'd sacrificed . . . all the things Tia had lost in her months of therapy. Her hands clenched into fists as she turned a corner and spotted the small building that housed the police station two blocks ahead. And now she had to go sit in a police station and be babysat by Brenda the dispatcher. Talk about loss of freedom!

As the gravel of the precinct parking lot crunched under her feet, she noticed Coop's truck sitting there. Of course, he was off in the cruiser now.

But she had a key to his truck.

She paused as a window of opportunity presented itself. The hunter wouldn't be looking for her in Coop's truck. She could borrow it and move around under the radar.

Not a bad idea.

She took her keys out of her pocket, jumped into the cab, and fired up the engine.

The warm breeze swirling through the truck helped to cool her temper a bit. She turned onto Highway 12 with the intention of just driving for a while, but when she saw the sign for Ego Beach, she decided to turn into the Canadian Hole.

With the truck pulled up to the edge of the parking lot, she was able to watch the windsurfers in the cove. The strong breeze and flat water made for perfect conditions, and some of the masters were out there hotdogging, flipping their boards and banking so sharply their bodies seemed to scrape the water.

How she longed to get out there with a board and sail and catch the wind! Her days on Pamlico Sound, taking lessons from Coop, now seemed surreal—a paradise too good to be true.

Tears stung her eyes as she realized what she had to do. Coop would be angry with her, and rightly so, but this trouble was more than any small police department could handle. Hell, not even New York City could provide her the protection she'd needed.

She would have to go it alone . . . on the run.

She fired up the truck's engine, angry at the world. Her heart ached at the thought of leaving Coop and all this behind, but she didn't see that she had a choice.

As traffic slowed down the road, she picked up her cell phone and forced herself to dial his number. The man she loved had a right to know, though he'd probably hate her when she told him her plan. She was beginning to hate herself.

As her bad luck would have it, Coop didn't pick up. Swallowing hard, she left him a message.

"I'm sorry, but I've got to borrow your truck. You can use my Jeep as fair trade. I've got to leave town, Coop. It's better for everyone, all around. Thank you for . . . for everything. I'll be in touch when this is all over . . . if you're still speaking to me."

She ended the call and silenced her cell phone, not wanting any diversions to stop her now. She knew Coop would call back eventually and it broke her heart to ignore him, but she couldn't stay here, a walking target.

Sea Breeze Lane was abuzz with activity. The driveway of Coop's house was empty, of course, but across the lane Mrs. Lang was outside watering her garden. Isaiah's truck was parked by the Claytons'—probably servicing their hot tub. Old Mr. Mitty came up from the beach path leaning on his walking stick. His two black Labs circled around him, then darted ahead.

Funny how this street felt more like home than any street she'd lived on in New York.

She pulled into the driveway of Coop's house—her safe haven. If only she could stay . . .

But that wasn't possible. She needed to throw her stuff in a bag and hit the road. Drive till she couldn't see clearly anymore. Leave the hunter behind in her dust.

The key turned in the lock, and she pushed the door open and bent down to check her makeshift security system. The fishing line was still intact, strung across the entryway. At least she knew no one had come through that door.

In the kitchen she paused, her hands on the cool counter, her gaze out over the smooth waters of Pamlico Sound.

This place, this interlude, would forever be engraved upon her soul. Already she missed her dinners with Coop and the intimate nights in his bed.

But she had to go. She grabbed a cold can of Diet Pepsi from the fridge, cracked it open, and headed into the bedroom.

In the closet, she unzipped her duffel bag and tossed in shoes and flip-flops. She stripped garments from their hangers and dumped them in.

On her way to the dresser, something struck her about the bedroom window. Had she left it open like that? She moved closer and noticed that the screen wavered in the wind.

Someone had sliced through it.

From the corner of her eye, she caught a movement in the mirror. The bedroom door was swinging away from the wall.

She swung around, her arms flailing, spilling diet soda through the air.

And there he was: big and dark-haired and with fierce brown eyes.

Her killer.

CHAPTER 15

Where the hell was Jane?

She'd left him a strange message about taking off in his truck and now she wouldn't answer his calls. What the hell was going on? Cooper clicked his radio to signal the dispatcher. "Brenda, do you have Jane there with you?"

"No, Sheriff. I've been watching for her like you said, but no one's been in at all this afternoon."

"Copy." He ran the route from the Quickstop to the station house in his mind. Four, maybe five blocks. What could have happened to her?

That was a question he didn't want to think about.

Jane could smell his sweat now.

He held up a gun.

And suddenly she couldn't look away from the hollow, black barrel pointed right between her eyes.

"I don't want to shoot you here." His voice had a surprisingly high pitch, but the fast-clipped New York accent was unmistakable. "There's too many people around. Your street is like Grand Central Fucking Station, so we gotta get out of here."

So this guy wanted to get away with it . . . and he'd noticed the neighbors outside.

She wondered if she could distract him and make a run for it.

He shot a quick glance toward the door, then stepped closer to her and rammed the cold steel of the pistol to her forehead.

Explosive pain gave way to blackness as she fell back onto the bed and curled up. Her head . . . she rubbed the knot already forming there.

"That's just a little taste of what I'll do if you don't listen. One bad move on your part and I'll shoot and run. I'll be out of this hick town before any of those neighbors realize the noise wasn't fireworks."

Her head was still throbbing when he grabbed her arm and

yanked her to her feet. "Move it. I don't want to be hanging around when the boyfriend comes."

Coop floored it down Sea Breeze Road, frantic to find her. He had waited with the rescue team on the beach until he'd gotten confirmation from Dale that the missing boy had been located, fine and dandy and with his auntie on the waterslide at Rodanthe.

"We got another incident pending. Stay on Alert Fifteen," he'd told the guys from the Coast Guard as he'd jumped into the cruiser. Alert Fifteen kept the helicopter crew on call, ready to go back up in the air with a few minutes' notice.

Cooper had hit the Quickstop, then the station house, where he'd confirmed that his truck was missing.

Then he'd hightailed it over here, thinking she might still be packing.

He hit the brakes and the cruiser screeched to a stop in front of his driveway, where his truck sat gleaming in the sun. Good . . . she was still here.

He dashed up the walkway and took the porch steps two at a time. Her little string contraption was knocked out of place, so she'd been moving in a hurry.

"Jane! Where are you?" he called.

In the bedroom, he paused at the dark brown stains on the rug in a wild sort of zigzag pattern. The can of soda sat on its side, not far from her half-packed duffel bag. Using a tissue, he picked up the can and jiggled it. Still fizzy. It hadn't been here too long.

"Jane . . . sugar?" he called, searching the rest of her apartment, then bolting upstairs to tear through his place.

She was gone . . . but his truck was here . . . and so was her stuff.

Something had gone wrong.

And from that wild pattern of the spilled soda, he had to assume there'd been some sort of confrontation.

Fear tore at his gut as he pictured it.

The hit man had gotten her, right here.

But they couldn't be too far away yet.

He pressed the radio to call dispatch. "Brenda, notify the Coast Guard copters that we need to conduct another air search. They're to wait for me on the beach. We've got another missing person.

Jane Doyle, age twenty-eight, brown hair, Caucasian, a hundred and five pounds."

Beautiful, inside and out.

How could he have been so stupid? He should have responded immediately when she'd reached out to him.

"She never did turn up?"

"Looks like she's been kidnapped, Brenda. Can you post the APB?"

"Kidnapped? Oh my land! Will do, Sheriff."

"And I'm going to need some assistance here to canvass the neighborhood." He gave her the address, then sighed, realizing they were stretched thin with deputies at the far reaches of town, just ending the missing child operation. "See if you can gather up the paramedics for me—Skeeter and Roman were out there today. They'd be a big help."

"They're still on the air. I'll send them right over, Sheriff."

Her head was throbbing and tears streaked down her cheeks unchecked, but Jane swallowed back her fear and kept her eyes on the road, determined to outsmart the man who'd cracked her on the head.

The brute.

With her hands tied behind her back, Jane couldn't really sit back in the seat of the minivan, but she did have a clear view out the tinted glass windows.

Hope had burned inside her at the sight of Coop blazing down Sea Breeze in the cruiser, just missing them. The brute had howled in glee over that, and she would have kicked him if she'd thought she could do it and not be punished tenfold.

She didn't want to piss him off. Let him stay calm and think he was in control until she had a chance to turn the tables.

Yes, he'd tied her up, but he'd left her cell phone in the pocket of her shorts. With enough time, she thought she could get to it and call for help.

Till then, she had to bide her time and try to figure out where he was taking her.

"You know," she said over the hot whir of the van's engine, "if you take me to the police right now, they'll reduce the charges."

He shook his head and grunted. "That'll never happen."

They were heading south on Highway 12 and he was going under the speed limit. No chance of being pulled over.

"Can you turn on the air conditioner?" she asked, only to get him talking.

"Sorry, princess. This is the best we got."

"You know I'm no princess. I work hard for the things I've got."

"Well, that's bonus points for you," the brute said indifferently.

Her senses went on alert when he slowed the van, then made a right turn onto a familiar dirt road.

"Where are you taking me?" she asked, though she knew where this road led.

"There's a low spot here. Gets hit hard at low tide. The water comes in and washes all around it."

Dragon's Point, she thought.

"I know that place," she said. "You'd better watch it or your car will get stuck out there overnight."

"I got a chart of the tides," he said. "I got it all figured out. You'll be tied up when the tide comes in. In over your head, so to speak. And I won't even have to waste a bullet on you." He tapped his beefy fingers on the steering wheel. "The cops might even think it was an accident."

Death by drowning.

She yanked her arms in an attempt to either stretch the bristly rope or work her wrists loose.

No such luck. Already her skin was sore and raw from the friction.

She tried not to think about the cell phone in the pocket of her shorts. He hadn't noticed it before, and she might not be able to reach it, but it was still there. Her ace in the hole.

Her lifeline to Coop.

"A white minivan with New Jersey plates," Cooper told Brenda over the radio. "Post a bulletin for a white minivan, male driver, thirties, about six-two and two hundred pounds, Caucasian, dark hair."

Cooper had gotten the perp's description from Becca at the

Quickstop. Skeeter had learned that the man had also been seen poking around the van by Mr. Mitty. And the van's Jersey plates had been noted by Mrs. Lang when she was watering her lilies.

People always saw more than they realized. For the first time, Cooper was grateful for his nosy neighbors.

"I'm getting on the Coast Guard helicopter now." Coop spoke quickly, driven by a sense of urgency. "I'll be switching over to their radio channel."

"Copy, Sheriff," Brenda said.

The blades began to whir, kicking up sand on the beach. He pulled on a helmet with a built-in radio system and stepped into the chopper, hoping his desperation to find her would not diminish his objectivity. It was never good to work a case you were involved in, but there was no way he was going to hand this over to another law enforcement agency.

He gave a thumbs-up to the pilot and the big bird began to rise.

"Just so you know, I've got my gun right here on my waistband, so don't try anything cute," he said as he pushed her toward the spit of land leading to Dragon's Point.

Jane had been sorting through all sorts of things to try—none of them so cute. She had tried different strategies with the brute. She'd reasoned and cajoled and played the sympathy card. But when she looked in his eyes, there was no glimmer of compassion, no tiny light of humanity.

He was a contract killer and she was nothing more than a bounty to him.

"What if I wrote you a check for the amount of money you're getting to kill me?" she said, only half teasing.

"Shut the hell up."

She walked sullenly, the throbbing ache on her forehead a reminder of his penchant for violence. It wouldn't pay to tangle with him directly.

They plodded through the sand on the narrow spit of land leading out to the rocky point. Slicks of water were already beginning to cut channels across the low-lying sandbars. Jane stepped over the puddles, wondering how well he knew Dragon's Point. With his accent, he obviously wasn't from around here.

"Why don't you tie me up at the cove?" she suggested, knowing that the tide rarely came up over the rocks out on the point.

"Because the water might not get to you there," he said. "I wasn't born yesterday."

The brute was smarter than she'd thought. He actually knew about the tides, and somehow he'd found out about Dragon's Point.

"This is far enough," he said. "Stop. Now."

She paused at the edge of a tide pool. They were just out far enough to see the colorful sails of puffed kites moving parallel to the shoreline.

"Aren't you worried about kite boarders seeing me?" she asked. "Or are you going to kill all of them, too?"

"Shut up. You're going to be gagged and they're not going to notice a woman sitting alone on the shore."

He put a beefy hand on her shoulders and pushed down. "Go on, sit."

She sank down onto one knee, then onto her bottom. Cold water seeped into her shorts immediately and she was cognizant of sitting on the left side to keep the cell phone as dry as possible.

Water splashed from his feet as he paced in front of her, considering. "Where's the rope?" he said aloud, then cursed.

You left it in the car. The words burned on her tongue, but she kept silent.

"All right, stay there. I'll be right back."

Cold water cooled her legs and bottom as she stayed very still, watching him walk back toward the car. At one point, he turned and looked back to check on her, but she was frozen in place, still as a statue.

She gave no hint that her heart was racing and her mind was reeling with possibilities.

Run!

No, she couldn't run to safety back on the land. She would never get past him.

But she could run out to the point and hide amid the boulders. That would buy her some time.

And her cell phone . . . maybe she could use it to call for help.

She waited a full minute after he dropped from sight, then angled herself up off the sand and bolted for the rocks. Running was difficult with her hands bound behind her, but she focused on maintaining her balance as she plunged through tide pools and scaled the rise up to the jagged point.

The boulders slowed her progress, but she felt a glimmer of hope when she reached the more secluded area. She climbed to a spot where sand had collected between two massive boulders and dropped down to her knees.

Sweat beaded on her forehead as she groaned and stretched her hands around to her side pocket. She couldn't reach inside, but she could feel the phone through the fabric of her shorts.

Every cell in her body strained as she massaged the phone to the edge of the pocket, pressing, pushing, scraping it to the opening of her pocket.

How long had it been?

The brute would be back any second.

"Come on," she breathed, her finger sore from the pressure. One more push, one more inch . . .

"Dispatch to Coast Guard One."

Cooper jerked away from the helicopter's window as Brenda's voice came over the air. "Coast Guard One, copy."

"Jane is at Dragon's Point, Sheriff. She's out on the point in the rocks. The male suspect is in the vicinity of the parking lot, but she says he's coming back. Armed and dangerous."

"Dragon's Point!" Coop shouted to the crew, but the aircraft was already banking to the left. The pilot had been listening on the same radio band.

"Copy," the pilot said.

"Brenda," Coop said, trying to picture the scene, "he left her on the Point? He's coming back?"

"He went back to the car for rope and a gag, she thinks. But he's going to be mad when he comes back and finds that she's moved her spot."

"And you've dispatched law enforcement on the ground to the Point?"

"Got two units on their way," Brenda said.

"Thanks, Bren. Copy." Coop moved back to the window and

thought through approaches. He could drop down to the water, but he couldn't bring a gun if he did that. They could buzz the perp if they spotted him far enough away from Jane, but the man was armed. Would he fire at the helicopter? And what if he had Jane hostage?

"How do you want me to approach?" the pilot asked over the radio.

"From inland . . . the parking area," Coop responded. "Let's see if we can ward the abductor off." *And keep Jane safe.* Let the bastard slip away; this was all about saving Jane.

The wait was agonizing.

Adrenaline thrummed through her as she peeked out over the rocks at the glassy water of the sound, trying to think of a way to escape as two kite boarders floated past.

"Help!" she cried. "Help me!"

They were too far away to hear her.

A guttural curse floated on the wind and she glanced down toward the path.

The brute crashed through the tide pools, furious that she was gone. His head twitched right and left as he scanned the horizon and . . .

Had he seen her?

She ducked again, and the air was rent by gunfire. Stones pinged nearby as bullets hit rock.

He was shooting at her.

Her body shook as she hobbled down onto her side, trying to stay low. But she imagined him running toward her, ready to fire. How many yards separated them?

And she was a sitting target.

All these months on the run, trying to hide and keep moving, and it had come to this.

A low growl sounded in the distance. She tried to focus on that noise, imagined it as a soothing mantra of normal life. A tractor on the road? A small fishing boat?

It grew louder, chopping the air overhead. A helicopter. She squinted up against the sun and spotted it—a Coast Guard helicopter. Was it still searching for the missing kid?

She wanted to jump up and try to signal, but she couldn't risk drawing fire from the brute.

Still . . . the helicopter gave her hope.

She hobbled up to her knees and peered over the rocks.

The brute saw the aircraft, too . . . and he realized that they could see him.

In one move, he holstered his gun and turned toward the parking lot . . .

Retreating.

A sob of relief quivered from Jane's chest as she pushed to her feet. They had saved her!

Tears of relief blurred her vision and she blinked them away, eager to see the aircraft circling overhead.

The copter hovered, descending over the cove. When it reached its lowest point, a rope ladder dropped out and a uniformed officer began to descend.

He was at least fifty yards away, but from his lithe movements and his strong, broad shoulders, she recognized him.

Coop.

Her heart swelled with love for this man, her protector, her soul mate. Tears streaked her face as she watched him drop into the water, wade into shore, and climb the rocks.

Coop had come to rescue her.

"Miss Jane?" His gaze combed over her, concerned, tentative. "Are you okay?"

"I am now."

He touched her shoulders gently, then cradled her in his arms as she sagged against him.

"Don't ever let go," she whispered. "Don't ever let me go."

EPILOGUE

"To safe haven," Rusty said, holding up a glass of sparkling apple cider.

"I'll drink to that," Jane said as she clinked glasses with Kailani and Coop.

The sun cast orange light on Coop's deck, where the table was spread with newspaper and a bag of steamed crabs sat ready to be cracked. The trauma of last week was beginning to fade to the back of Jane's mind, and Jane and Coop had decided it was time to invite Rusty and Kailani over to fill them in on Jane's story.

"I think your danger is gone, Jane," Kailani said, twirling her glass on the table. "I don't see it anymore."

"I sure hope so. I've had more than my share," Jane said.

"That state trooper who arrested your kidnapper came into the Quickstop today," Rusty said. "Ramsey was his name, right? Did you know he's got two other felony convictions for murder?"

"We heard that," Coop said, squeezing Jane's knee.

Jane had called him "the brute," but later they'd told her he was Anthony Ramsey and he had been apprehended that fateful day after a police chase on Highway 12.

"I hope he's off the streets for a long time," Jane said.

"He will be," Coop said, his voice quiet but confident. "He's got three strikes now."

Jane took a sip of the sweet apple juice and sighed. "It's good to be putting that whole chapter of my life behind me."

Coop nodded, bumping Rusty on the shoulder. "Jane just found out today that she doesn't have to go back to New York for that trial anymore. Turns out the killer, a thug named Canby, did some soul searching in prison. He's turning his life around. Confessed to the homicide."

Jane smiled. She had sobbed in relief after the call came from the Manhattan district attorney that day.

"So . . . instead of a trip to the city, we've decided on a September wedding here in Avon." Coop put his glass on the table, facing Kailani and Rusty. "We'd like you two to stand up for us."

Rusty bumped Coop on the shoulder. "I'm honored, man."

Kailani's dark eyes lit up. "And that explains why I've been seeing Jane barefoot on the beach in a white dress. You're having a beach wedding. And there are windsurfers behind you in the cove."

Jane laughed. "Okay, Kailani, now you're scaring me."

"I've been seeing that image all week," Kailani said seriously. "Now that you've said it, I can take it out of my head and make room for something else."

"Like your little baby girl?" Jane smiled.

Kailani rubbed her belly. "Two girls." She looked over at Rusty, who scraped his hair back. "I was right about the gender, wrong about the number. The doctor says we're having twins."

"I may never sleep again!" Rusty said.

Coop clapped him on the back. "Relax, buddy. You can sleep when you get old."

"Right." Rusty laughed. "I'll be aging fast."

"So . . ." Jane rose to pour out the steamed crabs. "Let's crack some crabs."

As they dug in, Jane leaned back and surveyed their relaxed faces, the quiet neighborhood with Mrs. Lang in her garden and Mr. Mitty walking his dogs out in the dunes. The orange ball of the sun was reflected on the water of the sound, where die-hard windsurfers worked their sails to capture the last ride of the day.

How she loved this place, this beach life, this Carolina charm . . . this man sitting beside her. Cooper had promised her protection, but he'd given her so much more.

A new life.

She looked down at the table as a vision popped into her head—a blue-eyed baby laughing up at her.

She darted a look at Kailani, who smiled. "Yes," Kailani said, nodding. "I see it, too. They'll play together."

Jane touched her belly, her heart beating in wonder. Yes, Cooper really had given her a new life.

THE BRASS RING

BY LISA JACKSON

CHAPTER 1

The old merry-go-round picked up speed, ancient gears grinding as black smoke spewed from the diesel engine and clouded the summer-blue Oregon sky.

Shawna McGuire clung to the neck of her wooden mount and glanced over her shoulder. Her heart swelled at the sight of Parker Harrison. Tall, with the broad shoulders of a natural athlete and brown hair streaked gold by the sun, he sat astride a glossy striped tiger. His blue eyes were gazing possessively at her and a camera swung from his neck.

Shawna grinned shamelessly. Tomorrow morning she and Parker would be married!

The carousel spun faster. Colors of pink, blue, and yellow blurred together.

"Reach, Shawna! Come on, you can do it!" Parker yelled, his deep voice difficult to hear above the piped music of the calliope and the sputtering engine.

Grinning, her honey-gold hair billowing away from her face, she saw him wink at her, then focus his camera and aim.

"Go for it, *Doctor!*" he called.

The challenge was on and Shawna glanced forward again, her green eyes fixed on the brass ring with fluttering pastel ribbons, the prize that hung precariously near the speeding carousel. She stretched her fingers, grabbed as she passed the ring and swiped into the air, coming up with nothing and nearly falling off her painted white stallion in the bargain. She heard Parker's laughter and looked back just in time to see him snatch the prize. A big, gloating smile spread easily across his square jaw and the look he sent her made her heart pound wildly.

She thought about her plans for the wedding the following morning. It was almost too good to be true. In less than twenty-four hours, under the rose arbor at Pioneer Church, she'd become Mrs. Parker Harrison and they would be bound for a weeklong honeymoon in the Caribbean! No busy hospital schedules, no double shifts, no phones or patients—just Parker.

She glimpsed Parker stuffing the ring and ribbons into the front pocket of his jeans as the merry-go-round slowed.

"That's how it's done," he said, cupping his hands over his mouth so that she could hear him.

"Insufferable, arrogant—" she muttered, but a dimple creased her cheek and she laughed gaily, clasping her fingers around the post supporting her mount and tossing back her head. Her long hair brushed against her shoulders and she could hear the warm sound of Parker's laughter. She was young and in love—nothing could be more perfect.

When the ride ended she climbed off her glazed white horse and felt Parker's strong arms surround her. "That was a feeble attempt if I ever saw one," he whispered into her ear as he lifted her to the ground.

"We all can't be professional athletes," she teased, looking up at him through gold-tipped lashes. "Some of us have to set goals, you know, to achieve higher intellectual and humanistic rewards."

"Bull!"

"Bull?" she repeated, arching a golden brow.

"Save that for someone who'll believe it, Doctor. I won and you're burned."

"Well, maybe just a little," she admitted, her eyes shining. "But it is comforting to know that should I ever quit my practice, and if you gave up completely on tennis, we could depend on your income as a professional ring-grabber."

"I'll get you for that one, Dr. McGuire," he promised, squeezing her small waist, his hand catching in the cotton folds of her sundress. "And my vengeance will be swift and powerful and drop you to your knees!"

"Promises, promises!" she quipped, dashing away from him

and winding quickly through the crowd. Dry grass brushed against her ankles and several times her sandals caught on an exposed pebble, but she finally reached a refreshment booth with Parker right on her heels. "A bag of buttered popcorn and a sack of peanuts," she said to the vendor standing under the striped awnings. She felt out of breath and flushed, and her eyes glimmered mischievously. "And this guy," she motioned to Parker as he approached, "will foot the bill."

"Henpecked already," Parker muttered, delving into his wallet and handing a five-dollar bill to the vendor. Someday—" he said, blue eyes dancing as he shucked open a peanut and tossed the nut into his mouth.

"Someday what?" she challenged, her pulse leaping when his eyes fixed on her lips. For a minute she thought he was going to kiss her right there in the middle of the crowd. If he did, she wouldn't stop him. She couldn't. She loved him too much.

"Just you wait, lady—" he warned, his voice low and throaty, the vein in the side of his neck pulsing.

Shawna's heart began to thud crazily.

"For what?"

A couple of giggling teenage girls approached, breaking the magical spell. "Mr. Harrison?" the taller, red-haired girl asked, while her friend in braces blushed.

Parker looked over his shoulder and twisted around. "Yes?"

"I told you it was him!" the girl in braces said, nearly jumping up and down in her excitement. Her brown eyes gleamed in anticipation.

"Could we, uh, would you mind"—the redhead fumbled in her purse—"could we get your autograph?"

"Sure," Parker said, taking the scraps of paper and pen that had been shoved into his hand and scribbling out his name.

"I'm Sara and this is Kelly. Uh—Sara without an 'h.' "

"Got it!" Parker finished writing.

"Is, um, Brad here?"

" 'Fraid not," Parker admitted, the corner of his mouth lifting as he snapped the cap back onto the pen.

"Too bad," Sara murmured, obviously disappointed as she tucked her pen and paper into her purse.

But Kelly smiled widely, displaying the wires covering her teeth. "Gee, thanks!"

The two girls waved and took off, giggling to themselves.

"The price of fame," Parker said teasingly.

"Not too bad for a has-been," Shawna commented dryly, unable to hide the pride in her voice. "But it didn't hurt that you're Brad Lomax's coach. He's the star now, you know."

Parker grinned crookedly. "Admit it, McGuire, you're still sore 'cause you didn't get the ring." Draping his arm possessively around her shoulders, he hugged her close.

"Maybe just a little," she said with a happy sigh. The day had been perfect despite the humidity. High overhead, the boughs of tall firs swayed in the sultry summer breeze and dark clouds drifted in from the west.

Shawna's feet barely hit the ground as they walked through the "Fair from Yesteryear." Sprawled over several acres of farmland in the foothills of the Cascade Mountains, the dun-colored tents, flashy rides, and booths were backdropped by spectacular mountains. Muted calliope music filled the summer air, and barkers, hawking their wares and games, shouted over the noise of the crowd. The smells of horses, sawdust, popcorn, and caramel wafted through the crowded, tent-lined fields that served as fairgrounds.

"Want to test your strength?" Shawna asked, glancing up at Parker and pointing to a lumberjack who was hoisting a heavy mallet over his head. Swinging the hammer with all of his might, the brawny man grunted loudly. The mallet crashed against a springboard and hurled a hearty weight halfway up a tall pole.

Parker's lips curved cynically. "I'll pass. Don't want to ruin my tennis arm, you know."

"Sure."

Parker ran his fingers through his sun-streaked hair. "There is another reason," he admitted.

She arched an eyebrow quizzically. "Which is?"

"I think I'll save my strength for tomorrow night." His voice lowered and his eyes darkened mysteriously. "There's this certain lady who's expecting all of my attention and physical prowess."

"Is that right?" She popped a piece of popcorn into his mouth and grinned. "Then you'd better not disappoint her."

"I won't," he promised, his gaze shifting to her mouth.

Shawna swallowed with difficulty. Whenever he looked at her that way, so sensual and determined, her heart always started beating a rapid double-time. She had to glance away, over his shoulder to a short, plump woman who was standing in front of a tent.

Catching Shawna's eye, the woman called, "How about I read your fortune?" With bright scarves wrapped around her head, painted fingernails, and dangling hooped earrings, she waved Shawna and Parker inside.

"I don't know—"

"Why not?" Parker argued, propelling her into the darkened tent. Smelling of sawdust and cloying perfume, the tent was dark and close. Shawna sat on a dusty pillow near a small table and wondered what had possessed her to enter. The floor was covered with sawdust and straw, the only illumination coming from a slit in the top of the canvas. The place gave her the creeps.

Placing a five-dollar bill on the corner of the table, Parker sat next to Shawna, one arm still draped casually over her shoulders, his long legs crossed Indian style.

The money quickly disappeared into the voluminous folds of the Gypsy woman's skirt as she settled onto a mound of pillows on the other side of the table. "You first?" she asked, flashing Shawna a friendly, gold-capped smile.

Shrugging, Shawna glanced at Parker before meeting the Gypsy woman's gaze. "Sure. Why not?"

"Good!" Lady Fate clapped her wrinkled palms together. "Now, let me read your palm." Taking Shawna's hand in hers, she gently stroked the smooth skin, tracing the lines of Shawna's palm with her long fingers.

"I see you have worked long and hard in your job."

That much was true, Shawna thought wryly. She'd spent more hours than she wanted to count as a bartender while going to college and medical school. It had been years of grueling work, late shifts, and early morning classes, but finally, just this past year, she'd become a full-fledged internist. Even now, juggling time between her clinic and the hospital, she was working harder than she'd ever expected.

"And you have a happy family."

"Yes," Shawna admitted proudly. "A brother and my parents."

The woman nodded, as if she saw their faces in Shawna's palm. "You will live a long and fruitful life," she said thickly and then her fingers moved and she traced another line on Shawna's hand, only to stop short. Her face clouded, her old lips pursed and she dropped Shawna's wrist as quickly as she had taken it earlier. "Your time is over," she said gently, kindness sparking in her old brown eyes.

"What?"

"Next," Lady Fate said, calling toward the flap used as a door.

"That's all?" Shawna repeated, surprised. She didn't know much about fortune-telling, but she'd just begun to enjoy the game and some of her five-dollar future was missing.

"Yes. I've told you everything. Now, if you'll excuse me—"

"Wait a minute. What about my love life?" Glancing at Parker in the shadowed room, Shawna winked.

Lady Fate hesitated.

"I thought you could see everything," Shawna said. "That's what your sign says."

"There are some things better left unknown," the woman whispered softly as she started to stand.

"I can handle it," Shawna said, but felt a little uneasy.

"Really, you don't want to know," Lady Fate declared, pursing her red lips and starting to stand.

"Of course I do," Shawna insisted. Though she didn't really believe in any of this mumbo jumbo, she wanted to get her money's worth. "I want to know everything." Shawna thrust her open palm back to the woman.

"She's very stubborn," Parker interjected.

"So I see." The fortune-teller slowly sat down on her pillows as she closed Shawna's fingers, staring straight into her eyes. "I see there is a very important man in your life—you love him dearly, too much, perhaps."

"And?" Shawna asked, disgusted with herself when she felt the hairs on the back of her neck prickle with dread.

"And you will lose him," the woman said sadly, glancing at Parker and then standing to brush some of the straw from her skirt. "Now go."

"Come on," Parker said, his eyes glinting mischievously. "It's time you got rid of that love of your life and started concentrating on me." He took Shawna by the hand and pulled her from the dark tent.

Outside, the air was hot and muggy but a refreshing change from the sticky interior of the tiny canvas booth. "You set her up to that, didn't you?" Shawna accused, still uneasy as she glanced back at the fortune-teller's tent.

"No way! Don't tell me you believed all of that baloney she tried to peddle you!"

"Of course not, but it was kind of creepy." Shuddering, she rubbed her bare arms despite the heat.

"And way off base." Laughing, he tugged on her hand and led her through a thicket of fir trees, away from the crowd and the circus atmosphere of the fair.

The heavy boughs offered a little shade and privacy and cooled the sweat beading on the back of Shawna's neck.

"You didn't believe her, did you?" he asked, his eyes delving deep into hers.

"No, but—"

"Just wait 'til the medical board gets wind of this!"

She couldn't help but smile as she twisted her hair into a loose rope and held it over her head, and off her neck. "You're laughing at me."

"Maybe a little." Stepping closer, he pinned her back against the rough bark of a Douglas fir, his arms resting lightly on her shoulders. "You deserve it, too, after all that guff you gave me about that damned brass ring."

"Guilty as charged," she admitted. She let her hair fall free and wrapped her hands around his lean, hard waist. Even beneath his light shirt, she could feel the ripple of his muscles as he shifted.

"Good." Taking the brass ring from his pocket, he slipped the oversized band onto her finger. "With this ring, I thee wed," he said quietly, watching the ribbons flutter over her arm.

Shawna had to blink back some stupid tears of happiness that wet her lashes. "I can't wait," she murmured, "for the real thing."

"Neither can I." Placing his forehead against hers, he stared at the dimpled smile playing on her lips.

Shawna's pulse leaped. His warm breath fanned her face, his fingers twined lazily in a long strand of her honey-gold hair and his mouth curved upward in a sardonic smile. "And now, Dr. McGuire, prepare yourself. I intend to have my way with you!" he said menacingly.

"Right here?" she asked innocently.

"For starters." He brushed his lips slowly over hers and Shawna sighed into his mouth.

She felt warm all over and weak in the knees. He kissed her eyelids and throat and she moaned, parting her lips expectantly. His hands felt strong and powerful and she knew that Parker would always take care of her and protect her. Deep inside, fires of desire that only he could spark ignited.

"I love you," she whispered, the wind carrying her words away as it lifted her hair away from her face.

"And I love you." Raising his head, he stared into her passion-glazed eyes. "And tomorrow night, I'm going to show you just how much."

"Do we really have to wait?" she whispered, disappointment pouting her lips.

"Not much longer—but we had a deal, remember?"

"It was stupid."

"Probably," he agreed. "And it's been hell." His angular features grew taut. "But weren't you the one who said, 'Everything meaningful is worth the wait'?"

"That's a butchered version of it, but yes," she said.

"And we've made it this far."

"It's been agony," she admitted. "The next time I have such lofty, idealistic and stupid ideas, go ahead and shoot me."

Grinning, he placed a kiss on her forehead. "I suppose this means that I'll have to give up my mistress."

"Your *what!*" she sputtered, knowing that he was teasing. *His mistress!* This mystery woman—a pure fantasy—had always been a joke between them, a joke that hurt more than it should have. "Oooh, you're absolutely the most arrogant, self-centered, egotistical—"

Capturing her wrists, he held them high over her head with one hand. "Go on," he urged, eyes slowly inching down her body, past her flashing green eyes and pursed lips, to the hollow of her throat where her pulse was fluttering rapidly, then lower still, to the soft mounds of her breasts, pushed proudly forward against apricot-colored cotton, rising and falling with each of her shallow breaths.

"—self-important, presumptuous, insolent bastard I've ever met!"

Lowering his head, he kissed the sensitive circle of bones at the base of her throat and she felt liquid inside. "Leave anything out?" he asked, his breath warm against her already overheated skin.

"A million things!"

"Such as?"

"Mistress," she repeated and then sucked in a sharp breath when she felt his moist tongue touch her throat. "Stop it," she said weakly, wanting to protest but unable.

"Aren't you the woman who was just begging for more a few minutes ago?"

"Parker—"

Then he cut off her protest with his mouth slanting swiftly over hers, his body pressed urgently against her. He kissed her with the passion that she'd seen burning in him ever since the first time they'd met. Her back was pinned to the trunk of the tree, her hands twined anxiously around his neck, wanton desire flowing from his lips to hers.

His hips were thrust against hers and she could feel the intensity of his passion, his heat radiating against her. "Please—" she whispered and he groaned.

His tongue rimmed her lips and then tasted of the sweetness within her open mouth.

"Parker—" She closed her eyes and moaned softly.

Suddenly every muscle in his body tensed and he released her as quickly as he'd captured her. Swearing, he stepped away from her. "You're dangerous, you know that, don't you?" His hands were shaking when he pushed the hair from his eyes. "I—I think we'd better go," he said thickly, clearly trying to quell the desire pounding in his brain.

Swallowing hard, she nodded. She could feel a hot flush staining her cheeks, knew her heart was racing out of control, and had trouble catching her breath. "But tomorrow, Mr. Harrison—you're not going to get away so easily."

"Don't tease me," he warned, his mouth a thin line of self-control.

"Never," she promised, forest-green eyes serious.

Linking his fingers with hers, he pulled her toward the parking lot. "I think we'd better get out of here. If I remember correctly, we have a wedding rehearsal and a dinner to get through tonight."

"That's right," she groaned, combing her tangled hair with her fingers, as they threaded their way through the cars parked in uneven rows. "You know, I should have listened to you when you wanted to elope."

"Next time, you'll know."

"There won't be a next time," she vowed as he opened the door of his Jeep and she slid into the sweltering interior. "You're going to be stuck with me for life!"

"I wouldn't have it any other way." Once behind the wheel, he cranked open the windows and turned on the ignition.

"Even if you have to give up your mistress?"

Coughing, he glanced at her. One corner of his mouth lifted cynically as he maneuvered the car out of the bumpy, cracked field that served as a parking lot. "The things I do for love," he muttered and then switched on the radio and shifted gears.

Shawna stared out the window at the passing countryside. In the distance, dark clouds had begun to gather around the rugged slopes of Mount Hood. Shadows lengthened across the hilly, dry farmland. Dry, golden pastures turned dark as the wind picked up. Grazing cattle lifted their heads at the scent of the approaching storm and weeds and wildflowers along the fencerows bent double in the muggy breeze.

"Looks like a storm brewing." Parker glanced at the hard, dry ground and frowned. "I guess we could use a little rain."

"But not tonight or tomorrow," Shawna said. "Not on our wedding day." *Tomorrow,* she thought with a smile. She tried to ignore the Gypsy woman's grim prediction and the promise of rain. "To-morrow will be perfect!"

"...and may you have all the happiness you deserve. To the bride and groom!" Jake said, casting a smile at his sister and holding his wineglass high in the air.

Hoisting her glass, Shawna beamed, watching her dark-haired brother through adoring eyes.

"Here, here," the rest of the guests chimed in, glasses clinking, laughter and cheery conversation filling the large banquet room of the Edwardian Hotel in downtown Portland. The room was crowded with family and friends, all members of the wedding party. After a rehearsal marred by only a few hitches, and a lovely veal dinner, the wine, toasts and fellowship were flowing freely in the elegant room.

"How was that?" Jake asked, taking his chair.

"Eloquent," Shawna admitted, smiling at her brother. "I didn't know you had it in you."

"That's because you never listened to me," he quipped, and then, setting his elbows on the table, winked at Parker. "I hope you have better luck keeping her in line."

"I will," Parker predicted, loosening his tie.

"Hey, wait a minute," Shawna protested, but laughed and sipped from a glass of cold Chablis.

"I can't wait until tomorrow," Gerri, Shawna's best friend, said with a smile. "I never thought I'd see this day, when someone actually convinced the good doctor to walk down the aisle." Shaking her auburn hair, Gerri leaned back and lit a cigarette, clicking her lighter shut to add emphasis to her words.

"I'm not married to my work," Shawna protested.

"Not anymore. But you were. Back in those days when you were in med school, you were no fun. I repeat: *No fun!*"

Parker hugged his bride-to-be. "I intend to change all that, starting tomorrow!"

"Oh, you do, do you?" Shawna said, her gaze narrowing on him. "I'll have you know, Mr. Harrison, that *you'll* be the one toe-ing the line."

"This should be good," Jake decided. "Parker Harrison under a woman's thumb."

"I'll drink to that!" Brad Lomax, Parker's most famous student, leaned over Shawna's shoulder, spilling some of his drink on the linen tablecloth. His black hair was mussed, his tie already lost, and the smell of bourbon was heavy on his breath. He'd been in a bad mood all evening and had chosen to drown whatever problems he had in a bottle.

"Maybe you should slow down a little," Parker suggested, as the boy swayed over the table.

"What? In the middle of this celebration? No way, man!" To add emphasis to his words, he downed his drink and signaled to the waiter for another.

Parker's eyes grew serious. "Really, Brad, you've had enough."

"Never enough!" He grabbed a glass of champagne from a passing waiter. "Put it on his tab!" Brad said, cocking his thumb at Parker. "This is his las' night of freedom! Helluva waste if ya ask me!"

Jake glanced from Parker to Brad and back again. "Maybe I should take him home," he suggested.

But Brad reached into his pocket, fumbled around and finally withdrew his keys. "I can do it myself," he said testily.

"Brad—"

"I'll go when I'm damned good and ready." Leaning forward, he placed one arm around Parker, the other around Shawna. "You know, I jus' might end up married myself," he decided, grinning sloppily.

"I'd like to be there on the day some girl gets her hooks into you," Parker said. "It'll never happen."

Brad laughed, splashing his drink again. "Guess again," he said, slumping against Shawna.

"Why don't you tell me about it on the way home?" Parker suggested. He helped Brad back to his feet.

"But the party's not over—"

"It is for us. We've got a pretty full schedule tomorrow. I don't want you so hung over that you miss the ceremony."

"I won't be!"

"Right. 'Cause I'm taking you home right now." He set Brad's drink on the table and took the keys from his hand. Then, leaning close to Shawna, he kissed her forehead. "I'll see you in the morning, okay?"

"Eleven o'clock, sharp," she replied, looking up at him, her eyes shining.

"Wouldn't miss it for the world."

"Me, neither," Brad agreed, his arm still slung over Parker's broad shoulders as they headed for the door. " 'Sides, I need to talk to you, need some advice," he added confidentially to Parker.

"So what else is new?"

"Be careful," Jake suggested. "It's raining cats and dogs out there—the first time in a couple months. The roads are bound to be slick."

"Will do," Parker agreed.

Jake watched them leave, his eyes narrowing on Parker's broad shoulders. "I don't see why Parker puts up with Brad," he said, frowning into his drink.

Shawna lifted a shoulder. "You know Brad is Parker's star student, supposedly seeded ninth in the country. Parker expects him to follow in his footsteps, make it to the top—win the grand slam. The whole nine yards, so to speak."

"That's football, sis. Not tennis."

"You know what I mean."

"He's that good?" Obviously, Jake didn't believe it, and Shawna understood why. As a psychiatrist, he'd seen more than his share of kids who'd gotten too much too fast and couldn't handle the fame or money.

Leaning back in her chair, Shawna quoted, "The best natural athlete that Parker's ever seen."

Jake shook his head, glancing again at the door through which Parker and Brad had disappeared. "Maybe so, but the kid's got a temper and a chip on his shoulder the size of the Rock of Gibraltar."

"Thank you for your professional opinion, Dr. McGuire."

"Is that a nice way of saying 'butt out'?" Jake asked.

Shawna shook her head. "No, it's a nice way of saying, let's keep the conversation light—no heavy stuff, okay? I'm getting married tomorrow."

"How could I forget?" Clicking the rim of his glass to hers, he whispered, "And I wish you all the luck in the world." He took a sip of his wine. "You know what the best part of this marriage is, don't you?"

"Living with Parker?"

"Nope. The fact that this is the last day there will be two Dr. McGuires working at Columbia Memorial. No more mixed-up messages or calls."

"That's right. From now on, I'll be Dr. Harrison." She wrinkled her nose a bit. "Doesn't have the same ring to it, does it?"

"Sounds great to me."

"Me, too," she admitted, looking into her wineglass and smiling at the clear liquid within. "Me, too."

She felt a light tap on her shoulder and looked up. Her father was standing behind her chair. A tall, rotund man, he was dressed in his best suit, and a sad smile curved his lips. "How about a dance with my favorite girl?" he asked.

"You've got it," she said, pushing back her chair and taking his hand. "But after that, I'm going home."

"Tired?"

"Uh-huh, and I want to look my best tomorrow."

"Don't worry. You'll be the prettiest bride ever to walk down that aisle."

"The wedding's going to be in the rose garden, remember?" She laughed, and her father's face pulled together.

"I don't suppose I can talk you into saying your vows in front of the altar?"

"Nope. Outside," she said, glancing out the window into the dark night. Rain shimmered on the windowpanes. "I don't care if this blasted rain keeps falling, we're going to be married under the arbor in the rose garden of the church."

"You always were stubborn," he muttered, twirling her around the floor. "Just like your mother."

"Some people say I'm a chip off the old block, and they aren't talking about Mom."

Malcolm McGuire laughed as he waltzed his daughter around the room. "I know this is the eleventh hour, but sometimes I wonder if you're rushing things a bit. You haven't known Parker all that long."

"Too late, Dad. If you wanted to talk me out of this, you shouldn't have waited this long," she pointed out.

"Don't get me wrong; I like Parker."

"Good, because you're stuck with him as a son-in-law."

"I just hope you're not taking on too much," he said thoughtfully. "You're barely out of med school and you have a new practice. Now you're taking on the responsibilities of becoming a wife—"

"And a mother?" she teased.

Malcolm's eyebrows quirked. "I know you want children, but that can come later."

"I'm already twenty-eight!"

"That's not ancient, Shawna. You and Parker, you're both young."

"And in love. So quit worrying," she admonished with a fond grin. "I'm a big girl now. I can take care of myself. And if I can't, Parker will."

"He'd better," her father said, winking broadly. "Or he'll have to answer to me!"

When the strains of the waltz drifted away, he patted Shawna's arm and escorted her back to her chair. He glanced around the room as she slipped her arms through the sleeves of her coat. "So where is that husband-to-be of yours? Don't tell me he already skipped out."

"Very funny." She lifted her hair out of the collar of her raincoat and said, "He took Brad Lomax home a little earlier. But don't worry, Dad, he'll be there tomorrow. I'll see you then."

Tucking her purse under her arm, she hurried down the stairs, unwilling to wait for the elevator. On the first floor, she dashed through the lobby of the old Victorian hotel, and shouldered open the heavy wood door.

The rain was coming down in sheets and thunder rumbled through the sky. Just a summer storm, she told herself, nothing to worry about. Everything will be clean and fresh tomorrow and the roses in the garden will still have dewy drops of moisture on their petals. It will be perfect! Nothing will ruin the wedding. Nothing can.

CHAPTER 2

Shawna stared at her reflection as her mother adjusted the cream-colored lace of her veil. "How's that?" Doris McGuire asked as she met her daughter's gaze in the mirror.

"Fine, Mom. Really—" But Shawna's forehead was drawn into creases and her green eyes were dark with worry. *Where was Parker?*

Doris stepped back to take a better look and Shawna saw herself as her mother did. Ivory lace stood high on her throat, and creamy silk billowed softly from a tucked-in waist to a long train that was now slung over her arm. Wisps of honey-colored hair peeked from beneath her veil. The vision was complete, except for her clouded gaze. "Parker isn't here yet?" Shawna asked.

"Relax. Jake said he'd let us know the minute he arrived." She smoothed a crease from her dress and forced a smile.

"But he was supposed to meet with Reverend Smith half an hour ago."

Doris waved aside Shawna's worries. "Maybe he got caught in traffic. You know how bad it's been ever since the storm last night. Parker will be here. Just you wait. Before you know it, you'll be Mrs. Parker Harrison and Caribbean-bound."

"I hope so," Shawna said, telling herself not to worry. So Parker was a few minutes late; certainly that wasn't something to be alarmed about. Or was it? Parker had never been late once in the six weeks she'd known him.

Glancing through the window to the gray day beyond, Shawna watched the yellow ribbons woven into the white slats of the arbor in the church garden. They danced wildly over the roses of the outdoor altar as heavy purple clouds stole silently across the sky.

Doris checked her watch and sighed. "We still have time to move the ceremony inside," she said quietly. "I'm sure none of the guests would mind."

"No!" Shawna shook her head and her veil threatened to come loose. She heard the harsh sound of her voice and saw her mother stiffen. "Look, Mom, I'm sorry, I didn't mean to snap."

"It's okay—just the wedding-day jitters. But try to calm down," her mother suggested, touching her arm. "Parker will be here soon." But Doris's voice faltered and Shawna saw the concern etched in the corner of her mother's mouth.

"I hope you're right," she whispered, unconvinced. The first drops of rain fell from the sky and ran down the windowpanes. Glancing again out the window to the parking lot, Shawna hoped to see Parker's red Jeep wheel into the lot. Instead, she saw Jake drive up, water splashing from under the wheels of his car as he ground to a stop.

"Where did Jake go?" she asked. "I thought he was in the rose garden . . ." Her voice drifted off as she watched her brother dash through the guests who were moving into the church.

"Shawna!" Jake's voice boomed through the door and he pounded on the wood panels. "Shawna!"

The ghost of fear swept over her.

"For God's sake, come in," Doris said, opening the door.

Jake burst into the room. His hair was wet, plastered to his head, his tuxedo was rumpled, and his face was colorless. "I just heard—there was an accident last night."

"An accident?" Shawna repeated, seeing the horror in his gaze. "No—"

"Parker and Brad were in a terrible crash. They weren't found until a few hours ago. Right now they're at Mercy Hospital—"

"There must be some mistake!" Shawna cried, her entire world falling apart. Parker couldn't be hurt! Just yesterday they were at the fair, laughing, kissing, touching . . .

"No mistake."

"Jake—" Doris reproached, but Jake was at Shawna's side, taking hold of her arm, as if he were afraid she would swoon.

"It's serious, sis."

Disbelieving, Shawna pinned him with wide eyes. "If this is true—"

"Damn it, Shawna, do you think I'd run in here with this kind of a story if I hadn't checked it out?" he asked, his voice cracking.

The last of her hopes fled and she clung to him, curling her fingers over his arm as fear grew in her heart. "Why didn't anyone tell me? I'm a doctor, for God's sake—"

"But not at Mercy Hospital. No one there knew who he was."

"But he's famous—"

"It didn't matter," Jake said soberly. His eyes told it all and for the first time Shawna realized that Parker, her beloved Parker, might die.

"Oh, my God," she whispered, wanting to fall to pieces, but not giving in to the horror that was coldly starting to grip her, wrenching at her insides. "I've got to go to him!"

"But you can't," her mother protested weakly. "Not now—"

"Of course I can!" Flinging off her veil, she gathered her skirts and ran to the side door of the church.

"Wait, Shawna!" Jake called after her, running to catch up. "I'll drive you—"

But she didn't listen. She found her purse with the car keys, jumped into her little hatchback, and plunged the keys into the ignition. The car roared to life. Shawna rammed it into gear and tore out of the parking lot, the car wheels screeching around the curves as she entered the highway. She drove wildly, her every thought centered on Parker as she prayed that he was still alive.

Jake hadn't said it, but it had been written in his eyes. *Parker might die!* "Please, God, no," she whispered, her voice faltering, her chin thrust forward in determination. "You can't let him die! You can't!"

She shifted down, rounding a curve and nearly swerving out of her lane as the car climbed a steep street. Fir trees and church spires, skyscrapers and sharp ravines, a view of the Willamette River and the hazy mountains beyond were lost to her in a blur of rainwashed streets and fear.

Twice her car slid on the slick pavement but she finally drove into the parking lot of the hospital and ignored a sign reserving the first spot she saw for staff members. Her heart hammering with dread, she cut the engine, yanked on the brake and ran toward the glass doors, oblivious to the fact that her dress was dragging through mud puddles and grime.

As she ran to the desk in the emergency room, she wiped the water from her face. "I need to see Parker Harrison," she said breathlessly to a calm-looking young woman at the desk. "I'm Dr. McGuire, Columbia Memorial Hospital." Flashing credentials in the surprised woman's face, she didn't wait for a response. "I'm also Mr. Harrison's personal physician. He was brought in here early this morning and I have to see him!"

"He's in surgery now—"

"Surgery!" Shawna said, incredulous. "Who's the doctor in charge?"

"Dr. Lowery."

"Then let me see Lowery." Shawna's eyes glittered with authority and determination, though inside she was dying. She knew her requests were unreasonable, against all hospital procedures, but she didn't care. Parker was in this hospital, somewhere, possibly fighting for his life, and come hell or high water, she was going to see him!

"You'll have to wait," the nurse said, glancing at Shawna's wet hair, her bedraggled wedding dress, the fire in her gaze.

"I want to see him. Now."

"I'm sorry, Dr. McGuire. If you'd like, you could wait in the doctors' lounge and I'll tell Dr. Lowery you're here."

Seeing no other option, Shawna clamped her teeth together. "Then, please, tell me how serious he is. Exactly what are his injuries? How serious?"

"I can't give out that information."

Shawna didn't move. Her gaze was fixed on the smaller woman's face. "Then have someone who can give it out find me."

"If you'll wait."

Swallowing back the urge to shake information out of the young woman, Shawna exhaled a deep breath and tried to get a grip on her self-control. "Okay—but, please, send someone up to the lounge. I need to know about him, as his physician and as his fiancée."

The young nurse's face softened. "You were waiting for him, weren't you?" she asked quietly, as she glanced again at Shawna's soiled silk gown.

"Yes," Shawna admitted, her throat suddenly tight and tears springing to her eyes. She reached across the counter, took the nurse's hand in her own. "You understand—I have to see him."

"I'll send someone up as soon as I can," the girl promised.

"Thank you." Releasing her grip, Shawna suddenly felt the eyes of everyone in the waiting room boring into her back. For the first time she noticed the group of people assembled on the molded-plastic couches as they waited to be examined. Small children whined and cuddled against their mothers and older people, faces set and white, sat stiffly in the chairs, their eyes taking in Shawna's disheveled appearance.

Turning back to the young nurse, she forced her voice to remain steady. "Please, I want to know if there's any change in his condition." *Whatever that is,* she added silently.

"Will do, Dr. McGuire. The doctors' lounge is just to the left of the elevator on the second floor."

"Thank you," Shawna said, scooping up her skirts and squaring her shoulders as she started down the hall. The heels of her soaked satin pumps clicked on the tile floor.

"Shawna! Wait!" Jake's voice echoed through the corridor. In a few swift strides he was next to her, oblivious to the eyes of all the people in the waiting room. Still dressed in his tuxedo, his wet hair curling around his face, he looked as frantic as she felt. "What did you find out?" he asked softly.

"Not much. I'm on my way to the lounge on the second floor. Supposedly they'll send someone up to give me the news."

"If not, I'll check around—I've got connections here," Jake reminded her, glancing at all the pairs of interested eyes.

"You what?"

"Sometimes I consult here, at Mercy, in the psychiatric wing. I know quite a few of the staff. Come on," he urged, taking her elbow and propelling her toward the elevators. "You can change in the women's washroom on the second floor."

"Change?" she asked, realizing for the first time that he was carrying her smallest nylon suitcase, one of the suitcases she'd packed for her honeymoon. Numb inside, she took the suitcase from his outstretched hand. "Thanks," she murmured. "I owe you one."

"One of many. I'll add it to your list," he said, but the joke fell flat. "Look, Mom went through that," he gestured at the bag, "and thought you could find something more suitable than what you're wearing." Frowning, he touched her dirty gown.

The sympathy in Jake's eyes reached out to her and she felt suddenly weak. Her throat was hot, burning with tears she couldn't shed. "Oh, Jake. Why is this happening?" she asked, just as the elevator doors whispered open and they stepped inside.

"I wish I knew."

"I just want to know that Parker will be all right."

"I'll find out," he promised as the elevator groaned to a stop and Shawna stepped onto the second floor. Pushing a button on the control panel, Jake held the doors open and pointed down the hallway. "The lounge is right there, around the corner, and the washroom—I don't know where *that* is, but it must be nearby. I'll meet you back in the lounge as soon as I find Tom Handleman—he's usually in charge of ER—and then I'll be back to fill you in."

"Thanks," she whispered. The brackets around Jake's mouth deepened as he grimaced. "Let's just hope Parker and Brad are okay."

"They will be! They have to be!"

"I hope so. For your sake."

Then he was gone and Shawna, despite the fact that she was shaking from head to foot, found the washroom. Trying to calm herself, she sluiced cold water over her face and hardly recognized her reflection in the mirror over the sink. Two hours before she'd been a beaming bride, primping in front of a full-length mirror. Now, she looked as if she'd aged ten years. Eyes red, mouth surrounded by lines of strain, skin pale, she stripped off her wedding dress, unable to wear it another minute. Then she changed into a pair of white slacks, a cotton sweater, and a pair of running shoes, the clothes she had thought she would wear while holding hands with Parker and running along the gleaming white beach at Martinique.

Parker. Her heart wrenched painfully.

Quickly folding her dress as best she could and stuffing it into the little bag, she told herself to be strong and professional. Parker would be all right. He had to be.

Quickly, she found the lounge. With trembling hands, she poured herself a cup of coffee. Groups of doctors and nurses were clustered at round tables chattering, laughing, not seeming to care that Parker, her Parker, was somewhere in this labyrinthine building clinging to his very life. Forcing herself to remain calm, she took a chair in a corner near a planter filled with spiky leafed greenery. From there she could watch the door.

Doctors came and went, some with two days' growth of beard and red-rimmed eyes, others in crisply pressed lab coats and bright smiles. Each time the door opened, Shawna's gaze froze expectantly on the doorway, hoping that Jake would come barging into the room to tell her the entire nightmare was a hellish mistake; that Parker was fine; that nothing had changed; that later this afternoon they would step on a plane bound for white sand, hot sun, and aquamarine water...

"Come on, Jake," she whispered to herself, watching the clock as the second hand swept around the face, the minutes ticking by so slowly the waiting had become excruciating. She eavesdropped, listening to the conversations buzzing around her, dreading to overhear that Parker was dead, hoping to hear that his injuries were only superficial. But nothing was said.

Please, let him be all right! Please.

Somehow she finished her coffee and was shredding her cup when Jake pushed open the door and headed straight for her. Another young man was with him—tall and lean, with bushy salt and pepper hair, wire-rimmed glasses, and a sober expression. "Dr. McGuire?" he asked.

Bracing herself for the worst, Shawna met the young man's eyes.

"This is Tom Handleman, Shawna. He was just in ER with Parker," Jake explained.

"And?" she asked softly, her hands balling into fists.

"And he'll live," Tom said. "He was pinned in the car a long time, but his injuries weren't as bad as we'd expected."

"Thank God," she breathed, her voice breaking as relief drove aside her fears.

"He has several cracked ribs, a ruptured spleen, a concussion and a fractured patella, including torn cartilage and ripped ligaments. Besides which, there are facial lacerations and contusions—"

"And you don't think that's serious!" she cut in, the blood draining from her face.

Jake met her worried eyes. "Shawna, please, listen to him."

"I didn't say his condition wasn't serious," Tom replied. "But Mr. Harrison's injuries are no longer life-threatening."

"Concussion," she repeated, "ruptured spleen—"

"Right, but we've controlled the hemorrhaging and his condition has stabilized. As I said, his concussion wasn't as bad as Lowery and I had originally thought."

"No brain damage?" she asked.

"Not that we can tell. But he'll have to have knee surgery as soon as his body's well enough for the additional trauma."

She ran a shaking hand over her forehead. *Parker was going to be all right!* She felt weak with relief. "Can I see him?"

"Not yet. He's still in recovery," Tom said quietly. "But in a few hours, once he's conscious again—then you can see him."

"Was he conscious when he was brought in?"

"No." Dr. Handleman shook his head. "But we expect him to wake up as soon as the anesthetic wears off."

Jake placed his hand on Shawna's shoulder. "There's something else," he said quietly.

His grim expression and the fingers gripping her shoulder warned her. For the first time, she thought about the other man in Parker's car. "Brad?" she whispered, knowing for certain that Parker's star pupil and friend was dead.

"Brad Lomax was DOA," Tom said softly.

"Dead on arrival?" she repeated, the joy she'd felt so fleetingly stripped away.

"He was thrown from the car and his neck was broken."

"No!" she cried.

Jake's fingers tightened over her shoulders as she tried to stand and deny everything Tom was saying. She could see heads swing in her direction, eyes widen in interest as doctors at nearby tables heard her protest.

"I'm sorry," Tom said. "There was nothing we could do."

"But he was only twenty-two!"

"Shawna—" Jake's fingers relaxed.

Tears flooded her eyes. "I don't believe it!"

"You're a doctor, Miss McGuire," Tom pointed out, his eyes softening with sympathy. "You know as well as I do that these things happen. Not fair, I know, but just the way it is."

Sniffing back her tears, Shawna pushed Jake's restraining hands from her shoulders. Still grieving deep in her heart, she forced her professionalism to surface. "Thank you, Doctor," she murmured, extending her hand though part of her wanted to crumple into a miserable heap. As a doctor, she was used to dealing with death, but it was never easy, especially at a time like this, when the person who had lost his life was someone she'd known, someone Parker had loved.

Tom shook her hand. "I'll let you know when Mr. Harrison is awake and in his room. Why don't you go and rest for a couple of hours?"

"No—I, uh, I couldn't," she said.

"Your choice. Whatever I can do to help," he replied before turning and leaving the room.

"Oh, Jake," she said, feeling the security of her brother's arm wrap around her as he led her from the lounge. "I just can't believe that Brad's gone—"

"It's hard, I know, but you've got to listen to me," he urged, handing her the nylon suitcase he'd picked up and helping her to the elevator. "What you'll have to do now is be strong, for Parker. When he wakes up and finds out that Brad is dead, he's going to feel guilty as hell—"

"But it wasn't his fault. It couldn't have been."

"I know," he whispered. "But Parker won't see the accident that way—not at first. The trauma of the accident combined with an overwhelming sense of guilt over Brad's death might be devastating for Parker. It would be for anyone." He squeezed her and offered a tight smile. "You'll have to be his rock, someone he can hold on to, and it won't be easy."

She met his gaze and determination shone in her eyes. "I'll do everything I can for him," she promised.

One side of Jake's mouth lifted upward. "I know it, sis."

"The only thing that matters is that Parker gets well."

"And the two of you get married."

Her fingers clenched around the handle of her suitcase and she shook a wayward strand of hair from her eyes. "That's not even important right now," she said, steadfastly pushing all thoughts of her future with Parker aside. "I just have to see that he gets through this. And I will. No matter what!"

* * *

The next four hours were torture. She walked the halls of the hospital, trying to get rid of the nervous tension that twisted her stomach and made her glance at the clock every five minutes.

Jake had gone back to the church to explain what had happened to the guests and her parents, but she'd refused to give up her vigil.

"Dr. McGuire?"

Turning, she saw Dr. Handleman walking briskly to her.

"What's happened?" she asked. "I thought Parker was supposed to be put in a private room two hours ago."

"I know," he agreed, his face drawn, "but things changed. Unfortunately, Mr. Harrison hasn't regained consciousness. We've done tests, the anesthesia has worn off, but he's still asleep."

Dread climbed up her spine. "Meaning?"

"Probably that he'll come to in the next twenty-four hours."

"And if he doesn't?" she asked, already knowing the answer, panic sending her heart slamming against her rib cage.

"Then we'll just have to wait."

"You're saying he's in a coma."

Tom pushed his glasses up his nose and frowned. "It looks that way."

"How long?"

"We can't guess."

"How long?" she repeated, jaw clenched, fear taking hold of her.

"Come on, *Dr.* McGuire, you understand what I'm talking about," he reminded her as gently as possible. "There's no way of knowing. Maybe just a few hours—"

"But maybe indefinitely," she finished, biting back the urge to scream.

"That's unlikely."

"But not out of the question."

He forced a tired smile. "Prolonged coma, especially after a particularly traumatic experience, is always a possibility."

"What about his knee?"

"It'll wait, but not too long. We can't let the bones start to knit improperly, otherwise we might have more problems than we already do."

"He's a tennis pro," she whispered.

"We'll take care of him," he said. "Now, if you want, you can see him. He's in room four-twelve."

"Thank you." Without a backward glance, she hurried to the elevator, hoping to stamp down the panic that tore at her. On the fourth floor, she strode briskly down the corridor, past rattling gurneys, clattering food trays, and the soft conversation of the nurses at their station as she made her way to Parker's room.

"Excuse me, miss," one nurse said as Shawna reached the door to room four-twelve. "But Mr. Harrison isn't allowed any visitors."

Shawna faced the younger woman and squared her shoulders, hoping to sound more authoritative than she felt. "I'm Dr. McGuire. I work at Columbia Memorial Hospital. Mr. Harrison is my patient and Dr. Handleman said I could wait for the patient to regain consciousness."

"It's all right," another nurse said. "I took the call from Dr. Handleman. Dr. McGuire has all privileges of a visiting physician."

"Thank you," Shawna said, entering the darkened room and seeing Parker's inert form on the bed. Draped in crisp, white sheets, lying flat on his back, with an IV tube running from his arm and a swath of bandages over his head, he was barely recognizable. "Oh, Parker," she whispered, throat clogged, eyes suddenly burning.

She watched the slow rise and fall of his chest, saw the washed-out color of his skin, the small cuts over his face, noticed the bandages surrounding his chest and kneecap, and she wondered if he'd ever be the same, wonderful man she'd known. "I love you," she vowed, twining her fingers in his.

Thinking of the day before, the hot sultry air, the brass ring, and the Gypsy woman's grim fortune, she closed her eyes.

You love him too much—you will lose him, the fortune-teller had predicted.

"Never," Shawna declared. Shivering, she took a chair near the bed, whispering words of endearment and telling herself that she would do everything in her power as a doctor and a woman to make him well.

CHAPTER 3

A breakfast cart rattled past the doorway and Shawna started, her eyelids flying open. She'd spent all day and night at Parker's bedside, watching, waiting, and praying.

Now, as she rubbed the kinks from her neck and stretched her aching shoulder muscles, she looked down at Parker's motionless form, hardly believing that their life together had changed so drastically.

"Come on, Parker," she whispered, running gentle fingers across his forehead, silently hoping that his eyelids would flutter open. "You can do it."

A quiet cough caught her attention and she looked up to the doorway, where her brother lounged against the door frame. "How's it going?" Jake asked.

She lifted a shoulder. "About the same."

He raked his fingers through his hair and sighed. "How about if I buy you a cup of coffee?"

Shaking her head, Shawna glanced back at Parker. "I don't think I could—"

"Have you eaten anything since you've been here?"

"No, but—"

"That's right, no buts about it. I'm buying you breakfast. You're not doing Parker any good by starving yourself, are you, Doctor?"

"All right." Climbing reluctantly to her feet, she stretched again as she twisted open the blinds. The morning rays of late summer sun glimmered on the puddles outside. Deep in her heart, Shawna hoped the sunlight would wake Parker. She glanced back at him, her teeth sinking into her lower lip as she watched the steady rise and fall of his chest, noticed the bandage partially covering his head. But he didn't move.

"Come on," Jake said softly.

Without protest, she left the room. As she walked with Jake to the cafeteria, she was oblivious to the hospital routine: the nurses and orderlies carrying medication, the incessant pages from the intercom echoing down the corridors, the charts and files, and the ringing phones that normally sounded so familiar.

Jake pushed open the double doors to the dining room. Trays and silverware were clattering, and the smell of frying bacon, sizzling sausages, maple syrup, and coffee filled the air. Despite her despondency, Shawna's stomach grumbled and she let Jake buy her a platter of eggs, bacon, and toast.

Taking a seat at a scarred Formica table, she sat across from her brother and tried to eat. But she couldn't help overhearing the gossip filtering her way. Two nurses at a nearby table were speaking in a loud whisper and Shawna could barely concentrate on her breakfast.

"It's a shame, really," a heavyset nurse was saying, clucking her tongue. "Parker Harrison of all people! You know, I used to watch his matches on TV."

"You and the rest of the country," her companion agreed.

Shawna's hands began to shake.

"And on his wedding day!" the first woman said. "And think about that boy and his family!"

"The boy?"

"Brad Lomax. DOA. There was nothing Lowery could do."

Shawna felt every muscle in her body tense. She was chewing a piece of toast, but it stuck in her throat.

"That explains the reporters crowded around the front door," the smaller woman replied.

"For sure. And that's not all of it. His fiancée is here, too. From what I hear she's a doctor over at Columbia Memorial. Been with him ever since the accident. She came charging over here in her wedding dress, demanding to see him."

"Poor thing."

Shawna dropped her fork and her fists curled in anger. *How dare they gossip about Parker!*

"Right. And now he's comatose. No telling when he'll wake up."

"Or if."

Shawna's shoulders stiffened and she was about to say something, but Jake held up his hand and shook his head. "Don't bother," he suggested. "It's just small talk."

"About Parker and me!"

"He's a famous guy. So was Brad Lomax. Loosen up, Shawna, you've heard hospital gossip before."

"Not about Parker," she muttered, her appetite waning again as she managed to control her temper. The two nurses carried their trays back to the counter and Shawna tried to relax. Of course Parker's accident had created a stir and people were only people. Jake was right. She had to expect curiosity and rumors.

"I know this is hard. But it's not going to get much better, at least for a while." He finished his stack of pancakes and pushed his plate to one side. "You may as well know that the reporters have already started calling. There were several recordings on your phone machine this morning."

"You were at my apartment?"

"I took back your bag and I gave the wedding dress to Mom. She's going to have it cleaned, but isn't sure that it will look the same."

"It doesn't matter," Shawna said. She wondered if she'd ever wear the gown again. "How're Mom and Dad?"

"They're worried about you and Parker."

"I'll bet," she whispered, grateful for her parents and their strength. Whereas Parker was strong because he'd grown up alone, never knowing his parents, Shawna had gotten her strength from the support and security of her family.

"Mom's decided to keep a low profile."

"And Dad?"

"He wants to tear down the walls of this hospital."

"It figures."

"But Mom has convinced him that if you need them, you'll call."

"Or you'll tell them, if I don't," Shawna guessed.

Smiling slightly, he said. "They're just trying to give you some space—but you might want to call them."

"I will. Later. After Parker wakes up."

Jake raised one brow skeptically, but if he had any doubts, he kept them to himself. "Okay, I'll give them the message."

She quit pretending interest in her food and picked up her tray. She'd been away from Parker for nearly half an hour and she had to get back.

"There's something you should remember," Jake said as they made their way through the tightly packed Formica tables, setting their trays on the counter.

"And what's that?"

"When you leave the hospital, you might want to go out a back entrance, unless you're up to answering a lot of personal questions from reporters."

"I understand. Thanks for the warning."

She turned toward the elevator, but Jake caught her elbow.

"There is one other thing. Brad Lomax's funeral is the day after tomorrow. Mom already arranged to send a spray of flowers from you and Parker."

Shawna winced at the mention of Brad's name. His death was still difficult to accept. And then there was the matter of Parker and how he would feel when he found out what had happened to his protégé. "Mom's an angel," Shawna decided, "but I think I'd better put in an appearance."

"The funeral's for family only," Jake told her. "Don't think about it."

Relieved, Shawna said, "I'll try not to. I'll see you later." Waving, she dashed to the stairwell, unable to wait for the elevator. She had to get back to Parker and make sure she was the one who broke the news.

Parker felt as if his head would explode. Slowly he opened an eye, ignoring the pain that shot through his brain. He tried to lift a hand to his head, but his cramped muscles wouldn't move and his struggling fingers felt nothing save cold metal bars.

Where am I? he wondered, trying to focus. There was a bad taste in his mouth and pain ripped up one side of his body and down the other. His throat worked, but no sound escaped.

"He's waking up!" a woman whispered, her voice heavy with relief. The voice was vaguely familiar, but he couldn't place it. "Call Dr. Handleman or Dr. Lowery! Tell them Parker Harrison is waking up!"

What the hell for? And who are Lowery and Handleman? Doctors? Is that what she said?

"Parker? Can you hear me? Parker, love?"

He blinked rapidly, focusing on the face pressed close to his. It was a beautiful face, with even features, pink-tinged cheeks, and worried green eyes. Long, slightly wavy honey-colored hair fell over her shoulders to brush against his neck.

"Oh, God, I'm so glad you're awake," she said, her voice thick with emotion. Tears starred her lashes and for the first time he noticed the small lines of strain near her mouth and the hollows of her cheeks.

She's crying! This beautiful young woman was actually shedding tears. He was amazed as he watched her tears drizzle down her cheeks and one by one drop onto the bedsheets. She was crying for him! But why?

Her hands were on his shoulders and she buried her face into the crook of his neck. Her tenderness seemed right, somehow, but for the life of him, he couldn't understand why. "I've been so worried! It's been three days! Thank God, you're back!"

His gaze darted around the small room, to the television, the rails on the bed, the dripping IV hanging over his head, and the baskets and baskets of flowers sitting on every available space in the room. It slowly dawned on him that he was in a hospital. The pain in his head wasn't imagined, this wasn't all a bad dream. Somehow he'd landed in a hospital bed, completely immobilized!

"Good morning, Mr. Harrison!" a gruff male voice called.

The woman straightened and quickly brushed aside her tears.

Shifting his gaze, Parker saw a man he didn't recognize walk up to the bed and smile down at him. A doctor. Dressed in a white lab coat, with an identification tag that Parker couldn't make out, the man stared down at Parker from behind thick, wire-framed glasses. Taking Parker's wrist in one hand, he glanced at his watch. "I'm Dr. Handleman. You're a patient here in Mercy Hospital and have been for the past three days."

Three days? What in God's name was this man talking about? Partial images, horrible and vague, teased his mind, though he couldn't remember what they meant.

Drawing his brows together in concentration, Parker tried to think, strained to remember, but his entire life was a blur of disjointed pieces that were colorless and dreamlike. He had absolutely no idea who these people were or why he was here.

"You're a very lucky man," the doctor continued, releasing his wrist. "Not many people could have survived that accident."

Parker blinked, trying to find his voice. "Accident?" he rasped, the sound of his own voice unfamiliar and raw.

"You don't remember?" The doctor's expression clouded.

"Wh-what am I doing here?" Parker whispered hoarsely. His eyes traveled past the doctor to the woman. She was leaning against the wall, as if for support. Wearing a white lab coat and a stethoscope, she had to be a member of the staff. *So why the tears?* "Who are you?" he asked, his bruised face clouding as he tried to concentrate. He heard her muted protest and saw the slump of her shoulders. "Do I know you?"

CHAPTER 4

Shawna's heart nearly stopped. "Parker?" she whispered, struggling to keep her voice steady as she took his bandaged hand in hers. "Don't you remember me?"

His gaze skated over her face and he squinted, as if trying to remember something hazy, but no flash of recognition flickered in his eyes.

"I'm Shawna," she said slowly, hoping to hide the tremble of her lips. "Shawna McGuire."

"A doctor?" he guessed, and Shawna wanted to die.

"Yes—but more than that."

Tom Handleman caught her eye, warning her not to push Parker too hard, but Shawna ignored him. This was important. Parker had to remember! He couldn't forget—not about the love they'd shared, the way they had felt and cared about each other.

"We were supposed to be married," she said quietly, watching his thick brows pull together in consternation. "The day after your accident, at Pioneer Church, in the rose arbor . . . I waited for you."

He didn't say a word, just stared at her as if she were a complete stranger.

"That's enough for now," Tom Handleman said, stepping closer to the bed, snapping on his penlight, trying to end the emotional scene. "Let's take a look at you, Mr. Harrison."

But before Tom could shine his penlight into Parker's eyes, Parker grabbed the doctor's wrist. The crisp sheets slid from one side of the bed, exposing his bare leg and the bandages, still streaked with dried blood. "What the hell's going on?" he demanded, his voice gruff and nearly unrecognizable. "What happened to me? What's she talking about?" He glanced back to Shawna. "What marriage? I've never even been engaged—" Then his eyes dropped to Shawna's left hand and the winking diamond on her ring finger.

"Mr. Harrison, please—"

"Just what the hell happened to me?" Parker repeated, trying to sit up, only to blanch in pain.

"Parker, please," Shawna whispered, restraining him with her hands. She could feel his shoulder muscles, hard and coiled, flexing as he attempted to sit upright. "Just calm down. We'll straighten this all out. You'll remember, I promise." But she had to fight the catch in her throat and her professionalism drained away from her. She couldn't be cool or detached with Parker. "Dr. Handleman's your physician."

"I don't *know* any Handleman. Where's Jack Pederson?"

"Who?" Handleman asked, writing quickly on Parker's chart.

Shawna glanced nervously to the doctor. "Jack was Parker's trainer."

"Was?" Parker repeated, his features taut from pain and the effort of trying to remember those tiny pieces of his past that teased him, rising just to the surface of his mind only to sink deeper into murky oblivion. "Was?"

"That was a couple of years ago," Shawna said quickly.

"What're you talking about? Just last Saturday, Jack and I—" But he didn't finish and his features slackened suddenly as he turned bewildered blue eyes on Handleman. "No, it wasn't Saturday," he whispered, running one hand through his hair and feeling, for the first time, the bandages surrounding his head. Involuntarily his jaw tightened. "Maybe you'd better fill me in," he said, dropping his hand and pinning Tom Handleman with his gaze. "What the hell happened to me?"

"You were in an accident. Several days ago."

Parker closed his eyes, trying vainly to remember.

"From what the police tell me, a truck swerved into your lane, your Jeep crashed through the guardrail, and you were pinned inside the vehicle for several hours. They brought you in here, we performed surgery, and you've been unconscious ever since."

Parker seemed about to protest, but didn't. Instead he listened in stony silence as Tom described his injuries and prognosis.

"So, now that you're awake and the swelling in your leg has gone down, we'll do surgery on that knee. It will all take a little time. You'll be in physical therapy for a while, then you'll be good as new—or almost."

"How long is 'a while?' "

"That depends upon you and how everything heals."

"Just give me an educated guess."

Handleman crossed his arms over his chest, folding Parker's chart against his lab coat. "I'll be straight with you, Mr. Harrison."

"I'd appreciate that—and call me Parker."

"Fair enough, Parker. It could take anywhere from three months to a year of physical therapy before you can play tennis again. But, if you set your mind to it, work hard, I'll bet you'll be walking without crutches in six months."

Parker's jaw was rock hard and his eyes, clouded, moved from Tom's face to Shawna's. "Okay. That answers one question. Now, tell me about the driver of the truck—is he okay?"

"Not a scratch," Tom replied. "You missed him completely, even though he was all over the road. He was too drunk to report the accident."

A muscle jerked in Parker's jaw as he tried to remember. Horrifying images taunted him, but he couldn't quite make them out. Nonetheless his heart began to beat unsteadily and his hands, beneath bandages, had started to sweat. "There's something else, though," he said, rubbing his eyes. "Something—I can't remember. Something . . . important." *God, what is it?*

Shawna cleared her throat. Though she tried to appear calm,

Parker read the hint of panic in the way she glanced at Handleman and toyed with the strand of pearls at her neck. "Maybe that's enough for you right now," she said.

"You know something, both of you. Something you're keeping from me."

Shawna, feeling the urge to protect him, to lie if she had to, to do anything to keep him from the horrid truth, touched his arm. "Just rest now."

"Is that your professional advice?" Parker asked. "Or are you trying to put me off?"

"Professional," Tom said quickly, rescuing Shawna. "A nurse will be in to take your temperature and order you some lunch—"

"Wait a minute." Parker's voice was stern. "Something's wrong here, I can feel it. There's something you're not telling me about the accident." *What the hell is it?* Then he knew. "Someone else was involved," he said flatly. "Who?"

Shawna's shoulders stiffened a bit and her fingers found his on the cold metal railing.

Handleman offered a professional smile. "Right now all you have to worry about is—"

Parker sat bolt upright, tearing the IV tubing from the rail of the bed and ignoring the jab of pain in his knee. He kicked off the sheets and tried to climb out of bed. "What I have to worry about is who was with me. Where is he—or she?" Fire flared in his eyes as Handleman tried to restrain him. "I have the right to know!"

"Whoa—Parker, settle down," Handleman said.

"Who, damn it!"

"Brad Lomax," Shawna whispered, unable to meet the confused torture in his eyes.

"Lomax?"

"He was in the car with you. He drank too much at our wedding rehearsal dinner and you were taking him home."

"But I don't remember—" He swallowed then, his eyes clouding. Somewhere deep in his mind he remembered the squeal of tires, the shatter of glass, felt his muscles wrench as he jerked hard on the steering wheel, heard a terrifying scream. "Oh, God," he rasped. "Who is he?"

"A tennis pro. Your student." Shawna felt her eyes grow moist as she watched the skin over his cheekbones turn white and taut.

"I was driving," he said slowly, as if measuring each agonizing word. "Lomax. How is he?"

"I'm afraid he didn't make it," Tom replied, exchanging glances with Shawna.

"He was killed in the wreck?" Parker's voice was sharp and fierce with self-loathing. "I killed him?"

"It was an accident," Shawna said quickly. "An unfortunate one—his seat belt malfunctioned and he was pinned under the Jeep."

Parker blinked several times, then lay back on the pillows as he struggled with his past. This couldn't be happening—he didn't even know these people! Maybe if he just went back to sleep he'd wake up and this hellish dream with the beautiful woman and clouded jags of memory would go away. "Does Lomax have any family?"

Just you, Shawna thought, but shook her head. "Only an uncle and a couple of cousins, I think."

"I think you'd better get some rest now," Tom advised, motioning to a nurse standing by the door. "I want Mr. Harrison sedated—"

"No!" Parker's eyes flew open.

"This has all been such a shock—"

"I can handle it," Parker said tightly, his face grim and stern. "No sedative, no painkillers. Got it?"

"But—"

"Got it?" he repeated, some of his old fire returning. "And don't try slipping anything into this!" He lifted his fist with the IV tubes attached.

Handleman's mouth became a thin white line. "Lie back down, Mr. Harrison," he said sternly, waiting until Parker reluctantly obeyed. "Now, it's my job to see that you're taken care of—that you rest. But I'll need your help. Either you contain yourself or I'll have the nurse sedate you."

Muscles rigid, eyes bright with repressed fury, Parker stared at the ceiling.

"Good. Just let me know if you change your mind about the

sedatives or the painkillers. Now, Shawna, I think Mr. Harrison needs his rest."

"Wait a minute," Parker insisted, reaching for Shawna's hand again. "I want to talk to you. Alone." His gaze drilled past Handleman's thick glasses, and fortunately, the doctor got the message. With a nod of his head, he tucked his clipboard under his arm, left the room, and closed the door.

"Tell me," he said, forcing himself to be calm, though his fingers clenched tightly over hers.

"About what?"

"Everything."

Shawna sighed and sagged against the bed. How could she begin to explain the whirlwind fantasy that had been their relationship? How could she recount how Parker had seen the potential in a streetwise juvenile delinquent and had turned him into one of the finest young tennis players in the nation—a boy who had become a younger brother to him?

"Tell me," he insisted, hungry for knowledge of himself.

"First things first. What do you remember?"

"Not enough!" he said sharply, then took a deep breath. "Not nearly enough."

"I'll tell you what I can," she said, "but you've got to promise to stay calm."

"I don't know if that's possible," he admitted.

"Then we haven't got a deal, have we?"

Swearing under his breath, he forced a grin he obviously didn't feel. "Okay," he said. "Deal."

"Good."

"Something tells me I should remember you."

"Most definitely," she agreed, feeling better than she had since the accident and grinning as she blinked back tears. Then, as all her bravado crumbled, she touched him gently on his forehead. "Oh, Parker, I've missed you—God, how I've missed you." Without thinking, she leaned forward and kissed him, brushing her lips suggestively over his and tasting the salt from her own tears.

But Parker didn't respond, just stared at her with perplexed blue eyes.

Shawna cleared her throat. "Fortunately, that part—the loneliness—is over now," she said, quickly sniffing back her tears. "And once you're out of here, we'll get married, and go to the Bahamas, have a ton of children, and live happily ever after!"

"Hey, whoa. Slow down," he whispered. Rubbing one hand over his jaw, he said, "Tell me about Brad Lomax."

Shawna realized he wouldn't give up. Though she felt the urge to protect him, she decided he had to face the truth sooner or later. She wanted to soften the blow, but she had to be honest with him. "Brad Lomax," she said uneasily, "was a hellion, and he was a terror on the tennis courts, and you saw something in him. You recognized his raw talent and took him under your wing. You and he were very close," she admitted, seeing the pain in his eyes. "You knew him a lot longer than you've known me."

"How close?" Parker asked, his voice low.

"You were his mentor—kind of a big brother. He looked up to you. That night, the night of the accident, he'd had too much to drink and wanted to talk to you. You offered to take him home."

A muscle worked in his jaw. "Why did he want to talk to me?"

Shawna lifted a shoulder. "I don't know. No one does. I suppose now that no one ever will."

"I killed him," Parker said quietly.

"No, Parker. It was an accident!" she said vehemently.

"How old was he?"

"Don't do this to yourself."

"How old was he?" His eyes drilled into hers.

"Twenty-two," she whispered.

"Oh, God." With a shudder, he closed his eyes. "I should have been the one who died, you know."

Shawna resisted the overpowering urge to cradle his head to her breast and comfort him. The torture twisting his features cut her to the bone. "Don't do this, Parker. It's not fair."

Parker stared up at her with simmering blue eyes. His expression was a mixture of anguish and awe, and his hand reached upward, his fingers slipping beneath her hair to caress her nape.

She trembled at his touch, saw the torment in his gaze.

"I don't remember where I met you. Or how. Or even who you are," he admitted, his voice husky, the lines near his mouth softening as he stared up at her. "But I do know that I'm one lucky son of a bitch if you were planning to marry me."

"Am—as in present tense," she corrected, her throat hot with unshed tears. "I still intend to march down the aisle with you, Parker Harrison, whether you're in a cast, on crutches, or in a wheelchair."

She felt his fingers flex as he drew her head to his, and he hesitated only slightly before touching his lips to hers. "I will remember you," he promised, eyes dusky blue. "No matter what it takes!"

Her heart soared. All they needed was a little time!

Tom Handleman, his expression stern behind his wire-rimmed glasses, poked his head into the room. "Doctor?"

"That's my cue," Shawna whispered, brushing her lips against Parker's hair. "I'll be back."

"I'm counting on it."

She forced herself out of the room, feeling more lighthearted than she had in days. So what if Parker didn't remember her? What did it matter that he had a slight case of amnesia? The important consideration was his health, and physically he seemed to be gaining strength. Although mentally he still faced some tough hurdles, she was confident that with her help, Parker would surmount any obstacle fate cast his way. It was only a matter of time before he was back on his feet again and they could take up where they'd left off.

Jake was waiting for her in the hallway. Slouched into one of the waiting-room chairs, his tie askew, his shirtsleeves rolled over his forearms, he groaned as he stretched to his feet and fell into step with her. "Good news," he guessed, a wide grin spreading across his beard-stubbled jaw.

"The best!" Shawna couldn't contain herself. "He's awake!"

"About time!" Jake winked at her. "So, when's the wedding?"

Shawna chuckled. "I think Parker and I have a few bridges to cross first."

"Meaning Brad's death?"

"For one," she said, linking her arm through her brother's and pushing the elevator button. "You can buy me lunch and I'll explain about the rest of them."

"There's more?"

"A lot more," she said as they squeezed into the crowded elevator and she lowered her voice. "He doesn't remember me—or much else for that matter."

Jake let out a long, low whistle.

"You're used to dealing with this, aren't you, in your practice?" she asked eagerly.

"I've seen a couple of cases."

"Then maybe you can work with him."

"Maybe," he said, his gray eyes growing thoughtful.

As the elevator opened at the hallway near the cafeteria, Shawna sent him a teasing glance, "Well, don't trip all over yourself to help."

"I'll do what I can," he said, massaging his neck muscles. "Unfortunately, you'll have to be patient, and that's not your strong suit."

"Patient?"

"You know as well as I do that amnesia can be tricky. He may remember everything tomorrow, or . . ."

"Or it may take weeks," she said with a sigh. "I can't even think about that. Not now. I'm just thanking my lucky stars that he's alive and he'll be all right."

Maybe, Jake thought, steering Shawna down the stainless steel counter and past cream pies, pudding, and fruit salad. Only time would tell.

Parker tried to roll off the bed, but a sharp pain in his knee and the IV tube stuck into his hand kept him flat on his back. He had a restless urge to get up, walk out of the hospital, and catch hold of the rest of his life—wherever it was.

He knew who he was. He could remember some things very clearly—the death of his parents in a boating accident, the brilliance of a trophy glinting gold in the sun. But try as he might, he couldn't conjure up Brad Lomax's face to save his soul.

And this Shawna woman with her honey-gold hair, soft lips, and intense green eyes. She was a doctor and they'd planned to be married? That didn't seem to fit. Nor did her description of his being some heroic do-gooder who had saved a boy from self-destruction while molding him into a tennis star.

No, her idealistic views of his life didn't make a helluva lot of sense. He remembered winning, playing to the crowd, enjoying being the best; he'd been ruthless and unerring on the court—the "ice man," incapable of emotion.

And yet she seemed to think him some sort of modern-day Good Samaritan. No way!

Struggling for the memories locked just under the surface of his consciousness, he closed his eyes and clenched his fists in frustration. Why couldn't he remember? Why?

"Mr. Harrison?"

He opened one eye, then the other. A small nurse was standing just inside the door.

"Glad you're back with us," she said, rolling in a clattering tray of food—if that's what you'd call the unappetizing gray potatoes-and-gravy dish she set in front of him. "Can I get you anything else?"

"Nothing," he replied testily, his thoughts returning to the beautiful doctor and the boy whose face he couldn't remember. *I don't want anything but my past.* Sighing, the nurse left.

Parker shoved the tray angrily aside and closed his eyes, willing himself to remember, concentrating on that dark void that was his past. Shawna. Had he known her? How? Had he really planned to marry her?

Sleep overcame him in warm waves and bits of memory played with his mind. Dreaming, he saw himself dancing with a gorgeous woman in a mist-cloaked rose garden. Her face was veiled and she was dressed in ivory silk and lace, he in a stiff tuxedo. Her scent and laughter engulfed him as they stopped dancing to sip from crystal glasses of champagne. Sweeping her into his arms again, he spilled champagne on the front of her gown and she tossed back her head but her veil stayed in place, blocking his view of her eyes as he licked the frothy bubbles from the beaded lace covering her throat.

"I love you," she vowed, sighing. "Forever."

"And I love you."

Light-headed from the drink and the nearness of her, he captured her lips with his, tasting cool, effervescent wine on her warm lips. Her fingers toyed with his bow tie, loosening it from his neck, teasing him, and he caught a glimpse of her dimpled smile before she slipped away from him. He tried to call out to her, but he didn't know her name and his voice was muted. Desperate not to lose her, he grasped at her dress but clutched only air. She was floating away from him, her face still a guarded mystery. . . .

Parker's eyes flew open and he took in a swift breath. His hand was clenched, but empty. The dream had been so real, so lifelike, as if he'd been in that garden with that beautiful woman. But now, in his darkened hospital room, he wondered if the dream had been part of his memory or only something he wanted so fervently he'd created the image.

Had the woman been Shawna McGuire?

Dear God, he hoped so. She was, without a doubt, the most intriguing woman he'd ever met.

The next evening, in her office at Columbia Memorial Hospital on the east side of the Willamette River, Shawna leaned back in her chair until it creaked in protest. Unpinning her hair, letting it fall past her shoulders in a shimmering gold curtain, she closed her eyes and imagined that Parker's memory was restored and they were getting married, just as they planned.

"Soon," she told herself as she stretched and flipped through the pages of her appointment book.

Because she couldn't stand the idea of spending hour upon hour with nothing to do, she had rescheduled her vacation—the time she had meant to use on her honeymoon—and today had been her first full day of work since the accident. She was dead tired. The digital clock on her desk blinked the time. It was eight-fifteen, and she hadn't eaten since breakfast.

She'd finished her rounds early, dictated patient diagnoses into the tiny black machine at her desk, answered some correspondence and phone calls, and somehow managed to talk to the amnesia specialist on staff at Columbia Memorial. Her ears still rang with his advice.

"Amnesia's not easy to predict," Pat Barrington had replied to her questions about Parker. A kindly neurosurgeon with a flushed red face and horn-rimmed glasses, he'd told Shawna nothing she hadn't really already known. "Parker's obviously reacting to the trauma, remembering nothing of the accident or the events leading up to it," Barrington had said, punching the call button for the elevator.

"So why doesn't he remember Brad Lomax or me?"

"Because you're both part of it, really. The accident occurred right after the rehearsal dinner. Subconsciously, he's denying everything leading up to the accident—even your engagement. Give him time, Shawna. He's not likely to forget you," Barrington had advised, clapping Shawna on her back.

Now, as Shawna leaned back in her chair, she sighed and stared out the window into the dark September night. "Time," she whispered. Was it her friend or enemy?

CHAPTER 5

Two weeks later, Shawna sipped from her teacup and stared through the kitchen window of her apartment at the late afternoon sky. Parker's condition hadn't changed, except that the surgery on his knee had been a success. He was already working in physical therapy to regain use of his leg, but his mind, as far as Shawna and the wedding were concerned, was a complete blank. Though Shawna visited him each day, hoping to help him break through the foggy wall surrounding him, he stared at her without a flicker of the warmth she'd always felt in his gaze.

Now, as she dashed the dregs of her tea into the sink, she decided she couldn't wait any longer. Somehow, she had to jog his memory. She ached to touch him again, feel his arms around her, have him talk to her as if she weren't a total stranger.

"You're losing it, McGuire," she told herself as she glanced around her kitchen. Usually bright and neat, the room was suffering badly from neglect. Dishes were stacked in the sink, the floor was dull, and there were half-filled boxes scattered on the counters and floor.

Before the wedding she'd packed most of her things, but now she'd lost all interest in moving from the cozy little one-bedroom apartment she'd called home for several years. Nonetheless, she had given her notice and would have to move at the end of the month.

Rather than consider the chore of moving, she stuffed two packets of snapshots into her purse and found her coat. Then, knowing she was gambling with her future, she grabbed her umbrella and dashed through the front door of her apartment.

Outside, the weather was gray and gloomy. Rain drizzled from the sky, ran in the gutters of the old turn-of-the-century building, and caught on the broad leaves of the rhododendron and azaleas flanking the cement paths.

"Dr. McGuire!" a crackly voice accosted her. "Wait up!"

Shawna glanced over her shoulder. Mrs. Swenson, her landlady, clad in a bright yellow raincoat, was walking briskly in her direction. Knowing what was to come, Shawna managed a smile she didn't feel. "Hi, Mrs. Swenson."

"I know you're on your way out," Mrs. Swenson announced, peering into the bushes near Shawna's front door and spying the lurking shadow of Maestro, Shawna's yellow tabby near the steps. Adjusting her plastic rain bonnet, Mrs. Swenson pursed her lips and peered up at Shawna with faded gold eyes. "But I thought we'd better talk about your apartment. I know about your troubles with Mr. Harrison and it's a darned shame, that's what it is—but I've got tenants who've planned to lease your place in about two weeks."

"I know, I know," Shawna said. If her life hadn't been shattered by the accident, she would already have moved into Parker's house on the Willamette River. But, of course, the accident had taken care of that. "Things just haven't exactly fallen into place."

"I know, I know," Mrs. Swenson said kindly, still glancing at the cat. "But, be that as it may, the Levertons plan to start moving in the weekend after next and your lease is up. Then there's the matter of having the place painted, the drapes cleaned, and whatnot. I hate to be pushy . . . but I really don't have much choice."

"I understand," Shawna admitted, thinking over her options for the dozenth time. "And I'll be out by Friday night. I promise."

"That's only four days away," Mrs. Swenson pointed out, her wrinkled face puckering pensively.

"I've already started packing." Well, not really, but she did have some things in boxes, things she'd stored when she and Parker had started making wedding plans. "I can store my things with my folks and live either with them or with Jake," she said. The truth of the matter was, deep down, she still intended to move into Parker's place, with or without a wedding ring. In the past few weeks since the accident, she'd discovered just how much she loved him, and that a certificate of marriage wasn't as important as being with him.

"And what're you planning to do about that?" the old woman asked, shaking a gnarled finger at Maestro as he nimbly jumped onto the window ledge. With his tail flicking anxiously, he glared in through the window to the cage where Mrs. Swenson's yellow parakeet ruffled his feathers and chirped loudly enough to be heard through the glass.

"He's not really mine—"

"You've been feeding him, haven't you?"

"Well, yes. But he just strayed—"

"Two years ago," Mrs. Swenson interjected. "And if he had his way my little Pickles would have been his dinner time and time again."

"I'll take him with me."

"Good. Saves me a trip to the animal shelter," Mrs. Swenson said. Shawna seriously doubted the old woman had the heart to do anything more dastardly than give Maestro a saucer of milk—probably warmed in the microwave. Though outwardly a curmudgeon, Myrna Swenson had a heart of gold buried beneath a crusty layer of complaining.

"I'll tell Eva Leverton she can start packing."

"Good!" Shawna climbed into her car and watched as Mrs. Swenson cooed to the bird in the window. She flicked on the engine, smothered a smile, and muttered, "Pickles is a dumb name for a bird!" Then slamming the car into gear, she drove away from the apartment complex.

More determined than ever to help Parker regain his memory,

Shawna wheeled across the Ross Island bridge and up the steep grade of the west hills to Mercy Hospital.

Today Parker would remember her, she decided with a determined smile as she pulled on the emergency brake and threw open the car door. Sidestepping puddles of rainwater, she hurried inside the old concrete and glass of Mercy Hospital.

She heard Parker before she saw him. Just as the elevator doors parted on the fourth floor, Parker's voice rang down the gray-carpeted hallway.

"Hey, watch out, you're killing me!" he barked and Shawna smothered a grin. One of the first signs of patient improvement was general irritability, and Parker sounded as if he was irritable in spades.

"Good morning," Shawna said, cautiously poking her head into the room.

"What's good about it?" Parker grumbled.

"I see our patient is improving," she commented to the orderly trying to adjust the bed.

"Not his temperament," the orderly confided.

"I heard that," Parker said, but couldn't help flashing Shawna a boyish grin—the same crooked grin she'd grown to love. Her heart did a stupid little leap, the way it always did when he rained his famous smile on her.

"Be kind, Parker," she warned, lifting some wilting roses from a ceramic vase and dropping the wet flowers into a nearby trash basket. "Otherwise he might tell the people in physical therapy to give you the 'torture treatment,' and I've heard it can be murder."

"Humph." He laughed despite his ill humor and the orderly ducked gratefully out the door.

"You're not making any friends here, you know," she said, sitting on the end of his bed and leaning back to study him. Her honey-colored hair fell loose behind her shoulders, and a small smile played on her lips.

"Am I supposed to be?"

"If you don't want your breakfast served cold, your temperature to be taken at four a.m., or your TV cable to be mysteriously tampered with."

"I'd pay someone to do it," Parker muttered. "Then maybe I

wouldn't have to watch any more of that." He nodded in the direction of the overhead television. On the small screen, a wavy-haired reporter with a bright smile was sitting behind a huge desk while discussing the worldwide ranking of America's tennis professionals.

"—and the tennis world is still reeling from the unfortunate death of Brad Lomax, perhaps the brightest star in professional tennis since his mentor, Parker Harrison's, meteoric burst onto the circuit in the midseventies."

A picture of Brad, one arm draped affectionately over Parker's broad shoulders, the other hand holding a winking brass trophy triumphantly overhead, was flashed onto the screen. Brad's dark hair was plastered to his head, sweat dripped down his face, and a fluffy white towel was slung around his neck. Parker, his chestnut hair glinting in the sun, his face tanned and unlined, his eyes shining with pride, stood beside his protégé.

Now, as she watched, Shawna's stomach tightened. Parker lay still, his face taut and white as the newscaster continued. *"Lomax, whose off-court escapades were as famous as his blistering serves, was killed just over two weeks ago when the vehicle Parker Harrison was driving swerved off the road and crashed down a hundred-foot embankment.*

"Harrison is still reported in stable condition, though there're rumors that he has no memory of the near-collision with a moving van which resulted in the—"

Ashen-faced, Shawna snapped the television off. "I don't know why you watch that stuff!"

Parker didn't answer, just glanced out the window to the rain-soaked day and the gloomy fir boughs visible through his fourth-floor window. "I'm just trying to figure out who I am."

"And I've told you—"

"But I don't want the romanticized version—just the facts," he said, his gaze swinging back to hers. "I want to remember—for myself. I want to remember *you.*"

"You will. I promise," she whispered.

He sighed in frustration, but touched her hand, his fingers covering hers. "For the past week people have been streaming in here—people I should know and don't. There have been friends, reporters, doctors, and even the mayor, for heaven's sake! They ask questions, wish me well, tell me to take it easy, and all the time I'm thinking, 'Who the hell are you?' "

"Parker—" Leaning forward, she touched his cheek, hoping to break through the damming wall blocking his memory.

"Don't tell me to be patient," he said sharply, but his eyes were still warm as they searched her face. "Just take one look around this room, for crying out loud!" Everywhere there were piles of cards and letters, huge baskets of fruit, tins of cookies and vases of heavy-blossomed, fragrant flowers. "Who *are* these people?" he asked, utterly perplexed.

Shawna wanted to cry. "People who care, Parker," she said, her voice rough as her hands covered his, feeling the warmth of his palms against her skin. She treasured the comfort she felt as his fingers grazed her cheekbones. "People who care about us."

He swore under his breath. "And I can't remember half of them. Here I am with enough flowers to cover all the floats in the Rose Parade and enough damned fruit and banana bread to feed all the starving people in the world—"

"You're exaggerating," she charged.

"Well, maybe just a little," he admitted, his lips twisting into a wry grin.

"A lot!"

"Okay, a lot."

She stroked his brow, hoping to ease the furrows in his forehead. "Unfortunately, neither of us can undo what's happened. Don't you think that I would change things if I could? That I would push back the hands of the clock so that I could have you back—all of you?" She swallowed against a huge lump forming in her throat.

He rested his forehead against hers. His gaze took in every soft angle of her face, the way her lashes swept over her eyes, the tiny lines of concern etching the ivory-colored skin of her forehead, the feel of her breath, warm and enticing against his face. Old emotions, cloaked in that black recess of the past, stirred, but refused to emerge. "Oh, why can't I remember you?" His voice was so filled with torment and longing, she buried her face in his shoulder and twisted her fingers in the folds of his sheets.

"Try," she pleaded.

"I have—over and over again." His eyes were glazed as he stroked her chin. "If you believe anything, believe that I want to re-member you . . . everything about you."

The ache within her burned, but before she could respond, his palms, still pressed against her cheeks, tilted her face upward. Slowly, he touched her lips with his. Warm and pliant, they promised a future together—she could feel it!

Shawna's heart began to race.

His lips moved slowly and cautiously at first, as if he were ex-ploring and discovering her for the first time.

Tears welled unbidden to her eyes and she moaned, leaning closer to him, feeling her breath hot and constricted in her lungs.

Love me, she cried mutely. *Love me as you did.*

The kiss was so innocent, so full of wondering, she felt as flus-tered and confused as a schoolgirl. "I love you," she whispered, her fingers gripping his shoulders as she clung to him and felt hot tears slide down her cheeks. "Oh, Parker, I love you!"

His arms surrounded her, drawing her downward until she was half lying across him, listening to the beat of his heart and feeling the hard muscles of his chest.

The sheets wrinkled between them as Parker's lips sought hers, anxious and moist, pressing first against her mouth and then lower, to the length of her throat as his hands twined in the golden sun-bleached strands of her hair. "I have the feeling I don't deserve you," he murmured into her ear, desire flaring in his brilliant blue eyes.

From the hallway, Jake cleared his throat. Shawna glanced up to see her brother, shifting restlessly from one foot to the other as he stood just outside the door.

"I, uh, hope I'm not disturbing anything," he said, grinning from one ear to the other, his hands stuffed into the pockets of his cords as he sauntered into the small room.

Shawna hurriedly wiped her cheeks. "Your timing leaves a lot to be desired."

"So I've been told," he replied, before glancing at Parker. "So, how's the patient?"

"Grumpy," Shawna pronounced.

"He didn't look too grumpy to me." Jake snatched a shiny red apple from a fruit basket and polished it against his tweed sports jacket.

"You didn't see him barking at the orderly."

One side of Jake's mouth curved cynically as he glanced at Parker. "Not you, not the 'ice man.' " Still grinning, he bit into the apple.

"This place doesn't exactly bring out the best in me," Parker said, eyeing the man who had almost become his brother-in-law.

"Obviously," Shawna replied. "But if everything goes well in physical therapy today and tomorrow, and you don't get on Dr. Handleman's bad side again, you'll be out of here by the end of the week, only doing physical therapy on an outpatient basis."

"No wonder he's in a bad mood," Jake said, taking another huge bite from the apple. "Outpatient physical therapy sounds as bad as the seventh level of hell, if you ask me."

"No one did," Shawna reminded him, but smiled at her brother anyway. Jake had a way of helping her find humor in even the most trying times. Even as children, she could count on him and his cockeyed sense of humor to lift her spirits even on her worst days.

Jake tossed his apple core deftly into a trash can. "Two points—or was that three?" he asked. When neither Parker nor Shawna answered, he shoved his fingers through his hair. "Boy, you guys are sure a cheery group."

"Sorry," Shawna said. "As I told you, Grumpy isn't in a great mood."

Jake glanced from Shawna to Parker. "So, what can we do to get you back on your feet?"

"You're the psychiatrist," Parker replied stonily. "You tell me."

Shawna reached into her purse. "Maybe I can help." Ignoring her brother's questioning gaze, she reached into her purse and withdrew a thick packet of photographs. "I thought these might do the trick."

Her hands were shaking as one by one, she handed him the snapshots of the fair. Her heart stuck in her throat as she saw the pictures of herself, her long blond hair caught in the breeze, her green eyes filled with mischief as she clung to the neck of that white wooden stallion on the carousel and stretched forward, reaching and missing the brass ring with the fluttering ribbons.

Other photos, of Parker trying to catch a peanut in his mouth, of Parker flaunting his prized brass ring, and of the dark-eyed fortune-teller beckoning them inside her ragtag tent, brought back her memories of the fair. Now, in the hospital room, only a little over two weeks later, the old-time fair seemed ages past, and the fortune-teller's prediction loomed over Shawna like a black cloak.

Parker studied each picture, his eyes narrowed on the images in the still shots. His brow furrowed in concentration.

Shawna held her breath. Couldn't he see the adoration shining in her eyes as she gazed into the camera? Or the loving way he had captured her on film? And what about the pictures of him, grinning and carefree? Wasn't it obvious that they had been two people hopelessly head over heels in love?

For a minute, she thought he reacted, that there was a flicker of recognition in his gaze, but as suddenly as it had appeared, it was gone.

"Nothing?" she asked, bracing herself.

He closed his eyes. "No—not nothing," he said, his voice dry and distant. "But what we shared—what was there at the fair—it's . . . gone."

"Just misplaced," Jake said quickly as if feeling the searing wound deep in Shawna's soul. "You'll find it again."

"I'd like to think so," Parker admitted but he still seemed vexed, his thick brows knitted, his chin set to one side, as if he were searching for a black hole in the tapestry her pictures had woven.

"Look, I've got to run," Jake said quickly, looking at his sister meaningfully. "Mom and Dad are expecting you for dinner tonight."

"But I can't," she said, unable to leave Parker. She felt that if she were given just a few more minutes, she could cause the breakthrough in Parker's memory.

"Don't stay on my account," Parker cut in, glaring angrily at the pictures spread across his bed.

Shawna saw them then as he did, pictures of a young couple in love, their future bright and untarnished, and she cringed inside, knowing instinctively what he felt—the anger and the resentment, the pain and the blackness of a time he couldn't remember.

"Maybe I shouldn't have brought these," she said hurriedly, scooping the photographs into the purse.

He snatched one out of her hands, the photo of her with her face flushed, her long hair billowing over the neck of the glossy white carousel horse. "I'll keep this one," he said, his features softening a little, "if you don't mind."

"You're sure?"

"Positive."

"Let's go." Jake suggested. "You can come back later. But right now, Mom and Dad are waiting."

Shawna felt her brother's hand over her arm, but she twisted her neck, craning to stare at Parker, who didn't move, just studied the photograph in his hands. Impatiently, Jake half dragged her through the building.

"That was a stupid move!" Jake nearly shouted, once they were outside the hospital. "He's not ready for pictures of the past, can't you see that?" Jake's expression turned dark as he opened the car door for her, then slid behind the wheel and shoved the Porsche into gear.

"You can't just skip into his room and hand him pictures of a rose-colored future that could have been, you know. It takes time! Think about him, not just yourself! Where's your professionalism, *Doctor?*"

"Back in my medical bag, I guess," Shawna said, staring blindly out the windows. "I'm sorry."

"It's not me you have to apologize to." He let out a long, disgusted breath, then patted her shoulder. "Just hang in there. Try to think of Parker as another patient—not your fiancé, okay?"

"I will, but it's hard."

"I know," he said, "but he needs all your strength now—and your patience." Jake turned off the main highway and veered down the elm-lined driveway of his parents' house. "Okay, sis. Show's on. Stiff upper lip for Mom and Dad," he teased, reaching across her and pushing open the car door.

As Shawna walked up the flagstone path, she steadfastly shoved all her doubts aside. Tomorrow she'd see Parker again and when she did, she wouldn't push too hard. She'd be patient and wait until the walls blocking his memory eroded—even if it killed her.

Long after Shawna left his room, Parker stared at the small photograph in his hand. Without a doubt, Dr. Shawna McGuire was the most fascinating, beautiful, and stubborn woman he'd ever met.

He knew now why he'd fallen in love with her. Though he was loath to admit it and despite all the problems he now faced, he was falling in love with her again. The depth of his feelings was a surprise. She aroused him sensually as well as intellectually. Doctor McGuire, though she professed her love, was a challenge. Just being near her, smelling her perfume, seeing the glimmer of mystique in her intelligent green eyes, was enough to drive him to distraction and cause an uncomfortable heat to rise in his loins.

Unfortunately, he had to be careful. No longer was he a recent tennis star with a future bright as the sun, acting in commercials and coaching younger, upcoming athletes. Now his future was unsure.

He glanced down and the woman in the photograph smiled up at him. She swore she loved him and he believed her. And, if he let himself, he could easily get caught in her infectious enthusiasm. Several times, when he'd kissed her, he'd seen images in his mind—smelled the salty air of the beach, or fresh raindrops in her hair, heard the tinkle of her laughter, felt the driving beat of her heart. Reality mixed with sights and smells that were as elusive as a winking star—bright one minute, dim and clouded the next.

And now, lying in the hospital bed, with months, perhaps years of physical therapy staring him in the face, what could he offer her?

A big, fat nothing. Because no matter how she deluded herself, Shawna was wrong about one thing: Parker would never be the man he was before the accident. His perception, with his memory, had changed.

Brad Lomax was gone, as was Parker's ability to coach and play tennis. The man Shawna McGuire had fallen in love with no longer existed and this new man—the one who couldn't even remember her—was a pale substitute. How long could she love a faded memory? he wondered. When would that love, so freely given, turn to duty?

Glancing again at the woman in the picture, Parker ached inside. Yes, he wanted her, maybe even loved her. But he wouldn't let her live a lie, sacrifice herself because she believed in a dream that didn't exist.

Gritting his teeth, Parker took the snapshot of Shawna and crushed it in his fist—then feeling immediately contrite, he tried to press the wrinkles from the photo and laid it, facedown, in a book someone had left by his bed.

"Help me," he prayed, his voice echoing in the empty room. "Help me be whole again."

CHAPTER 6

Shawna snatched a patient's chart from the rack next to the door of the examination room. She was running late and had to force herself into gear. "Get a move on, Doctor," she muttered under her breath as she glanced quickly over the patient information file. The patient, Melinda James, was new to the clinic, had an excellent health record, and was eighteen years old.

"Good afternoon," Shawna said, shoving open the door to find a beautiful black-haired girl with round eyes perched on the edge of the examination table. She looked scared as her fingers clamped nervously over a sheet she'd pulled over her shoulders, and Shawna felt as if the girl wanted to bolt. "I'm Dr. McGuire," she said calmly. "And you're Melinda?"

Melinda nodded and chewed nervously on her lip.

"So what can I do for you?"

"I, uh, saw your name in the paper," Melinda said quickly,

glancing away. "You're the doctor who's engaged to Parker Harrison, right?"

Shawna's stomach tightened at the mention of Parker. Was Melinda a reporter, pretending to be a patient just to get an inside story on Parker, or was there something else?

"That's right, but I really don't see what that has to do with anything." She clamped the chart to her chest. "Do you know Parker?"

"He's got amnesia, doesn't he?"

Shawna tried to keep her tongue in check. Obviously the girl was nervous—maybe she was just making conversation. "I can't discuss Parker's condition. Now—" she glanced down at her chart. "Is there a reason you came to see me? A health reason?"

The girl sighed. "Yes I, uh, I've only been in Portland a few months so I don't have a doctor here. I went to a pediatrician in Cleveland," Melinda continued, "but I'm too old for a pediatrician now and I've got this problem, so I made an appointment with you."

"Fair enough." Shawna relaxed a little and took a pen from the pocket of her lab coat. "What was the pediatrician's name?"

Melinda seemed hesitant.

"I'll need this information in case we need to contact him for his files," Shawna explained, offering the girl an encouraging smile.

"Rankin, Harold Rankin," Melinda said quickly and Shawna scrawled the physician's name in the appropriate spot on the form. "Thanks." Pushing her suspicions aside, Shawna set the chart on a cabinet. "You said you had a problem. What kind of problem?"

Melinda twisted the sheet between her fingers. "I'm sick." Avoiding Shawna's eyes, she said in a rush, "I can't keep anything down and I'm not anoretic or whatever it's called. I don't understand what's wrong. I've had the flu for over a month and it just won't go away. I've never been sick for this long."

"The flu?" Shawna said, eyeing the girl's healthy skin color and clear eyes. "You're feverish? Your muscles ache?"

"No, not really. It's just that one minute I'm feeling great; the next I think I might throw up."

"And do you?"

"Sometimes—especially in the afternoon." Melinda wrung her hands anxiously together and sweat beaded her forehead. "And sometimes I get horrible cramps."

"Anything else? Sore throat?"

Shaking her short glossy hair, Melinda sighed. "I kept hoping I would get better, but—" She shrugged and the sheet almost slipped from her fingers.

"Well, let me take a look at you. Lie down." Shawna spent the next fifteen minutes examining Melinda carefully, as the girl nearly jumped off the examination table each time she was touched.

"When was the date of your last menstrual period?" Shawna finally asked, once the examination was over and Melinda was sitting, sheet draped over her on the table.

"I don't know. A couple of months ago, I guess."

"You *guess?*" Shawna repeated.

"I don't keep track—I'm real irregular."

"How irregular?"

"Well, not every month. I skip around a little."

"Could you be pregnant?"

Melinda's eyes widened and she licked her lips. "I—I don't get sick in the morning. Never in the morning."

Shawna smiled, trying to put the girl at ease. "It's different with everyone. I had a patient who only was sick at night."

Melinda chewed on her lower lip. "I—uh, it's possible, I guess," she whispered.

"Why don't we run a quick test and see?" Shawna asked.

"When will I know?"

"In a little while. I have a friend in the lab. The pregnancy test is relatively easy; but if there's something else, we won't know about it for a couple of days. Now, why don't you try to remember the date of your last period."

Melinda closed her eyes as Shawna drew a small vial of blood from her arm and had a nurse take the filled vial to the lab.

"I don't know. I think it was around the Fourth of July."

Shawna wasn't surprised. All of Melinda's symptoms pointed toward pregnancy. "This is nearly October," she pointed out.

Melinda's lower lip protruded defiantly. "I said I was irregular."

"Okay. No need to worry about it, until we know for sure." She checked her watch. "It's still early—the hospital lab can rush the results if I ask."

"Would you?"

"Sure. You can get dressed and meet me in my office in a few hours—say four o'clock?"

"Fine." Melinda grudgingly reached for her clothes and Shawna, feeling uneasy, left the room.

By the time Shawna returned to her office after seeing the rest of her patients and finished some paperwork, she was ready to call it a day. It was four o'clock and she was anxious to drive to Mercy Hospital to spend some time with Parker.

But first she had to deal with Melinda James.

"Well?" Melinda asked as she plopped into the chair opposite Shawna's desk.

Shawna scanned the report from the lab, then glanced at the anxious girl.

"Your test was positive, Melinda. You're going to have a baby."

Melinda let out a long sigh and ran her fingers through her hair. "I can't believe it," she whispered, but her voice lacked conviction and for the first time Shawna wondered if Melinda had been suspicious of her condition all along. "There's no chance that"—she pointed to the pink report—"is wrong."

"Afraid not."

"Great," Melinda mumbled, blinking back tears.

"I take it this isn't good news."

"The worst! My dad'll kill me!"

"Maybe you're underestimating your dad," Shawna suggested.

"No way!"

"What about the father of your child?" Shawna asked.

Tears flooded the girl's eyes. "The father?" she repeated, swallowing with difficulty and shaking her head.

"He has the right to know."

"He can't," Melinda said, her voice low and final, as if she had no choice in the matter.

"Give him a chance."

Melinda's eyes were bright with tears. "I can't tell him," she said. "He thinks this is all my responsibility. The last thing he wants is a baby."

"You don't know—"

"Oh, yes I do. He said so over and over again."

Shawna handed her a couple of tissues and Melinda dabbed her eyes but was unable to stem the flow of her tears.

"I—I was careful," she said, blinking rapidly. "But he'll blame me, I know he will!"

"Sometimes a man changes his mind when he's actually faced with the news that he's going to be a father."

"But he can't!" Melinda said harshly, obviously hurting deep inside.

Shawna walked around the desk and placed her arm around the young woman's shaking shoulders. "I don't want to pry," she said evenly. "What's going on between you and the father isn't any of my business—"

"If you only knew," Melinda whispered, glancing at Shawna with red-rimmed eyes, then shifting her gaze. Standing, she pushed away Shawna's arm. "This is my problem," she said succinctly. "I—I'll handle it."

"Try not to think of the baby as a problem, okay?" Shawna advised, reaching for a card from a small holder on her desk. "Take this card—it has Dr. Chambers's number. He's one of the best obstetricians in the city."

"What I need now is a shrink," Melinda said, still sniffing.

"My brother's a psychiatrist," Shawna said quietly, locating one of Jake's business cards. "Maybe you should talk with him—"

Melinda snatched the cards from Shawna's outstretched hand. "I—I'll think about it. After I talk with the father."

Shawna offered the girl an encouraging smile. "That's the first step."

"Just remember—this was *your* idea!"

"I'll take full responsibility," Shawna replied, but read the message in the young woman's eyes. More clearly than words, Melinda had told her Shawna didn't know what she was saying. Anger and defiance bright in her eyes, Melinda James walked briskly out the door.

Shawna watched her leave and felt the same nagging doubts she had when she'd first talked to the girl. "You can't win 'em all," she told herself thoughtfully as she hung her lab coat in the closet and quickly ran a brush through her hair. But she couldn't shake the feeling that Melinda, despite her vocal doubts, had known she was pregnant all along.

She reached for her purse and slung it over her shoulder, but stopped before slipping her arms through her jacket. Feeling a little guilty, she called directory assistance in Cleveland and asked for the number of Harold Rankin, Melinda's pediatrician.

"There are several H. Rankins listed," the operator told her.

"I'm looking for the pediatrician. He must have an office number." The operator paused. "I'm sorry. There is no Doctor Rankin listed in Cleveland."

"Unlisted? Look, I'm a doctor myself. I need to consult with him about a patient and I don't have his number," Shawna said, new suspicions gnawing at her.

The operator muttered something under her breath. "I really can't—"

"It's important!"

"Well, I guess I can tell you this much, there's no Dr. Harold Rankin listed or unlisted in Cleveland. Just a minute." For a few seconds all Shawna could hear was clicking noises. "I'm sorry—I checked the suburbs. No Dr. Harold Rankin."

"Thank you," Shawna whispered, replacing the receiver. So Melinda had lied—or the doctor had moved. But that was unlikely. Shawna remembered Melinda's first words. *I saw your name in the paper. . . . You're the doctor who's engaged to Parker Harrison, aren't you? . . . He's got amnesia, right?*

Without thinking about what she was doing, Shawna buttoned her jacket and half ran out the door of her office. She waved good-bye to the receptionist, but her mind was filled with Melinda's conversation and the girl's dark, grudging glances. No, Melinda James wasn't a reporter, but she was hiding something. Shawna just couldn't figure out what it was. As she took the elevator down to the underground parking garage, she was alone, her keys gripped in one hand. What did a pregnant eighteen-year-old girl have to do with Parker? she asked herself, suddenly certain she wouldn't like the answer.

* * *

Parker's leg throbbed, rebelling against his weight as he attempted to walk the length of the physical therapy room. His hands slipped on the cold metal bars, but he kept himself upright, moving forward by sheer will. Every rigid, sweat-covered muscle in his body screamed with the strain of dragging his damned leg, but he kept working.

"That's it, just two more steps," a pert therapist with a cheery smile and upturned nose persuaded, trying to encourage him forward.

Gritting his teeth he tried again, the foot slowly lifting from the floor. Pain ripped through his knee and he bit his lower lip, tasting the salt of his sweat. *Come on, Harrison,* he said to himself, squeezing his eyes shut, *do it for Shawna, that beautiful lady doctor who's crazy enough to love you.*

In the past few weeks, he'd experienced flashes of memory, little teasing bits that had burned in his mind. He could remember being with her on a sailboat—her tanned body, taut and sleek. She'd been leaning against the boom as the boat skimmed across clear green water. Her blond hair had billowed around her head, shimmering gold in the late afternoon sun, and she'd laughed, a clear sound that rippled across the river.

Even now, as he struggled to the end of the parallel bars, he could remember the smell of fresh water and perfume, the taste of her skin and the feel of her body, warm and damp, as she'd lain with him on the sand of some secluded island.

Had they made love? That one delicious recollection escaped him, rising to the surface only to sink below the murky depths of his memory, as did so much of his life. Though he knew—he could sense—that he'd loved her, there was something else stopping him from believing everything she told him of their life together— something ugly and unnamed and a part of the Brad Lomax tragedy.

"Hey! You've done it!" the therapist cried as Parker took a final agonizing step.

While thinking of the enigma that was his relationship with Shawna, he hadn't realized that he'd finished his assigned task. "I'll be damned," he muttered.

"You know what this means, don't you?" the therapist asked, positioning a wheelchair near one of the contraptions that Parker decided were designed for the sole purpose of human torture.

"What?

"You're a free man. This is the final test. Now, if your doctor agrees, you can go home and just come back here for our workouts."

Parker wiped the sweat from his eyes and grinned. He'd be glad to leave this place! Maybe once he was home he'd start to remember and he could pick up the pieces of his life with Shawna. Maybe then the dreams of a mystery woman that woke him each night would disappear, and the unknown past would become crystal clear again.

The therapist tossed him a white terry towel and a nurse appeared.

Parker wiped his face, then slung the towel around his neck.

Placing her hands on the handles of the wheelchair, the nurse said, "I'll just push you back to your room—"

"I'll handle that," Shawna said. She'd been standing in the doorway, one shoulder propped against the jamb as she watched Parker will himself through the therapy. She'd witnessed the rigid strength of his sweat-dampened shoulders and arms, seen the flinch of pain as he tried to walk, and recognized the glint of determination in his eyes as he inched those final steps to the end of the bars.

"If you're sure, Doctor—" the nurse responded, noting Shawna's identification tag.

"Very sure." Then she leaned over Parker's shoulder and whispered, "Your place or mine?"

He laughed then. Despite the throb of pain in his knee and his anguish of not being able to remember anything of his past, he laughed. "Get me out of here."

"Your wish is my command." Without further prompting, she rolled him across the polished floors of the basement hallway and into the waiting elevator, where the doors whispered closed. "Alone at last," she murmured.

"What did I do to deserve you?" he asked, glancing up at her, his eyes warm and vibrant.

Her heart constricted and impulsively she jabbed the stop button before leaning over and pressing her lips to his. "You have been, without a doubt, the best thing that ever happened to me," she said, swallowing back a thick lump in her throat. "You showed me there was more to life than medical files, patient charts, and trying to solve everyone else's problems."

"I can't believe—"

"Of course not," she said, laughing and guessing that he was going to argue with her again, tell her he didn't deserve her love. "You've been right all along, Parker," she confided. "Everything I've been telling you is a lie. You don't deserve me at all. It's just that I'm a weak, simple female and you're so strong and sexy and macho!"

"Is that so?" he asked, strong arms dragging her into his lap.

She kissed him again, lightly this time. "Well, isn't that what you wanted to hear?"

"Sounded good," he admitted.

Cocking her head to one side, her blond hair falling across his shoulder, she grinned slowly. "Well, the strong and sexy part is true."

"But somehow I don't quite see you as a 'weak, simple female.' "

"Thank heaven. So just believe that you're the best thing in my life, okay? And no matter what happens, I'm never going to take the chance of losing you again!"

"You won't," he murmured, pulling her closer, claiming her lips with a kiss so intense her head began to spin. She forgot the past and the future. She could only concentrate on the here and now, knowing in her heart the one glorious fact that Parker, her beloved Parker, was holding her and kissing her as hungrily as he had before the accident—as if he did indeed love her all over again.

Her breath caught deep in her lungs and inside, she was warming, feeling liquid emotion rush through her veins. She felt his hands move over her, rustling the lining of her skirt to splay against her back, hold her in that special, possessive manner that bound them so intimately together. Delicious, wanton sensations whispered through her body and she tangled her hands in his hair.

"Oh, what you do to me," he whispered in a voice raw and raspy as his fingers found the hem of her sweater and moved upward to caress one swollen breast. Hot and demanding, his fingers

touched the soft flesh and Shawna moaned softly as ripples of pleasure ran like wildfire through her blood.

"Parker, please—" She cradled his head against her, feeling the
warmth of his breath touch her skin. His lips teased one throbbing
peak, his tongue moist as it caressed the hard little button.

Shawna was melting inside. Rational thought ceased and she
was only aware of him and the need he created.

"Oh, Shawna," he groaned, slowly releasing her, his eyes still
glazed with passion as a painful memory sizzled through his desire.
"You're doing it again," he whispered, rubbing his temple as if it
throbbed. "Shawna—stop!"

She had trouble finding her breath. Her senses were still spinning out of control and she stung from his rejection. Why was he
pulling away from her? "What are you talking about?"

Passion-drugged eyes drilled into hers. "I remember, Shawna."

Relieved, she smiled. Everything was going to be fine. She tried
to stroke his cheek but he jerked away. "Then you know how much
we loved each—"

"I remember that you teased me, pushed me to the limit in public places. Like this."

"Parker, what are you talking about?" she cried, devastated.
What was he saying? If he remembered, then surely he'd know
how much she cared.

"It's not all clear," he admitted, helping her to her feet. "But
there were times, just like this, when you drove me out of my
mind!" He reached up and slapped the control panel. The elevator
started with a lurch and Shawna nearly lost her footing.

"I don't understand—" she whispered.

The muscles of his face tautened. "Remember the fair?" he said
flatly. "At the fir tree?"

She gasped, recalling rough bark against her bare back, his
hands holding her wrists, their conversation about his "mistress."

"It was only a game we played," she said weakly.

"Some game." His eyes, still smoldering with the embers of recent passion, avoided hers. "You know, somehow I had the impression that you and I loved each other before—that we were lovers.
You let me think that." His eyes were as cold as the sea.

"We were," she said, then recognized the censure in the set of his jaw. "Well, almost. We'd decided to wait to get married before going to bed."

Arching a brow disdainfully, he said through clenched teeth, *"We* decided? You're a doctor. I'm a tennis pro. Neither one of us is a kid and you expect me to believe that we were playing the cat-and-mouse game of waiting 'til the wedding."

"You said you remembered," she whispered, but then realized his memory was fuzzy. Certain aspects of their relationship were still blurred.

"I said I remembered part of it." But the anger in his words sounded hollow and unsure, as if he were trying to find an excuse to deny the passion between them only moments before.

The elevator car jerked to a stop and the doors opened on the fourth floor. Shawna, her breasts still aching, reached for the handles of the wheelchair, but Parker didn't wait for her. He was already pushing himself down the corridor.

In the room, she watched him shove the wheelchair angrily aside and flop onto the bed, his face white from the effort.

"Your memory is selective," she said, leaning over the bed, pushing her face so close to his that she could read the seductive glint in his blue eyes.

"Maybe," he admitted and stared at her lips, swallowing with difficulty.

"Then why won't you just try to give us a chance? We were good together, sex or no sex. Believe me." She heard him groan.

"Don't do this to me," he asked, the fire in his eyes rekindling.

"I'll do whatever I have to," she whispered, leaning closer, kissing him, brushing the tips of her breasts across his chest until he couldn't resist.

"You're making a big mistake." He pressed her close to him.

"Let me."

"I'm not the same man—"

"I don't care, damn it," she said, then sighed. "Just love me."

"That would be too easy," he admitted gruffly, then buried his face in her hair, drinking in the sweet feminine smell that teased at his mind every night. He held her so fiercely she could feel the heat of his body through her clothes. Clinging to him, she barely heard the shuffle of feet in the doorway until Parker dragged his lips from hers and stared over her shoulder.

Twisting, half expecting to find Jake with his lousy sense of timing, she saw a young black-haired girl standing nervously on one foot, then the other.

"Melinda?" Shawna asked, her throat dry. "Are you looking for me?"

"No," Melinda James said quietly, her large, brown eyes lifting until they clashed with Parker's. "I came to see him, on your advice."

"My advice—what—?" But a dark doubt steadily grew in her heart and she gripped Parker's shoulders more tightly, as if by clinging to him, she could stop what was to come. "No—there must be some mistake," she heard herself saying, her voice distant, as if in a dream.

"You told me to talk to him and that's . . . that's why I'm here," Melinda said, her eyes round with fear, large tears collecting on her lashes. "You see, Parker Harrison is the father of my child."

CHAPTER 7

"He's what?" Shawna whispered, disbelieving.

"It's true."

"Wait a minute—" Parker stared at the girl, not one flicker of recognition in his eyes. "Who are you?"

Shawna wanted to tell him not to believe a word of Melinda's story, but she didn't. Instead she forced herself to watch his reaction as Melinda, hesitantly at first, then with more conviction, claimed she and Parker had been seeing each other for several months, long before he'd started dating Shawna, and that she'd become pregnant with his child.

Parker blanched, his mouth drawing into a tight line.

"This is absurd," Shawna finally said, praying that Parker would back her up.

"How old are you?" he asked, eyes studying the dark-haired girl.

"Eighteen."

"Eighteen?" he repeated, stunned. His eyes narrowed and he forced himself to stand. "And you're saying that you and I—"

"—were lovers," Melinda clarified.

Shawna couldn't stand it a minute more. "This is all a lie. Parker, this girl came into my office, asked all sorts of questions about you and your amnesia, and then had me examine her."

"And?"

"And she *is* pregnant. That much is true. But . . . but . . . she's lying . . . you couldn't have been with her. *I* would have known." But even though her words rang with faith, she couldn't help remembering all the times Parker had taunted her by pretending to have a mistress. *I suppose this means that I'll have to give up my mistress,* he'd said at the fair, teasing her, but wounding her just the same. Her old doubts twisted her heart. Was it possible that he'd actually been seeing someone and that the person he'd been with had been this girl?

"You don't remember me?" Melinda asked.

Parker closed his eyes, flinching a bit.

"I saw you the night of the accident," she prodded. "You . . . you were with Brad and he was drunk."

Parker's eyes flew open and pain, deep and tragic, showed in their vibrant blue depths.

"You stopped by my apartment and Brad became violent, so you hauled him back to the car."

"She's making this up," Shawna said. "She must have read about it in the papers or heard it on the news." But her voice faltered as she saw Parker wrestling with a memory.

"I've met her before," he said slowly. "I was at her apartment."

"No!" Shawna cried. She wouldn't believe a word of Melinda's lies—she couldn't! Parker would never betray her! She'd almost lost Parker once and she wasn't about to lose him again, not to this girl, not to anyone. "Parker, you don't honestly believe—"

"I don't know *what* to believe!" he snapped.

"But we've been through so much together..." Then she turned her eyes on Melinda and all of her professionalism and medical training flew out the window. No longer was Melinda her patient, but just a brash young woman trying to tarnish the one man Shawna loved. "Look," she said, her voice as ragged as her emotions. "I don't really know who you are or why you're here torturing him or even how you got into this room, but I want you out, now!"

"Stop it, Shawna," Parker said.

But Shawna ignored him. "I'll call the guards if I have to, but you have no right to come in here and upset any of the patients—"

"I'm *your* patient," Melinda said, satisfaction briefly gleaming in her eyes.

"I referred you to—"

"He's the father of my child, damn it!" Melinda cried, wilting against the wall and sobbing like the girl she was.

"She can stay," Parker pronounced as Tom Handleman, his lab coat flapping behind him, marched into the room. "What the devil's going on here?" he demanded, eyeing Shawna. "Who's she?" He pointed an accusing finger at the huddled figure of Melinda.

"A friend of mine," Parker said, his voice ringing with quiet authority.

"Parker, no!" Shawna whispered, ignoring Tom. "She lied to me this morning—told me the name of her previous physician in Cleveland. I tried to call him—there is no Dr. Harold Rankin in the area."

"Then he moved," Melinda said, stronger because of Parker's defense. "It's—it's been years."

"She has to leave," Shawna decided, turning to Tom, desperation contorting her face.

"Maybe she can help," Tom suggested.

"Help?" Shawna murmured. "She's in here accusing him, lying to him, lying to me—"

Melinda stood, squaring her shoulders and meeting Parker's clouded gaze. "I—I understand why you feel betrayed, Dr. McGuire. First Parker lied to you and then I had to lie this morning. But I just wanted to find out that he was all right. No one would let me in here. Then *you* convinced me that I had to tell him about the baby—"

"Baby?" Handleman asked, his face ashen.

"—and I decided you were right. Every father has the right to know about his child whether he wants to claim him or not."

"For cryin' out loud!" Tom whispered. "Look, Miss—"

"James," Melinda supplied.

"Let her stay," Parker said.

"You remember me," she said.

Shawna wanted to die as they stared at each other.

"I've met you," Parker admitted, his face muscles taut. "And I don't mean to insult you, Miss James—"

"Melinda. You called me Linnie. Don't you remember?" Her chin trembled and she fought against tears that slid from her eyes.

"I'm sorry—"

"You have to remember!" she cried. "All those nights by the river—all those promises—"

Good Lord, what was she saying? Shawna's throat closed up. "Parker and I were—are—going to be married, and neither one of us believes that he's the father of your child. This is obviously just some way for you and your boyfriend to take advantage—"

"No!" Melinda whispered. "I don't care what *you* believe, but Parker loves me! He—he—" Her eyes darted quickly around the room and she blinked. "Oh, please, Parker. Remember," she begged.

Parker gripped the arms of his wheelchair. "Melinda," he said softly. Was it Shawna's imagination or did his voice caress the younger woman's name? "I don't remember ever sleeping with you."

"You deny the baby?"

He glanced at Shawna, his eyes seeming haunted. She could only stare back at him. "Not the baby. I'm just not sure it's mine."

Shawna shook her head. "No—"

"Then maybe you'd want a simple paternity test," Melinda suggested.

"Hey—hold the phone," Tom Handleman cut in. "Let's all just calm down. Right now, Miss James, I'm asking you to leave." Then he glanced at Shawna. "You, too, Dr. McGuire. This has been a strain on Parker. Let's all just give it a rest."

"I'm afraid I can't do that," Melinda said staunchly, seeming to draw from an inner reserve of strength. "Don't get me wrong, Parker. I'm not interested in ruining your reputation or trying to damage your professional image, but my baby needs his father."

"So you want money," Parker said cynically.

"Money isn't what I'm after," Melinda said, and Shawna felt a chill as cold as a December wind cut through her. "I want to give my baby a name and I want him to know who his father is. If it takes a paternity test to convince you or a lawsuit, I don't care." Swallowing back a fresh onslaught of tears, she walked unsteadily out of the room.

Shawna turned a tortured gaze to Parker. "You remember her?"

He nodded and let his forehead drop to his hand. "A little."

Dying inside, Shawna leaned against the bed. After all these weeks, Parker still barely admitted to remembering her—only disjointed pieces of their relationship. And yet within fifteen minutes of meeting Melinda James he conceded that he recognized her. Dread settled over her.

Sick inside, she wondered if Melinda's ridiculous accusations could possibly be true. Did Parker remember Melinda because they had slept together? Was her face so indelibly etched in his mind because of their intimacy? But that was ridiculous—she knew it and deep down, so did he!

She felt that everything she'd believed in was slowly being shredded into tiny pieces.

"You—you and Brad. You saw her that night?" she asked, her voice barely audible over the sounds of the hospital.

He nodded, his jaw extending. "Yes."

"And you remember?"

"Not everything."

"Maybe she was Brad's girl. Maybe the baby is his."

Parker's eyes narrowed. "Maybe. I don't know."

Tom placed his hand over Shawna's arm and guided her to the door. "Don't torture yourself," he said in a concerned whisper. "Go home, think things through. I guarantee you Parker will do the same. Then tomorrow, come back and take him home."

"Home?" she repeated dully.

"Yes, I'm releasing him tomorrow." He glanced over his shoulder to Parker. "That is, unless Miss James's visit sets him back."

"I hope not," Shawna said, staring at Parker with new eyes, trying to smile and failing miserably. "Look, I really need to talk to him. Just a few minutes, okay?"

"I guess it won't hurt," Tom decided, "but keep it short. He's had one helluva shock today."

"Haven't we all?" Shawna said as Tom closed the door behind him.

Parker didn't look at her. He scowled through the window to the gray day beyond.

Had he betrayed her? Shawna couldn't believe it. Melinda had to be lying. But why? And why had Parker gone to visit the young girl before taking Brad home? Was it to call off their affair? Or had he needed to see her just one more time before the wedding? Shawna's stomach churned at the thought of them lying together, kissing—

"So much for the knight in shining armor, huh?" he mocked.

"I don't believe a word of her lies. And I really don't think you do, either."

"That's the tricky part," he admitted, staring up at the ceiling. "I know I've seen her—been with her, but—"

"—But you don't remember." Tossing her hair over her shoulder, she leaned against the bed.

"She has no reason to lie."

"Neither do I, Parker. I don't know anything about that girl, but I know what we shared and we didn't cheat or lie or betray one another."

"You're sure of that?"

"Positive," she whispered, wishing that awful shadow of doubt would disappear from her mind. "I only wish I could prove it."

Parker watched her blink back tears, saw her fine jaw jut in determination, and loved her for all of her pride and faith in him. Her blond hair draped across her shoulder to curl at her breast, and her eyes, fierce with indignation and bright with unshed tears, were as green as a night-darkened forest. How he loved her. Even lying here, charged with fathering another woman's child, he loved Shawna McGuire. But not because of any memories that had surfaced in his mind. No, this love was new, borne from just being near her. Never had he met any woman so proud and free-spirited, so filled with giving and fighting for what she believed in. And what she believed in was him.

"Do you think you're the father of Melinda's baby?" she finally asked, so close he could touch her.

"I don't know."

She blanched, as if in severe pain. Without thinking he took her hand in his and pulled her gently forward, so that she was leaning over him.

"But I do know that if I ever did anything that would hurt you this much, I have to be the worst bastard that ever walked the earth."

She swallowed. "You . . . you wouldn't."

"I hope to God you're right." His throat felt dry, and though the last thing he intended to do was kiss her again, he couldn't stop himself. He held her close, tilting her chin up with one finger and molding his mouth possessively over hers. "I don't want to ever hurt you, Shawna," he rasped hoarsely. "Don't let me."

"You won't." She felt the promise of his tongue as it gently parted her lips, then heard the sound of voices in the hall. She couldn't think when he held her, and she needed time alone to recover from the shock of Melinda James's announcement. Besides, she'd promised Dr. Handleman she wouldn't upset Parker. "Look, I don't want to, but I've got to go. Doctor's orders."

"To hell with doctor's orders," he muttered, his arms flexing around her, thwarting her attempts at escape.

"Don't mess with the medical profession," she warned, but the lilt she tried for didn't materialize in her voice.

"Not the whole profession," he said slowly, "just one very beautiful lady doctor."

Oh, Parker! Her throat thickened. "Later," she promised, kissing him lightly on the tip of the nose and hearing him moan in response.

"You're doing it again," he whispered.

"What?"

"Driving me crazy." His gaze slid down her body and stupidly, like a schoolgirl, she blushed and ran for the door.

As she drove home, her thoughts were tangled in a web of doubt and despair. Was it possible? Could Melinda's story be true?

"Don't be absurd," she told herself as she maneuvered her little car through the twisted streets of Sellwood. Maple and alder trees had begun to drop their leaves, splashing the wet streets with clumps of gold, brown, and orange.

As Shawna climbed out of the car, a cold autumn breeze lifted her hair from her face, cooled the heat in her cheeks.

"Hey, about time you showed up!" Jake accosted her as he climbed out of a battered old Chevy pickup. "I thought you'd be home half an hour ago."

She'd forgotten all about him, and the fact that he'd offered to help her move. "I—I'm sorry. Uh, something came up," she said, trying to concentrate.

"Oh, yeah?" Jake's brows raised expectantly. "Don't tell me the coach is gonna be released."

"Tomorrow," Shawna said, her voice catching before her brother saw the pain in her eyes.

"Hey—whoa. What happened?" Jake grabbed both her shoulders, then forced her chin upward with one finger and stared down at her.

"You wouldn't believe it."

"Try me." One arm over her shoulders, Jake walked her to the front door and unlocked the dead bolt. The apartment was a mess. Boxes and bags were scattered all over the living-room floor, piled together with pictures, furniture, and clothes.

Shawna flopped in the nearest corner and told Jake everything, from the moment Melinda James had walked into her office until the time when she'd dropped the bomb about Parker being the father of her unborn child.

"And you bought that cockamamy story?" Jake asked, flabbergasted.

"Of course not." Shawna felt close to tears again.

"I hope not! It's ridiculous."

"But Parker did."

"What?"

"He claims to remember her, and admits that he visited her the night Brad was killed!"

Stricken, Jake sat on a rolled carpet. His eyes narrowed thoughtfully. "I don't believe it."

"Neither did I, but you should have been there." Outside, Maestro meowed loudly. "I'm coming," Shawna called, every muscle in her body suddenly slack as she tried to stand and couldn't.

"I'll let him in." Jake opened the door and the bedraggled yellow tabby, wet from the rain, dashed into the house and made a beeline for Shawna. He cried until she petted him. "At least I can trust you," she said, her spirits lifting a little as the tabby washed his face and started to purr noisily.

"You can trust Parker, too," Jake said. "You and I both know it. That guy's crazy about you."

"Tell him," she said.

Jake frowned at his sister. "Okay, so this lunatic girl has made some crazy claims and Parker can't remember enough to know that she's lying. It's not the end of the world." He caught her glance and sighed. "Well, almost the end," he admitted, and even Shawna had to smile. "Now, come on. What's your next step?"

"You're not going to like it," Shawna said, opening a can of cat food for the cat.

"Try me."

"When the movers come tomorrow, I'm going to have them take my things to Parker's."

"His house?" Jake asked, his brows shooting up. "Does he know about this?"

"Nope." She straightened and her gaze narrowed on her brother. "And don't you tell him about it."

"I wouldn't dare," Jake said with obvious respect for Parker's volatile temper. "What about Mom and Dad?"

"I'll explain."

"Good luck. That's one dogfight I don't want any part of."

"I don't blame you." Why was this happening, and why now? She couldn't help thinking back to the Gypsy fortune-teller and her grim prediction.

"Shawna?" Jake asked, concern creasing his brow. "Are you okay?"

She nodded, her chin inching upward proudly. "I'm fine," she said. "I just have to stick by Parker 'til all of this is resolved one way or the other."

"Can I help?"

"Would you mind taking care of Maestro, just for a few days?"

Jake eyed the tabby dubiously. As if understanding he was the center of attention, Maestro leaped to the counter and arched his back as he rubbed up against the windowsill.

"I'm allergic to cats."

"He's outside most of the time."

"Bruno will eat him alive."

Shawna couldn't help but laugh. Bruno was a large mutt who was afraid of his own shadow. "Bruno will stick his big tail between his legs and run in the other direction."

"Okay."

"By the way," she said, feeling better. "You should work on that dog's obvious case of paranoia!"

"Maybe I should work on yours," Jake said, clapping her on the back. "You and I both know that Parker wasn't unfaithful to you."

"But he doesn't know it," Shawna replied, her convictions crumbling a little.

"You'll just have to convince him."

"I'm trying. Believe me." She pushed her hair from her eyes and rested the back of her head against the wall. "But that's not the only problem. What about Melinda and her baby? Why is she lying? How does Parker know her? As much as this mess angers me, I can't forget that Melinda is only eighteen, unmarried, and pregnant."

"Does she have any family?"

"I don't know." Shawna blew a strand of hair from her eyes. "All she said was that her dad would kill her when he found out. I think she was just using a turn of phrase. At least I hope so."

"But you're not sure."

"That's one of the most frustrating things about all of this. I don't know a thing about her. I've never even heard her name before and now she claims to be carrying my fiancé's child."

"Maybe there's something I could do."

"Such as?"

"I don't know, but *something.*"

"Not this time," she decided, grateful for his offer. "But thanks. This one I've got to handle by myself."

"I don't believe it!" Doris McGuire exclaimed. Sitting on her antique sofa, she stared across the room at her daughter. "Parker, and some, some girl?"

"That's what she claims," Shawna said.

"She's lying!"

"Who is?" Malcolm McGuire opened the front door and shook the rain from his hat, then tossed the worn fedora over the arm of an oak hall tree in the foyer. "Who's lying?" he repeated as he strode into the den and kissed Shawna's cheek. "You're not talking about Parker, are you?"

"Indirectly," Shawna admitted.

"Some young girl claims she's pregnant with Parker's child!" Doris said, her mouth pursed, her eyes bright with indignation. "Can you believe it?"

"Hey, slow down a minute," Malcolm said. "Let's start at the beginning."

As Shawna explained everything that had happened since she'd first met Melinda, Malcolm splashed a stiff shot of Scotch into a glass, thought twice about it, and poured two more drinks, which he handed to his daughter and wife.

"You don't believe it, do you?" he finally asked, searching Shawna's face.

"Of course not."

"But you've got doubts."

"Wouldn't you?"

"Never!" Doris declared. Malcolm's face whitened a bit.

"Sometimes a man can make a mistake, you know," he said.

"He was *engaged* to Shawna, for goodness sake!"

"But not married to her," Malcolm said slowly.

"Dad?" Did he know something? She studied the lines of her father's face as he finished his drink and sat heavily on the edge of the couch.

"I have no idea what Parker was up to," Malcolm said. "But I warned you that we didn't know all that much about him, didn't I? Maybe he had another girlfriend, I don't know. I would never have believed it before, but now? Why would she lie?"

Why indeed?

"But let's not judge him too harshly," Malcolm said. "Not until all the facts are in."

"I don't think you understand the gravity of the situation," Doris replied.

"Of course I do. Now, tell me about Parker. What does he have to say?"

"Not much." Shawna told her parents about the scene in the hospital room.

Malcolm cradled his empty glass in both hands and frowned into it. Doris shook her head and sighed loudly, though her back was ramrod stiff. "He'll just have to submit to a paternity test— prove the child isn't his and then get on with his life."

"Maybe it's not that simple," Malcolm said quietly. "He has a career to think of. All this adverse publicity might affect it."

"We're talking about the man Shawna plans to marry," Doris cut in, simmering with fury, "and here you are defending his actions—if, indeed, he was involved with that . . . that *woman!*"

"She's barely more than a girl," Shawna said.

"Eighteen is old enough to know better!"

Malcolm held up his hand to calm his wife. "I'm just saying we should all keep a level head."

Now that she'd said what she had to say, Shawna snatched her jacket from the back of a wing chair. "I think Dad's right—we should just low-key this for now."

"The girl is pregnant!"

"I know, I know. But I've decided that what I'm going to do is try and help Parker through this. It's got to be as hard on him as it is on me. That's one of the reasons I've decided to move in with him."

"Do what?" Doris was horrified. She nearly dropped her drink and her pretty face fell.

"He's being released from the hospital tomorrow. And I'm taking him home—to his house—with me."

"But you can't—you're not married. And now, with that girl's ridiculous accusations—"

"All the more reason to try and help jog his memory." Shawna saw the protests forming on her mother's lips and waved them off.

"Look, I've already made up my mind. If things had turned out differently, I'd already be married to him and living in that house. He and I would still have to deal with Melinda—unless this is all a convenient story of hers just because he's lost his memory. So, I'm going to stand by him. I just wanted you to know how to get in touch with me."

"But—"

"Mom, I love him." Shawna touched her mother's shoulder. It felt stiff and rigid under Doris's cotton sweater. "I'll call you in a couple of days."

Then, before her mother or father could try to change her mind, she walked out of the room, swept her purse off an end table, and opened the front door. She was glad to drive away from her parents' house because she needed time alone, time to think and clear her head. Tomorrow she'd have the battle of her life with Parker. He'd already told her he didn't want her tied to him as a cripple, that they couldn't marry until he was strong enough to support them both. Now, after Melinda's allegations, he'd be more adamant than ever.

Well, that was just too damned bad. Shawna intended to stand by him no matter what, and if he never walked again, she still intended to marry him. All she had to do was convince him that she was right. Involuntarily, she crossed her fingers.

Parker shoved the dinner tray aside. He wasn't hungry and didn't feel like trying to force food down his throat. With a groan, he reached for the crutches near his bed.

Dr. Handleman and the idiot down in physical therapy didn't think he was ready for crutches, but he'd begged them off a candy striper. Tomorrow he was going home and he wasn't about to be wheeled down the hall like a helpless invalid.

Gritting his teeth against a stab of pain in his knee, he slid off the bed and shoved the crutches under his arms. Then, slowly, he moved across the room, ignoring the throbbing in his knee and the erratic pounding of his heart. Finally he fell against the far wall, sweating but proud that he'd accomplished the small feat of walking across the room.

Breathing hard, he glanced out the window to the parking lot below. Security lamps glowed blue, reflecting on the puddles from a recent shower. Parker had a vague recollection of another storm. . . .

Rain had been drizzling down a windshield, wipers slapping the sheeting water aside as he had driven up a twisting mountain road. Someone—was it Brad?—had been slumped in the passenger seat. The passenger had fallen against Parker just as the Jeep had rounded a corner and there, right in the middle of the road, a huge truck with bright glaring headlights was barreling toward them, out of control. The truck driver blasted his horn, brakes squealed and locked, and Parker, reacting by instinct alone, had wrenched hard on the wheel, steering the Jeep out of the path of the oncoming truck and through the guardrail into the black void beyond.

Now, as he stood with his head pressed to the glass, Parker squeezed his eyes shut tight, trying to dredge up the memories, put the ill-fitting pieces of his past into some order.

He remembered Melinda—he'd seen her that night. But she was just a girl. Surely he wouldn't have slept with her!

Impatient with his blank mind, he swore and knocked over one of his crutches. It fell against the table, knocking over a water glass and a book. From the pages of the book fluttered a picture—the single snapshot of Shawna on the carousel.

In the photograph, her cheeks were rosy and flushed, her eyes bright, her hair tossed wildly around her face. He'd been in love with her then. He could feel it, see it in her expression. And now, he'd fallen in love with her again and this time, he suspected, his feelings ran much deeper.

Despite the searing pain in his knee, he bent down, but the picture was just out of reach, in the thin layer of dust under the bed, and he couldn't coax the snapshot back to him, not even with the aid of his crutch.

He frowned at the irony. He couldn't reach the picture just as he couldn't have her, wouldn't chain her to a future so clouded and unsure. She deserved better than a man who might never walk without a cane—a man who couldn't even remember if he'd betrayed her.

CHAPTER 8

Bracing herself, knowing full well that she was in for the fight of her life, Shawna walked into Parker's hospital room. "Ready?" she asked brightly.

"For what?" Parker was standing near his bed, fully dressed in gray cords and a cream-colored sweater, and balancing precariously on crutches.

"To go home." She picked up his duffel bag and tossed it over her shoulder, overlooking the storm gathering in his eyes. "Hurry up, I'm double-parked."

"I'll call a cab," he said quietly.

"No reason. Your house is on my way."

"To where?"

"The rest of my life."

Taking in a swift breath, he shoved one hand through his hair and shook his head. "You're unbelievable," he muttered.

"So you've said. Come on."

"Mr. Harrison?" A nurse pushed a wheelchair into his room and Parker swore under his breath.

"I don't need *that.*"

"Hospital regulations."

"Change them," he said, jaw tight.

"Come on, Parker, don't buck the system now," Shawna said, grabbing the handles of the wheelchair from the nurse. "Everyone has to use these chairs in order to get out."

Muttering to himself he slid into the chair and grumbled all the way along the corridor.

"I see we're in good spirits today," Shawna commented drily.

"Don't start in with that hospital 'we' talk, okay? I'm sick to death of it."

"My mistake. But don't worry. I'll probably make a few more before the day is over." She wheeled him into the elevator and didn't say a word until they were through the emergency room doors— the same door she'd run through weeks ago in her soggy wedding dress. That day felt like a lifetime ago.

Once they were in the car and through the parking lot, Shawna drove south, down the steep fir-cloaked hills of west Portland toward Lake Oswego and Parker's rambling Tudor house on the cliffs.

He stared out the window in silence, his eyes traveling over the familiar landscape. Leaves of the maple and oak trees had turned vibrant orange and brown, swirling in the wind and hanging tenaciously to black branches as Shawna drove toward the river. She glanced at Parker and noticed the tight pinch at the corners of his mouth and the lines of strain on his forehead as his stone house loomed into view.

Rising a full three stories, with a sharply gabled roof and dormers, the Tudor stood high on the cliffs overlooking the green waters of the Willamette. Trees and shrubbery flanked a broad, pillared porch and leaded glass windows winked in the pink rays from a setting sun.

Shawna cut the engine in front of the garage. She was reaching for the handle of her door when his voice stopped her.

"Aren't you going to ask me about Melinda?"

She froze and her stomach twisted painfully. Inadvertently she'd been avoiding the subject. "Is there something you want to tell me?"

Swallowing, he glanced away, then stared straight into her eyes. "I—I'm starting to remember," he admitted, weighing his words. "Part of the past is getting a little more clear."

She knew what was coming and died a bit inside, her fingers wrapping around the steering wheel as she leaned back in her seat. "The part with Melinda," she guessed, fingers clenched tight over the wheel.

"Yes."

"You . . . remember being with her?"

"Partly."

"Sleeping with her?"

She saw him hesitate, then shake his head. "No, but there's something . . . something about her. If only I could figure it out."

Licking her lips nervously, she forced her gaze to meet his. "I don't believe you betrayed me, Parker," she admitted, her voice rough. "I just can't."

"Maybe it would be easier if you did," he whispered.

"Why?"

"Because I feel—this tremendous responsibility."

She touched him then, her fingers light on his sweater, beneath which she could feel the coiled tension in his shoulders. "Give it time."

"I think we're running out." Then, as quickly as he'd brought up the subject, he jerked on the door handle and shoved the car door open. Cool wind invaded the interior as he gripped the frame and tried to struggle to his feet.

"Hey—wait!" She threw open her door and ran around the car just as he extracted himself from his seat and balanced on one leg, his face white with strain. "What do you think you're doing?" she demanded.

"Standing on my own," he said succinctly.

She caught his meaning, but refused to acknowledge it. "Sure, but you were almost flat on your face," she chastised. "How do you think Dr. Handleman would like it if you twisted that knee again and undid all his work?"

"I don't really give a damn what he does or doesn't like."

"Back to your charming sweet self, I see," she said, though her heart was pounding a rapid double-time. "Personally I'd hate to see you back in that hospital bed—in traction or worse—all because of your stupid, bullheaded male pride." She opened the hatchback of her car and wrestled with the collapsible wheelchair, noting that he'd paled slightly at the mention of the hospital. Good! He needed to think that one over. "So, quit being a child and enjoy being pampered."

"Pampered by whom?"

"Me." She locked the wheelchair and rolled it toward his side of the car.

"I don't want to be pampered."

"Oh, I think you will. Think of it as a reward for all those grueling hours you'll be spending with the physical therapist. I already hired him—he starts tomorrow."

"You did *what?*" Parker was livid, the fire in his eyes bright with rage. "I'm not going to—"

"Sure you are. And you're going to get off this self-reliant-male ego kick right now!"

She pushed the wheelchair next to him, but he held up a hand, spreading his fingers in her face. "Hold on, just one minute. I may not remember a lot about my past, but I know one thing, I never let any woman—even a lady doctor—push me around."

"Not even Melinda James?" Shawna snapped, instantly regretting her words when she saw his face slacken and guilt converge over his honed features.

"I'll deal with Melinda," he said, his voice ringing with authority, "in my own way." Then, ignoring the wheelchair, he reached down and tugged on the crutches she'd wedged into the car.

"You can't—"

"I can damned well do as I please, Dr. McGuire," he said cuttingly. "I'm not in a hospital any longer. You're not the boss." He slammed the crutches under his arms and swung forward, landing on his good leg with a jarring thud as he started up the flagstone path leading to the back door.

"You'll be back in the hospital before you know it if you don't watch out," she warned. Walking rapidly, she caught up with him.

"You can go home now, Shawna," he advised.

"I am."

Cocking his head to one side, he asked testily, "You're what?"

"Home."

"What?" he roared, twisting to look at her, his crutch wedging in the chipped mortar to wrench out from under him. He pitched forward, grabbing frantically at the lowest branches of a nearby willow tree and landing with a thud on the wet grass.

"Parker!" Shawna knelt beside him. "I'm sorry—"

"Wasn't your fault." But he winced in pain, skin tight over his cheeks. "Now, tell me I heard wrong."

"I moved in this morning," she said, but her eyes were on his leg and without asking she pushed up his pant leg to make sure that the stitches in his knee hadn't ruptured.

"I'm all right." He caught her wrist. "You are *not* my doctor. And you're not moving in here."

"Too late," she said, reaching into her pocket with her free hand and extracting a key ring from which dangled the keys to his house, car, and garage. "You gave these to me—for better or for worse, remember."

"We didn't get married."

"Doesn't matter. I'm committed to you, so you'd better get used to it!" She met his gaze steadily, her green eyes bright with defiance and pride. His fingers were still circling her wrist, warm against her skin, and her breathing, already labored, caught in her throat as his eyes moved from hers to the base of her neck and lower still. "Whether the ceremony happened or not, I consider myself your wife, and it will take an act of God for you to get rid of me."

"What about another woman's child?"

Her heart constricted. "We'll just have to deal with that together, won't we?" Nervously, she licked her lips, her self-confidence slowly drifting away.

He studied her mouth. "Maybe I need to stand alone before I can stand with someone," he said, sun glinting off the burnished strands of his hair.

"Are you telling me you won't let me live here?" She could barely concentrate. Her thoughts centered on her wrist and the provocative movement of his fingers against her skin. And his eyes, blue as the sea, stared into hers, smoldering with desire, yet bewildered.

"I just don't think we—you and I—can act like this accident didn't happen, pretending that Melinda James doesn't exist, that our lives will mesh in some sort of fairy-tale happy ending, when there are so many things pulling us apart." He glanced down at her lips and then to her hair, shining a radiant gold in the afternoon sunlight.

"Please, Parker, just give me a chance. I—I don't mean to come on like gangbusters, but we need time alone together, to work things out."

He pulled her close, kissing her as passionately as she'd ever been kissed, his lips possessive and strong with a fire she knew burned bright in his soul.

Responding, she cradled his head to hers, feeling the texture of his hair and the warmth of his breath.

He shifted, more of his weight falling across her, his arms strong as they circled her waist.

"Parker, please—just love me," she whispered against his ear. He groaned a response. "Let me help you—help us." She placed both of her hands on his cheeks and held his head between her palms. "I can't let go, Melinda or no Melinda. Baby or no baby."

Before he could respond, Shawna heard the back door swing open and there, standing on the porch, her eyes dark with unspoken accusation, was Melinda James.

"What the devil?" Parker whispered. "How'd you—? Don't even answer! It doesn't matter."

Shawna realized that he'd probably given her a set of keys, too, long before he'd met Shawna, and the wound she'd tried so hard to bind opened again, fresh and raw.

"Remind me to have my locks changed," Parker muttered.

Shawna dusted off her skirt and tried to help him to his feet, but he pushed her hands aside, determined to stand by himself.

"I—I didn't know she would be here," Melinda said quietly, but her dark eyes darted quickly from Shawna to Parker and back again.

"I live here," Shawna said.

Melinda nearly dropped her purse. "You what?"

Parker's brows shot up. "Hold on a minute. I live here. Me. Alone."

"Not anymore," Shawna said, cringing at how brash she sounded. Two months ago she would never have been so bold, but now, with her back against the wall and Parker's physical and mental health at stake, she'd fight tooth and nail to help him.

"You invited her?" Melinda asked, surveying Parker with huge, wounded eyes.

"She invited herself." He forced himself upright and started propelling himself forward.

"Are—are you all right?" Melinda asked.

"Just dandy," he snapped, unable to keep the cynicism from his voice. "I think we'd all better go into the house, and straighten out a few things." He glanced over his shoulder to Shawna, who was attempting to comb the tangles from her hair with her fingers. "Coming, Doctor?"

"Wouldn't miss it for the world," she quipped back, managing a smile though her insides were shredding.

What would she do if he threw her out, insisted that he cared about Melinda, that the child was his?

"One step at a time," she reminded herself, following him inside.

Melinda was already halfway down the hall to the den. "I don't like this," Shawna confided in Parker as she caught up with him.

"Neither do I." His gaze wandered to her face and she could feel his eyes taking in the determined slant of her mouth. "But then there's a lot of things I don't like—things I'm not sure about."

"Such as?"

Before she could walk down the two steps to the den, he leaned forward, balanced on his crutches, and touched her shoulder. "Such as you," he admitted, eyes dark and tormented. "It would be easy to fall in love with you, Shawna—too easy. I must have been one helluva lucky guy—"

"You still are."

"—but now, things have changed. Look at me! I still can't walk. I may never walk without these infernal things!" He shook one crutch angrily, his expression changing to violent anger and frustration. "And then there's Melinda. I can't say her story isn't true. I don't know! I can't remember."

"I'll help you."

He let out a weary sigh and rested his forehead against hers. Involuntarily her fingers caught in the thick threads of his sweater. So desperately, she wanted him to understand, remember, recapture that fleeting love they'd shared.

One of his hands stroked her cheek, as if he couldn't quite believe she was real. "You—you've got a medical practice—a future, and you're a gorgeous, intelligent woman. Any man would count himself lucky if you just looked sideways at him."

"I'm not interested in 'any man,' " she pointed out. "Just one."

"Oh, Shawna," he moaned, his voice as low as the wind rustling through the rafters of the old house. Against her cheek, his fingers trembled.

A hot lump filled her throat. "How come I feel like you're trying to push me away?"

"Because I am. I have to. I can't tie you down to this!" He gestured to his legs, furious that they wouldn't obey his commands.

"Let me make that decision." Tears filled her eyes, but she smiled bravely just the same. "I'll decide if you're so horrible that any sane woman wouldn't be interested in you."

From the doorway to the den, Melinda coughed. She glanced guiltily away, as if she didn't mean to eavesdrop, but hadn't been able to stop herself from witnessing the tender scene between Parker and Shawna. "If you want me to, I'll leave," she said, chin quivering.

"Not yet." Straightening, Parker rubbed one hand around his shoulders, as if to relieve a coiled tension in his muscles. "Not yet." He swung his crutches forward and hobbled down the two steps into the den.

Steeling herself, Shawna followed, only to find that Melinda had already lit a fire in the grate and had placed a carafe of coffee on the table. "You've been here a while."

Melinda shrugged but resentment smoldered in her large brown eyes. "I, um, didn't expect you."

Parker met the questions in Melinda's gaze. "I think we'd better set a few ground rules. First of all, I don't remember you, not in the way you think I should," he said to Melinda. "But, if that child is really mine, I'll do right by you."

"That's all I'd expect," Melinda replied quickly. "I'm just concerned for my baby."

Shawna's hands shook. Just thinking that Parker might have a child with someone else, even a child conceived before they had met, tore at her soul. *I can handle this,* she told herself over and over again, trying to convince herself.

"Okay, so how did we meet?" Parker said, leaning forward and cringing a little when a jab of pain shot through him.

"I—I was a friend of Brad's. I, uh, used to watch him play and you coached him. Brad—he introduced us."

"How did you know Brad?"

Melinda looked down at her hands. "We went to school together in Cleveland, before he dropped out," she explained. "We, uh, used to date."

"But then you met Parker," Shawna prodded.

"Yes, and, well, Brad was seeing someone else, Parker and I hit it off, and then—" She licked her lips. "We fell in love. Until you came along."

Shawna exhaled slowly. How much of Melinda's story was fact and how much fantasy? If only Parker could remember! She wanted to hate the girl but couldn't. Melinda was afraid of something, or someone; it was written all over her downcast face.

"Do you have any family?" Parker asked.

"Not around here. My dad's a widower."

"Does he know that you're pregnant?"

"I didn't know until I saw *her* yesterday," Melinda said, then her shoulders slumped. "Though I guess I kinda expected it. But Dad, even if he did know, he wouldn't care. I haven't lived at home for a couple of years."

"I thought you said he'd kill you," Shawna whispered.

"I guess I was wrong." Melinda swallowed hard and Shawna almost felt sorry for her. "Look, I made a mistake. It's no big deal," she said, her temper flaring. "The thing is I'm in trouble, okay? And it's *his* fault. You know I'm not lying; you're the one who did the test."

Shawna slowly counted to ten. She couldn't lose her self-control. Not now. "Fine. Let's start over."

"I didn't come here to talk to you."

"This involves all of us," Parker said.

Shawna asked, "Did you finish high school?"

"Yep." Melinda flopped onto one of the cushions of the leather couch and stared at the ceiling. "I was going to be a model. Until I met Parker."

"After Brad."

"Right."

Shawna wondered how much, if any, of the girl's story were true. "And then you were swept off your feet?"

"That's about it," Melinda said, her smile faltering.

Parker's expression was unreadable. He stared at Melinda, his lips pressed together, as if he, too, were trying to find flaws in her words, some key to what had really happened. "Then you won't mind if I have a friend of mine look up your father, just to verify a few things," Parker said slowly.

Beneath her tan, Melinda blanched, but said, "Do what you have to do. It won't change anything, and at least then maybe she'll believe me." Disturbed, she slung her purse over her shoulder and left, the heels of her boots echoing loudly on the tiles of the foyer. A few seconds later Shawna heard the front door slam.

"Does anything she said sound true?" she asked.

"I don't know." Parker sighed heavily and, groaning, pushed himself to his feet. "I just don't know." Leaning one shoulder against the stones of the fireplace, he stared into the glowing red embers of the fire. "But she seemed pretty sure of herself. That seems to be a trait of the women I knew."

The firelight flickered on his face, causing uneven red shadows to highlight the hard angle of his jaw. He added, "You know you can't stay here."

"I have to."

"You don't owe me any debts, if that's what you think."

"You need someone to look after you."

"Like hell!" he muttered, his eyes blazing with the reflection of the coals. "What I don't need is anyone who thinks they owe me."

"You just don't understand, do you?" she whispered, so furious she was beginning to shake again. "You just don't understand how much I love you."

"Loved. Past tense."

Standing, she tossed her hair away from her face and met his fierce, uncompromising stare. "One accident doesn't change the depth of my feelings, Parker. Nor does it, in any way, shape or form, alter the fact that I love you for life, no matter what. Legally, I suppose, you can force me out of here. Or, you could make my life here so intolerable that I'd eventually throw in the towel and move. But you can't, *can't* destroy the simple fact that I love you and always will." Into the silence that followed, she said, "I've made up the guest room for you so you won't have to hassle with the stairs. I've moved all of your clothes and things down here."

"And you—where do you intend to sleep?"

"Upstairs—for now. Just until this Melinda thing is straightened out."

"And then?"

"Then, I hope, you'll want me to sleep with you."

"As man and wife?"

"Yes. If I can ever get it through that thick skull of yours that we belong together! So," she added fiercely, "if we're finished arguing, I'll make dinner." Leaving him speechless, she marched out of the room, fingers crossed, hoping that somehow, some way, she could help him remember everything.

Parker stared after her in amazement. Nothing was going as he'd planned. Ever since she'd bulldozed her way back into his life, he seemed to have lost control—not only of his past, but of his future.

Unfortunately, he admired her grit and determination, and even smiled to himself when he remembered how emphatic she'd become when she'd told him she intended to sleep with him. Any other man would jump at the chance of making love to her—but then any other man could jump and make love. So far he hadn't done either since the accident. He was sure he couldn't do one. As for the other, he hoped that he was experiencing only a temporary setback. He smiled a little. Earlier, when he'd fallen on the ground and he'd kissed Shawna, he'd felt the faintest of stirrings deep within.

Now, he found his crutches and pushed himself down the hallway toward the kitchen. Shawna was so passionate, so full of life. Why would he betray her with a woman who was barely out of childhood?

He leaned one shoulder against the wall and watched Shawna working in the kitchen. She'd tied a towel over her wool skirt, clipped her hair loosely away from her face, and kicked her shoes into a corner. In stocking feet and reading glasses, she sliced vegetables near the sink. She was humming—actually humming—as she worked, and she seemed completely at home and comfortable in his house, as though their argument and Melinda's baby didn't exist.

Watching her furtively, listening to the soft sound of her voice, seeing the smile playing upon her lips, he couldn't help feeling as lighthearted as she. She was a beautiful, intriguing woman—a woman with determination and courage—and she gave her love to him so completely.

So how could he have betrayed her? Deep inside, he knew he wouldn't have cheated on her. Yet he couldn't dismiss the fact that he vaguely remembered Melinda James.

She glanced up sharply, as if sensing him for the first time, and she blushed. "I didn't hear you."

"It's okay, I was just watching."

"Well, come in and take a center seat. No reason to hide in the hall," she teased.

Parker grinned and hobbled into the kitchen where he half fell into one of the caned chairs. "Don't let me disturb you," he said.

"Wouldn't dream of it!" She pushed her glasses onto the bridge of her nose and continued reading a recipe card. "You're in for the thrill of your life," she declared. *"Coq au vin* à la Shawna. This is going to be great."

"I know," he admitted, folding his arms over his chest, propping his bad leg on a nearby chair, and grinning to himself. Great it would be, but he wasn't thinking about the chicken in wine.

CHAPTER 9

Shawna eyed the dining room table critically. It gleamed with a fresh coat of wax and reflected the tiny flames of two creamy white candles. She'd polished the brass candlesticks and placed a fresh bouquet of roses and baby's breath between the flickering candles.

Tonight, whether Parker was agreeable or not, they were going to celebrate. She'd been living with him for over three weeks in a tentative truce. Fortunately, Melinda hadn't intruded, though Parker had spoken with her on the phone several times.

"Buck up," she told herself, as she thought about the girl.

Melinda was pregnant and they couldn't ignore her. Even though neither she nor Parker had brought up the subject of Melinda's baby, it was always in the air, an invisible barrier between them.

In the past weeks, Parker had spent his days in physical therapy, either at Mercy Hospital or here, at the house.

Shawna rearranged one drooping flower and frowned. As a doctor, she knew that Parker was pushing himself to the limit, forcing muscles and ligaments to work, as if regaining full use of his leg would somehow trip his memory. Though Shawna had begged him to slow down, he'd refused to listen, mule-headedly driving himself into a state of utter exhaustion.

Finally, at the end of the third week, he'd improved to the point that he was walking with only the aid of a cane.

To celebrate, she'd taken the afternoon off and had been waiting for him, cooking and cleaning and feeling nearly as if she belonged in his house—almost as if she were his wife.

She heard his car in the drive. Smiling, she hurried into the kitchen to add the last touches to the beef stroganoff simmering on the stove.

Parker opened the back door and collapsed into one of the kitchen chairs. His hair was dark with sweat and his face was gaunt and strained as he hung his cane over the back of his chair. He winced as he lifted his bad leg and propped it on a stool. Glancing up, he forced a tired smile. "Hi."

Shawna leaned over the counter separating kitchen from nook. "Hi, yourself."

"I thought you had the late shift."

"I traded so that we could have dinner together," she said.

"Sounds good." But he really wasn't listening. He was massaging his knee, his lips tightening as his fingers touched a particularly sensitive spot.

"You've been pushing yourself too hard again," she said softly, worried that he would do himself more damage than good.

"I don't think so."

"I'm a doctor."

He rolled his eyes. "Don't I know it?"

"Parker, please," she said, kneeling in front of him and placing a kiss on his sweat-dampened forehead. "Take it easy."

"I can't."

"There's plenty of time—"

"Do you really believe that?" He was staring at her suspiciously, as if he thought she was lying to him.

"You've got the rest of your—"

"Easy for you to say, *Doctor,*" he snapped. "You're not facing the rest of your life with this!" He lifted his cane, then, furious with the damned thing, hurled it angrily across the room. It skidded on the blue tiles and smashed into a far wall.

Shawna wanted to lecture him, but didn't. Instead she straightened and pretended interest in the simmering sauce. "I, uh, take it the session wasn't the best."

"You take it right, Doctor. But then you know everything, don't you?" He gestured toward the stove. "What I should eat, where I should sleep, how fast I should improve—all on your neat little schedule!"

His words stung, and she gasped before stiffening her back and pretending he hadn't wounded her. The tension between them had been mounting for weeks. He was disappointed, she told herself.

But he must have recognized her pain. He made a feeble gesture of apology with his hand, then, bracing his palms on the table, forced himself upright.

"I wish things were different," he finally said, gripping the counter with both hands, "but they're not. You're a good woman, Shawna—better than I deserve. Do yourself a favor and forget about me. Find yourself a whole man."

"I have," she whispered, her throat swollen tight. "He's just too pigheaded to know it."

"I mean it—"

"And so do I," she whispered. "I love you, Parker. I always will. That's just the way it is."

He stared at her in amazement, then leaned back, propping his head against the wall. "Oh, God," he groaned, covering his face with his hands. "You live in such a romantic dream world." When he dropped his hands, his expression had changed to a mask of indifference.

"If I live in a dream world," she said quietly, "it's a world that you created."

"Then it's over," he decided, straightening. "It's just . . . gone. It vanished that night."

Shawna ignored the stab of pain in her heart. "I don't believe you and I won't. Until you're completely well and have regained all of your memory, I won't give up."

"Shawna—"

"Remember that 'for better or worse' line?"

"We didn't get married."

Yet, she thought wildly. "Doesn't matter. In my heart I'm committed to you, and only when you tell me that you remember everything we shared and it means nothing to you—then I'll give up!"

"I just don't want to hurt you," he admitted, "ever again."

"You won't." The lie almost caught on her tongue.

"I wish I was as sure as you."

Her heart squeezed as she studied him, his body drenched in sweat, his shoulder balanced precariously against the wall.

As if reading the pity in her eyes, he swore, anger darkening his face. Casting her a disbelieving glance, he limped down the hall to his room and slammed the door so hard that the sound echoed through the old house.

Shawna stared after him. Why couldn't he remember how strong their love had been? *Why?* Feeling the need to break down and cry like a baby, she steeled herself. In frustration, she reached for the phone, hoping to call her brother or her friend Gerri or anyone to whom she could vent her frustrations. But when she placed the receiver to her ear, she heard Parker on the bedroom extension.

"That's right . . . everything you can find out about her. The name's James—Melinda James. I don't know her middle name. She claims to have been living in Cleveland and that she grew up with Brad Lomax."

Quietly, Shawna replaced the receiver. It seemed that no matter where she turned or how fiercely she clung to the ashes of the love she and Parker had once shared, the winds of fate blew them from her fingers.

Dying a little inside, she wondered if he was right. Maybe the flames of their love couldn't be rekindled.

"Give him time," she told herself, but she knew their time was running out. She glanced around the old Tudor house, the home she'd planned to share with him. She'd moved in, but they were both living a lie. He didn't love her.

Swallowing against the dryness in her throat, she turned toward the sink and ran water over the spinach leaves in a colander. She ignored the tears that threatened to form in the corners of her eyes. *Don't give up!* part of her insisted, while the other, more reasonable side of her nature whispered, *Let him go.*

So intent was she on tearing spinach, cutting a hard-boiled egg, and crumbling bacon that she didn't hear the uneven tread of his footsteps in the hall, didn't feel his gaze on her back as she worked, still muttering and arguing with herself.

Her first indication that he was in the room with her was the feel of his hands on her waist. She nearly dropped her knife as he bent his head and rested his chin on her shoulder.

"I'm not much good at apologies," he said softly.

"Neither am I."

"Oh, Shawna." His breath fanned her hair, warm and enticing, and her heart took flight. He'd come back! "I know you're doing what you think is best," he said huskily. "And I appreciate your help."

She dropped the knife and the tears she'd been fighting filled her eyes. "I've done it because I want to."

His fingers spanned her waist. "I just don't understand," he admitted, "why you want to put up with me."

She wanted to explain, but he cut her off, his arms encircling her waist, her body drawn to his. His breath was hot on the back of her head and delicious shivers darted along her spine as he pulled her close, so close that her back was pressed against the taut muscles of his chest. A spreading warmth radiated to her most outer limbs as his lips found her nape.

"I—I love you, Parker."

His muscles flexed and she silently prayed he would return those three simple words.

"That's why I'm working so hard," he conceded, his voice rough with emotion. "I want to be able to remember everything."

"I can wait," she said.

"But I can't! I want my life back—all of it. The way it was before the accident. Before—"

He didn't say it, but she knew. *Before Brad was killed, before Melinda James shattered our lives.*

"Maybe we should eat," she said, hoping to divert him from the guilt that ran rampant every time he thought about Brad.

"You've worked hard, haven't you?"

"It's a—well, it was a celebration."

"Oh?"

"Because you're off crutches and out of the brace," she said.

"I've still got that." He pointed to where the cane still lay on the floor.

"I know, but it's the final step."

"Except for my memory."

"It'll come back," she predicted, sounding more hopeful than she felt. "Come on, now," she urged. "Make yourself useful. Pour the wine before I ruin dinner and the candles burn out."

During dinner Shawna felt more lighthearted than she had in weeks. At the end of the meal, when Parker leaned forward and brushed his lips over hers, she thought fleetingly that together they could face anything.

"Thanks," he whispered, "for putting up with me."

"I wouldn't have it any other way." She could feel her eyes shining in the candlelight, knew her cheeks were tinged with the blush of happiness.

"Let's finish this—" he said, holding the wine bottle by its neck, "—in the gazebo."

A dimple creased her cheek. "The gazebo?" she repeated, and grinned from ear to ear as she picked up their wineglasses and dashed to the hallway where her down coat hung. Her heart was pounding with excitement. Just two months earlier, Parker had proposed in the gazebo.

Hand in hand, they walked down a flagstone path that led to the river. The sound of water rushing over stones filled the night air and a breeze, fresh with the scent of the Willamette, lifted Shawna's hair.

The sky was clear and black. A ribbon of silver moonlight rippled across the dark water to illuminate the bleached wood and smooth white rocks at the river's edge. On the east bank, lights from neighboring houses glittered and reflected on the water.

Shawna, with Parker's help, stepped into the gazebo. The slatted wood building was built on the edge of Parker's property, on the ridge overlooking the Willamette. The gazebo was flanked by lilac bushes, no longer fragrant, their dry leaves rustling in the wind.

As Shawna stared across the water, she felt Parker's arms slip around her waist, his breath warm against her head, the heat from his body flowing into hers.

"Do—do you remember the last time we were here?" she whispered, her throat swollen with the beautiful memory.

He didn't say anything.

"You proposed," she prodded.

"Did I?"

"Yes." She turned in his arms, facing him. "Late in the summer."

Squinting his eyes, fighting the darkness shrouding his brain, he struggled, but nothing surfaced. "I'm sorry," he whispered, his night-darkened eyes searching hers.

"Don't apologize," she whispered. Moonlight shifted across his face, shadowing the sharp angles as he lowered his head and touched his lips to hers.

Gently, his fingers twined in her hair. "Sometimes I get caught up in your fantasies," he admitted, his lips twisting cynically.

"This isn't a fantasy," she said, seeing her reflection in his eyes. "Just trust me."

He leaned forward again, brushing his lips suggestively over hers. "That's the trouble. I do." He took the wine and glasses and set them on the bench. Placing his palms on her cheeks, he stared into her eyes before kissing her again. Eagerly she responded, her heart pulsing wildly at his touch, her mouth opening willingly to the erotic pressure of his tongue on her lips.

She felt his hands quiver as they slid downward to rest near her neck, gently massaging her nape, before pushing the coat from her shoulders. The night air surrounded her, but she wasn't cold.

Together, they slid slowly to the weathered floorboards and Parker adjusted her down coat, using its softness as a mattress. Then, still kissing her, he found the buttons of her blouse and loosened them, slipping the soft fabric down her shoulders.

Slowly he bent and pressed his moist lips against the base of her throat.

In response, she warmed deep within, stretching her arms around him, holding him tight, drinking in the smell and feel of him.

"Shawna," he whispered.

"Oh, Parker, love," she murmured.

"Tell me to stop."

"Don't ever stop," she cried.

He shuddered, as if trying to restrain himself, then, in one glorious minute, he crushed his lips to hers and kissed her more passionately than ever before. His hands caressed her skin, tearing at her blouse and the clasp of her bra, baring her breasts to the shifting moonlight. Slowly he lowered his head and touched each proud nipple with his lips, teasing the dark peaks to impatient attention.

"Ooh," she whispered, caught up in the warm, rolling sensations of his lips and tongue as he touched her, stoking fires that scorched as they raced through her blood and burned wantonly in her brain.

Reckless desire chased all rational thought away.

Her breath tangled with his and his hands touched her, sweeping off her skirt until she was naked in the night. Her skin was as white as alabaster in the darkness. Despite the cool river-kissed wind, she was warm deep inside, as she throbbed with need for this one special man.

His moist lips moved over her, caressing her, arousing her, stealing over her skin and causing her mind to scream with the want of him.

She found the hem of his sweater and pushed the offending garment over his head. He groaned in response and she unsnapped his jeans, her fingers sliding down the length of his legs as she removed the faded denim until, at last, they lay naked in the tiny gazebo—his body gleaming with a dewy coat of sweat, hers rosy with the blush of desire.

"I will always love you," she promised as he lowered himself over her, twisting his fingers in her hair, his eyes blue, lusting flames.

"And I'll always love you," he vowed into her open mouth as his hands closed over her breasts, gently kneading the soft, proud nipples, still wet from his kiss.

Her fingers moved slowly down his back, touching firm, smooth muscles and the gentle cleft of his spine.

Though her eyes wanted to close, she willed them open, staring up at him, watching the bittersweet torment on his face as he delved inside, burying himself in her only to withdraw again and again. Her heart slamming wildly, her blood running molten hot, she arched upward, moved by a primitive force and whispering words of love.

Caught in her own storm of emotion and the powerful force of his love, she lost herself to him, surrendering to the vibrant spinning world that was theirs alone. She felt the splendor of his hands, heard him cry out her name.

In one glorious moment he stiffened, his voice reverberating through the gazebo and out across the river, and Shawna, too, convulsed against his sweat-glistened body.

His breath was rapid and hot in her ear. "This . . . could be dangerous," he whispered hoarsely, running a shaking hand through his hair.

Still wrapped in the wonder and glow of passion, she held him close, pressed her lips to his sweat-soaked chest. "Don't talk. For just tonight, let's pretend that it's only you and me, and our love."

"I'm not much good at pretending." Glancing down at her plump breasts, he sighed, then reached past her to a glass on the bench. Swirling wine in the goblet, he said, "I don't think we should let this happen again."

"I don't think we have a choice."

"Oh, Shawna," he whispered, drinking his wine and setting the empty glass on the floor before he reached behind her, to wrap the coat over her suddenly chilled shoulders before holding her close. "This isn't a question of love," he said.

Crushed, she couldn't answer.

"I just think we both need time."

"Because of Melinda's baby."

"The baby has something to do with it," he admitted, propping himself against the bench. He drew her draped body next to his and whispered against her neck. "But there's more. I don't want to tie you down."

"But you're not—"

"Shh. Just listen. I'm not the man you were in love with before the accident. Too much has changed for us to be so naive to think that everything will be just as we'd planned, which, for the record, I still can't remember."

"You will," she said, though she felt a gaping hole in her heart.

Parker slid from behind her and reached for his clothes. He'd never intended to make love to her, to admit that he loved her, for crying out loud, but there it was—the plain, simple truth: He loved her and he couldn't keep his hands off her.

"I think I'll go for a drive," he said, yanking his sweater over his head and sliding with difficulty into his jeans.

"Now?"

"I need time to think, Shawna. We both do," he said abruptly. Seeing the wounded look in her eyes he touched her cheek. "You know I care about you," he admitted, stroking her hair. "But I need a little space, just to work things out. I don't want either of us to make a mistake we'll regret later."

"Maybe we already have," she said, clutching her coat over her full breasts. She lifted her chin bravely, though deep inside, she was wounded to the core. Just minutes before he was loving her, now he was walking away!

"Maybe," he groaned, then straightened and hobbled to the door.

Shawna watched him amble up the path and shuddered when she heard the garage door slam behind him. He was gone. It was that simple. Right after making love to her for the first time, he'd walked away. The pain in her heart throbbed horribly, though she tried to believe that his words of love, sworn in the throes of passion, were the only real truth.

Brittle night wind raced through the car as Parker drove, his foot on the throttle, the windows rolled down. He pushed the speed limit, needing the cold night air to cool the passion deep in his soul. He was rocked to his very core by the depth of his feelings for Shawna. Never would he have believed himself capable of such all-consuming physical and mental torture. He wanted her—forever. He'd been on the verge of asking her to marry him back in the gazebo and damning the consequences.

"You're a fool," he chastised, shifting down, the car squealing around a curve in the road. Lights in the opposite lane dazzled and blinded him, bore down on him. "A damned fool."

The car in the oncoming lane passed, and memories crashed through the walls of his blocked mind. One by one they streamed into his consciousness. He remembered Brad, passed out and unconscious, and Melinda crying softly, clinging to Parker's shoulder. And Shawna—Lord, he remembered her, but not as he saw her now. Yes, he'd loved her because she was a beautiful, intelligent woman, but in the past, he hadn't felt this overpowering awe and voracious need that now consumed him.

He strained to remember everything, but couldn't. "Give it time," he said impatiently, but his fingers tightened over the wheel and he felt a desperate desire to know everything.

"Come on, come on," he urged, then realized that he was speeding, as if running from the black hole that was his past.

With difficulty, he eased up on the throttle and drove more cautiously, his hot blood finally cooled. Making love to Shawna had been a mistake, he decided, though a smile of satisfaction still hovered over his lips at the thought of her ivory-white body stretched sensually in the gazebo, her green eyes luminous with desire.

"Forget it," he muttered, palms suddenly damp. Until he remembered everything and knew she loved the man he was today, not the person she'd planned to marry before the accident, he couldn't risk making love to her again.

And that, he thought, his lips twisting wryly, was a crying shame.

CHAPTER 10

"He's pushing too hard," Bob Killingsworth, Parker's physical therapist, admitted to Shawna one afternoon. She had taken the day off and had intended to spend it with Parker, but he was still in his indoor pool, swimming, using the strength of his arms to pull himself through the water. Though one muscular leg kicked easily, the other, the knee that had been crushed, was stiff and inflexible and dragged noticeably.

"That's it!" Bob called, cupping his hands around his mouth and shouting at Parker.

Parker stood in the shallow end and rubbed the water from his face. "Just a couple more laps."

Glancing at his watch, Bob frowned. "I've got to get to the hospital—"

"I don't need a keeper," Parker reminded him.

"It's all right," Shawna whispered, "I'll stay with him."

"Are you sure?"

"I *am* a doctor."

"I know, but—" Bob shrugged his big shoulders. "Whatever you say."

As Bob left, Shawna kicked off her shoes.

"Joining me?" Parker mocked.

"I just might." The tension between them crackled. Since he'd left her the night they had made love, they had barely spoken. With an impish grin, she slid quickly out of her panty hose and sat on the edge of the pool near the diving board, her legs dangling into the water.

"That looks dangerous, Doctor," Parker predicted from the shallow end.

"I doubt it."

"Oh?" Smothering a devilish grin, Parker swam rapidly toward her, his muscular body knifing through the water. She watched with pride. In two weeks, he'd made incredible strides, physically if not mentally.

He'd always been an athlete and his muscles were strident and powerful. His shoulders were wide, his chest broad and corded. His abdomen was flat as it disappeared inside his swimming trunks to emerge again in the form of lean hips and strong legs—well, at least one strong leg. His right knee was still ablaze with angry red scars.

As he reached the deep end of the pool, he surfaced and his incredible blue eyes danced mischievously. He tossed his hair from his face and water sprayed on her blouse.

"What's on your mind?" she asked, grinning.

"I thought you were coming in."

"And I thought I'd change first."

"Did you?" One side of his mouth lifted into a crafty grin.

"Oh, Parker, no—" she said, just as she felt strong hands wrap over her ankles. "You wouldn't—"

But he did. Over her protests, he gently started swimming backward, pulling her off her bottom and into the pool, wool skirt, silk blouse, and all.

"You're despicable!" she sputtered, surfacing, her hair drenched.

"Probably."

"And cruel and . . . and heartless . . . and—"

"Adorable," he cut in, laughing so loudly the rich sound echoed on the rafters over the pool. His hands had moved upward over her legs to rest at her hips as she hung by the tips of her fingers at the edge of the pool.

"That, too," she admitted, lost in his eyes as he studied her. Heart pounding erratically, she could barely breathe as his head lowered and his lips brushed erotically over hers.

"So are you." One strong arm gripped her tighter, so fierce and possessive that her breath was trapped somewhere between her throat and lungs, while he clung to the side of the pool with his free hand. "Oh, so are you."

Knowing she was playing with proverbial fire, she warned herself to leave, but she was too caught up in the wonder of being held by him, the feel of his wet body pressed against hers, to consider why his feelings had changed. She didn't care that her clothes were ruined. She'd waited too long for this glorious moment—to have him hold her and want her again.

His tongue rimmed her mouth before parting her lips insistently. Moaning her surrender she felt his mouth crush against hers, his tongue touch and glide with hers, delving delicately, then flicking away as she ached for more. Her blood raced uncontrollably, and her heart hammered crazily against her ribs.

She didn't know why he had chosen this moment to love her again. She could only hope that he'd somehow experienced a breakthrough with his memory and could remember everything—especially how much they had loved each other.

His warm lips slid lower on her neck to the base of her throat and the white skin exposed between the lapels of her soggy blouse. The wet silk clung to her, and her nipples, proudly erect, were visible beneath the thin layer of silk and lace, sweetly enticing just above the lapping water.

Lazily, as if he had all the time in the world, his tongue touched her breast, hot as it pressed against her skin. She cried out, couldn't help herself, as he slowly placed his mouth against her, nuzzling her, sending white-hot rivulets of desire through her veins.

She could only cling to him, holding his head against her breast, feeling the warmth within her start to glow and a dull ache begin to throb deep at her center.

She didn't resist as with one hand he undid the buttons of her blouse, baring her shoulders, and letting the sodden piece of silk drift downward into the clear depths of the pool. Her bra, a flimsy scrap of lace, followed.

She was bare from the waist up, her breasts straining and full beneath his gaze as clear water lapped against her white skin.

"You are so beautiful," he groaned, as if her beauty were a curse. He gently reached forward, softly stroking her skin, watching in fascination as her nipple tightened, his eyes devouring every naked inch of her skin. "This is crazy, absolutely crazy," he whispered. Then, almost angrily, he lifted her up and took one bare nipple into his mouth, feasting hungrily on the soft white globe, his hand against her back, causing goose bumps to rise on her skin.

"Love me," she cried, aching to be filled with his spirit and soul. Her hands tangled in the hair of his chest and her eyes glazed as she whispered, "Please, Parker, make love to me."

"Right here?" he asked, lifting his head, short of breath.

"I don't care . . . anywhere."

His lips found hers again and as he kissed her, feeling her warm body in the cool water, a jagged piece of memory pricked his mind. Hadn't there been another time, another place, when Shawna—or had it been another woman—had pleaded with him to make love to her?

The sun had been hot and heat shimmered in vibrant waves over the river. They were lying in a canoe, the boat rocking quietly as he'd kissed her, his heart pounding in his ears, her suntanned body molded against his. She'd whispered his name, her voice rough with longing, then . . .

Just as suddenly as the memory had appeared, it slipped away again.

"Parker?"

He blinked, finding himself in the pool with Shawna, her green eyes fixed on his, her white skin turning blue in the suddenly cold water.

"What is it?"

"I don't know," he admitted, frustrated all over again. If only he could remember! If only he could fill the holes in his life! He released her and swam to the edge of the pool. "I think maybe you'd better get dressed," he decided, hoisting his wet body out of the water and reaching for a towel. "I—I'm sorry about your clothes."

"No—"

But he was already limping toward the door.

Dumbfounded, she dived for her blouse and bra, struggled into them, and surfaced at the shallow end. "You've got a lot of nerve," she said, breathing rapidly, her pride shattered as she climbed, dripping out of the pool. "What was *that?*" Gesturing angrily, she encompassed the entire high-ceilinged room to include the intimacy they'd just shared.

"A mistake," he said, wincing a little. Snatching his cane from a towel rack, he turned to the door.

"Mistake?" she yelled. "Mistake?" Boiling, her female ego trampled upon one too many times, she caught up to him and placed herself, with her skirt and blouse still dripping huge puddles on the concrete, squarely in his path. "Just like the other night was a mistake?"

His gaze softened. "I told you—we need time."

But she wasn't listening. "I know what you're doing," she said, pointing an accusing finger at him. "You're trying to shame me into leaving!"

"That's ridiculous!"

"Is it? Then explain what that scene in the pool was all about! We nearly made love, for crying out loud, and now you're walking out of here as if nothing happened. Just like the other night! That's it, isn't it? You're trying to mortify me!" All her pent-up emotions exploded, and without thinking she slapped him, her palm smacking as it connected with his jaw. The sound reverberated through the room.

"Thank you, Dr. McGuire," he muttered, his temper erupting. "Once again your bedside manner is at its finest!" Without another word he strode past her, limping slightly as he yanked open the door and slammed it shut behind him.

Shawna slumped against the brick wall. She felt as miserable and bedraggled as she looked in her wet clothes. Stung by his bitterness and the cruelty she'd seen in his gaze, she closed her eyes, feeling the cold of the bricks permeate her damp clothes. Had he set her up on purpose? Her head fell to her hands. Had he planned to make love to her only to throw her aside, in order to wound her and get her out of his life? "Bastard!" she cursed, flinging her wet hair over her shoulder.

Maybe she should leave. Maybe there was no chance of ever recovering what they had lost. Maybe, just maybe, their love affair was truly over. Sick at heart, she sank down against the wall and huddled in a puddle of water near the door.

Then her fists clenched tightly and she took a long, steadying breath. She wouldn't give up—not yet, because she believed in their love. She just had to get him to see things her way!

Parker slammed his bedroom door and uttered a quick oath. What had he been thinking about back there in the pool? Why had he let her get to him that way? He yanked off his wet swim trunks and threw them into a corner.

Muttering to himself, he started to struggle into a pair of old jeans when the door to his room swung open and Shawna, managing to hold her head high though her clothes were wet and dripping and her hair hung lankily around her face, said, "You've got company."

"I don't want—"

"Too late. She's here."

"She?" he repeated, seeing the pain in her eyes.

"Melinda. She's waiting in the den."

Parker zipped up his jeans, aware of her gaze following his movements. He didn't care, he told himself, didn't give one damn what she thought. Grabbing a T-shirt and yanking it over his head, he frowned and made a sound of disgust. "What's she doing here?" he finally asked, holding onto the rails of the bed as he hobbled toward the door.

"Your guess is as good as mine, but I don't think I'll stick around to find out. You know the old saying, three's a crowd."

He watched as she marched stiffly upstairs. He could hear her slamming drawers and he cringed as he made his way to the den.

Melinda was there all right. Standing next to the windows, she straightened as he entered. "So Shawna's still here," she said without any trace of inflection.

"So far."

"And she's staying?" Melinda asked, not meeting his eyes.

"That remains to be seen." He flinched as he heard Shawna stomping overhead. A light fixture rattled in the ceiling. Cocking his head toward an old rocker, he said, "Have a seat."

"No. I'm not staying long. I just came to find out what you intend to do—about the baby, I mean. You do remember, don't you? About the baby?"

Sighing wearily, he stretched his bad leg in front of him and half fell onto the raised hearth of the fireplace. The stones were cold and dusty with ash, but he couldn't have cared less. "What do you want to do?" he asked.

"I don't know." Her chin quivered a little and she chewed on her lower lip. "I suppose you want me to have an abortion."

His skin paled and he felt as if she'd just kicked him in the stomach. "No way. There are lots of alternatives. Abortion isn't one."

She closed her eyes. "Good," she whispered, obviously relieved as she wrapped her arms around herself. "So what about us?"

"Us?"

"Yes—you and me."

He heard Shawna stomp down the stairs and slam the front door shut behind her. Glancing out the window, he saw her, head bent against the wind as she ran to her car. Suddenly he felt as cold as the foggy day.

"Parker?"

He'd almost forgotten Melinda and he glanced up swiftly. She stared at him with wounded eyes and it was hard for him to believe she was lying—yet he couldn't remember ever loving her.

"We have a baby on the way." Swallowing hard, she fought tears that began to drizzle down her face and lowered her head, her black hair glossy as it fell over her face. "You still don't believe me," she accused, her voice breaking.

"I don't know what to believe," he admitted. Leaning his head back against the stones, he strained for images of that night. His head began to throb with the effort. Dark pieces emerged. He remembered seeing her that rainy night, thought she'd held him and cried into the crook of his neck. Had he stroked her hair, comforted her? God, if he could only remember!

"You're falling in love with her again," she charged, sniffing, lifting her head. When he didn't answer, she wiped at her eyes and crossed the room. "Don't be fooled, Parker. She'll lie to you, try to make you doubt me. But this," she patted her abdomen, "is proof of our love."

"If it's mine," he said slowly, watching for any sign that she might be lying. A shadow flickered in her gaze—but only for an instant—then her face was set again with rock-solid resolve.

"Just think long and hard about the night before you were supposed to get married, Parker. Where were you before the accident? In whose bed?"

His skin tightened. Surely he hadn't—Eyes narrowing, he stared up at her. "If I was in your bed, where was Brad?" he asked, as memory after painful memory pricked at his conscience only to escape before he could really latch on to anything solid.

"Passed out on the couch," she said bitterly, hiking the strap of her purse over her shoulder. "He'd drunk too much."

He almost believed her. Something about what she was saying was true. He could sense it. "So," he said slowly, "if I'd planned to stay with you that night, why didn't I take Brad home first?"

She paled a bit, then blinked back sudden tears. "Beats me. Look, I'm not trying to hassle you or Shawna. I just took her advice by giving you all the facts."

"And what do you expect to get out of it?" he asked, studying the tilt of her chin.

"Hey, don't get the wrong idea, you don't *have* to marry me—we never had that kind of a deal, but I do want my son to know his father and I would expect you to . . ." She lifted one shoulder. "You know . . . take care of us."

"Financially?"

She nodded, some of her hard edge dissipating. "What happened—the accident and you losing your memory—isn't really fair to the baby, is it?"

"Maybe nothing's fair," he said, then raked his fingers through his hair. He'd never let anyone manipulate him and he had the distinct feeling that Melinda James was doing just that. Scowling, he felt cornered, and he wanted to put her in her place. But he couldn't. No matter what the truth of the matter was, her unborn child hadn't asked to be brought into a world with a teenager for a mother and no father to care for him.

When the phone rang, she stood. "Think about it," she advised, swinging her purse over her shoulder and heading toward the door.

Closing his eyes, he dropped his face into his hands and tried to think, tried to remember sleeping with Melinda, making love to her.

But he couldn't remember anything. Though he strained to concentrate on the dark-haired young woman who claimed to be carrying his child, the image that swam in front of his eyes was the flushed and laughing face of Shawna McGuire as she clung to the neck of a white carousel stallion.

Once again he saw her laughing, her blond hair billowing behind her as she reached, grabbing blindly for a ribboned brass ring.

Or was the image caused by looking too long at photographs of that fateful day?

Think, Harrison, think!

A fortune-teller with voluminous skirts sat by a small table in a foul-smelling tent as she held Shawna's palm. Gray clouds gathered overhead, rain began to pepper the ground, the road was dark and wet, and Brad was screaming. . . .

Parker gritted his teeth, concentrating so much his entire head throbbed. He had to remember. He had to!

The phone rang again, for the fourth or fifth time, and he reached to answer it just in time to hear the smooth voice of Lon Saxon, a friend and private detective. "That you, Parker?"

"Right here," Parker replied.

"Good. I've got some of the information you wanted on Melinda James."

Parker's guts wrenched. Here it was. The story. "Okay, tell me all about her."

Shawna's fingers were clammy on the wheel as she turned into the drive of Parker's house. After driving aimlessly through the damp streets of Portland, she decided she had to return and confront him. She couldn't run from him and Melinda's baby like some wounded animal.

Silently praying that Melinda had already left, Shawna was relieved to see that the girl's tiny convertible wasn't parked in the drive.

"Remember that he loves you," she told herself as she flicked off the engine and picked up the white bags of hamburgers she'd bought at a local fast-food restaurant. "Just give him time."

Inside, the house was quiet, and for a heart-stopping minute, Shawna thought Parker had left with Melinda. The den was dark and cold, the living room empty. Then she noticed a shaft of light streaming from under the door of his bedroom.

She knocked lightly on the panels, then poked her head inside.

He was still dressed in the old jeans but his shirt was hanging limply from a post on the bed, and his chest was stripped bare. His head was propped by huge pillows and he stared straight at her as if he'd never seen her before.

"Truce?" she asked, holding up two white bags of food.

He didn't move, except to shift his gaze to the bags.

"Was it bad? With Melinda?"

"Did you expect it to be good?"

Hanging on to her emotions, she walked into the room and sat on the bed next to him. The mattress sagged a little, but still he didn't move.

Though her hands were trembling, she opened one bag and held out a paper-wrapped burger. When he ignored the offering she set it, along with the white sacks, on the nightstand. "I didn't expect anything. Every day has a new set of surprises," she admitted, tossing her hair over her shoulders and staring straight at him, refusing to flinch. "Look, let's be completely honest with each other."

"Haven't we been?"

"I don't know," she admitted. "I—I just don't know where I stand with you anymore."

"Then maybe you should move out."

"Maybe," she said slowly, and saw a streak of pain darken his eyes. "Is that what you want?"

"Honesty? Isn't that what you said?"

"Yes." She braced herself for the worst.

His jaw grew rock hard. "Then, *honestly,* I want to do the right thing. If the baby's mine—"

"It isn't," she said.

The look he gave her cut straight through her heart. "Do you know something I don't?"

"No, but—*Yes.* I do know something—something you don't remember—that we loved each other, that we would never have betrayed each other, that Melinda's baby *can't* be yours."

"I remember her," he said softly.

She gave a weak sound of protest.

His throat worked. "And I remember being with her that night—holding her. She was crying and—"

"No! This is all part of her lies!" Shawna screamed, her stomach twisting painfully, her breath constricted and tight. She wanted to lash out and hit anyone or anything that stood in her way. "You're lying to me!"

"Listen to me, damn it!" he said, grabbing her wrist and pulling her forward so that she fell across his chest, her hair spilling over his shoulders. "I remember being with her that night. Everything's not clear, I'll grant you that. But I was in her apartment!"

"Oh, no," she whispered.

"And there's more."

"Parker, please—"

"You were the one who wanted honesty, remember?" His words were harsh, but there wasn't any trace of mockery in his eyes, just blue, searing torment.

"No—"

"Her story checks out, at least part of it. I had a private detective in Cleveland do some digging. Her mother's dead. Her father is an unemployed steelworker who hasn't held a job in ten years! Melinda supported him while she went to high school. He was furious with her when he found out she was pregnant."

Shawna's fingers clenched over the sheets. "That doesn't mean—"

"It means she's not a chronic liar and she obviously has some sense of right and wrong."

"Then we'll just have to wait, won't we?" she asked dully, her entire world black. "Until you regain your memory or the baby's born and paternity tests can be run."

"I don't think so," he said thoughtfully. She didn't move, dread mounting in her heart, knowing the axe was about to fall. "She told me she wants me to recognize the baby as mine and provide support."

"She wants you to marry her, doesn't she? She expects it?"

"No—" he let his voice drop off.

"But you're considering it!" Shawna gasped, all her hopes dashed as the realization struck her. Parker was going to do the noble deed and marry a girl he didn't know! Cold to the bone, she tried to scramble away, but he held her fast. "This is crazy—you *can't* marry her. You don't even remember her!"

"I remember enough," he said, his voice oddly hollow.

For the first time Shawna considered the horrid fact that he might be the baby's father, that he might have betrayed her the week and night before their wedding, had one last fling with a young girl. "I . . . I don't think I want to hear this," she whispered.

"You wanted the truth, Shawna. So here it is: I'm responsible for Melinda's predicament and I can't ignore that responsibility or pretend it doesn't exist, much as I might want to." His eyes searched her face and she recognized his pain—the bare, glaring fact that he still loved her. She could smell the maleness of him, hear the beating of his heart, feel the warmth of his skin, and yet he was pushing her away.

"Please, Parker, don't do this—"

"I have no choice."

"You're claiming the baby," she whispered, eyes moist, insides raw and bleeding.

"Yes." His jaw was tight, every muscle in his body rigid as he took in a long, shaky breath. "So—I think it would be better for everyone involved if you moved out."

She closed her eyes as her world began spinning away from her. All her hopes and dreams were just out of reach. She felt his grip slacken. Without a word, she walked to the door. "I—I'll start packing in the morning," she whispered.

"Good."

Then, numb from head to foot, she closed the door behind her. As she slowly mounted the stairs, she thought she heard him swear and then there was a huge crash against one of the walls, as if a fist or object had collided with plaster. But she didn't pay any attention. All she could think about was the horrid emptiness that was her future—a future barren and bleak without Parker.

CHAPTER 11

Tossing off the covers, Shawna rolled over and stared at the clock. Three a.m. and the room was pitch black except for the green digital numbers. Tomorrow she was leaving, giving up on Parker.

Before a single tear slid down her cheek, she searched in the darkness for her robe. Her fingers curled in the soft terry fabric and she fought the urge to scream. How could he do this? Why couldn't he remember?

Angry with herself, Parker, and the world in general, she yanked open the door to her room and padded silently along the hall and down the stairs, her fingers trailing on the banister as she moved quietly in the darkness. She didn't want to wake Parker, though she didn't really know why. The thought that he was sleeping peacefully while she was ripped to ribbons inside was infuriating.

In the kitchen she rattled around for a mug, the powdered chocolate, and a carton of milk. Then, while her cocoa was heating in the microwave, she felt a wild need to escape, to run away from the house that trapped her with its painful memories.

Without really thinking, she unlocked the French doors of the dining room and walked outside to the balcony overlooking the dark Willamette. The air was fresh and bracing, the sound of the river soothing as it flowed steadily toward the Columbia.

Clouds scudded across a full moon, filtering thin beams of moonlight, which battled to illuminate the night and cast shadows on the river. Leaves, caught in the wind, swirled and drifted to the ground.

Shivering, Shawna tightened her belt and leaned forward over the rail, her fingers curling possessively around the painted wood. This house was to have been hers, but losing the house didn't matter. Losing Parker was what destroyed her. She would gladly have lived in a shack with him, if only he could have found his way back to her. But now it was over. Forever.

She heard the microwave beep. Reluctantly she turned, her breath catching in her throat when she found Parker staring at her, one shoulder propped against the open French door.

"Couldn't sleep, either?" he asked, his night-darkened gaze caressing her face.

"No." She lifted her chin upward, unaware that moonlight shimmered silver in her hair and reflected in her eyes. "Can I get you a cup?" she asked, motioning toward the kitchen. "Hot chocolate's supposed to do the trick."

"Is that your professional opinion?" For once there was no sarcasm in his voice.

"Well, you know me," she said, laughing bitterly at the irony. "At least you did. But maybe you don't remember that I don't put too much stock in prescriptions—sleeping pills and the like. Some of the old-fashioned cures are still the best. So, if you want, I'll fix you a cup."

"I don't think so."

Knowing she should leave, just brush past him, grab her damned cocoa and hightail it upstairs, she stood, mesmerized, realizing that this might be their last moment alone. She couldn't help staring pointedly at his bare chest, at his muscles rigid and strident, his jeans riding low over his hips. Nor could she ignore his brooding and thoughtful expression. His angular features were dark and his eyes, what she could see of them, were focused on her face and neck. As his gaze drifted lower to linger at the cleft of her breasts and the wisp of white lace from her nightgown, she swallowed against her suddenly dry throat.

"I thought you should have this," he said quietly as he walked across the balcony, reached into the pocket of his jeans, and extracted the brass ring he'd won at the fair. Even in the darkness she recognized the circle of metal and the ribbons fluttering in the breeze. "You should have caught this that day."

"You remember?" she asked quickly as her fingers touched the cold metal ring.

"Pieces."

Hope sprang exuberantly in her heart. "Then—"

"It doesn't change anything."

"But—"

His hand closed over hers, warm and comforting, as his fingers forced hers to curl over the ring. "Take it."

"Parker, please, talk to me!" Desperate, she pleaded with him. "If you remember—then you know the baby—"

His jaw grew rock hard. "I don't know for sure, but you have to accept that the baby is mine," he said, his eyes growing distant. He turned then, limping across the balcony and through the kitchen.

For a few minutes Shawna just stared at the damned ring in her hands as memory after painful memory surfaced. Then, unable to stop herself from trying one last time, she practically flew into the house and down the hall, her bare feet slapping against the wooden floors. "Parker, wait!"

She caught up with him in his bedroom. "Leave it, Shawna," he warned.

"But you remember!" Breathless, her heart hammering, she faced him. "You know what we meant to each other!"

"What I remember," he said coldly, though his gaze said differently, "is that you wouldn't sleep with me."

"We had an agreement," she said weakly, clasping the post of his bed for support. "Maybe it was stupid, but—"

"And you teased me—"

"I what?" But she'd heard the words before. Stricken, she could only whisper, "It was a joke between us. You used to laugh!"

"I told you then you'd drive me to a mistress," he said, his brows pulling down sharply over his eyes.

"You're doing this on purpose," she accused him. "You're forcing yourself to be cruel—just to push me away! All that business about having a mistress...you were kidding...it was just a little game...oh, God." She swayed against the post. Had she really been so blind? Had Parker and Melinda—? Numb inside she stumbled backward. Before she could say or do anything to further degrade herself, she scrambled out of the room.

"Shawna—"

She heard him call, but didn't listen.

"I didn't mean to—"

But she was already up the stairs, slamming the door shut, embarrassed to tears as she flipped on the light and jerked her suitcases from the closet to fling them open on the bed.

"Damn it, Shawna! Come down here."

No way! She couldn't trust herself, not around him. She wouldn't. She felt close to tears but wouldn't give in to them. Instead she flung clothes—dresses, sweaters, underwear, slacks—anything she could find into the first suitcase and slammed it shut.

"Listen to me—"

Dear God, his voice was closer! He was actually struggling up the stairs! What if he fell? What if he lost his balance and stumbled backward! "Leave me alone, Parker!" she shouted, snapping the second suitcase shut. She found her purse, slung the strap over her shoulder, slipped into her shoes, and hauled both bags to the landing.

He was there. His face was red from the exertion of the climb, and his eyes were blazing angrily. "Look," he said, reaching for her, but she spun out of his grasp and he nearly fell backward down the steep stairs.

"Stop it!" she cried, worried sick that he would stumble. "Just stop it!"

"I didn't mean to hurt you—"

"Too late! But it doesn't matter. Not anymore. It's over. I'm leaving you alone. That's what you want, isn't it? It's what you've been telling me to do all along. You've got your wish."

"Please—"

Her traitorous heart told her to stay, but this time, damn it, she was going to think with her head. "Good luck, Parker," she choked out. "I mean it, really. I—I wish you the best." Then she ran down the stairs, feeling the tears filling her eyes as she fled through the front door.

The night wind tore at her robe and hair as she raced down the brick path to the garage and the safety of her little hatchback. Gratefully, she slid behind the steering wheel and with trembling fingers flicked on the ignition. The engine roared to life just as Parker opened the kitchen door and snapped on the overhead light in the garage.

Shawna sent up a silent prayer of thanks that he'd made it safely downstairs. Then she shoved the gearshift into reverse and the little car squealed out of the garage.

Driving crazily along the empty highway toward Lake Oswego, she could barely breathe. She had to fight to keep from sobbing hysterically as she sought the only safe refuge she knew. Jake—her brother—she could stay with him.

Slow down, she warned herself, as she guided the car toward the south side of the lake where Jake lived in a small bungalow. *Please be home,* she thought as she parked, grabbed her suitcases, and trudged up the front steps to the porch.

The door opened before she could knock and Jake, his dark

hair falling in wild locks over his forehead, his jaw stubbled, his eyes bleary, grabbed the heavier bag. "Come on in, sis," he said, eyeing her gravely.

"You knew?"

"Parker called. He was worried about you."

She let out a disgusted sound, but when Jake kicked the door shut and wrapped one strong arm around her, she fell apart, letting out the painful sobs that ripped at her soul.

"It's okay," he whispered.

"I wonder if it will ever be," Shawna said, before emitting a long, shuddering sigh and shivering from the cold.

"Come on," Jake suggested, propelling her to the tiny alcove that was his kitchen. "Tell me what happened."

"I don't think I can."

"You don't have much choice. You talk and I'll cook. The best omelet in town."

Shawna's stomach wrenched at the thought of food. "I'm not hungry."

"Well, I am," he said, plopping her down in one of the creaky kitchen chairs and opening the refrigerator, "So, come on, spill it. Just what the hell happened between you and Parker tonight?"

Swallowing hard, Shawna clasped her hands on the table and started at the beginning.

Parker could have kicked himself. Angry with himself, the world, and one lying Melinda James, he ignored the fact that it was the middle of the night and dialed his lawyer.

The phone rang five times before he heard Martin Calloway's groggy voice. "Hello?" he mumbled.

"Hello. This is—"

"I know who it is, Harrison. Do you have any idea what time it is?"

"Vaguely."

"And whatever's on your mind couldn't wait 'til morning?"

"That's about the size of it," Parker said, his gaze roving around the dark, empty kitchen. Damn, but the house felt cold without Shawna. "I want you to draw up some papers."

"Some papers," Martin repeated dryly. "Any particular kind?"

"Adoption," Parker replied flatly, "and postdate them by about six or seven months."

"Wait a minute—what the hell's going on?"

"I've had a breakthrough," Parker said, his entire life crystal clear since his argument with Shawna. "Something happened tonight that brought everything back and now I need to straighten out a few things."

"By adopting a child that isn't born yet?"

"For starters—I don't care how you handle it—I just want to make sure the adoption will be legal and binding."

"I'll need the mother's signature."

"I don't think that will be a problem," Parker said. "Oh—and just one other thing. I want to keep the fact that I'm remembering again a secret."

"Any particular reason?"

"There's someone I have to tell—after we get whatever letters of intent for adoption or whatever it's called signed."

"I'll work on it in the morning."

"Great."

Parker hung up and walked restlessly to his bedroom. He thought about chasing Shawna down at Jake's and admitting that he remembered his past, but decided to wait until everything was settled. This time, he wasn't going to let anything come between them!

If Shawna had known the torment she was letting herself in for, she might have thought twice about leaving Parker so abruptly. Nearly a week had dragged by, one day slipping into the next in a simple routine of patients, hospitals, and sleepless nights. Though Shawna fought depression, it clung to her like a heavy black cloak, weighing down her shoulders and stealing her appetite.

"You can't go on like this," Jake said one morning as Shawna, dressed in a skirt and blouse, sipped a cup of coffee and scanned the newspaper without interest.

"Or *you* can't?" Shawna replied.

Jake's dog, Bruno, was lying under the table. With one brown

eye and one blue, he stared at Maestro and growled as the preco-
cious tabby hopped onto the window ledge. Crouching behind a
broad-leafed plant, his tail twitching, Maestro glared longingly past
the glass panes to the hanging bird feeder where several snowbirds
pecked at seeds.

Jake refused to be distracted. "If you don't believe that you're
moping around here, take a look in the mirror, for Pete's sake."

"No, thank you."

"Shawna, you're killing yourself," Jake accused, sitting angrily
in the chair directly across from hers.

"I'm leaving, just as soon as I find a place."

"I don't care about that, for crying out loud."

"I'm not 'moping' or 'killing myself' so don't you dare try to
psychoanalyze me," she warned, raising her eyes to stare at him
over the rim of her cup. He didn't have to remind her that she
looked bad, for heaven's sake. She could feel it.

"Someone's got to," Jake grumbled. "You and Parker are so
damned bullheaded."

Her heartbeat quickened at the sound of his name. If only he'd
missed her!

"He looks twice as bad as you do."

"That's encouraging," she muttered, but hated the sound of her
voice. Deep down, she wanted Parker to be happy and well.

"Talk to him."

"No."

"He's called twice."

Frowning, Shawna set her cup on the table. "It's over, Jake.
That's the way he wanted it, and I'm tired of being treated as if my
emotions don't mean a damned thing. Whether he meant to or not,
he found my heart, threw it to the ground, and then stomped all
over it."

"So now you don't care?"

"I didn't say that! And you're doing it again. Don't talk to me
like you're my shrink, for Pete's sake."

Jake wouldn't be silenced. "Okay, so I'll talk like your brother.
You're making one helluva mistake here."

"Not the first."

"Cut the bull, Shawna. I know you. You're hurting and you still love him even if you think he's a bastard. Isn't it worth just one more chance?"

She thought of the brass ring, still tucked secretly in the pocket of her robe. "Take a chance," Parker had told her at the fair that day. Dear Lord, it seemed ages ago.

"I'm out of chances."

Jake leaned over the table, his gaze fastened on her. "I've never thought you were stupid, Shawna. Don't change my mind, okay?" Glancing at the clock over the stove, he swore, grabbing his suit jacket from the back of a chair. "Do yourself a favor. Call him back." With this last bit of brotherly advice, Jake swung out the door, then returned, his face flushed. "And move your car, okay? Some of us have to work today."

She felt like sticking her tongue out at him, but instead she grabbed her purse and keys and swung her coat over her shoulders. The beginning of a plan had begun to form in her mind—and if Jake was right about Parker . . .

"You don't have to leave," Jake said as they walked down the frost-crusted path to the garage. "Just move that miserable little car of yours."

"I think I'd better get started."

"Doing what?" he asked. "You have the next couple of days off, don't you?"

She grabbed the handle of her car door and flashed him a secretive smile as she climbed inside, "Maybe you're right. Maybe I should do more than mope around here."

"What's that supposed to mean?" he asked suspiciously.

"I'm not sure. But I'll let you know." Waving with one hand, she rammed her car into gear and backed out of his driveway. With only the barest idea of what she was planning, she parked in front of the house and waited until Jake had roared out of sight.

Spurred into action, she hurried back inside Jake's house, called her friend Gerri, and threw some clothes into a bag.

Her heart was in her throat as she climbed back into her car. She could barely believe the plan that had formed in her mind. Ignoring the screaming protests in her mind, she drove through the fog, heading north until she slammed on the brakes at the street leading toward the Willamette River and Parker's house.

Her hands were damp. What if he wasn't home? Or worse yet, what if he had company? Perhaps Melinda? *Well, that would be too damned bad. Because it's now or never!*

Her muscles were so rigid they ached as she drove, her jaw firm with determination as Parker's huge house loomed to the side of the road. Without hesitation, she cranked the wheel, coasted along the long asphalt drive and parked near the brick path leading to the front door.

Then, with all the confidence she could gather, she marched up the path and rang the bell.

CHAPTER 12

Shawna held her breath as the door swung inward, and Parker, dressed in cords and a soft sweater, stared at her. Her heart started knocking against her rib cage as she looked into his eyes.

"Well, if this isn't a surprise," he drawled, not moving from the door. His face was unreadable. Not an emotion flickered in his eyes.

"I had a few things to sort out," she said.

"And are they sorted out?"

Nervously, she licked her lips. "Just about. I thought maybe we should talk, and I'm sorry I didn't return your calls."

Still suspicious, he pushed open the door. "Fair enough."

"Not here," she said quickly. "Someplace where we won't be disturbed."

"Such as?"

Shawna forced a friendly smile. "For starters, let's just drive."

He hesitated a minute, then shrugged, as if it didn't matter what she wanted to discuss—nothing would change. Yanking his fleece-lined jacket off the hall tree, he eyed his cane hanging on a hook but left it.

Striding back to the car, Shawna held her breath and felt his eyes bore into her back as he walked unsteadily after her and slid into the passenger side of the hatchback.

Without a word, she climbed behind the wheel and started out the drive. A surge of self-doubts assailed her. If he had any idea that she planned to kidnap him for the weekend, he'd be furious. She might have ruined any chance they had of ever getting back together again.

But it was a risk she had to take. The longer they were apart, she felt, the more likely stubborn pride would get in their way.

She put the little car through its paces, heading west amidst the fog still clinging to the upper reaches of the west hills. "So talk," Parker suggested, his arms crossed over his chest, his jean jacket stretched tight over his shoulders.

"I've had a lot of time to think," she said, gambling, not really knowing what to say now that he was sitting in the seat next to hers, his legs stretched close, his shoulder nearly touching hers. "And I think I acted rashly."

"We both behaved like children," he said, staring straight ahead as the city gave way to suburbs. Parker looked around, as if noticing for the first time that they'd left Portland far behind. Ahead the blue-gray mountains of the coast range loomed into view. "Where're we going?" he asked, suddenly apprehensive.

"To the beach." She didn't dare glance at him, afraid her emotions were mirrored in her eyes.

"The *beach?*" he repeated, stunned. "Why?"

"I think more clearly when I'm near the ocean." That, at least, wasn't a lie.

"But it's already afternoon. We won't be back until after dark."

"Is that a problem?"

"I guess not."

"Good. I know this great candy store in Cannon Beach—"

He groaned, and Shawna, glimpsing him from the corner of her eye, felt a growing sense of satisfaction. So he did remember—she could see it in his gaze. Earlier in the summer they'd visited Cannon Beach and eaten saltwater taffy until their stomachs ached. So just how much did he recall? Everything? What about Melinda? Shawna felt dread in her heart but steadfastly tamped it down. Tonight she'd face the truth—all of it. And so would Parker!

Once at the tiny coastal town, with its weathered buildings and cottages, they found a quaint restaurant high on the cliffs overlooking the sea. The beach was nearly deserted. Only a few hardy souls braved the sand and wind to stroll near the water's ragged edge. Gray-and-white seagulls swooped from a steely sky, and rolling white-capped waves crashed against jagged black rocks as Shawna and Parker finished a meal of crab and crusty French bread.

"Want to take a walk?" Shawna asked.

Deep lines grooved around his mouth. "Didn't bring my wheelchair," he drawled, his lips thinning.

She said softly, "You can lean on me."

"I don't think so. I really should get back." His eyes touched hers for a moment and then he glanced away, through the window and toward the sea.

"Melinda's expecting you?"

His jaw worked. "Actually, it's a case of my lawyer wants to meet with her attorney. That sort of thing."

She braced herself for the showdown. "Then we'd better get going," she said as if she had every intention of driving him back to Portland. "I wouldn't want to keep her waiting."

Parker paid the check, then ambled slowly toward the car. Shawna pointed across the street to a mom-and-pop grocery and deli. "I'll just be a minute. I want to pick up a few things," she said, jaywalking across the street.

"Can't you get whatever it is you need in Portland?"

Flashing him a mischievous smile, she shook her head. He noticed the luxuriant honey-blond waves that swept the back of her suede jacket. "Not fresh crab. Just give me a minute."

Rather than protest, he slid into the hatchback and Shawna joined him a few minutes later. She swallowed back her fear. Until this moment, she'd been fairly honest with him. But now, if she had the courage, she was going to lie through her teeth.

"It's almost sunset," she said, easing the car into the empty street.

The sun, a fiery luminous ball, was dropping slowly to the sea. The sky was tinged rosy hues of orange and lavender. "I'd noticed."

"Do you mind if I take the scenic route home, through Astoria?"

Frowning, Parker rubbed the back of his neck and shrugged. "I guess not. I'm late already."

So far, so good. She drove north along the rugged coastline, following the curving road that wound along the crest of the cliffs overlooking the sea. Contorted pines and beach grass, gilded by the sun's final rays, flanked the asphalt. Parker closed his eyes and Shawna crossed her fingers. Maybe, just maybe, her plan would work.

"Here we are," Shawna said, pulling up the hand brake as the little car rolled to a stop.

Parker awakened slowly. He hadn't meant to doze, but he'd been exhausted for days. Ever since Shawna had moved out of his house, he'd spent sleepless nights in restless dreams filled with her, only to wake up drenched with sweat and hot with desire. His days, when he wasn't consulting his lawyer about Melinda's child, had been filled with physical therapy and swimming, and he could finally feel his body starting to respond. The pain in his injured leg had slowly lessened and his torn muscles had grudgingly started working again. For the first time since the accident, he'd felt a glimmer of hope that he would eventually walk unassisted again. That knowledge was his driving force, though it was a small comfort against the fact that he'd given up Shawna.

But only temporarily, he reminded himself, knowing that one way or another he would make her love him, not for what he once was, but for the man he'd become. But first, there was the matter of Melinda's baby, a matter which should have been completed this afternoon. If he'd had any brains at all, he never would have agreed to drive to the beach with Shawna, but he hadn't been able to stop himself.

When he had opened the door and found her, smiling and radiant on his doorstep, he hadn't been able to resist spending a few hours with her.

Now, he blinked a couple of times, though he knew he wasn't

dreaming. "Where?" In front of her car was a tiny, weathered, run-down excuse of a cabin, behind which was the vibrantly sun-streaked ocean.

"Gerri's cabin."

"Gerri?"

"My friend. Remember?" She laughed a little nervously. "Come on, I bet you do. You seem to be remembering a lot lately. More than you're letting on."

But Parker still wasn't thinking straight. His gaze was glued to the gray shack with paned windows and a sagging porch. "What're we doing here?" Was he missing something?

She pocketed her keys, then faced him. "We're spending the weekend together. Here. Alone. No phone. No intrusions. Just you and me."

He smiled until he saw that she wasn't kidding. Her emerald eyes sparkled with determination. "Hey—wait a minute—"

But she wasn't listening. She climbed out of the car and grabbed the grocery bag.

"Shawna!" He wrenched open the door, watching in disbelief as she mounted the steps, searched with her fingers along the ledge over the porch, then, glancing back with a cat-who-ate-the-canary smile, held up a rusted key. *She wasn't joking!* "You can't do this— I've got to be back in Portland tonight!" Ignoring the pain in his knee, he followed after her, limping into the dark, musty interior of the cabin.

She was just lighting a kerosene lantern in the kitchen. "Romantic, don't you think?"

"What does romance have to do with the fact that you shang-haied me here?"

"Everything." She breezed past him and he couldn't help but notice the way her jeans fit snugly over her hips, or the scent of her hair, as she passed.

"I have a meeting—"

"It'll wait."

His blood was boiling. Just who the hell did she think she was— kidnapping him and then flirting with him so outrageously? If only she'd waited one more day! "Give me your keys," he demanded.

She laughed, a merry tinkling sound that bounced over the

dusty rafters and echoed in the corners as she knelt on the hearth of a river-rock fireplace and opened the damper.

"I'm serious," Parker said.

"So am I. You're not getting the keys." She crumpled up a yellowed piece of newspaper, plunked two thick pieces of oak onto the grate, and lit a fire. Immediately flames crackled and leaped, climbing hungrily over the dry wood.

"Then I'll walk to the road and hitchhike."

"Guess again. It's nearly a mile. You're still recovering, remember?"

"Shawna—"

"Face it, Parker. This time, you're mine." Dusting her hands, she turned to face him and her expression had changed from playful and bright to sober. "And this time, I'm not letting you go. Not until we settle things once and for all."

Damn the woman! She had him and she knew it! And deep in his heart he was glad, even though he worried about his meeting with Melinda James and her attorney. He glanced around the room, past the sheet-draped furniture and rolled carpets to the windows and the view of the sea beyond. The sky was painted with lavender and magenta and the ocean, shimmering and restless, blazed gold. Worried that he might be blowing the delicate negotiations with Melinda, Parker shoved his hands into the pockets of his cords and waited. Protesting was getting him nowhere. "I'll have to make a call."

"Too bad."

He swore under his breath. "Who knows we're here?"

"Just Gerri. She owns this place."

Since Gerri was Shawna's best friend, he didn't doubt that she'd keep her mouth shut. "What about Jake or your folks?"

She shook her head and rolled out the carpet. "As I said, it's just you, me, the ocean, and the wind. And maybe, if you're lucky, white wine and grilled salmon."

"I'm afraid you'll live to regret this," he said, groaning inwardly as he deliberately advanced on her. Firelight caught in her hair and eyes, and a provocative dimple creased her cheek. The very essence of her seemed to fill the empty cracks and darkest corners of the cabin. He hadn't realized just how much he'd missed her until now. "We probably both will."

"I guess that's a chance we'll just have to take." She met his gaze then, her eyes filled with a love so pure, so intense, he felt guilty for not admitting that he remembered everything—that he, at this moment, had he been in Portland, would be planning for their future together. Reaching forward, he captured her wrist in his hand, felt her quivering pulse. "I want you to trust me," he said, his guts twisting when he recognized the pain in her eyes.

"I do," she whispered. "Why do you think I kidnapped you?"

"God only knows," he whispered, but his gaze centered on her softly parted lips and he felt a warm urgency invade his blood. "You know," he said, his voice turning silky, "I might just mete out my revenge for this little stunt."

He was close to her now, so close she could see the flecks of blue fire in his eyes. "Try me."

Would she never give up? He felt an incredible surge of pride that this gorgeous, intelligent woman loved him so tenaciously she would fight impossible odds to save their relationship. A vein throbbed in his temple, his thoughts filled with desire, and he gave in to the overpowering urge to forget about the past, the present, and the future as he gazed hungrily into her eyes. "I do love you. . . ." he whispered, sweeping her into his arms.

Shawna's heart soared, though she didn't have time to catch her breath. The kiss was hard, nearly brutal, and filled with a fierce passion that caused her heart to beat shamelessly.

She moaned in response, twining her arms around his neck, her breasts crushed against his chest, her blood hot with desire. He pulled her closer still, holding her so tight she could barely breathe as his tongue pressed against her teeth. Willingly, her lips parted and she felt him explore the velvety recesses of her mouth.

"God, I've missed you," he whispered, his voice rough as his lips found her throat and moved slowly downward.

She didn't stop him when he pushed her jacket off her shoulders, nor did she protest when he undid the buttons of her blouse. Her eyes were bright when he kissed her lips again.

The fire glowed red and yellow and the sound of the sea crashing against rocks far below drifted through the open window as she helped him out of his clothes.

"Shawna—are you sure?" he asked, and groaned when she kissed his chest.

"I've always been sure," she whispered. "With you." Tasting the salt on his skin, feeling the ripple of his muscles, she breathed against him, wanton with pleasure when he sucked in his abdomen, his eyes glazing over.

"You're incredible," he murmured, moving suggestively against her, his arousal evident as her fingers played with his waistband, dipping lower and teasing him.

"So are you."

"If you don't stop me now—"

"Never," she replied and was rewarded with his wet lips pressing hard against hers. All control fled, and he pushed her to the carpet, his hands deftly removing her clothes and caressing her all over until she ached for more. Blood thundered in her ears, her heart slammed wildly in her chest, and she could only think of Parker and the desire throbbing hot in her veins. "I love you, Parker," she said, tears filling her eyes at the wonder of him.

Firelight gleamed on his skin as he lowered himself over her, touching the tip of her breasts with his tongue before taking one firm mound possessively with his mouth and suckling hungrily. His hand was on her back, spread wide over her skin, drawing her near as he rubbed against her, anxious and aroused.

"I should tell you—"

"Shh—" Twining her fingers in the hair of his nape, she drew his head down to hers and kissed him, moving her body erotically against his. She pushed his cords over his hips, her fingers inching down his muscular buttocks and thighs, a warm, primal need swirling deep within her. His clothes discarded, she ran her fingers over his skin and turned anxious lips to his.

If he wanted to stop, he couldn't. His muscles, glistening with sweat and reflecting the golden light from the fire, strained for one second before he parted her legs with one knee and thrust deep into her.

"Shawna," he cried, his hand on her breasts, his mouth raining kisses on her face. "Love me."

"I do!" Hot inside, and liquid, she captured him with her legs, arching against him and holding close, as if afraid he would disappear with the coming night.

With each of his long strokes, she felt as if she were on that carousel again, turning faster and faster, spinning wildly, crazily out of control.

Tangled in his passion, she shuddered, and the lights of the merry-go-round crackled and burst into brilliant blue and gold flames. Parker cried out, deeply and lustily, and it echoed with her own shriek of pleasure. Tears filled her eyes with each hot wave of pleasure that spread to her limbs.

Parker kissed the dewy perspiration from her forehead, then took an old blanket from the couch and wrapped it over them.

"My darling, I love you," he murmured, his voice cracking.

"You don't have to say anything," she whispered, but her heart fairly burst with love.

"Why lie?" Levering himself on one elbow, he brushed the honey-streaked strands of hair from her face and stared down at her. "You wouldn't believe me anyway. You've always insisted that I loved you." He kissed her gently on the cheek. "You just have no idea how much." His gaze lowered again, to the fullness of her breasts, the pinch of her waist, the length of her legs. "I love you more than any sane man should love a woman," he admitted, his voice thick with emotion.

"Now, we can forget about everything except each other," she whispered, winding her arms around his neck. "I love you, Parker Harrison. And I want you. And if all I can have of you is this one weekend—then I'll take it."

"Not good enough, Doctor," he said, his smile white and sensual as it slashed across his jaw. "With you, it has to be forever."

"Forever it is," she whispered, her voice breaking as she tilted her face eagerly to his.

Gathering her into his arms, he made love to her all night long.

CHAPTER 13

Shawna stretched lazily on the bed, smiling to herself as she reached for Parker again. But her fingers rubbed only cold sheets. Her eyes flew open. "Parker?" she called, glancing around the tiny bedroom. Where was he?

Morning light streamed into the room and the old lace curtains fluttered in the breeze.

"Parker?" she called again, rubbing her eyes before scrambling for her robe. The little cabin was cold and she didn't hear any sounds of life from the other room. There was a chance he'd hobbled down to the beach, but she doubted he would climb down the steep stairs of the cliff face. Worried, she crossed the small living room to peer out a side window, and her fears were confirmed. Her hatchback was gone. He'd left. After a night of intense lovemaking, he'd gone.

Maybe he's just gone to the store, or to find a phone booth, she told herself, but she knew better, even before she found a hastily scrawled note on the table. Her hands shook as she picked up a small scrap of paper and read:

Had to run home for a while. I'll be back or send someone for you. Trust me. I do love you.

She crumpled the note in her hand and shoved it into the pocket of her robe. Her fingers grazed the cold metal of the brass ring he'd won at the fair all those weeks ago and she dropped into one of the old, dilapidated chairs. Why had he returned to Portland?

To settle things with Melinda.

And after that?

Who knows?

Her head fell to her hands, but she tried to think positively. He did love her. He had admitted it over and over again the night before while making love, and again in the note. So why leave? Why take off and abandon her now?

"Serves you right," she muttered, thinking how she'd shang-haied him to this cabin.

She had two options: she could walk into town and call her brother, or trust Parker and wait it out. This time, she decided to give Parker the benefit of the doubt.

To pass the time, she cleaned the house, stacked wood, even started lamb stew simmering on the stove before changing into clean clothes. But at five-thirty, when he hadn't shown up again, she couldn't buoy her deflated spirits. The longer he was away, the more uncertain she was of the words of love he had whispered in the night.

"He'll be back," she told herself, knowing he wouldn't leave her stranded, not even to pay her back for tricking him. Nonetheless, she slipped into her shoes and jacket and walked outside.

The air was cool and as the sun set, fog collected over the waves. A salty breeze caught and tangled in her hair as she threaded her way along an overgrown path to the stairs. Brambles and skeletal berry vines clung to her clothes and dry beach grass rubbed against her jeans before she reached the weathered steps that zigzagged back and forth along the cliff face and eventually led to the beach. She hurried down, her shoes catching on the uneven boards and exposed nails, to the deserted crescent-shaped strip of white sand. Seagulls cried over the roar of the surf and foamy waves crashed against barnacle-riddled shoals. Far to the north a solitary light-house knifed upward, no light shining from its gleaming white tower.

Shawna stuffed her hands in her pockets and walked along the water's edge, eyeing the lavender sky and a few stars winking through tattered wisps of fog. She walked aimlessly, her thoughts as turbulent as the restless waves.

Why hadn't Parker returned? Why? Why? Why?

She kicked at an agate and turned back toward the stairs, her eyes following the ridge. Then she saw him, standing at the top of the cliff, balanced on the weather-beaten stairs. His hair ruffling in the wind, Parker was staring down at her.

He'd come back!

Her heart took flight and she started running along the water's edge. All her doubts were washed away with the tide. He waved, then started down the stairs.

"Parker, no! Wait!" she called, her breath short. The steps were uneven, and because of his leg, she was afraid he might fall. Fear curled over her heart as she saw him stumble and catch himself. "Parker—don't—"

But her words were caught in the wind and drowned by the roar of the sea. Adrenaline spurred her on, her gaze fastened on the stairs. He was slowly inching his way down, his hands gripping the rail, but she was still worried.

Her legs felt like lead as she raced across the dry sand toward the stairs, her heart hammering, slamming against her ribs, as his eyes locked with hers. He grinned and stepped down, only to miss the final sun-bleached stairs.

"No!" she cried, as he scrambled against the rail, swore, then pitched forward. In an awful instant, she watched as he fell onto the sand, his strong outstretched arms breaking his fall. But his jeans caught on a nail, the fabric ripped, and his bad leg wrenched.

He cried out as he landed on the sand.

"Parker!" Shawna flew to his side, dropping to her knees in the sand, touching his face, her hands tracing the familiar line of his jaw as his eyes blinked open.

"You—you were supposed to catch me," he joked, but the lines near his mouth were white with pain.

"And you weren't supposed to fall! Are you all right?" She cradled his head to her breast, her eyes glancing down to his leg.

"Better now," he admitted, still grimacing a little, but his blue gaze tangled in hers.

"Let me see—"

Ignoring his protests, she ripped his pant leg further and probed gently at his knee.

He inhaled swiftly.

"Well, you didn't do it any good, but you'll live," she thought aloud, relieved that nothing seemed to have torn. "But you'll have to have it looked at when we get back." She tossed her hair over her shoulder and glared at him. "That was a stupid move, Harrison—" she said, noticing for the first time a crisp white envelope in the sand. "What's this?"

"The adoption papers," he replied, stretching his leg and grimacing.

"Adoption—?" Her eyes flew to his.

"Melinda's agreed to let me adopt the baby."

"You—?"

"Yep." Forcing himself to a standing position, he steadied himself on the rail as Shawna scanned the legal forms. "It didn't even take much convincing. I agreed to send her to school and take care of the baby. That's all she really wanted."

Shawna eyed him suspiciously and dusted off her hands to stand next to him. "Are you sure you're okay?"

His eyes darkened with the night. "I'm fine, now that everything's worked out. You know the baby isn't really mine. Melinda was Brad's girlfriend. I just couldn't remember the connection for a while."

She couldn't believe her ears. "What triggered your memory?"

"You did," he said affectionately. "You literally jarred me to my senses when you moved out."

Dumbstruck, she felt her mouth open and close—then her eyes glimmered furiously. "That was days ago!"

"I called."

Trying to hold on to her indignation, she placed her hands on her hips. "You could have said something last night!"

"I was busy last night," he said and her heart began to pound. "So, do you want to know what happened?"

"Of course."

"The night of the wedding rehearsal, I drove Brad to Melinda's apartment and they had a knock-down-drag-out about her pregnancy. He didn't want to be tied down to a wife and kid—thought it would interfere with his career." Parker whitened at the memory. "Melinda was so upset she slapped him and he passed out on the couch. That's why I remembered her, because I held her, told her everything would work out, and tried to talk some sense into her. Later, I intended to give Brad the lecture of his life. But," he sighed, "I didn't get the chance."

"So why did she claim the baby was yours?"

"Because she blamed me for Brad's death. It was a scheme she and her father cooked up when they read in the papers that I had amnesia. But she couldn't go through with it."

"Because you remembered."

"No, because she finally realized she had to do what was best for the baby. Nothing else mattered."

"That's a little hard to believe," Shawna whispered.

He shrugged. "I guess the maternal instinct is stronger than either of us suspected. Anyway, I told her I'd help her through school, but I want full custody of the child." His eyes narrowed on the sea and now, as if to shake off the past, he struggled to stand. "It's the least I can do for Brad."

"Be careful," she instructed as she brushed the sand from her jeans. She, too, was reeling. Parker was going to be a father!

Wincing a little, he tried his leg, then slung his arm over Shawna's shoulders. "I guess I'll just have to lean on you," he whispered, "if you'll let me."

"You think I wouldn't?"

Shrugging, he squeezed her shoulder. "I've been kind of an ass," he admitted.

"That's for sure," she agreed, but she grinned up at him as they walked toward the ocean. "But I can handle you."

"Can you? How about a baby?"

She stopped dead in her tracks. "What are you saying, Parker?" They were at the water's edge, the tide lapping around her feet.

"I'm asking you to marry me, Shawna," he whispered, his gaze delving deep into hers. "I'm asking you to help me raise Brad's baby, as if it were ours, and I'm begging you to love me for who I am, not the man I was," he said, stripping his soul bare, his eyes dark with conviction.

"But I do—"

"I'm not the same man you planned to marry before," he pointed out, giving her one last door to walk through, though his fingers tightened possessively around her shoulders.

"Of course you are. Don't you know that no matter what happens in our lives, what tragedy strikes, I'll never leave you—and not just out of some sense of duty," she explained, "but because I love you."

She saw the tears gather in his eyes, noticed the quivering of his chin. "You're sure about this?"

"I haven't been chasing you down for weeks, bulldozing my way into your life just because I thought it was the right thing to do, Parker."

"I know, but—"

" 'I know but' nothing. I love *you*—not some gilded memory!"

"All this time I thought—"

"That's the problem, Parker, you didn't think," she said, poking a finger into his broad chest and grinning.

"Oh, how I love you," he said, his arms pulling her swiftly to him, his lips crashing down on hers, his hands twining in the long silky strands of her hair.

The kiss was filled with the wonder and promise of the future and her heart began to beat a wild cadence. "I'll never let you go now," he vowed.

"I don't want to."

"But if you ever decide to leave me," he warned, his eyes drilling into hers, "I'll hunt you down, Shawna, I swear it. And I'll make you love me again."

"You won't have to." She heard the driving beat of his heart over the thrashing sea, saw pulsating desire in his blue eyes, and melted against him. "I'll never leave." She tasted salt from his tears as she kissed him again.

"Good. Then maybe we can exchange this—" Reaching into his pocket, he withdrew the beribboned brass ring.

"Where did you get that?"

"In the cabin, where you were supposed to be."

"But what're you going to do?"

"We don't need this anymore." Grinning wickedly, he hurled the ring with its fluttering ribbons out to sea.

"Parker, no!" she cried.

But the ring was airborne, flying into the dusk before settling into the purple water.

"As I was saying, we'll exchange the brass ring for two gold bands."

She watched as pastel ribbons drifted beneath the foaming

waves. When he tilted her face upward, her eyes were glistening with tears. Finally, Parker had come home. Nothing separated them.

"Will you marry me, Dr. McGuire?"

"Yes," she whispered, her voice catching as she flung her arms around his neck and pressed her eager lips to his. He loved her and he remembered! Finally, they would be together! "Yes, oh, yes!" Her green eyes shimmered in the deepening shadows, her hands urgent as desire and happiness swept through her.

"Slow down, Shawna," he whispered roughly. But even as he spoke, her weight was dragging them both down to the sea-kissed sand. "We've got the rest of our lives."

Dear Reader,

I can't tell you how thrilled I am that "The Brass Ring" has been republished by Kensington. When I first wrote this story I didn't anticipate it becoming a "classic romance" or that my career would take the twists and turns it has to the point that I'm now writing mainstream romantic suspense.

"The Brass Ring" really is a favorite of mine. I remember thinking as I wrote the story, What would happen if a woman who has it all, including the man of her dreams, loses everything right before her wedding? How would she react? Would her love survive? From there, the characters came to mind and the story was born! "The Brass Ring" is a story of true love, and I hope you liked it.

Let's talk about my next book. In *You Don't Want to Know* you'll meet Ava Church Garrison, a woman who fears she's losing what's left of her mind. Once strong and decisive, a business-woman, Ava is now reduced to a shell of her former self. She trusts no one, not even her husband, Wyatt, or the pretty psychologist, Evelyn McPherson, he's hired to "help her."

Ava's paranoia has its roots in the loss of Noah, her two-year-old child, a boy who went missing and who most presume is dead. Ava, though, hasn't given up hope and she still sees Noah's image not only haunting her dreams but appearing in the rising mists that swirl over Church Island. Is he really alive? Or a hallucination borne of false hope and guilt? Is someone intent on driving her out of her mind by somehow torturing her with his image? Whom, if anyone, can she trust? Certainly not Wyatt; or her cousin, Jewel-Anne, trapped in a wheelchair; or her once-upon-a-time best friend, Tanya Denton, who lives on the mainland and has ties to the island; or the new man that her husband hired, Austin Dern, a handyman of sorts with a murky past and a killer smile.

The fact that Ava's trapped on an island where only a smattering of people live and an old, decrepit former asylum lies rotting and abandoned only adds to her mounting fears. Desperately she tries to hold on to her rapidly deteriorating mind while finding out what really happened to her only child.

I think you'll like *You Don't Want to Know*. I really enjoyed writing it (even if I did get creeped out a time or two!).

I've included an excerpt from the book here, in the following pages, and if you'd like to learn more about *You Don't Want to Know* or any of my other projects, please visit me at www.lisajackson.com or on Facebook, where I have the latest info on all of my books, upcoming projects, appearances, and the like. I've got contests running, and I'd love to hear what you think of the books and the characters. We have some lively conversations going on!

Okay, so I promised you a sneak peek of *You Don't Want to Know*, and here it is! Just turn the page. . . .

Hope you like it!

Lisa

From #1 New York Times bestselling author Lisa Jackson comes a gripping novel of suspense in which a mother's worst fear is only the beginning of a terrifying nightmare. . . .

In Ava's dreams, her son, Noah, looks just the way she remembers him: a sweet two-year-old in rolled-up jeans and a red sweatshirt. When Ava wakes, the agonizing truth hits her all over again. Noah went missing two years ago, and his body has never been found. Almost everyone, including Ava's semi-estranged husband, Wyatt, assumes the boy drowned after falling off the dock near their Church Island home.

Ava has spent most of the past two years in and out of Seattle mental institutions, shattered by grief and unable to recall the details of Noah's disappearance. Now she's back at Neptune's Gate, the family estate she once intended to restore to its former grandeur. Slowly, her strength is returning. But as Ava's mind comes back into focus, her suspicions grow. Despite their apparent concern, Ava can't shake the feeling that her family, and her psychologist, know more than they're saying. But are they really worried for her well-being—or anxious about what she might discover?

Unwilling to trust those around her, Ava secretly visits a hypnotist to try to restore her memories. But the strange visions and night terrors keep getting worse. Ava is sure she's heard Noah crying in the nursery and glimpsed him walking near the dock. Is she losing her mind, or is Noah still alive? Ava won't stop until she gets answers, but the truth is more dangerous than she can imagine. And the price may be more than she ever thought to pay. . . .

**Please turn the page for an exciting sneak peek of
Lisa Jackson's
You Don't Want to Know
coming in August 2012!**

PROLOGUE

Again, the dream creeps in.

It's a foggy, gray day and I'm in the kitchen, on the phone, talking to someone . . . but that part changes. Sometimes it's my husband, Wyatt; other times it's Tanya, and sometimes it's my mother, though, I know she's been dead a long, long time. But that's how it is. . . .

From the family area, the room right next to the kitchen, here in this house, I hear the television, soft cartoon voices speaking, and I know that Noah's playing with his toys on the rug in front of the flat screen.

I've baked some bread—the kitchen is still warm from the oven—and I'm thinking about Thanksgiving. As I glance out the window, I notice that it's nearly dark outside, dusk at hand. It must be cold, too, as the trees shiver in the wind, a few stubborn leaves hanging on to thin, skeletal branches. Across the bay, the town of Anchorville is invisible, shrouded by fog.

But inside this old mansion, the one my great-great-grandfather built, it's cozy.

Safe.

Smelling of cinnamon and nutmeg.

And then, from the corner of my eye, I see movement outside.

It's Milo, our cat, I think, but I remember Milo, a prince of a tabby, is dead. Has been for years.

I squint, suddenly fearful. It's hard to see through the fog rolling in from the sea, but I *know* something's out there, in the yard, behind the hedgerow of roses where the scraggly bushes are thin and bedraggled, a few shriveled petals visible in the dead blooms and thorns.

Creeeaaaak!

My skin crawls as a shadow passes near the porch.

For the briefest of seconds I fear there's something evil lurking just beyond the vertical, arrow-shaped spikes of the surrounding wrought-iron fence.

Creeeaaaak! Bang! The gate's open, swinging in the buffeting wind.

That's when I catch a glimpse of Noah, my son, in his little hooded sweatshirt and rolled-up jeans. He's gotten out of the house somehow and wandered through the open gate. Now, in the twilight, he's running joyfully, as if he's chasing something, down the path to the dock.

"NO!" I drop the phone.

It knocks over my water glass in slow motion.

I spin around and think I'm mistaken, that surely he's in front of the couch by the TV, that . . . I see the room is empty, some Disney thing—*Aladdin?*—still playing. "Noah!" I scream at the top of my lungs and take off at a dead run.

I'm in my pajamas and my feet feel as if they're in quicksand; I can't get through this damned house fast enough, but as I race past each of the windows looking out at the bay, I see him, running through the descending darkness, getting closer and closer to the water.

I pound on an old pane with a fist.

The window shatters!

Glass sprays.

Blood spurts!

Still, he doesn't hear me. I try to open the French doors to the veranda overlooking the bay. They don't move. It's as if they're painted shut. Blood drizzles down the panes.

I slog forward. Screaming at my son, and for Wyatt, I run in slow motion to the doors. They're unlocked, one swinging open and moaning loudly as I push myself onto the porch. "Noah!"

I'm crying now. Sobbing. Panic burns through me as I nearly trip on the steps, then run past the dripping rhododendrons and windswept pines of this godforsaken island, the place I've known as home for most of my life. "Noah!" I scream again, but my voice is lost in the roar of the sea, and I can't see my boy—he's disappeared beyond the dead roses in the garden, no sight of him in the low-hanging mist.

Oh, please, God, no . . . let him be all right!

The chill of the Pacific sweeps over me, but it's nothing compared to the coldness in my heart. I dash down the path strewn with oyster and clam shells, sharp enough to pierce my skin, and onto the slick planks of the listing dock. Over the weathered boards to the end, where the wharf juts into the mist as if suspended in air. "Noah!" *Oh, for God's sake!* "NOAH!!!"

No one's there.

The pier is empty.

He's gone.

Vanished in the mist.

"Noah! Noah!" I stand on the dock and scream his name. Tears run from my face, blood trickles down my cut palm to splash in the brackish water. "NOAH!"

The surf tumbles beyond the point, crashing and roaring as it pummels the shore.

My boy is missing.

Swallowed up by the sea or into thin air, I don't know which.

"No, no . . . *no.*" I'm wretched and bereft, my grief intolerable as I sink onto the dock and stare into the water, thoughts of jumping into the dark, icy depths and ending it all filling my mind. "Noah . . . please. God, keep him safe. . . ."

My prayer is lost in the wind. . . .

Then I wake up.

I find myself in my bed in the room I've occupied for years.

For the briefest of instants, it's a relief. A dream . . . only a dream. A horrible nightmare.

Then my hopes sink as I realize my mistake.
My heart is suddenly heavy again.
Tears burn my eyes.
Because I know.
My son really is gone. Missing. It's been two years since I last saw him.
On the dock.